RITUAL INCOME

A WITCH OF THE DEMESNE NOVEL

B.L. BROWN

GOOD INTENT PRESS

The opinions expressed by the witches in this novel in regard to burnt ends, Tiki bars, and the City of New Orleans do not reflect the views or positions of the author.

Book Cover by GetCovers

Illustrations by Lindsey Staton

1st edition 2023

ISBN 979-8-9879716-3-5 (pbk)

ISBN 979-8-9879716-2-8 (ebook)

Please don't forget to feed the raw-head.

To Oliver – for telling me to shut up and write the damn thing.
I wrote the damn thing.

This novel is the slowest of burns. That being said, if you're related to me, feel free to skim chapters twenty-eight and thirty-four. If you aren't related to me, please enjoy chapters twenty-eight and thirty-four.

AUTHOR'S NOTE

Ritual Income is book one of *Witch of the Demesne*, a series within the World of C.R.O.W. *Shady Depths: A Witches of C.R.O.W. Novella* acts as a prequel to *Ritual Income*. It is not required reading (but, if you'd like to know more about Darkly, I do recommend it).

Content Warnings
Depression, grieving, self-harm, on-page sexual acts (consensual), mental and emotional abuse, gore, profanity.

St. Augustine Florida
Fort Mose
Vilano Beach
The Best Tacos in St. Augustine
Fountain of Youth
Huguenot Cemetery
Castillo de San Marcos
Darkly's Rental
Tolomato Cemetery
Southern Gothic
Government House
Flagler College
Plaza de la Constitucion
Bridge of Lions
St. Augustine Distillery
Milla's Duplex
Julie's Apartment
N
W
E
S
LINDSEY STATON

Ways
Fine and Faire

Aragon

sound
Audiomantic

Augurist *crystal witch*

Fortune tellers Chiromantic

Chronomantic *timey-wimey*

Hippocromantic *doctors/nurses*

Meteomantic

weather witch (Donny) Obfuscari' *mind witches*

Obnubilari'

Technomantic

Vinefica' *poisons + potions (Rai)*

Corpomantic⁺

Český-Krumlov

good herb
Green Witch

Kitchen Witch

Light Witch *soul, truth*

animal handling (shepherds) Pastýř

Vestic *diviners*

Spalování *Flame witch (Toby)*

Stitch Witch

Svítilna *wee sparks*

Ways
Forbidden and Foule

To be reported immediately to C.R.O.W.

~~Corpomantic~~
Dark Witch *Master of shades*
Death Witch

⁺ numerous historical incidences identify the marked Ways as At-Risk. Witches of the noted Ways are observed closely by their demesne's Aural Insurance Adjusters and assessed for Fine and Faire aura every five years.

"Most of the evil in this world is done by people with good intentions."

T.S. Eliot, Ink Witch

Lake Pontchartrain

New Orleans, LA

He turns his back. He always turns his back.

Every single time she relives this moment, he turns his back with the surety and unassailable faith in his own ability that only narcissism can provide. And that is his fatal mistake every damn time. That unswerving trust in himself and the natural extension of that trust to her.

Ezra glances back, the teal crackle of magic bright and painful in his eyes. "No matter what you See, Milla, believe in me."

"I will."

"That's my Millapet." He takes a step. Another and another, and for a heartbeat, she thinks he might manage it this time. He might succeed in pulling the world apart. And then her vision fractures into three, the pain in her head debilitating. The tether between them frays; it rips out of her grip and shreds her to her soul.

"Ezra!" Her feet slide in the silt, and she grabs the tether with both hands, bearing her weight down on her heels.

"Hold tight, Milla, believe in me!"

Snap. Snapsnap.

"Ezra, come back!" Strands snap and coil away, the tether slips and tears her palms, lashing her forearms and spraying blood across her face and her clothes. Her vision continues fracturing; nine, twenty-seven, eighty-one. A bone in her arm shatters, and she closes her eyes against the scream. "I can't hold on. I don't-I don't know—"

Snap.

"Ezra, please!" The tether burns against her palms, and the tension fails, whipping against her wrists and the back of her hands. His scream echoes hers, a pain cut deep to the center of their very being. "Come back!"

And then he is gone. The only sound is her ragged breathing and the staggered cessation of chanting as she struggles to piece together what is left. Of her, of him.

No. That wasn't right.

There was nothing left of him.

ONE

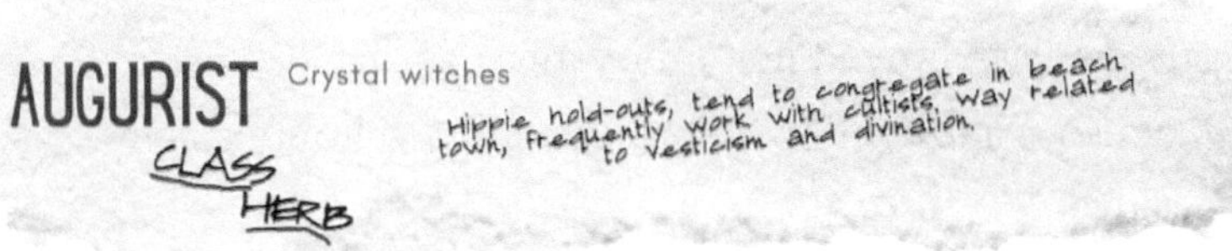

IF IT WEREN'T FOR the customers, Milla's job would be ideal.

There were days when all she did was sit at the front counter, sipping her drink and waiting for something to happen when she wished nothing would. Glorious days when the only person she spoke to was her roommate and co-worker, Diego, and all their sales were made online.

"Hey, hon!"

And then there were days like today when Milla had to remain calm in the face of Southern passive aggression.

"Me, again." Her sole customer approached the counter, flapping the garment in her hand. Milla paused mid-sip, identifying the vintage nineteenth-century asymmetrical bathing costume being treated as a handkerchief as The Pinkerton.

She frowned into her bubble water. The Pinkerton was an antique bathing costume she had painstakingly restored under Diego's watchful eye. It had been the first magick she'd attempted in months. Her blood, sweat, and the echoes of her curse words lived on in each thread of the asymmetrical banding and delicate frill on the collar.

The woman was still talking, probably complaining about the ventriloquists' dummies being creepy or the Tiffany lamp in the corner flickering whenever she walked by. Tourists had no end of complaints when it came to Milla's store and its eclectic collection.

She took another small sip, let the sharp tang roll over her tongue, and swallowed her annoyance. "What."

Okay, so maybe she wasn't so good at swallowing her annoyance.

"Excuse me?" The woman's eyebrows arched, which was a feat. Milla honestly did not think eyebrows drawn with Crayola could arch with such disdain.

"You're excused?" She extended a hand, palm up, gesturing at the Pinkerton. "Did you want to buy that?"

"Well, sort of." The woman's eyes dropped to her hand, indignation wrestling with and losing to sick curiosity. Her hands had that effect on people. It had been over a year, and even Milla wasn't entirely used to the webs of spidery white tissue marring her palm.

The woman sneered, shoving the Pinkerton into Milla's waiting hand. Her fingers brushed Milla's palm, and the unnatural chill had her darting away, the sneer widening to alarm.

Even before the incident that earned her those scars, people said she was too cold, her skin clammy when it should be warm from the Florida sun—chilled when it should be flushed from heat or exertion.

No one had liked touching Milla until Ezra.

Ezra who ran hot and wore bags of ice tucked into the waist of his running shorts. Ezra who slept in the buff and sweat through the night, even with the a/c running itself to exhaustion.

Ezra who was Gone.

"Sort of?" Milla raised her eyebrows.

"I was wondering if you had this in a larger size?"

She held up the garment, using it as a shield to hide the incredulous look on her face. "A larger size."

"You know how it is when you've had kids." The woman patted a hip in a manner that might have been cute had Milla not noticed a torn seam on the bathing costume.

"Did you—this is a 19th-century bathing costume, originally sold by Pinkerton's on the Boardwalk in Atlantic City." The woman smiled, nodding. "Atlantic City, New Jersey." Another nod. "In 1886."

"Uh-huh." She smiled broadly, still not understanding.

Oh, Horned God.

"This is an antique." Milla prodded the torn seam and tried counting backward from ten. She made it to seven, which, truth be told, was an achievement. "One-of-a-kind. I had to outbid a collector in New Haven for this."

"Incredible." The woman nodded, clearly not picking up what Milla was putting down. "So, do you have it in a bigger size? Maybe in the back?" Eyelashes fluttered, her lips pressed together in a pink, glossy pout. "I won a cruise through my company. I'm a Diamond Qualifying Executive for Icy Me, and this little bathing suit"—Milla's eye twitched—"is just perfect." She paused, lips pursed like a sturgeon, and Milla could have sworn she was holding for questions.

She had just the one, but Diego would be pissed if Milla asked this woman, this customer, if she was fucking serious.

So she cleared her throat and reached for her sparkling water. "Nope."

"Aren't you even going to check?"

"What part of 'one-of-a-kind' is confusing you?"

"I …" The woman's smile finally faltered. Milla relished the war of emotions playing out on perfectly contoured cheeks. The eyes lost it first, then the right corner of her mouth, followed by the left, disappointment altering the scenery of a lovingly painted face until the final transformation from cheerful Southern Gal to Bitch Queen was complete. It was utterly mesmerizing. "I would like to speak to your manager."

Had Milla not been the owner and operator of Southern Gothic Antiquities and Curios, she might have quaked in her boots.

Might have.

But the point remained: it was the *Pinkerton*. She couldn't sell it to just anyone.

"I'm afraid I'm the only one here."

"I see." The woman whipped her phone from the oversized beach tote on her shoulder, thumb swiping at the screen. She was no doubt crafting a rude post of her experience for Yap! Reviews, which was fine. Milla didn't need in-person sales to survive; the store was mostly a way to fill her days and keep her mind from wandering.

Believe in me, Milla.

Not that it was working very well.

A shutter snapped, and Milla blinked, jaw hanging open at the sheer *gall*. "Did you just take my picture?"

"You don't have any signs saying I can't."

"I…wha…you…" Milla fumbled, her usually sharp tongue struck dumb. "I think you should leave. *Ma'am*." The woman's nostrils flared at the layers of insult Milla added to the honorific. "Maybe Shopaholic has something more in line with what you're looking for." She gestured to the front door. "They usually carry plus sizes."

"Did you just *body shame* me?" The woman flushed, though it was hard to tell beneath the caked-on makeup. Her neck turned an alarming shade of red, as did her ears, but her face remained the same painstakingly contoured shades of peach and pink shimmer.

"I—shit," Milla stammered. "No, it's just, that's an antique. People in the 1800s were, um, smaller."

The woman slammed her palms down on the glass. "I've decided I don't want that moth-eaten fabric you call an antique," she snarled, which would have been intimidating were it not for the beach tote choosing that exact moment to slide down her arm. She jogged her shoulder to readjust the bag. "You've made a big mistake. Huge. I'm going to tell everyone I know about the appalling customer service at …" She squinted at the business cards beside the register and snorted. "Southern Gothic? Guess I shouldn't expect someone who designed their entire personality off of Wednesday Addams to be creative."

"Whatever," Milla rolled her eyes, "Karen."

"Kayleigh." She sniffed, then screwed her mouth into a purse of disgust. "This entire establishment reeks like the gin in your coke."

"It's juniper-scented bubble water," Milla huffed.

"Whatever." Kayleigh jabbed her phone screen with a finger. "What kind of trash store only sells clothing in one size."

"An antique store." Milla swept her arm at the curio cabinet behind her, pointing out the porcelain figurines, heirloom jewelry, and the broken but beautiful Berthoud marine clock. "Full of antiques, which this bathing suit—I mean *costume*—is."

"Do yourself a favor, sweetpea, and sell something people actually want to buy," Kayleigh hissed. "Not like it'll do any good by the time I'm done with you." She whirled in a swirl of floral polyester and shoved the door open, muttering insults under her breath. "You body shaming piece of …"

Milla fumed, palms itching, as Kayleigh stormed across the road and disappeared down Toques Place.

"That went well." Diego's mocking voice hummed from the hallway to the rear office, bathroom, and sewing room.

She drummed her fingers on the glass display case, chewing on her lip. "She wanted to buy the Pinkerton."

"Diosa forbid we sell anything." Diego sidled in front of the display, slipping a hand beneath the bathing costume and whisking it from the counter with a flourish. "You are obscenely attached to this shift."

He was shorter for a man but tall for an Iberian, or so he claimed. Thick, shoulder-length black hair was pulled into a bun at the nape of his neck, and the shadow of a beard clung to his jaw, adding warmth to an already deep olive complexion. From the wireless headphones looped around his neck, Milla caught the synth-loop refrain of Chaka Khan's "I Feel For You."

"Already in 1985?" Milla asked. For the past few months, after he'd figured out his smartphone, streaming services, and Bluetooth, Diego had been painstakingly reviewing music of the twenty-first century, in order.

Diego made a face, squinting behind his thick-framed glasses. "Chaka's later catalog is so frivolous. I much preferred her collaboration with Rufus." He held the bathing costume at arm's length, examining the torn seam with a critical tailor's eye. "Not much can compare to Cher's Best Works of the 1970s."

"Obviously," Milla agreed. "Nothing beats 'Dark Lady'."

"How you can say that when 'Rescue Me' is on the same album, I do not know." Diego turned his attention to the Pinkerton, shaking out the garment and muttering an allure. "*Muéstrame.*"

The fabric swelled and curved in the intended places, tapering around a modest waist and flaring over sweet hips as though it clung to the body of a turn-of-the-century model. As a Stitch Witch, Diego had a Way with fabrics, especially those from previous centuries, and he delighted in these impromptu displays of his magick.

He tilted his head, pressed a finger to the torn seam, and muttered a second quiet intent. A faint crackle of magick rose the hair along Milla's arms, and the stitching at the hip wove itself back together. Diego smiled, releasing his Way, and the bathing costume sagged in the way of all woolen things.

"She wanted it in a bigger size." Milla leaned against the curio cabinet. The figurines, jewelry busts, and vases rattled, and Diego lurched to steady the hutch. "Oh, calm down, I'm not that heavy." The broken clock thumped off of its display, and Milla flinched.

"Not at all what I was suggesting." Diego gripped the glass vial he wore around his neck, unable to completely wash away the sick look on his face. "You should have called for me, pequeña bruja, rather than frighten away a customer."

"Right, because I'm so scary." Milla rolled her eyes. "I can handle an angry customer."

"Like you handled that one?"

"It's not my fault that Karen tried to squeeze herself into an antique bathing suit."

"Kayleigh," Diego corrected.

"Whatever. We don't even have a dressing room; where did she even try it on? *And* she tore a seam."

"Which I have fixed."

"Well, aren't you special," Milla grumbled. "Not all of us have the luxury of old age and Stitch Witchery to fall back on."

"Old age?" Diego narrowed his eyes and flicked his fingers at her with a hiss. "Do not start insulting me because *you* were rude to a customer."

"I—" Milla started. And stopped, immediately regretting her words. She covered her face with her hands. "Shit, I'm sorry. That was … that was unacceptable."

"I will not say it is alright." Diego held her eye, forcing a weak smile. "But I understand you are frustrated, Milla."

He did. The Horned God and the Triple Goddess knew he did.

"Doesn't excuse it." Milla peered at him over her fingertips. "I'm sorry."

Diego's smile warmed. He stepped around the glass display, grabbing her cold, clammy hands and tracing his thumbs over the ruin of her palms. Not for the first time, she wondered if a Stitch Witch could see the seams beneath the scars.

"What sort of tío would I be if I did not forgive you?" Milla managed a tiny smile. He let go and fixed her bangs before tucking a dark lock of hair behind one ear. "Si, I forgive you," he smiled, eyes crinkling. "Also, there is a rat stuck in the trap."

Milla set the rat free in the alley and clung to the store's corners while Diego worked the register. Another attempt was made at getting the Berthoud to work, which ended with Milla storming out the rear door, hollering with the ship's clock in hand, "To the dumpster with you!"

Diego wrestled her for the clock, cursing a stream of Spanish as he stalked inside, and finally, it was sunset—closing time.

"Big plans tonight?" Diego called from his sewing room.

"Feed the raw-head, cup of tea, and my regularly scheduled ugly cry." She turned the lock on the front door, flipped the sign, and headed down the hall.

"Ah, yes. The Tuesday Special. Is this an R.E.M. 'Everybody Hurts' or Taylor Swift 'White Horse' kind of night? So I am prepared."

"I was leaning more towards something by Heart or Adele." Milla tugged open Diego's mini-fridge to grab a can of sparkling water and a hunk of raw meat wrapped in paper. "Or My Chemical Romance."

"Oh, please let it be an Adele night." Diego grinned with a sewing needle clenched in his teeth. A beaded collar stretched across his work table beside a handful of black and white pearls piled on a velvet cloth. Placed with some reverence beside them was an antique cameo—the centerpiece of the genuine Whaler's Wife mourning collar from the early twentieth century. He pulled the needle from his teeth, threading it with ease and wiggling his fingers over the pearls. "She always brings out the good wine."

"Because I do this for you." Milla pulled the tab off her can and flicked it at him. Diego winked, brown eyes twinkling.

"Naturally." He plucked a pristine black pearl from the pile and threaded it through with the needle.

Diego had spotted the collar on one of the many occult boards he trolled. Milla didn't know how he selected the gold from the veritable sea of pyrite that was online browsing, but he always knew which pieces to bid on, their essence speaking to him through the computer.

Or something.

She stopped questioning his skill after the third purchase in a row, a nineteenth-century top hat worn by an usher at the final performance of *Our American Cousin* at Ford's Theater, had proved legit. The black silk stovepipe arrived, and at a glance, Milla knew the hat carried a scrap of emotional memory—a Shade of terror—imbued in the very fabric of its being. After restoration, the antique hat was sold to a collector in Belgium for five times the purchasing price.

"I am only going to be here a few more hours," Diego said. "Not long enough for you to get into any trouble."

"Noted; I'll hold off on my tea until you get home."

She left the shop to his care, hurrying onto Spanish Street and keeping a wide berth around the mortals ambling the cobblestones or crowding under wisteria arches and narrow Spanish balconies.

Agatha waved her down from her usual spot on the corner of Spanish Street and Treasury. The old augurist was a holdover from the influx of hippies in the sixties and seventies and a St. Augustine institution. Her cart boasted an assortment of crystal necklaces, earrings, charms, and purple geodes sparkling under the orange-yellow glow of gaslight and salt lamps.

Things in St. Augustine changed, but Agatha did not.

The witch and her augury cart had sat on the corner of Spanish and Treasury for half a century, ready to ensnare inebriated tourists stumbling into the daylight after having gorged themselves on alcoholic slushies. It was one of the first places Milla's foster mother had brought her when she was a girl and nearly twenty years later, she still wore the lavender-hued geode shard the old augurist had gifted her.

Milla returned the wave, lifting her necklace to show Agatha the smudged and cloudy amethyst shard dangling next to a woven dreamcatcher.

"Your aura is looking a bit thin, dear!" Agatha cried out.

"I'll be sure to drink more tea," Milla replied, veering
onto Treasury Street. The crowd bled from sunburned tourists
to tanned, laughing Flagler students. Skirting the Governor's
House, she crossed Plaza de la Constitucion and pointed towards
the Bridge of Lions, a two-lane drawbridge stretching across the
Matanzas River.

A pair of Medici Lions protected the St. Augustine side, their
teeth bared in what Milla thought resembled pained laughter. As
if the city were a bad joke they were forced to protect. She often
felt the same and, over the years, had developed a kinship with
the lions. Named Firm and Faithful, Milla could never remember
which was properly which, so she'd designated the right-hand
lion as Faithful and ran a tingling palm over his paw whenever
she passed by.

Tuesday night was Feed the Raw-head Night, a task Milla
neither relished nor forewent. A task that, unfortunately, fell to
her as the Witch of the Demesne.

Raw-heads were nasty pieces of work brought over to the
Americas by Cornish sailors. How one had ended up in her
Spanish Floridian demesne remained a mystery but nevertheless,
here it was.

Humanoid in design, the raw-head in question was all knobby
knees and elbows, a gaunt belly, and skin stretched tight over a
frame too lean. Flaps of flayed skin dangled around its neck like a
macabre daisy, and the wretched thing had the habit of taunting
mortals and witches alike through fleshless lips.

"Bad words, bad deeds," the raw-head hissed when Milla
stepped onto the bridge. The rasp of jagged nails against metal
followed her every step. She only went far enough to place herself
over water and in danger. It was the only way the raw-head

would come close, Milla being a thing Forbidden and Foule as she was.

"Nice to see you, too." She picked at the tape keeping the paper closed around the raw meat. The horrid flap-slap of the raw-head's flayed skin scuttled closer, and the fine hairs along the back of her neck rose.

"Unpunished." A blood-blistered eye reeled at Milla through a metal grate.

"Not for long, pal." She curled her lip, pinching the—*Oh, Goddess, ew*—chuck roast between two fingers. Thrusting her arm through a gap in the pale-green iron bars, Milla dangled the meat over the water. The raw-head edged closer, and when she felt the heat of its breath on her wrist, she released the steak and jerked her hand back through the guard rail.

"You invite grief," the raw-head grumbled, its version of a curse … or a threat. Milla hadn't quite figured that one out. The raw-head might have meant it as a compliment.

The meat ka-ploshed in the Matanzas River, followed by the heavier ker-splash of the raw-head chasing its dinner. Milla allowed herself one full-body shudder before power-walking off the bridge.

The house she shared with Diego was a one-hundred-and-change-year-old Victorian across the street from Flagler College. Painted a pale yellow Milla likened to room temperature butter, the dangling trim, now more of a mossy light green with gray dust edging, was due for some attention, as was the sagging front porch. At some point in its more than a century of existence, the house had been split into a duplex. Milla had rented the left half of the property since her freshman year at Flagler, while the owner, an elderly woman from New England, leased the other half as a vacation property.

Electric candles flickered warmly in the windows of her half, a welcoming light for the wandering and the lost. She paused at the front door, bracing herself before stepping inside an empty house haunted by a ghost that wasn't there. Even now, she caught Ezra's scent in the heavy, humid air: bourbon and praline, the herbal bite of his shampoo, and the subtle sweetness of his lotion.

She dropped her forehead against the fogged glass pane in the door, closing her eyes and counting to ten before thrusting her key into the lock. The door swung open at the gentlest pressure.

The door of the duplex she shared with Diego and Ezra's not-ghost ... a not-ghost that was in no way capable of unlocking a door, which meant—

"Horned Goddammit, I left the door open again." She thunked her head against the frame twice before stepping inside, helping the door close with a heel kick.

Milla headed down the hall, stopping in the kitchen to grab a tub of hummus, bell pepper slices, and a beer. She stepped out of her checkered slip-ons in the hallway and charged into a dining room that had long ago been converted into her bedroom, complete with built-in cupboards and drawers in the closet that had once served as a butler's pantry.

A wingback upholstered chair sat by the bay window opposite her bed turned to overlook the small yard she shared with the other half of the duplex. A low bookcase formed a window seat, and in a brief spurt of get-it-done-ness, Milla had added shelves along the walls framing the window.

Her grimoire sat on one of these shelves, opened to an unassuming page on the benefits of hemlock and drawbacks of hawthorn in regards to the limbic system and aural display, and waiting patiently in her chair, with the poise of a witch who expected to be noticed as soon as she entered a room, was the Morgenhexe.

Two

how did a vestic win St. A?

"Hello, Ludmilla." The Morgenhexe's lips twisted upwards in a sadistically feline manner. She rose from the chair with straight-backed grace and crossed the room in three gliding steps, whisking the can of beer from Milla's hand. "How kind of you to remember my preference for a crisp lager."

"Blessed be," Milla squeaked, setting her hummus and veggies on the edge of the bed to proffer a bow to her *jezibaba*—her first mentor and foster mother.

"Blessed be," Morgen cracked open the can and took a tentative sip. A Black Forest witch, Morgen was as tall and imposing as the trees blanketing the hills of her birthplace. She had a look of austerity about her, with the cunning kindness that forms around the eyes from a life well lived. A master conjurer and illusionist, the Morgenhexe was a former Aural Insurance Investigator—an Enforcer—for the Coven Aural Review Board, conversationally known as C.A.R.B. They were the witches called in when magick Forbidden and Foule reared its ugly head, hunting down the those who dared practice the illegal craft.

In this room with Milla, however, she was a mentor first, a mother second, and an Enforcer never.

Morgen brought light to hand, illuminating the room as she studied the label on the can. The art depicted a cartoon image of Ponce de Leon guzzling a can of beer bearing the same image. "Ferment of Youth, *bezaubernd*." Smiling at the recursive headache that was the label, she took another sip and smacked her lips. "It is good to see you, Ludmilla."

"What brings you all the way up from the Keys?"

"Can a mother not visit her daughter?"

"When the mother is you, there tends to be a reason." Milla sat on the bed, drawing her feet up and crossing them at the ankles. "I take it my dues are due?"

"Tch," she waved a hand, "I took care of those last month. And the month before that, before that, and before that ..."

"I get it." Milla pulled the tub of hummus closer and pried off the lid, ignoring the dour glare from her foster mother. She opened the bag of bell peppers and plucked out a slice. "Doesn't necessitate a visit." She swept the bell pepper through the hummus and popped it into her mouth. "So, to what do I owe the honor?"

"To good standing."

Milla choked on her bell pepper.

To be a witch in good standing, one was expected to renew their Practical License every five years with an appearance before C.A.R.B., which was managed by the Coven for the Regulation and Oversight of Witches, or C.R.O.W., for the word adverse. An aural reading was performed, the witch demonstrated the Fine and Faire application of their Way and, ideally, walked out of the coven headquarters as a witch in good standing, able to fly under the radar for another decade.

Morgen sipped the beer, eyed Milla, and examined the room and tchotchkes on the bookshelf. Her eyes skimmed over an origami tiger, settling on a chunk of graffiti-ed cement taken from the ruins of a wall.

"Is it wise to have this on display?"

"Like anyone even comes in here." Milla tried to keep the annoyance from her voice. Her face, on the other hand, was a lost cause. "Can't you speak on my behalf to C.A.R.B.?" She jabbed another slice of bell pepper into the hummus and shoved it into her mouth. "As you can see, I'm doing marvelously. Couldn't be better. It was nice to see you, now please return my Jericho Stone to the bookshelf and leave me and my hummus in peace."

Morgen replaced the stone and moved her hands, face impassive. The beer can vanished from the left while her right scoured the air, conjuring a fist-sized pale yellow sun out of nothing. With less than a glance her way, the Morgenhexe lobbed the glowing sphere at Milla. She dove from the bed, flinging the container of hummus at her *jezibaba*. The tub twisted and rolled in on itself a foot away from the witch, disappearing altogether.

"Hey!" Milla clambered to her feet. "That was my dinner."

In response, Morgen conjured a second orb, flicking her wrist to send it flying. This time, however, Milla's hands were free. She braced her feet and cupped her palm, digging at the air as she swept her arm like a lacrosse stick. The orb tingled against her scars, and Milla tossed it to her right hand, redirecting the energy with a grunt and sending it flying back at the Morgenhexe.

Morgen bent to the side, and the orb curved around her. She held out the back of her hand, and the gaseous yellow ball alighted on her wrist as a tweeting yellow canary like the witch was a damn Disney princess. Nary a hair was out of place; even her clothing was unruffled.

Not. Fair.

Milla panted, glaring at her mentor. The exertion of absorbing, re-shaping, and redirecting Morgen's magick was tiring on a good day, and Milla was out of shape. She hadn't sparred with her foster mother for years and had barely touched magick since Ezra.

At least, not the combative sort. Her magick these days was quiet and contemplative. Stitches and lace. Simple mechanics and sachets of hawthorn, hellebore, hemlock, and clove. Not surprise brawls in her bedroom with a master illusionist.

"Milla," Morgen tutted, "you used to spar with me for hours."

"Yeah, when I was seventeen and hormonally enraged that My Chemical Romance had broken up. Then you apprenticed me to a twenty-one-year-old Mind Witch. You think we spent our time sparring?" Milla spat the last word, trying to keep her thoughts from what she and Ezra *had* spent much of their time doing.

Morgen cocked her head. With a flick of her fingers, the beer can wobbled to rest at Milla's feet. She eyed the summoned lager and gazed up to meet her foster mother's.

"Was there a point to that gross display of magick?"

"Of course." Morgen flapped a hand between them, gesturing to the beer. "My apologies for startling you." Chair legs screeched over the hardwood as she turned the wingback to face the bed. Milla sat without being told. It was her room, her house, and Horned God-dammit she was a grown-ass witch of twenty-six. She didn't need permission from Cate Blanchett's magickal doppelganger to sit on the edge of her bed; thank you very much. "I am worried about you, Ludmilla. C.R.O.W. is worried about you." Morgen began. Milla drank.

C.R.O.W.

Of course, it was C.R.O.W.

Their sole aim was to keep every witch under their jurisdiction in line and to eradicate those who dared to push against the narrow confines of their covenants.

"Why would C.R.O.W. be worried about me?"

"You are the unregistered Witch of a Demesne, you have clearly not been using your magick and, judging from your grimoire, have been experimenting with"—Morgen glanced over at the book. A curl of her finger turned the page to an entry on the benefits of lilies—"warding and banishment?"

"At least you know you're welcome in my home," Milla muttered into her beer.

An exquisite eyebrow raised. "Or you performed the incantation wrong."

Milla snorted.

"You stopped returning my calls, you have stopped using the magick I taught you while pursuing that which Ezra desired you to perfect, and the worn pages of your grimoire lead me to believe you wish to disappear." Morgen pursed her lips, waiting.

But what was there to say? That her body was slowly heading down the same path as her dead heart?

Two years. She had survived without Ezra for two years, keeping her head low, her magick muffled, and avoiding the notice of C.R.O.W. What more did they want from her?

"Is that it, Ludmilla? Should I have left you in that filthy apartment in New Orleans?"

"No," she whispered.

"Ludmilla." Morgen had moved across the room and stared down at her, fingers laced at her front. "You were meant to recover here, not claim the title of Witch of the Demesne."

"It was an accident."

"I am beginning to think your return to St. Augustine was a mistake." She curled a lock of Milla's hair around a finger, the gesture one of maternal care borne from years as a foster mother. "There are too many ghosts wandering these streets. One too many shadows in your mind. It was my wish that you return with me to Key West, where I could keep an eye on you."

"*What?*" Milla's heart clenched at the veiled threat. It took a moment for the implication of her words to settle, and Milla lurched to her feet when they did. "Wait, what do you mean *was*."

"C.R.O.W., however, has different ideas."

Milla snorted. "Because they've known what's best for me in the past."

"After seeing what you have made of yourself, Ludmilla, I am inclined to agree with them." Dread curdled in Milla's stomach. She pressed her lips together and clenched her fists, willing the tingle in her palms to cease. "As of now, you are being promoted to *polednice*"—Milla blinked. A *polednice* was a Mid-day Witch, the intermediary membership level with C.R.O.W.— "and will be assigned a *čarodějnice* of your own."

"An *apprentice*? How can I have an apprentice? *I'm* still a *čarodějnice*." Milla rattled the Czech title off her tongue, the word as familiar as her own name.

Little Witch, entry-level.

Nothing and no one to be concerned with as far as C.R.O.W. and their Enforcers were concerned.

"Considering your status as Witch of the Demense, C.R.O.W. feels it necessary to promote—"

"This is insane. I'm barely managing the demesne; how am I expected to manage a witchling? Look at me. I'm a mess!"

Morgen acquiesced, dragging her deep blue eyes from Milla's ankle-socked feet to her pale legs with their assortment of random bruises from working in the store, running into cabinets, and climbing under displays. A corner of the Morgenhexe's mouth twitched at Milla's high-waisted black shorts, fallen suspenders, and her cropped band t-shirt. Self-conscious under that critical eye, Milla ran her fingers through tangled hair. Thick, black, falling just past her shoulders. She exhaled, fluttering blunt bangs, and forced herself to meet Morgen's eye.

"True, you do not look the part of a *polednice*," her foster mother began, "but perhaps a youthful bent in leadership is what C.R.O.W. needs."

"You can't be serious. Morgen, please." Milla's voice cracked, and the sound finally pulled something like emotion from the Morgenhexe. "Don't make me do this."

The elder witch flinched, her cold exterior crumbling. She embraced Milla, smoothing her hair as the younger witch leaned against her.

It was odd, being held. Letting herself be held. Milla relaxed into the embrace, wrapping her arms around Morgen and holding tight. Touch was such a simple thing, and while her friends often gave quick hugs or high-fives to Milla, no one had truly held her since Ezra had … Gone.

"Shh, shh, *Millamäuschen*," Morgen whispered. "It will be alright. Goddess knows you have had enough experience with magick, both Faire and Foule, to set another young witchling successfully on the right path." Milla sniffled against the velvet of Morgen's gown. The older woman gripped her shoulders and pushed Milla away to look her in the eye. "It is already done; all that remains is to prepare yourself and convince C.R.O.W."

"Convince C.R.O.W.?"

"I am only a summons away, Ludmilla. You understand?"

She managed a nod, and Morgen shared a soft smile, the kind that brooked no argument but managed to convey sympathy all the same. "We cannot have you fading away, *Millamäuschen*. Give it a try for this old witch, hm?"

Milla nodded, and Morgen let go, striding to the bay window and staring out at the moon-drenched yard, the out-of-season lilies, and the pale green burst of petals on the witch hazel tree. Her mouth pinched as a bushel of crumpled hay tottered out of the shadows and tossed an empty plastic bottle on the patio table. "A *polevik*?"

"He showed up a year ago." Milla shrugged.

"Hm." Disapproval drew a tiny line between Morgen's eyebrows. "Your *čarodějnice* was previously assigned to a technomantic who trained with me on Big Torch Key."

"Why is she moving to Florida?"

"A disturbance Forbidden and Foule in her home demesne." Morgen rapped her knuckles on the window, startling the *polevik*. What resembled an arm of hay rose, stalks bending into the imitation of a middle finger before the Slavic field sprite toddled back into the shadows. "Or so I am told. The official story should hit our grimoires in a day or so, though the rumor in Český-Krumlov is that C.A.R.B. has dispatched an elite team of Enforcers to handle the matter."

Milla's skin prickled at the mention of Enforcers, and she wondered if Morgen wished she were among them. "So something happens elsewhere, necessitating the presence of Enforcers, and you thought *I* was the best choice to take over as a mentor?"

Morgen waved a dismissive hand. "The girl has relatives in Vilano Beach, and as St. Augustine is your demesne, her education in the Ways falls to you. Congratulations on your promotion, Ludmilla." Morgen lay a hand against the glass. Ice spiraled out from her fingertips, crawling across the pane. It was a simple piece of illusory magick Morgen had performed time and time again, always to prove a point. Present enough pieces of reality, ice gathering on a window pane, a well-placed shiver, a puff of cloudy air as one spoke, and a person could and would believe whatever they were shown. An old lesson but one Milla took to heart.

Believe that you can do this, Milla. Or, barring that, fool yourself until you do.

Right on schedule, Milla shivered from the imagined cold. "Understood."

The Morgenhexe smiled.

"There is one more thing." She spun and folded her arms, slender fingers resting near the crook of each elbow. "C.R.O.W. remains to be convinced of your qualifications as *čarodějnice* and Witch of the Demesne. They are sending an Aural Insurance Adjuster down to St. Augustine. You will be expected to meet with him—"

"I'm sorry, what?"

"—and allow him access to the demesne." Morgen hooked her finger under one of Milla's suspenders and placed it back on her shoulder. "Will that be a problem?"

"Is an A.I.A. necessary?" She gripped her beer in both hands to hide how they shook. "My demesne was reviewed by an aural adjuster when I took over stewardship. I thought they only did that on, like, a ten-year cycle."

"Indeed. Regardless, it is a condition of your promotion—"
"Which I didn't ask for."
"—and for your having a *čarodějnice*."
"Which, again, I did not ask for."

"Consider, then, the mystery behind the witch involved in the disappearance of Master Ezra Lightner winning stewardship of a demesne. And not only that but stealing it from a witch that had successfully held the territory for nearly four decades." Milla suddenly found her ankle socks very fascinating. "The ritual you and Ezra performed required massive magick, *Millamäuschen*. It cost a witch in good standing his life. That is not an act easily forgotten." Milla bit her lips to keep from correcting Morgen on all the details she had gotten wrong. "C.R.O.W. is willing to ascribe your participation to youthful ignorance; as such, they require assurance that you are sound enough in mind and magick to tend the demesne."

"Or else?" Because there was always an "or else" where C.R.O.W. was involved.

"Or else you will have to account for your actions." Morgen pinched between her eyes. "And no one lies to C.R.O.W., Ludmilla. Not even me."

"But I haven't done anything," Milla said too quickly. Morgen raised an eyebrow. "I've been leading a low-C.A.R.B. lifestyle."

"That is, at least to me, painfully obvious." The elder witch ran a finger along the top of Milla's grimoire. The book made a sound like a too-long ignored dog on the receiving end of a solid ear-scratch. "It is C.R.O.W. you must convince, Ludmilla, so I suggest you put yourself together."

THREE

MORGEN DEPARTED AFTER HER dire warning, leaving Milla with an uncomfortable amount of self-realization to attend to and little desire for her tea. Morning light dripped through the window too soon, and the demesne beckoned. She struggled into her running clothes and staggered from the bedroom, making it all of two steps before tripping over her discarded shoes in the hallway.

"Agh, fuck." She caught herself on the kitchen counter, avoiding faceplanting on the linoleum.

"O, por Diosa!" Diego whirled around with an egg pan in his hand. He ripped an earbud out and glared at Milla with an expression devoid of pity. The same expression he'd worn the last time she tripped on the stairs. He had given her that look, tended to her bloody nose, and packed up all of Ezra's things the next morning, moving into the upstairs bedroom and banishing Milla to the ground floor.

"Morning, Diego." Milla hoisted herself to her feet. His nostrils flared, eyes narrowing, and Gloria Estefan hit a high note underscored by samba horns in his headphones.

"How much did you drink last night?"

"Like half a beer, I tripped over my shoes." She rubbed her knee, jerking her chin at the offending footwear.

"No tea?" Diego blinked at the shoes in the middle of the hall. Milla wasn't sure which hurt worse: seeing that tired, angry look or the utter surprise that she was sober and had indeed tripped over a pair of shoes.

"Morgen dropped by for a surprise visit." She quickly filled him in on the news, emphasizing that she, and therefore *he*, would be under the observation of an aural insurance adjuster. "Tea didn't seem like a good idea after that."

"Oh." Diego's eyes went wide behind his glasses. "What are you going to do?"

"What can I do?" She pouted. "They've already made their decision, and Morgen backed it."

"Why would she do that? She knows what you—"

"I know," Milla cut him off. "I've kept us hidden this long; we just have to be extra careful for a few weeks, is all."

"Well," Diego exhaled, clearly unhappy. "Outside of *that*, you left the door open again."

"No, I didn't." Milla grabbed a fresh coffee filter from the stack. Gone were the days of Ezra's French press and pour-over with hand-ground beans. Making coffee had been a ritual for him, one that he delighted in perfecting, like the good witch he was. Before Ezra, Milla had been satisfied with cans of double espresso energy drinks, stating, "They have ginseng and Vitamin B, and you can hardly taste the coffee at all." He'd ruined that within a week of her apprenticeship, and it was like they said: once you go hand-ground fair trade Colombian, you never go back. "I specifically remember kicking it closed after Morgen left."

"It was wide open when I got home," Diego retorted. "Bruja, you have to remember to lock up."

"I lock the door at the store."

"Yes, my mistake. One locked door makes up for you leaving our home open to criminals."

"We live in St. Augustine."

"Si," he countered, "and they let anyone open a store these days."

Milla pressed the button on the burr grinder and glared at Diego. He leveled a smile her way, popping the earbud back in and returning his egg to the stove.

Coffee prepped, she headed down the hall, hollering at Diego, "Off for a run!" before closing the door hard enough to rattle the glass in its frame.

The sun had climbed midway up the palm trees, and the first snatches of commuter traffic along Cordova set a pleasant soundtrack for her run.

She set her pace to the drone of cars and random bursts of music: snippets of Mellencamp and The Boss, the newest auto-tuned pop hit, and the deep bass and wobble of Dirty South hip hop. To chatter floating through open windows and from sidewalk cafes until circling the park turned the music into children's laughter. The songs of her demesne fueled the witch, who fed power back into the city with each footfall and brush of tingling fingers against trees, gates, and lampposts.

The loop around Maria Sanchez Lake was always where Milla felt her best. Legs limber, breathing steady, she opened up her stride. The gentle lapping of the reservoir and call of the birds focused her mind and pushed her through to home, finishing her charge of the demesne with a clear head and peaceful heart. Her Way settled for the time being.

Diego was already gone when she finished her run, though he had left a note on the kitchen counter reminding her to lock the door. The urge to roll her eyes rose, but next to the note was a mug of coffee topped with the appropriate amount of milk and a swirl of Redi-Whip.

"You are forgiven," she told the note, tapping a cupboard door closed as she left the kitchen.

She showered quickly, not wanting to be alone with the not-ghost of Ezra. It was infrequent, but whenever she was tired, sad, or lonely—like right now—Milla swore she could see him out of the corner of her eye, reading in a chair or opening a cupboard. The echo of his footsteps would creak on the stairs, or the ghost of his fingers would brush her spine.

But Ezra was Gone.

Not dead, Gone.

People who died left behind bodies that could be found and mourned or an echo to be traced. A Shade or a fragment of Soul. An aural stain where they had last stood.

Ezra had left nothing.

Nothing but Milla.

She dressed, took care to lock the front door, refreshed a few of the sigils protecting the house, and began her walk into the Colonial Quarter. The day was cooler, reaching the low seventies around noon and lingering on into the perpetual stasis of Floridian twilight, so she had chosen her outfit accordingly: cuffed black shorts, an a-line halter in bold black and white stripes, a floppy black sun hat, and clunky ankle boots.

In black, of course.

She was a witch, after all.

Diego was already hunched over his sewing table when she entered through Southern Gothic's rear. Milla rapped her knuckles on the frame in greeting as she passed by, and he raised two fingers in a wave.

She opened the store, flicking on lights, unlocking the door, and powering up the tablet that served as their register, and was on her second can of sparkling water when the bells over the door tinkled merrily. Glancing up from her phone, she smiled as Julie Kettler waved hello.

"I thought you worked today."

"Mm-mm," Julie shook her head, red curls bobbing. She dropped her purse on the counter and shrugged off an Army Green bomber jacket, revealing a loose-fit v-neck and worn jeans. "Took the day off to meet a friend from out of town."

"Nice," Milla tucked her phone away and propped an elbow on the counter. "Taking her to Fountain of Youth?"

"Coffee first," Julie said, "then after that, maybe. I'm not sure what she wants to get up to." She eyed the earrings, necklaces, and rings in the display case. "She evacuated or something from Hattiesburg, got in town a couple of days ago."

"Evacuated?" Milla straightened. "What's going on in Mississippi?"

"Haven't you watched the news today?" Julie frowned when Milla shook her head. "There's been an outbreak of something in the Delta; a bunch of people were hospitalized, and someone died. I think. Ooh, can I try that one on?" She pointed to a large square-cut emerald in a white gold cathedral setting with black diamonds running along the band. "It's the Art Deco, right?"

"Nah." Milla crouched to unlock the display. "The Art Deco is the one with the triangles. This is the Victorian. Do they think it's going to be serious, like COVID?"

"No idea." Julie drummed her fingers on the glass. "I just hope I don't get furloughed again."

"Ahead of an outbreak?" She set the ring in front of Julie, who excitedly clapped her hands. Her wandering in to try on a ridiculous amount of the ridiculous items in Southern Gothic had become a ritual. Secretly, Milla loved it. Outwardly, she had a carefully curated persona of gloom to defend. Julie knew her well enough to tell when Milla was having fun, and seeing the nurse strutting around in a can-can skirt and beaded headdress tugged over her red hair was always a delight.

"You remember what it was like when everything calmed down, too many nurses, not enough patients. I'm still trying to pay off my credit card debt from that side hustle I started to make ends meet."

"I told you it was a bad idea," Milla said. The bells over the door tinkled, halting Julie's reply. Both women looked over—Julie with a delighted squeak and clap of her hands and with Milla a wide-mouthed look of surprise. "When did you leave?"

"Half an hour ago." Diego grinned at her, balancing two stacked cups of coffee in one hand and holding a bag of Old City Biscuits in the other. "You were doom-scrolling Blather; I did not wish to interrupt." He raised the bag. "Left my phone in the back, but I got your favorite: sundried tomato, spinach, red onion, and a fried egg. Light aioli."

"Oh, my Goddesssssss," Milla danced out from behind the register, grabbing the topmost coffee and reaching for the bag. "Bless you."

He swept his arm back, taking the bag out of reach. "Did you really not know I had left?"

"Nope." She popped her lips on the *p*. He chuckled and shook his head, dropping the bag on the counter. Milla pulled it closer, peering within. "Been quiet, haven't had a single customer."

"Um, hello?" Julie waved.

"Are you going to buy anything?"

Julie gave the store a speculative scan. "No?"

"Not a single customer." Milla doubled down.

"I am not surprised." Diego grabbed the bag from Milla's greedy hands. "The line at Shopaholic is out the door, though from what I saw of the window display, I do not understand why."

Milla snorted, smirking. "What hideousness are they shilling now?"

"Birds of Paradise floral spandex *everything*." He gave an exaggerated eye roll and headed for the rear of the store. "Some new brand I have never heard of."

"Ooh?" Julie arched back from the counter, peering out the window. "What's the label?"

"Excuse me, you are my customer." Milla fake pouted, and Julie laughed.

"Thought you hadn't had a single customer today."

"Semantics."

"I'm just saying," Julie put her hands up in surrender, "Southern Gothic is very … niche."

"And that's a problem, why?"

The nurse paled, stammering as she backpedaled. "It–it's not. Everything in the Quarter right now is neon leggings and pastel scarves. It's what sells, that's all. Colorful Florida florals, not the … the specialty shops like you and the crystal cart."

"And the torture museum."

"That is not a shop, Milla," Diego called from down the hall.

"Could be, if that's your thing," she hollered back.

Julie poked the glass in front of the diamond and sapphire band. "Well, if you want to spice up what you sell, let me know. I still have boxes of inventory."

"I don't see why we should change what we sell to please a crowd," Milla replied, ducking low to grab the Art Deco ring.

She set it in front of Julie, who squeaked and clapped her hands. "We don't need the foot traffic; Diego makes most of our sales online."

"Lucky you, then." The nurse slid both rings on her finger. "But as someone who spends twelve hours a day in scrubs and a sports bra, cheerful tights are kinda nice now and then."

"Okay, so buy them at Shopaholic," Milla unwrapped her biscuit and took a large bite, speaking around her food, "and let me sell my antiques in peace."

"Only saying, if you wanted to broaden your market at all, you could—"

"What did you do?" Diego stormed out of his sewing room and slammed his phone on the display case. Julie jumped back, covering a startled yelp with her hand. "Lo siento, Julie. Sorry. For that. And for this." He turned the full brunt of his righteous Iberian anger on Milla. "What did you say to that woman?"

"What woman?"

"The one from yesterday, to whom you refused to sell the bathing suit."

"Who," Milla corrected.

"The *customer*," he seethed.

"No, you used 'whom,' not—never mind. Are you talking about the Pinkerton bathing *costume*? I didn't refuse to sell it to her; it didn't fit. I told her to go to Shopaholic to find something in her size."

"Yikes," Julie whispered.

"We are a shop, Milla. We sell things." Diego pressed a punctuative finger against the display case. "It is a time-honored transactional sequence of events. Customer enters, customer selects an item, shopkeeper keeps their opinions to themselves and takes their money. Shopkeeper does *not* send customer to another store!"

Julie glanced between the pair. "What happened?"

"Some Karen got mad at me," Milla explained.

"*Kayleigh*." Diego hollered.

"Kayleigh?" Julie asked.

"Whatever." Milla waved a dismissive hand.

"Whatever?" Diego jerked his head back, eyes blinking rapidly. He picked up his phone and shoved it in her face. "Look. Scroll. Read. Absorb." Milla startled back, hesitantly taking the phone. The screen was open to their Yap! page, which had been flooded with new reviews. "Fix."

The first review was harsh but not out of line. "Weird shop, weird owner, go in with low expectations."

"Fair enough," she muttered.

From there, however, they got progressively worse.

"Shitty clothes and broken furniture," "buncha dead flies," "reeks of mildew," "questionable stains on the carpet."

She looked at Diego. "We don't even have carpet in here."

"You have the Persian rug," Julie offered.

"Hyderabadi," Milla and Diego corrected. "Keep reading," he continued.

Milla scrolled until her eyes landed on a novel-length review, each sentence worse and more fabricated than the last.

My girls and I stopped in here on a port call during a recent cruise. While promising at the outset with an eclectic and funky owner—

"Not so bad." Milla attempted to smile and kept reading.

— Southern Gothic quickly disappointed. Not only did the owner refuse to help us find items in our size, but the store is absolutely disgusting. Cockroaches everywhere, I saw a dead rat in the bathroom, the whole place reeks of gin and, I hate to be so rude, but, a morgue. It

smells like dead bodies in there. Maybe it's all the old crap, maybe it's the risk of operating an antique store in the Colonial Quarter but Jesus Christ, have some pride. Take a shower and sober up when you get to work.

Milla looked at Diego, stunned. His glower told her to keep reading.

The next review was worse, calling her illiterate and saying they would never trust the store to give out the correct change. Accusations of turning away customers of a certain racial make-up, refusal to allow returns on vintage Keds ("I have never in my life sold a pair of Keds."), out of date and out of touch ("We sell antiques! It says so on the sign!"), more accusations of a drunk salesgirl, an especially creative review that compared the store to a unicorn in that they could not believe it existed, and finally, a review from Kayleigh Masterson.

"At least she's kind of honest," Milla muttered, reading her account of their argument.

"Who is?" Julie peered at the screen, squinting to read the poster's name.

"The Karen."

"Kayleigh," Diego corrected.

"Whatever," Milla snapped.

Julie cleared her throat. "What does it say?"

"It's only half the story," Milla protested. "And that bathing costume is one of a kind. We literally don't have it in any other size."

"Again, Milla, not your problem." Diego snatched his phone out of her hand. "You take money from the customer. The customer leaves with an ill-fitting garment, we keep our ratings up and then sell more ill-fitting garments to the next batch of idiots that wander in." He paused and glanced at the two rings on Julie's finger. "Those look lovely on you, by the way."

"Thank you?"

Milla covered her face with her hands and groaned. She had messed up. Again. Another mistake added to her very long list of mistakes.

"I hate to leave when you are obviously having a … thing," Julie shot Milla a sympathetic look, sliding the rings off her finger, "but I need to head out to meet my friend. Want me to bring you back anything?"

She shook her head, face still covered in her hands. The bells tinkled as her friend left, and Milla slid her hands down, covering her mouth with her fingers. "Diego, I am so sorry."

"No, you are not."

"Yes, I am. I had no idea that woman was serious."

Diego's warm, brown eyes were hard behind his glasses, his laughing mouth a thin, angry line. "My tailoring is quite literally all I have. You saw to that when you, you —," he curled his fingers into claws, tearing at the air between them and appealing to the ceiling. "Tonto del culo … fix this. Call Yap!, apologize to this Kayleigh woman, I do not care what you do, but fix it."

"It's not that big a deal," she protested. "They don't even know Bimini Bespoke is attached to my store."

"Oh?" He raised an eyebrow and stole his phone back. Within a second, he had the profile for his tailor services, Bimini Bespoke, pulled up.

Someone needs to call ICE on Southern Gothic. The owner is clearly smuggling aliens into our country.

"What the fuck—" Milla stole the phone back, scrolling, her eyes catching snippets.

Send him back to where he came from...immigrant stealing our jobs...sorta faggot owns a sewing shop...can someone say 'slave labor'?

Diego snatched his phone, gripping it hard and pointing at Milla. She could not help but notice the tears limning his eyes and the tremble of his finger. "Fix it."

Four

SHE SPENT THE AFTERNOON cleaning dead flies, cockroaches, and spiderwebs from the corners of her store while trying to get a customer service representative for Yap! on the phone. After a final effort at number mashing to get around the automated "Thank you for calling Yap! Reviews, please hold for the menu of options." Milla gave up.

This dilemma called for space, grace, and alcohol in her face.

She grabbed her bag and floppy hat in a huff, storming out of Southern Gothic and heading to the nearest bar to brainstorm and drink until she didn't care about Diego and stupid Yap! with its stupid reviews planted by stupid Kayleigh Masterson.

Drake's Fire was a half-assed attempt at a Tiki bar sandwiched between BoVine Creamery (selling hand-churned ice cream and wine from a fridge) and WineNot (selling hand-selected wine and ice cream from a freezer).

Lit by the late afternoon sun streaming through large picture windows and a row of television screens hung over the bar, the walls of Drake's Fire were decorated with low-ABV beer ads and faded posters depicting random tropical islands. Grass skirts were pinned to the edges of torn vinyl booths, the front of the bar was plastered in faded bamboo wallpaper, and the bartender wore an ill-fitted button-down Tommy Bahama shirt. It smelled of coconut, pineapple juice, stale beer, and vomit, making it the perfect match for Milla's miserable mood.

She stalked in, rolled her eyes at the closing strains of "Cheeseburger in Paradise," and flung herself onto a stool at the corner of the bar. The only other customers were a young couple wearing air-brushed Mr and Mrs t-shirts. They mooned over the flame of their volcano bowl while being broadly ignored by the bartender. He was a witch, a Mix Witch, to be specific, but a stranger to Milla, which she considered a small blessing.

Strangers were safe. Strangers did not wander off script when talking to an off-putting witch. The most she would get from Tiki Tommy, as she immediately dubbed him in her head, was "What's your order," "Want another," and "Here you go" in that safely predictable order.

It was too early in the day for hard liquor, and alcoholic slushies made her teeth hurt, so Milla ordered an IPA from a craft brewery in Tampa. A beer would get her far less drunk over time as she pondered how to earn Diego's forgiveness.

He was right, of course. The store and his bespoke tailoring was all Diego had; all he could have, thanks to her. The Stitch Witch had put his life into refurbishing the items she bought, scouring the internet for curios, and running his shop from the workroom in the back, and Milla's bad attitude had put all of that at risk. She had completely misread a situation, misunderstood how to navigate the social cues, and ruined something that had been good for a time. And what was worse, she had hurt Diego in the process.

Her eyes drifted up to the mounted television screens. Being early, they were showing a variety of programs as opposed to the standard Florida college sports—a NASCAR race, a televangelist preaching about Horned God knew what, the internet witches episode of the old vampire slayer show, and national news on the screen directly in front of Milla.

She half watched the muted interview of a woman in her mid-forties, identified in the banner as Sarah Sanderson, daughter of the deceased. Her face was shiny and swollen-eyed from crying, and she kept gesturing angrily at the wall of boxes filling the garage at her back.

"That would suck," she told her beer. Cleaning up after a dead or Gone person was hard enough, but having to deal with a hoarding situation? Milla thought of the store, shuddered at the amount of crap she had shoved within her four hundred square feet, and decided a fire would be the best way to handle that poor woman's garage.

Then she wondered who would go to the effort of setting her store on fire if she died, dropped a coaster on her half-finished beer, and went to the bathroom for a good stall cry.

Feeling slightly less like a piece of shit, Milla left the bathroom and froze midstep at the sight of a new person in the bar. He occupied the stool next to hers, eyes on the television, but Milla could tell he was tall, fit, and a tourist. Too pale to be local and too nice-looking to frequent this hole in the wall, which meant he was from out of town and the sort of stranger who would want to chat.

"Great, just great," she grumbled, pinching her mouth into a thin line when the tourist looked over at the sound of her voice.

A tiny smile curved the corner of his mouth, and he returned to the screen, giving Milla free rein to look him over as she approached: broad shoulders and a trim torso in an almost-too-tight black v-neck. Auburn hair styled in the undercut pompadour so many men favored. A shadow of stubble dusted his jaw, and he was polite enough not to glance at Milla as she slid onto her stool.

She angled herself away just enough to make it clear that conversation was not an option. He took the hint, sipping a slushie drink, drumming his fingers on the bar, and bouncing his leg in time to the song on the jukebox. It changed from country rock to a classic, and he started singing along. Quietly, like he thought she couldn't hear him, but sing-a-long he did.

"Daylight comes, and I want to go home."

Milla cocked her head, watching him from the corner of her eye. His attention was on the vampire slayer show, but he was enjoying the calypso cool of Harry Belafonte far more than the stilted fight choreography on-screen.

And then he did it again.

"It's a day, oh. Daylight comes, and I want to go home." His accent was thick and rolling; a Scottish brogue Milla hadn't heard outside of old movies and TV shows about time-traveling housewives from the 1940s.

"'Me wan' go home'," she muttered, too bewildered to stop herself.

The stranger stilled. A disbelieving smile dimpled his cheek. "Pardon?"

"The lyric, it's 'me wan' go home.'"

He scoffed. "Dinnae ken about that."

"You can not ken about it all you want, but that's the lyric." Milla returned to her beer, ignoring the Scotsman as he pulled out his phone and tapped on the screen. Definitely kept ignoring him when he covered his mouth with a hand and said, "Huh." It was harder to ignore him when he slid his phone over to show her the lyrics to the song. "*Beetlejuice* is my favorite film, cannae believe I've been singing this wrong my entire life."

"You know 'Banana Boat' from *Beetlejuice*?" Milla leveled an incredulous stare at him. "The old movie about ghosts and the afterlife?"

"First, it's the Neitherworld, and second, the song is called 'Day-Oh.'" He smiled fully, sat up straight, and Milla's mouth went dry. He didn't just straighten his back and sit up so much as sit up and keep sitting up. He was so tall that Milla had to tilt her head back to look him in the eye.

"Well," she swallowed, "wrong again, Mac. It's called 'Banana Boat'." His smile dropped as she tapped his phone where "Banana Boat (Day-Oh)" was displayed. "It's an old Jamaican working song. They're invoking the tallyman as a placeholder for a Loa of wealth and fortune. Erzulie, maybe? I was never that great with the Rada and Petro." The stranger stared blankly at her. "Anyways, the black tarantula refers to the punishment doled out by the Loa should they betray it."

"Loa?"

"Voodoo spirit, still really big in the Mississippi delta and Caribbean nations."

He grabbed the phone as she spoke, scrolling, tapping back a screen, re-doing his search, and sitting back, defeated.

"I feel like I owe you a drink," he mumbled, staring into the middle distance. Milla half smiled, and his eyes tracked to her. It was dark in the bar, and the sunlight clawing its way through the doors and windows back-lit the Scotsman made his eyes appear a deep, disturbing shade of black.

"Only if I don't owe you anymore chit-chat."

"Chit-chat."

"Small talk. It's a skill all Southern women are supposed to possess." Milla grabbed her half-full IPA, finished it in one great swallow, and signaled the bartender. "I suck at it."

"Do you?" An eyebrow twitched, and the corner of his mouth curved.

"Absolutely."

"You're certain?"

"No," Milla deadpanned. "I'm Czechian."

He blinked, and that tiny curve broadened into a grin. He shook his head and faced the bar, relinquishing Milla from any further chitchat. She mumbled "thank you" when her beer arrived, received no reply, and chalked up the brief exchange as a successful step towards being a decent human.

Fifteen minutes later, she was swaying slightly from two strong IPAs on an empty stomach and staring at the protective sigil she had drawn in the pooled sweat from her glass. Specifically, one that warded against those who intended harm. A low pulse of power hummed from the sigil, enough to make a person with ill intent move to the opposite corner of the room. Stunned, Milla wiped the ward away and subtly scanned the bar.

The Scotsman was still there, working on a jar of Diesel Fuel, a Florida Panhandle specialty made from varying amounts of gin, rum, vodka, and triple sec. He glanced at her, eyes flicking to the smear where the sigil had been, her empty glass, and then to the bartender. Without a word, he raised his hand in the international sign for, "Oh barkeep, I would fancy another beverage," and went back to his drink.

Milla's new beer arrived, and she wriggled on the barstool. "I suppose," she began, then closed her mouth, pursed her lips to the side, and tried again. "I suppose the proper response to the social contract I've just entered into would be to say thank you and initiate a conversation."

"Thought you didnae wish to chit-chat." The Scotsman chuckled at her scowl. He winked a dark eye. "No need to put yourself out on my behalf; just looked like you were a little lost."

"What?" Milla sat up, wondering if it was that obvious.

"In your head, a little lost in your head," he clarified. "Seemed like you could use a little kindness. No need to have a conversation you dinnae fancy, just pay it forward some time, aye?"

"Yeah," Milla nodded. "Yeah." They drank in companionable silence, like two friends who had never met. Half an hour passed. The TV changed to a stupid human tricks compilation underscored by the Scotsman's quiet chuckling. Milla spun the glass in her hands, flinching when he bumped his shoulder against hers and pointed to the screen where a stunt was replaying.

"Absolutely mental." He grinned, dark eyes hazy from drink, and Milla's entire world narrowed down to the dimple that grin drove into his cheek. "Fancy another?"

Milla blinked, her head cotton-soft and cozy from the beer as an idea formed.

She told herself it was because her warding sigil hadn't frightened him away, that it had to do with how this stranger wasn't asking anything of her that made Milla want to give him more.

That it didn't have anything to do with being too afraid to connect with another person after Ezra or that a simple hug from her foster mother threatened to reduce her to a puddle of tears. That it wasn't because she was lonely. She had Diego. She had Julie. She wasn't alone. Not truly. Not unless someone looked closer at how she had met Julie or how Diego had entered her

life. So maybe it was because of her frustrations with the Yap!
Reviews.

That was it. The Yap! Reviews. *Not* that she was a sad witch
looking for a distraction.

She should leave. Closeout her tab, thank the Scotsman, and
head home, but going home alone meant facing Ezra's not-ghost
who wasn't really there because he was Gone and Milla was alone,
and if there was one thing Milla was overwhelmingly certain of
in this moment, it was that she did not want to be alone.

She bumped her shoulder against his as words tumbled free.
"I'm fancyin' somethin', alright."

"Are you, then?" The Scotsman watched her, his dark eyes and
half smile answering the question she had yet to ask.

"It should be said, this isn't for the beer," Milla brushed his calf
with her foot, "or the second one."

"Aye, because that would make this 'paying it forward'."

"Exactly," she nodded. "I've just had a bad … year or two, and
you look like you'd be a lot of fun."

His dark gaze dropped, flitting over Milla and lingering in
places that made her skin heat. He bit his lower lip and edged
closer, bringing with him an intoxicating waft of cologne: clove
and clean smoke edged with the faintest alcoholic bite of a moist
towelette.

A tourist, she confirmed. *Just landed. Only in town for a night or
two. No connections, no strings attached.*

"Aye," he rumbled, extending a hand for Milla to take. "That I
am, hen."

Shadows caught in the hollow of his palm, and she could just
barely read the run of his head and heart lines, both steady, deep
rents in his skin.

A level-headed person, they told her. Logical but emotionally driven. Her eyes flicked to his thumb. Will ruled over logic, so level-headed *and* logical, but with a strong personal justice system susceptible to his own will. She flicked her gaze back to his heartline, noting the slightly bowed curve and medium length.

Open to emotional expression but not overly sensitive; someone who needs affection but is afraid to ask for it.

A puzzle that would be fun for a night. Maybe two, but she didn't want to get ahead of herself.

Milla shrugged the reading away. Palmistry wasn't her strength, and she wasn't here to do magick; she was here for fun, and so she took his hand, her skin tingling at the touch. His smile warmed further, fingers curling without the slightest reaction to her warped, clammy palm.

"Think you'd like to find out?"

Plaster scraped her shoulders, abrading her skin with a pain that had Milla gasping. She dug her nails into his back, clinging to the Scotsman for leverage. He didn't let her think, didn't let her breathe, as he pressed his palm flat between her shoulders and pulled Milla onto her tiptoes.

This was insane. Utterly out of character and exactly what she needed. A fun escape, a means to burn through the pent-up energy her tea hadn't been able to quell, and this man, this *tourist*, was turning out to be a hell of a lot of fun.

He let her lead him from the bar, commenting on the restaurants and gaslamps before pulling Milla into an alleyway a few blocks later. And then her back was against a wall, and his tongue was in her mouth, and Horned *God*, the man kissed like he was starving and fucking at the same time. Plunging deep again and again until her head spun and her nails pinched his skin, only to withdraw and tug her lower lip with his teeth. A flash of pain elicited a gasp, and then he was back, drowning Milla in sensation and heat and the decadent clove and smoke scent of *him*.

"This was a good idea," she gasped against his jaw, stubble burning her lips. He wormed his fingers into her hair, tugging just-*so* to earn a startled moan. "Such a good fucking idea."

His answering rumble shot down to Milla's toes. Heat bloomed in her belly and her chest, ribboning down to the tips of her fingers. He angled her head back, kissing her hard. His hand slid down her spine, pressing Milla against a long, lean body. "Best idea I've had in a while," he panted in her ear, nipping the lobe. Milla shivered, which only prompted the Scotsman to do it again before trailing his lips down her throat. "D'ye live nearby?"

"About a half—"

"Too far." He cut her off with another kiss, gripping her by the hips, her rear, and then Milla was hoisted from the ground. She wrapped her legs around his waist, and the Scotsman rumbled, pressing her shoulders against the wall.

"Your hotel?" she managed.

"Nae in a hotel," he muttered, drowning Milla in his scent, heat, and tongue. A part of her brain tracked his words, warning Milla to stop. Walk away. Abort! Because not a hotel meant a rental, or worse, a *lease*, and this was only supposed to be fun for a night or two. Then he rocked his hips and tugged Milla's hair, chuckling at her gasp before swallowing her moan and holy—

"Horned God, you're fun." His brogue trickled down her spine like whisky in a glass. Milla arched her back, pressing against the Scots—wait.

"What did you just—"

"What's your name?" He released her hair, running his hand down her back, under her shirt. Rough callouses prickled her skin, and more delicious heat sizzled in her limbs, her palms, chased by the coarse chill of his touch.

"Milla," she gasped. "Ludmilla."

"Ludmi—" The Scotsman jerked his head back, dark eyes searching Milla's face, his entire body taut and still. "*Mo bhandia.*"

Slowly, oh so slowly, he slid his hands to Milla's waist, bracing her as she dropped her legs and leaned against the wall. The heat soured, churning unpleasantly in her gut and crawling up her chest and neck like a cancerous rot. His hands lingered at her waist, no longer the self-assured grip of a man knowing what came next. His hold now was tentative. Uneasy. "I should go."

Milla snorted, retreating behind a protective veil of sarcasm. "Sure."

"This was fun?"

"Why are you saying it like a question?"

"I…"

"Nevermind." She twisted out of his hands, putting space between herself and the Scotsman. "I really, *really* don't want to know." Too pissed at herself for this stupid idea, Milla spun away, charging down the alley.

"Could I have your number?" he called after her. "I'm in town for a few weeks on business; we could do lunch."

"My number?" Milla spun on her heels. "We were just dry-humping in an alleyway, and you want my number for *lunch*?" She gaped at the Scotsman, daring him to say something, anything, that was less ludicrous than that. He shoved a hand in his pocket, sweeping the other through his hair and letting it rest at the base of his neck. Silently. Milla rolled her eyes and flipped him both middle fingers. "Lunch on that."

FIVE

BOOM. BOOM. BOOMBOOM.

The sugar-sweet liquor store muscadine wine had been a bad idea. She knew it when she opened the bottle, but that didn't stop Milla from filling and refilling her glass. When Diego got home, she extended an olive branch by digging out a bottle of Ezra's beloved Blaufränkisch, an Austrian red wine, for them to drink with her tea. She didn't even know if it was the last bottle, not that it mattered.

But it did.

Two and a half years had passed since Ezra's last visit to C.R.O.W. to renew his Practical License, so it very well may have been the last bottle of Blaufränkisch. If so, it deserved a better fate than being thrown up in a trashcan by a sad, pathetic witch who couldn't even wrangle a one-night stand.

Boom. BoomBoom. Boom.

She groaned, pressing the heel of her palm between her eyes. Wine hangovers were the worst. Coupled with her tea, they brought on a sharp pain from bright lights and an incessant pounding in her head. Her mouth tasted like bile, her neck hurt from the way she had passed out on the couch, and that pounding would not stop.

BoomBoom. Boom. Boom.

Milla rolled over, reached for a pillow to cover her head, and fell off the couch.

"Diego?" She croaked from the floor, frowning down at herself. At some point during her pity party, Milla had changed into one of Ezra's old Joy Division shirts and lost her pants.

At least she'd passed out on the couch and not the floor. Small wins.

She hauled herself onto wobbly legs and scanned the living room. A blanket had tumbled off the couch with her, which meant Diego had tucked her in when she passed out.

"I do not deserve you," she told the living room. The room creaked in reply as if folding its arms and nodding in agreement.

Boom. Boomboom.

Boom.

The demanding pounding changed its tempo, and while it was not a physical manifestation of the pounding in her head, it certainly wasn't helping. She tiptoed to the front window and peered through the blinds, sighting a long shadow pouring down the stairs. The pillars framing the front porch made it impossible to see who was standing outside without venturing into the hallway, where they could see her blurry form through the warped glass pane in the door.

One last rattling *boom* sounded; the shadow did not turn into a retreating form, and Milla sighed.

"Alright, alright." She padded to the hallway, running a hand down her face. Whoever it was clearly wanted to talk to her. Or Diego. The shape at the door was tall, wearing a light blue shirt, tan pants, and finally turning for the stairs. As Milla didn't normally treat with people who wore pastels, there was a high likelihood that they were here for Diego. She hurried to unlock the door, not wanting to miss the opportunity to send something good her roommate's way.

"Did you need something?"

The man turned, looked up at Milla with an appropriately chagrined expression, and she slammed the door.

What the fuck what the fuck what the fuck.

She scrunched her face, pressing her back against the glass, her heart pounding wildly as the Scotsman tapped on the glass.

"Ludmilla?"

"Milla, quien diablos is at the door?" Diego appeared at the top of the stairs, his hair tousled from sleep and glasses askew.

"I don't know. I mean, I do, but I-I don't know how he got here."

"Jesucristo, what did you do before I got home last night?"

"Nothing!"

"Ludmilla?" Another tap on the glass. "Let me explain."

Diego's eyebrows climbed up his forehead.

"Okay, maybe, maybe I wanted to do him, but I didn't. You saw me." She gestured to herself, over-sized band t-shirt, bare legs and all. "Is this the look of a woman who has achieved satisfaction?"

Diego took her in, head-to-toe, and headed back into his room. "Either let him in or tell him to vete a la mierda."

Milla dropped her head back against the glass and closed her eyes.

"I can see your, ehm, arse," the Scotsman mumbled through the warped pane. Milla yelped and whirled around, yanking the door open.

"How the hell did you find me," she hissed in his face.

He retreated and threw his hands up in surrender. The motion pulled the fabric of his light blue polo shirt—tucked into chinos and paired with a braided belt, of course—tight against the trim torso she'd wrapped her legs around the night before, straining the sleeves against the swell of his biceps. "Let me explain, please. That got out of hand."

"Out of hand? We were thirty seconds away from committing a misdemeanor, and you call that *out of hand?*"

"If the misdemeanor in question is indecent exposure, then by all appearances" —he gestured to Milla, braless, oversized Joy Division shirt, no pants— "you're nae too concerned about it." The door creaked as Milla gripped it tighter, fuming at the Scotsman. He glanced past her, leaning slightly to look inside the duplex. "Who were you talking to?"

"My roommate." He raised onto his toes, peering inside. "Did you want something?" She pulled the door partly closed, half hiding herself and half hiding the interior of her home.

"Can I come inside?"

"No."

"Please?" He pulled his sunglasses off, and they disappeared entirely. Milla gaped at him. "What?"

"Your eyes are green."

"...aye?"

"They weren't green yesterday."

His brows drew together. "Are you certain? It was dark in that bar, and you werenae exactly sober."

"No, I'm sure. You had dark eyes, like deep brown. Almost black."

"I have green eyes." His expression eased to a snake oil salesman's easy charm. He twisted his left hand in the air, magicking a card from nothing and offering it to her. "Family trait. Here."

Milla narrowed her eyes at the card. One side was a black so deep it absorbed the morning light, while the other was bone white with three lines of text written in the same disconcerting Stygian shade. She read the words and covered her mouth to keep laughter from spilling. It was too rich, too ridiculous to be real.

"No," she giggled, handing the card back. His eyes dropped to her hand, scanning the warped palm and the surgical scar running from her wrist to the crook of her elbow, and that slick smile melted away.

"No?"

"No. I refuse to accept that this" —Milla flicked the card— "is my reality. So please, take this back, tell my foster mother, 'congratulations, you got me,' and have a nice stay in St. Augustine." She held the card out between them. He slid both hands into his pockets, waiting. Milla grumbled and thrust the card at him again. He shook his head.

"Read the card, Ludmilla." His tone was authoritative and unwavering; final in a way that had Milla swallowing and doing as she was bid. The card shook in her hand, but those three lines of deep, black ink were painfully legible:

DARKLY SIMMONS, MCLP

AURAL INSURANCE ADJUSTER

C.R.O.W., EDINBURGH

"You lied to me." She couldn't look at him. It was too embarrassing.

"Nae technically."

"I asked you to ... we almost ..."

"It's alright." She jerked her face up to meet his gaze and Darkly—seriously, *Darkly*. Utterly ridiculous—grinned. He slid a hand free from his pocket, gesturing at his tall, lanky mass. "Have you seen me?"

"Oh, my *Goddess*." Milla groaned and walked inside her house, slamming the door behind her.

"Who was it?" Diego called from the kitchen.

"No one."

"That did not look like no one." He popped his head out into the hallway with a sly, mocking smile. His hair had been tamed into a low tail, and the witch had donned mid-calf capris and one of Milla's silk robes without bothering to tie it closed. "It looked like you are not as dead inside as you pretend to be."

"Can I come in?" Darkly said through the door.

"No."

"Si! Si, por favor entra!" Diego called. Milla glowered and crossed her arms.

Darkly slid through the narrowly opened door like a shadow, standing a few feet away from Milla with the good grace to seem uncomfortable. She glared at him, he gazed at the crown molding, and Diego returned to cooking breakfast. The morning news trickled down the hallway, punctuating the awkward quiet with depressing coverage.

"—ing news out of Hattiesburg; a woman identified as Mrs. Jennifer Sanderson was found dead in her home. Medical authorities are attributing the death to carbon monoxide poisoning while family members cry foul play. Our local affiliate has the details." The news anchor cut out, and a wet-sounding voice started speaking. "They said it was carbon monoxide, but my sister and my daddy was in the house. They're just fine, and that don't make any sense. None of it makes any sense. She was hardworking, you know? Worked two jobs, *two* to make sure we was comfortable, and then collapses from poisoning none of us got. I-I can't believe she's gone, what are we going to do with all of—"

The sound cut off, and Milla sagged against the wall. Diego mumbled a quiet "Sorry, neteř," from the kitchen, and a second egg hit the pan.

"Are you alright?" Darkly looked down at her, speaking softly.

"Yes," she said. Then sighed. "No. I don't like death."

"Understandable." A beat. "Can I please explain?"

Milla gestured for him to follow her to the living room. Diego, bless him, had tidied the space, and the only evidence of their night was the thick knit hygge blanket artfully draped over the couch's armrest. Milla grabbed a pillow, folded her legs beneath her, and dragged the blanket around her shoulders.

Darkly remained standing, his bright green gaze taking in the room. The framed art deco travel posters of Key West, Munich, Hong Kong, and Prague snagged his attention, which then flittered over the potted plants and shelves crammed with books that hadn't made the cut for the store: some newer best-selling novels, a full run of *The Babysitter's Club*, an embarrassing amount of YA fantasy novels, and a stack of well-worn teeny-bopper magazines.

The singular remaining photo of Milla and Ezra was in a frame on the bookshelf. She pulled the blanket over her head as Darkly sauntered over and picked up the picture. It was taken on a Hong Kong trip just months before Ezra was … Gone. The two of them smiling in a selfie on top of Victoria's Peak with the city skyline rising like dragon's teeth in the background. It had been a clear, windy day, so Milla was pressing down on her black floppy sunhat, grinning up at Ezra, who was flashing a broad, white-toothed smile that crinkled his amber eyes.

"Dinnae ken I ever saw him this happy," Darkly muttered, still studying the photograph in his hand.

"You know Ezra?"

That earned her a look. One that had Milla silently berating herself for phrasing and improper use of tenses.

"I knew him." He nodded, then amended, "A little. My sister worked with him a few times." A faint smile. "He came by for tea."

"Huh." That wasn't surprising. Ezra was engaging and outgoing, easily charming everyone he met. It wasn't unusual for him to get called in by the different agencies of C.R.O.W. He had consulted on the aural readings of other obnubilari and obfuscatio—Mind Witches who could plant illusions and ideas in your head or obscure reality—like himself, worked alongside C.A.R.B.'s Enforcers on a few high-profile missions, and even presented a paper on the benefits of polygraph testing in conjunction with divination and spectral-aura scoping in determining uses of black magick among witches in poor standing.

Ezra Lightner was a household name among witches, even before he—

Milla pulled the blanket tighter across her shoulders and tried to melt into the wool.

"I'm sorry," he blurted, rushing the frame back to the shelf.

"Why are you sorry?"

"For last night and just now?" Darkly frowned at the picture. "It looked like you two were … close."

Milla had no idea what to do with that, so she deferred. "You're here to investigate me. Isn't talking about my dead mentor part of the whole deal?"

"Observing," he corrected. "And yes."

"Well, doing a bang-up job so far, gumshoe." She pulled an arm free from her blanket cave and saluted. Letting an Aural Insurance Adjuster into her demesne might be the only way to keep C.A.R.B. off her back, but it didn't mean she had to be polite about it.

"Milla, does your guest want any eggs?" Diego called from the kitchen. Milla looked to Darkly, who shook his head and mouthed, "No, thank you".

"No," Milla called.

"Okaaay," Diego sang. His bare feet padded against the linoleum, entering the living room. Darkly jerked still, his eyes widened, and the shadows behind him twitched. Milla twisted around to see Diego frozen in the entryway, the plate in his hand tilting precariously and her breakfast sliding off.

"Diego!" She leaped from her blanket cave and bolted over the couch, half aware that, yes, she was only wearing a t-shirt and underwear and had just flashed an ass-full of star-spangled black briefs at the witch sent to investigate her. The eggs hit the floor, and she caught the plate before it fell from Diego's hand. He blinked, shook his head, and began backing away.

"Lo siento, olvidé que tengo que-que … I have to go." He dropped the second plate on the counter and darted out of sight. The back door creaked open, and his feet thudded down the steps.

"What in the nine rings," she muttered, scooping the egg from the floor and dropping it on the plate. Darkly cleared his throat. She looked up to see him towering over the sofa, staring in the direction Diego had disappeared.

"Who was that?"

"My roommate, Diego. You heard him through the door." She scooped up more eggs, stood, and froze. Darkly's shadow was long, cast on the wall behind him in a deep, near impenetrable midnight black. She blinked, and the illusion vanished. Darkly settled in the love seat, seemingly recovered from his first look at Diego Gregorio de Bimini, bespoke witch and cad.

"Oh, that explains it then." She tossed out the flippant remark and passed into the kitchen to dispose of the ruined eggs. "Should I have led with the fact my roommate is a man and I'm the non-judgmental sort?" She grabbed Diego's discarded plate and returned to the living room, forking a pile of fluffy scrambled eggs and popping it into her mouth. She was being churlish; she *knew* she was being churlish, but seriously. What the fuck. "Maybe that would've gotten you to my house."

"Pardon?"

"Diego's a good-looking man. Considering how you two just gawked at each other, well"—she swept her fork over him in a mockery of his earlier gesture—"have you seen you?"

Darkly cleared his throat. "Let's get to the point of my visit, aye?"

Milla sat, pulled the blanket over her legs, and continued eating.

"I owe you an apology."

"Oh, do you?"

His gaze dropped to the blanket wrapped around Milla's shoulders, then lower, before drifting back to her face. "For stopping by unannounced." His cheeks flushed. "I thought it best to properly introduce myself before I bring your *čarodějnice* around."

"Kind of you."

"I should have done so last night," he continued in an even tone. Overly steady as if he had rehearsed this little speech on the way to her house. "It was improper of me to … and it hadnae occurred to me you wouldnae ken who your Aural Insurance Adjuster would be."

"Honestly? I was expecting Eduardo." The Aural Insurance Adjuster she had first registered with was a harried witch who had come into the Ways late in life. A boon, considering Milla was an unregistered witch with a demesne she had little to no idea what to do with at the time. "What happened to him?"

"It was suggested he entertain an early retirement," Darkly answered.

"Fired, then."

He stared at her, expression blank. "It was unprofessional of me to be in a bar, behaving as I did."

"You mean picking up a stranger and dry-humping her in an alleyway." She tried to keep her tone light, but this conversation was hitting a little too close to reality for so early in the morning.

"I …yes." He watched her, waiting for the outburst, the denial. Or maybe he thought she would skip straight ahead to bargaining. It was hard to tell, his eyes had gone dark again, and his face was a stone wall.

"So, is this an official warning? Sober up and fly right, kid, or you're booted from the Witches Only Club."

"Things arenae so dire for you, Ludmilla." She made a face and forked another mound of egg. "But I am here to ensure the stability of your demesne and understand how it is you came to be its steward. It would behoove"—Milla snorted—"you to think about your behavior in relation to your position as Witch of the Demesne."

Milla scanned his face for the disdain, the disappointment, and, worst of all, the pity that so many people cast in her direction.

She found none of it.

That's not to say his face was expressionless, but it lacked anything resembling what she expected. His eyes held hers, his mouth twitched reassuringly, and Milla realized he was concerned. For her.

He's an A.I.A.; it's what they're paid to do. Pretend to care and then slap people with a label, screaming Blackened Aura! Burn the Witch!

Still, there was something about the patient way he waited for her to speak …

She swallowed her bite and looked down at the plate, suddenly very tired. "So, how do we start?"

When he spoke, his tone was soft with a hint of a smile. "Put on a bra and some shorts, aye? Maybe take a shower first?"

She looked up, befuddled by the absolute lack of cruelty or suspicion in any line, shadow, or swell of him. Even on Ezra's best days, when Milla performed to his expectations, there was an edge of danger to the twist of his lips when he kissed her. A prowl to his walk that she found both dangerous and irresistible.

Not so with Darkly Simmons, the Aural Insurance Adjuster who sat there and seemed genuinely kind.

"Baby steps, Ludmilla. Shower, get dressed." He rose, pulling a scrap of paper out of nowhere as he crossed the room and set it on the arm of the couch. Milla glanced at the lines scrawled in a carefully neat hand. An address on Lemon Street, not more than a mile away. "Meet me here at noon and I'll mark that up as a win for the day."

Six

"Bruja, please!" Diego's eyes rounded. He covered his mouth with a hand to hide the laughter. "Please tell me you did not—"

"I did," Milla groaned. She thunked her head against the doorway to the sewing room. "Why did he have to be my A.I.A.?"

"Only you would make advances on the witch sent to investigate us."

"We say 'hit on,' or 'pick up,' in the twenty-first century, and shut up," she snapped. "It's not funny."

"Disagree. Es gracioso." He jabbed a sewing needle in her direction. "And brilliant. I have seen this on CineNet; sleep with him, and he will not be inclined to tell C.R.O.W. how you tend the demesne."

Milla replied with her middle finger. Hours later, standing at one end of a flagstone path, Diego's teasing buzzed like a flea in her ear. She adjusted her shoulder bag, stink-eyeing the cheerful pink Key West-style cottage sandwiched between a cat café and a tattoo shop and weighing the pros and cons of walking away.

"You keen to air the demesne's laundry on the sidewalk?"

At the other end of the path, Darkly leaned against the cottage's doorframe in a jaunty pose: one ankle crossed over the other, holding a quesadilla in one hand, a cup with a bright red straw in the other, and looking for all the world like a Yacht Bro in seersucker shorts, a white fitted button down, and boat shoes.

"I didn't know I was supposed to bring lunch," Milla retorted.

"Werenae." He took a bite, chewed, grinned at her with cheeks full of food like a chipmunk, and walked inside.

"What the fuck does that mean." Milla approached the cottage, avoiding cracks in the flagstone and pausing at the base of the whitewashed stairs. Cutesy beach signs and an obscene number of seashells cluttered the walls, and wicker chairs padded with floral cushions clustered together at one end of the porch. A paint can propped the storm door open, and light blue drops of paint speckled the whitewash from the underside of the porch ceiling having been painted a pale, pleasant hue she recognized as Haint Blue.

There were instances where a witch or mortal passed, and their Shade, or haint, remained topside, chasing people to exhaustion for want of a corporeal body. The ghosts of emotion, Shades, clung to dying thoughts, whether vicious, mournful, or confused.

As creepy as Shades were, the Dark Witches associated with them were even more terrifying. Mortals would call them exorcists, but witches knew better. Dark Witches were the pinnacle of the Forbidden and Foule, capable of controlling Shades and bending them to their will, both the wandering and the still very much attached to their body and Soul.

Ghosts and ghasts. Haints, thralls, and wraiths.

Blanket terms for Shades enslaved and compelled by the Dark Witches deemed too dangerous to exist by C.R.O.W. and hunted by their Enforcers with extreme prejudice.

In Gullah tradition, practiced heavily in the Carolinas, practitioners believed haints could not cross flowing water. As a precautionary measure against both haints and Dark Witches, the low-country witches painted their porch ceilings in this particular hue. Seeing it now, Milla had to admit that the color was an exact match to that of the ocean under a clear blue sky. Still, the practice wasn't common in St. Augustine, which spoke to the practical nature of her A.I.A.

A dream-catcher swaying in a river breeze snagged her attention next. The sigil woven in the band was intended to ward off evil spirits, ghouls, and Shades. Across the porch, an identical sigil was hidden in the seashells of a wind chime. On a hunch, Milla scanned the front yard. Cast in full shadow, a sundial was visible between a cluster of short, plump jelly palms. A useless decoration. Unless …

She climbed the steps, gripped the banister, and rose onto tiptoes. Sure enough, inlaid in the concrete sundial was a third matching sigil.

So the witch was practical and thorough, both traits which made for a good investigator.

Still, the wards were unsettling. She had her own surrounding the duplex: two at the base of her stairs—one a ward against solicitors, the other to warn of unwanted guests—a tightly rolled scroll affixed to the door frame appealing to the Triple Goddess for protection, and another just past the threshold for fortune and happiness. Wards and sigils she refreshed after Morgen's brief visit, which *should* have alerted her to Darkly's presence before he even climbed the stairs.

Milla lowered her heels and faced the cottage, wary.

The open door revealed pale walls rising to a vaulted ceiling, drawing the eye to a driftwood shelf hung over a flatscreen television. Seashells, a school of ceramic fish, and a basket of twigs clustered around letter blocks spelling out "Beachy Keen". A throw pillow-covered sofa faced the flatscreen, and at the opposite end of the room, a floor lamp, end tables, and two armchairs framed a bookshelf. The back wall was split by a narrow hallway leading to the bedrooms and bathroom, and a bar-height cut-out with a marble counter peeked into the kitchen.

It was cute, quaint, and obnoxiously perfect for the witch in seersucker and linen, hunched over the kitchen sink and shoveling an overstuffed quesadilla into his mouth. A news anchor's voice trickled out from the cottage, reading the midday report while Milla and Darkly stared at each other.

"—iesburg, Laurel, Columbia, and Biloxi. Public health officials urge homeowners to replace the batteries in their carbon monoxide alarms, and local fire stations are available to schedule home visits—" the anchor's voice cut off. Darkly winced as he swallowed a half-chewed bite of quesadilla, bright eyes wide and cheeks pinkening.

"Sorry about that." He dropped a television remote on the counter. "We can do this on the porch if you fancy, or I've an office in the back."

Milla eyed the sigils dangling to the east and the west, their invisible net of power tickling the nape of her neck and raising the skin on her arms. "Is that an invitation?"

"So she does practice." He stepped into the hallway, wiping his hands on a towel.

"Not really."

"Caution, that is." The towel vanished, and a broad grin lit up his face. "Blessed be."

"Blessed be," she mumbled.

"Come on in." Darkly sealed her invitation as a wanted guest with a twitch of his left ring finger.

The air around the door fizzled, and Milla took a deep breath, fighting the urge to duck as she crossed the threshold. Passing through a warded liminal space always made her skin itch, and the feel of magickal pressure gave her the irrational fear that something was about to drop on her head, like a brick or a wampus cat.

Nothing happened, thanks to the twitch of his finger. Darkly waved for her to follow him down the narrow hall, striding away without checking to see if she followed. Milla lingered in the living room long enough for his over-tall figure to be swallowed by shadows. She cast one last wistful look at the front yard and flagstone path, took a Big Girl Breath, and powered down the hall.

Buttery sunlight gleamed through a storm door leading to an unfinished patio and modest garden, bare save for a pair of Adirondacks facing a circular fire pit with a metal grate. The fire pit made her skin prickle, and Milla was certain she would find a fourth sigil hidden beneath the ash. To her left was a bedroom, and to the right was what she assumed to be Darkly's temporary office.

Like any good witch, Milla stuck her head in the bedroom and was immediately disappointed.

Bed: made. Dresser: tidy. Suitcase: upright in a corner. Closet: open. An organized array of button-down short-sleeved shirts, polos, a light coat, and a windbreaker hung inside. What looked to be two weeks' worth of t-shirts was folded on a shelf, and in a neat little row on the floor were running shoes, a packed naval seabag, and a pair of well-worn Chuck Taylor's in the classic black.

The bedside table held slightly more in the way of clues: a brass dish candle holder with a fresh mauve candle, unburnt, a box of matches, and, considering its placement on his makeshift altar, what she assumed to be his grimoire. Where hers was oversized and bound in leather from a questionable source, his was an e-book embossed with the official C.R.O.W. sigil.

All of which told Milla nothing beyond the fact he was a well-funded witch.

She popped back out, relieved he hadn't been watching her snoop, and stepped across the hall to his empty office.

This room smelled heavily of a not-unpleasant incense and was even more boring than the bedroom. An achievement, considering the wicker loveseat in front of the window and the massive bean bag filling a corner. A desk was against the wall hosting a thin folder and a small rectangular wooden box, but no chair. A wicker side table sat beside the loveseat, complete with a glass surface over a seashell mosaic. Milla glared at the bean bag, spinning around as the plastic on the loveseat cushions—because *of course* they were covered in plastic—creaked beneath Darkly's weight.

"Where did you—?"

"Have a seat." He gestured to the bean bag.

"I am not sitting there."

"You can sit next to me if you like." He patted the cushion.

Her glower bent into a scowl, and she tried to settle on the bean bag with something resembling dignity. Thankfully, Milla had worn black moto leggings, a French tucked heather purple t-shirt, and black boots, which offered vastly more coverage than an old t-shirt. Not that it mattered. He'd already gotten an eyeful of her hungover ass and a handful before that. Still, bean bags for a proper young witch. It was offensive on several levels.

To start, why did this old woman of a cottage even have a bean bag?

The minutes passed.

Milla would be damned before she started speaking without being prompted. It was the principle of the thing. She didn't want to work with an Aural Insurance Adjuster. She hadn't asked for a demesne or a *čarodějnice*. She hadn't asked for any of this; it was thrust upon her. So she would endure Darkly's self-assured gaze and quiet smirk for the required hour. By her count, there were fifty-five minutes left to go.

After another five minutes, she was uncomfortable. She hooked the heel of one foot under the thigh of the other and tried to lean to the side. Her seat, being a bean bag, had other plans and sent her tumbling onto the floor.

"Mother fu—"

"Fancy a cuppa?" With one arm stretched across the back of the loveseat and an ankle propped on a knee, Darkly watched her with a grin he no longer tried to hide.

"Cuppa?"

"Tea. I only have unsweetened, dinnae ken how you Southerners tolerate that sugary filth."

"Czechian," Milla corrected. He waited. "Not Southern, that is, I would like some tea. Please."

Darkly nodded and rose, disappearing to the kitchen. An electric kettle clicked on, followed by the sound of his rifling through cupboards.

"Peppermint," he called out, "lemon-ginger, or … a winter blend with a rather offensive depiction of Father Christmas on the package?"

"Oh, um, the blend, please," Milla replied, wandering to the window.

Shaded by the rear porch, the window had only a flimsy gauze curtain. Pleasant midday light filled the room, highlighting motes dancing in the air. She was considering asking if she could drag in one of the Adirondacks when Darkly cleared his throat.

"Milk?" Milla shook her head, and he shrugged. "Ach, well, cannae be helped."

The mug was just on the hot side of warm, and she accepted it with a quiet thanks. Darkly smiled, resuming his seat and leaving her to the bean bag. Milla passed her cup from hand to hand, suffering his patient gaze. After another three minutes, she gave up.

"Can I use your restroom?"

Darkly extended two fingers in a lazy point towards the hall.

Milla wasted another ten minutes playing on her phone before he lightly knocked on the door. "Are we alright?"

"Something I ate." She flushed the toilet, washed her hands to the sound of his pacing, and opened the door to an empty hallway. "What?"

Tapping a finger on the frame, Milla thought back to his candle, mentally cursing that it had yet to be burned. She cataloged what she knew of the witch, which was obnoxiously very little.

He did close-up magick, but any kid could master pulling a card from thin air. He was an Aural Insurance Adjuster, so possibly an empath and likely to have some latent skill as a vestic, which wasn't of any concern to Milla. He was cocky and annoying, which were character flaws, not magick, and he had eyes that (allegedly) changed color, a marker of no less than five different Ways Milla could rattle off, none of which would explain the empty hallway.

"Hello?" She called out, feeling stupid, then relieved, and then stupid again when he replied from the office.

"Alright?"

He was back in the loveseat, having drawn the curtains to darken the room. Milla hesitated in the doorway, only re-entering the twilight of Darkly's office when he pointedly checked the time on his phone.

"You've wasted half of my hour. Can we talk about something for the last bit? We could start with something simple if you like." Milla collected her mug from the desk and slurped her tea, pleased when Darkly's eye twitched in annoyance. "How did you end up in St. Augustine?"

Milla glared at him over the rim. "Skilled in the art of subtlety, I see."

Darkly sat up, tugging at the collar of his shirt and clearing his throat. "I'm sorry?"

"Isn't this all in a dossier somewhere?" She mimed looking around the room. "Hard to believe C.R.O.W. would send you here unprepared. I've got to have a file three inches thick by now."

"They did prep me, but I'd rather hear the story from you."

"What story is there to tell?"

"Yours." The calm voice reigned again, and Milla sensed he felt like he had just won a battle. In a way, she supposed he had—he had gotten her to talk by asking about the one thing she didn't want to talk about. "How does a vestic end up as Witch of the Demesne?"

"You're just going to ask?"

"Aye."

"You're a terrible detective," she leveled.

Darkly tipped his head forward. "Aural Insurance Adjuster."

"Whatever."

"Why St. Augustine," he pressed.

Milla gripped the mug in both hands. She didn't want to talk about why she came back. Is this what C.R.O.W. wanted from her? A confession? She deserved punishment for her part in Ezra's scheme, but stealing a confession by making her relive the years she spent with him—how was that fair when none of it was her fault?

Blood rushed in her ears as the old panic took root. She closed her eyes and took deep, steadying breaths in through the mouth, one-two-three-four-five. Out through the nose, one-two-three. In and out, in and out.

The plastic cushions crinkled, and the mug was gently pulled from her hands.

"How about this." Darkly's voice was close and low, as if the witch stood directly before her, ready to catch Milla should she pass out. That he thought her so weak made her furious. If he did, it meant Morgen thought she was weak, and C.R.O.W. must think her useless. Worthless. Fit for the torment of isolation she had condemned herself to. Unfit to be the witch of a demesne she didn't even want. "Tell me about Key West."

His breath puffed against her cheek and her eyes flew open.

Darkly lounged on the loveseat, ankle propped on a knee, mug in hand, watching her with a half-cocked eyebrow. At that, Milla had to finally admit that she was dealing with a witch of an unusual Way.

"How are you doing that?"

"Doing what?" He smiled, but it did not meet his eyes.

She waved her hand in the air. "Skitzing around so quickly."

"Skitzing?"

"Technical term." Milla put her hands on her hips. "How are you doing it?"

"Dinnae ken what you're on about."

"Liar."

"Nae technically."

She glowered. Darkly threw his head back and laughed. *Laughed*. At her. At her frustration and her loss.

"You're a shitty detec—"

"Aural Insurance Adjuster." He leveled his gaze at Milla and stretched a lanky arm along the back of the loveseat, drumming his fingers and looking for all the world like a wolf that had cornered its prey and felt like playing. "Have you seen that old movie about the FBI Agent and the cannibal?"

Milla took a large sidestep for the door. "I have suddenly decided that I do not want to hear the rest of whatever you're about to say."

"Quid pro quo."

She froze. "I'm listening."

"One for one. You tell me something; I'll tell you something. Fair?"

She scoffed. "Hardly."

Darkly rose and crossed the room in one sure stride, stopping close enough that Milla could see the slow, steady pulse on his throat. "I need you, Ludmilla."

Her name was liquid in his mouth, the brogue rolling over the double-l's and sending a shiver down her spine. For a fleeting moment, she thought he might reach for her. Might wind his fingers in her hair and tug her head back. Thought he might slam her up against the floral wallpaper and finish what they'd started the night before. Her belly flipped, traitorous thing that it was.

"What," Milla croaked.

"And I ken I've the right of it when I say you need me." His voice lowered further, and then he did reach out, looping a lock of hair around his finger, frowning, and letting it slip away.

"Just because we hooked up in an alley doesn't mean that—"

"There was a surge of magick tracked by C.R.O.W. a little over two weeks ago." Green eyes locked onto hers. "The sort this demesne hasn't seen in over a year since you assumed the role of Witch of the Demesne." Milla startled back, her heel coming down on the bean bag. "We cannae determine where the surge came from or which witch cast it. As of now, the Demesne of St. Augustine is being watched very closely by all manner of C.R.O.W. agents."

Enforcers, he meant, because who else could he mean?

"I haven't done anything—"

"You need to work with me." His eyes went hard as gemstones, and the smirk vanished. "Answer my questions and show me the demesne is in good hands so I can set C.R.O.W.'s hive mind at ease."

"And why do you need me?"

Her words surprised him, rounding out that stern glare. He lifted his gaze over her head, and in the low light, she tracked a flush blooming on his cheeks. "I, ehm, well—"

"Oh, this is gonna be good."

Darkly scowled, retreating out of her space. "I was benched for a time, if you must know." He plucked at the buttons on his shirt. "This is my first assignment back in the field, and, honestly, I need it to go well."

She scanned him from head to toe, following that with a flick of her finger for good measure. "They had you pushing paperwork?"

He flexed his left hand. "Something like that."

"And you want me to work with you to … what, fix your reputation with the home office?"

His scowl ebbed away. "I want you to work with me so I can deliver your *čarodějnice*, assure C.R.O.W. that the demesne is safe and secure in the hands of a capable witch, and get back to my life as soon as possible."

Milla lowered herself to the beanbag and looked pointedly at her phone. "You have fifteen minutes." Which only seemed fair, considering the amount of exposition he'd just given for free.

Darkly shot her a cautious smile and settled on the loveseat, leaning over his knees. "Your parents. Quadmilla and Hector, why did they send you to the Morgenhexe?"

"She's an old family friend." He waited, and Milla sighed, taking the hint. "My father and Morgen were Enforcers together; apparently, there was some sort of debt between them, and he called it in when I was eight."

"Why?"

"Mm-mm. That was two, technically three. Your turn."

"Hit me." Darkly smiled.

"Tempting." Milla mulled her many questions about this formerly benched Aural Insurance Adjuster: why did they send you? What do you know about me? What got you benched? What work did you do with Ezra?

That one gave her pause. The ravenous need she still held for any shred of Ezra's life beyond her was staggering. It had driven Milla to scour his notebooks and, in one shameful instance, call a number scrawled on the corner of a page only to hang up when a woman answered.

She settled instead on something safe. Easy.

"Do you have any siblings?"

"One." Darkly sat back. "A sister, as I mentioned."

"Oh." Milla hadn't remembered until he said it. He had a sister who had worked with Ezra. A lump formed in her throat, and a full minute passed before she realized Darkly was waiting for her to speak. "No siblings. An only child."

He slouched on the loveseat. "She's older. My Mum and Da passed when I was eleven. She took over my guardianship and became my *polednice*. Our Ways are similar, after a fashion. You could say I followed in her footsteps in working for C.R.O.W."

"That was five."

Darkly ran a hand through his hair, mussing the wavy strands. "So it was."

Milla tried to anticipate his next question, and when it finally came, she was legitimately surprised.

"After all you've been through, why didnae you stay in Český-Krumlov?" He paced out the question as if afraid she'd make a run at the door. Maybe that was the reason she answered honestly. Or maybe it was the way he spoke so reverently of his sister.

"There was an incident when I was young that scared my mom. My dad blamed me; I was shipped off to Florida, and the rest is history." She scratched the surgical scar on her right arm, just below the crook of her elbow. It tingled sometimes, a phantom memory of the pain she had endured. "Those months back in Český-Krumlov, after Ezra, didn't help. My relationship with my mom has been pretty bad since, well, *him*." She scanned her palms, the ruin of her lifeline, and the utter destruction of her head and heart lines. "It felt like I had unfinished business in St. Augustine, and my presence in Český-Krumlov wasn't doing anyone any good."

"Six." Darkly was tense and pale, his attention hovering somewhere over her head.

"You okay?"

He blinked, shaking free from whatever had grabbed him. "Dinnae have to go into it if you're nae ready."

"Isn't that the whole point of this?"

"No." He frowned, scratching idly at the center of his chest and shifting uncomfortably on the plastic cushions. "Perhaps it would be better if we discussed your future."

"My future?" Milla snorted. "You know my mom is a vestic, right?"

"Aye," he snapped. "And we both know I meant a future in your demesne without C.R.O.W. interference."

Milla stared at him, stunned that a stranger like Darkly would be concerned with her potential for a future in anything. Milla's story was told. It featured a meet-cute, a training montage, a falling-for-each-other sequence, and everything. There were even steamy shower scenes for crying out loud—a beginning, middle, and end. Love and loss, fade to black and roll credits.

Milla's story was over.

Darkly plucked the tan folder from the desk and pulled a pencil out of nowhere. "So, how did a vestic win this demesne?"

"Isn't that in my file?"

"Quid pro quo, Ludmilla." He crooned her name with a sharp slash of a smile that unfurled something dark in her belly. A malevolence darkened his eyes, and his grin turned cruel. "Wouldnae want me to report back to C.R.O.W. with anything Forbidden or Foule, would we?"

*

"Asshole." Bells jangled as Milla stormed into Southern Gothic. She slapped her hands on the display case, half-aware of the sandy grit growing beneath her palms. "Cocky, self-assured, Highland-coo-loving asshole." Diego stared at her over his thick black frames, eyebrows firmly pinned at his hairline. "I can't believe I have to endure that quesadilla eating, boring clothes having, Tiki drink loving, card-pulling-out-of-nowhering—"

"Asshole?" Diego ventured.

"Yessss," Milla dragged her hands in the air. "He's the wooooooorsssssst."

"Be that as it may, you should save this little whatever-it-is for later. First of all"—Diego ran a finger through the sugar-fine sand on the display and showed it to Milla—"you need to drink your tea. There was another rat kicking in the trap today."

"Goddess." She dropped her arms. "Remind me to place an order from Savannah."

Diego nodded. "And two, you should see to your friend."

"My friend?"

Diego pointed over Milla's shoulder at Julie, hovering by the corkboard. She was in her scrubs, stained with what, exactly, Milla didn't care to know. Her shoes were worn from the rub of bunions, and one had a completely different lace.

"Is this a bad time?" She winced.

"Oh! No, this is a great time." Milla waved her over. "I just … I started seeing a, um," she glanced to Diego for help. He offered none. "A therapist." Julie's eyes darted to Milla's hand and back to her face. The witch couldn't blame her; she'd been the nurse on duty when Milla was brought in for the injury. "The sessions are really, uh, tough."

Julie's face relaxed, a soft smile easing the strain on her eyes. "Milla, that's wonderful. I'm proud of you."

"Thanks." Milla's responding smile was weaker. "So, what's up?"

"I just … I had an idea after y'all's argument yesterday."

"Oh." Her stomach sank. She had yet to puzzle a way out of the mess she caused, and the way Diego's nails scratched the display case, told her he was still angry about the Yap! Reviews. "Shit, I guess you did hear all of that."

Julie inhaled and unleashed a stream of prattle. "I didn't mean to eavesdrop but cheese and rice, those reviews are awful! I know you're not racist, and anyone who takes half a second to look at the books you sell would never think you couldn't read! Anyways, it got me thinking: do you remember my friend? From out of town?" She didn't wait for Milla to answer, hardly pausing for a breath before pressing onward. "Well, I was talking to her about what happened, which I know I should have asked you first, but the whole thing makes me so sick, and then she offered some advice."

"Okay?"

"Milla, I think this is the answer."

"What?"

"Icy Me. I know you hate the florals and pastels, but I think it would work."

"I'm sorry," Diego blinked rapidly. "Icy who?"

"Icy Me," Julie smiled. "She has this extra inventory she can sell me, and I thought…" Julie looked between Diego and Milla.

Milla, for her part, was completely lost. Diego, however, had the beginnings of a smile and a scheme in his eyes. He pointed at Julie. "I think I see where you are going with this." He faced Milla. "Milla, yes."

"Diego, what?" Milla shook her head. "Julie, what?"

"Leggings, scarves, nothing too gaudy, and Diego can pick out future stock once we off-load the initial inventory."

"Milla, yessss," Diego bounced on the balls of his feet, slapping his hands against the glass counter, which caused Julie to do the same. "Think of the foot traffic!"

"And you can upsell your trinkets and creepy stuff, gain new clientèle, new reviews …" Julie kept talking, selling Milla on an idea that she was just now coming to understand.

She took in her store: the totally not haunted mirror, bookshelves with editions both rare and foreign, Victorian gowns and a cluster of traveling trunks, clocks, pocket watches, dolls that followed you around the room with their eyes, a true Berthoud chronometer that she could never get to work. All the antiques and vintage memorabilia wielding a magick of their own. Her gaze drifted to the window, where she tracked a moth flitting up from the trap on the sill. Finally, she turned to Diego, her mind made up before he spoke.

"Milla, you promised you would fix this." He showed her their Yap! reviews. Southern Gothic had lost two more stars, a death knell for a store in a city that thrived on tourist-backed wallets and word of mouth.

It felt like an ending, an admission that the past was truly over. It was time to leave it where it belonged and move on.

"Alright."

SEVEN

CLOVE Protection and cleansing. Grind and burn in censer for exorcism and to drive away hostile forces. Steep in tea/potions to protect love and cleanse aura.

(protect from dwindling? threat? or to maintain? ask ~~rai~~)

"VARSITY IN HIGH SCHOOL and on partial scholarship at Flagler."

"D'ye still run?" Darkly reclined on the beanbag, long legs stretched out. The room was small enough, and he was long enough, that his feet were almost touching her boots. Milla had considered skipping their meeting until Diego pointed out Darkly knew where they lived.

"He has a file on you, bruja. I would not be surprised if that file has the address of our store and a list of your favorite bars."

She gloomed over that for her walk from the Colonial Quarter to his rented cottage, storming down the hallway to claim the loveseat. In the last three days, she had succeeded twice, her victory muffled by an unbothered Darkly flopping onto the bean bag and lounging like a co-ed rather than interrogating her as the somewhere near thirty Aural Insurance Adjuster he claimed to be.

Milla was unconvinced. His easy approach to their meetings, the quid pro quo, and the fact that he had yet to present her *čarodějnice* or follow along while she worked the demesne was entirely unlike her previous experience with an A.I.A.

Eduardo was a witch in over his head, being eaten alive by mosquitoes while trudging after Milla as she hunted skunk apes. Middle-aged and soft around the middle, Eduardo made sense. Handsome Scottish witches who looked like they stepped out of a J. Crew brochure did not grow up to become occult insurance claims adjusters.

She gave him a pointed look, crossed her arms, and waited.

He chuckled. "Fitba."

"I'm sorry, what?" Milla sputtered.

"Football," he over-enunciated. "Soccer. Though now it's mostly boxing thanks to a torn ACL." He gestured to his right knee. "Never quite healed all the way. How often do you run?"

"Every day, when I can manage," she supplied, adding in a rare bout of generosity, "keeps me in decent shape, and it's a low-effort way to charge the demesne."

"Two spells, one cauldron, I like it," Darkly said. "One question, though."

"Yeah?"

"D'ye run before the sun rises?"

"What?"

Darkly laughed, extending his foot and tapping her bare shin with the toe of a boat shoe. "Paler 'n death's horse."

Milla's stomach plummeted.

Darkly must have mistaken her stricken expression for something else. He winked. *Winked.* And caught himself. "Just, ehm, pale for a runner. In Florida." He tugged the sleeve of his polo shirt and drew his legs in to adopt yet another effortlessly casual pose—forearms on his knees, fingers of one hand lightly circling the opposite wrist— and the chagrined smile he sent her way made Milla's neck crawl with heat.

"Oh, my Goddess, I'm beginning to see why they benched you."

"Dinnae ken the half of it." His phone chimed in a pocket, and Darkly slid it free, frowning at whatever message or notification he had received.

"I mean, you're clearly awful at your job," Milla continued, trying to get a rise out of the witch. "Treating these like shitty therapy sessions."

"Paranormal psychiatry," he muttered, swiping a response into the phone. "I've clearance to bring around your *čarodějnice* tomorrow." He shot her an apologetic look, though apologetic for what, Milla had no idea. His eyes drifted to the window, and whatever he saw made him frown. "We should call it for today. Afraid I've kept you longer than our hour."

Milla glanced at her phone. "Only by a minute."

"Aye?" Darkly double-checked the time, a line forming between his brows, and frowned at the window. The sky had darkened to a hazy, overcast twilight, slowly enough that her eyes had adjusted to the fading light without notice.

Milla started to … thank Darkly for his time or maybe say goodbye? Whatever she had been about to say, however, vanished at his expression. It wasn't fear, but something had spooked him. Eyes wide, lips parted, Darkly had risen from the bean bag and positioned himself in the furthest corner of the room. The dark eyes were back, and his cheeks had paled to a shade closer to hers.

"You alright?"

"M'fine," he snapped, black eyes finding hers. He cleared his throat, rubbing a hand over his face. "Fine, just … I need to make a call."

"Okaaay." Milla rose from the loveseat and grabbed her bag. "So, see you tomorrow?"

"Hmm?" Darkly was staring out of the window again, holding his phone in his right hand while the left summoned and banished a large black coin. "Yeah, tomorrow. Aye."

"Right. Bye." Milla left down the narrow hallway. The front door banged closed behind her, and she stopped short of the stairs, cursing at the blinding brightness of the midday sun.

"If he's such a terrible therapist, why are you still seeing him?" asked Julie.

"I don't know," Milla lied, reaching across her coffee table for the bottle of wine.

"I knooow," Diego sang from the kitchen. "You should see him. Better yet, you should see her after she sees him."

Julie pursed her lips, her eyes rounded, and a little squeak escaped, the dam breaking. "Oh. My. Lanta. Does Milla have a crush?"

"No."

"She propositioned him in a bar." Diego sauntered into the living room, a charcuterie board in one hand and a full glass of wine in the other.

"No!" Julie exhaled.

"Shut. Up." Milla's neck crawled red. "And that was *before* he became my—"

"You *do* have a crush! It's about time." The nurse jogged her shoulder against Milla, causing her to spill wine on the coffee table. "Oh, sugarsnaps, sorry!" Julie grabbed her scrub top from the floor and wiped up the mess, beaming at Milla the entire time.

"I'm super proud of you for seeing a therapist, even if you did develop the world's most inadvisable crush—"

"I don't have a crush on him."

"—so long as you don't act on it. Ohmygosh, did I tell you about the ED Counselor who started dating a patient? He proposed before anyone found out, and then they invited his boss to the wedding, and an HR assistant saw the invite on her desk. It was super awkward because she and the counselor used to date—" She paused, sipping her wine and waving a hand as she swallowed. "Anyways, one thing led to another, and now they live in New Mexico and raise goats."

Milla blinked at the nurse, clutching her glass in both hands. "The … HR Assistant and the boss?"

"No!" Julie cackled, dancing her feet on the ground. "The patient and her ex-husband."

"Who is … the counselor?" she tried again.

"Oh, no, he's up in Valdosta now. I think. I'm not really sure, anyways, just don't act on anything, and you'll be fine."

"Noted." Milla nodded, grinning at the mortal. One of these days, she'd manage to wrangle an entire story from the woman, but for now, she was content to let her chatter on in her uniquely Julie way. She leaped from topic to topic, dropping key exposition to share another juicy bit of gossip or interesting thing she'd learned that day.

Once, early in their friendship, Milla had complained to the nurse about a blackened toenail earned from running in old shoes. By the end of the conversation, she'd learned about fungal remedies, the importance of changing out your insoles halfway through a fourteen-hour shift in the emergency department, and that Eun-Ji from the salon in the Colonial Quarter had moved to Tampa with her dachshund and a woman named Katie.

As always, story time with Julie was a delight, so long as the focus wasn't on her.

"So." Milla sipped her rosé, pointedly addressing Julie head-on. "Let me down easy. What of my vintage curios—"

"Your creepy shit," Julie muttered into her wine glass, eyes bright with laughter.

"—I need to move for this inventory."

"¡Espere!" Diego rushed in, a newly opened bottle of Garnacha in hand. He settled on the corner of the coffee table and leaned forward, placing a hand on Milla's knee. "Wait. Waitwaitwait, we get to move your creepy shit?"

"Some of my creepy shit," Milla acceded. "I am still a dealer of curios and antiques."

"And leggings and blouses and jewelry," Julie added. "We also need to think about our web presence and how to incorporate the seasonal displays best."

Milla and Diego shared a look.

"Is that wrong?" The nurse shrank in on herself. "I was researching marketing on the internet." In the silence that followed, Julie looked down at her feet. "I'm sorry, that was probably overstepping. You're doing me a favor by hosting my inventory—"

"No, no." Milla sat up, absolutely unwilling to let her friend stew in misappropriated defeat. "You are doing us"—Diego cleared his throat— "me the favor. I messed up, and you were the one to find a solution. *Julie.*" She layered intent into her words. A little bit of witchiness to gain the full attention of her mortal friend. "Thank you. Truly. What do we need to move in the store?"

The nurse's blue eyes rounded, her lips parting in surprise. Diego brushed his hand against Milla's knee, warning her to lay off on the intent. She released a heavy sigh, settling back against the cushions.

"Why don't I leave you to it?" she prompted.

Julie blinked, shook her head, and smiled dazedly. "Really?" Hope threaded softly in that singular word, thawing a cold, embittered piece of Milla.

"Really. I trust you." She grinned at Diego, then the nurse. "Both of you."

And leave them to it, she did, reading a book about wizards in Chicago while they planned the displays. The sting of having to move around some of her favorite urns, mantel clocks, and the ventriloquist's dummies that absolutely were not possessed by the souls of their former owners was a bit harsher than she expected, and she finally headed into her room when the Garnacha was gone, waving off a farewell from Julie and a hollered reminder from Diego.

"Do not forget to place that order from Savannah!"

When Milla wandered into Southern Gothic the next morning, tired from her run and hungover from the wine, the store was a riot of one witch action. Diego had already re-arranged some of her eclectic wares to accommodate the new inventory. Teal, pink, yellow, and lime green stood in sharp contrast to the muted browns, navy blues, and worn brass palette of the antiques—garish and lip-curling.

Milla hated it, but her roommate was utterly in his element, tearing open boxes and judging the clothing with the critical eye of a Stitch Witch. He had begun organizing the merchandise in piles she recognized as Passing Fair, Wretched, and What Were

They Thinking, the last of which held a mountain of leggings and a-line dresses compared to the others.

Cardboard boxes filled any available space on the floor, and printed on the side of each, in a boldly flourished style, were the letters I-C-Y-M-I, each "i" capped with a tittle of unfurling flower petals. The logo was vaguely familiar, but Milla couldn't place where she'd seen it before. She cocked her head, mouthing the letters, and then groaned. "ICYMI. Icy Me. Ugh."

At her disdain, Diego surfaced from his fast-fashion fugue state and gestured to the stack of boxes beside the register. "Bangles, earrings, scrunchies, and headbands. There are a few stands in the back you can use. Make it look like you did not decorate it."

"You got it, boss." She saluted and dropped her bag on the floor behind the counter. She popped up after digging around in a few baskets beneath the China hutch. "Where's the box cutter?"

"Use the safety scissors in the arts and crafts bin."

"It's not an arts and crafts bin," Milla grumbled.

"Then why do you have children's scissors?"

"I got them the last time I made tea." She dug through the plastic tub filled with permanent markers, stickers, tape, and tags, withdrawing a pair of bright pink safety scissors, the rounded blades covered by a plastic butterfly cover. "It was all Shopaholic had."

"Hmm." Diego withdrew the box cutter from his fanny pack. He stooped low and swept the blade across the top of a box. "Speaking of tea, did you remember to place an order?"

"Oh, shit, no. I've got to do that today."

"Bruja." He rolled his eyes in exasperation. "You *do* remember what happened the last time you made it yourself, si?"

"I was desperate!"

"And I had just gotten here!" Diego crossed his arms. "It was hard enough trying to figure out how to work the television, much less what to do with you."

"Alright, alright." She threw her hands up in surrender. "I'll order more tea."

"Si. Do that." Diego pointed the box cutters at Milla, blew her a kiss, and returned to sorting clothing. Julie arrived with coffee and pastries, unloading her goodies on the glass display and rushing to help Diego shove an armoire into the furthest corner of the store. Within a few hours, Southern Gothic was transformed from eclectic and wonderfully weird into a pastel nightmare.

Pinching a scrunchie between her fingers, Milla's lip curled at the slippery feel of the fabric. "This makes us no better than Shopaholic."

"I do not disagree, but look." He hooked a thumb at the door where some of the post-brunch tourist crowd had stopped to eye the new displays. Julie was in front of the window, waving at the tourists and adjusting the dress on a headless mannequin Milla had tracked down in an abandoned department store in central Georgia. It liked to move when your back was turned, so she was fairly certain it wouldn't be pleased to wear a sky-blue dress plastered in white and yellow daisies.

"This is what we need," Diego continued. "If there is one thing I know, it is how to adapt to the times."

They sold five hundred dollars of hideous leggings in the first hour.

Milla staggered out into the St. Augustine sun, dazed and disbelieving. Southern Gothic rarely cleared that amount in a day, save an hour. Her index finger was sore from the register, and her hands were riddled with paper cuts from crisp twenties. When her stomach growled, Diego issued his lunch order and waved her away. She returned from Old City Biscuits, brushing crumbs from her lips, to find Julie redressing the mannequin, her phone pinched between her cheek and shoulder.

"You weren't kidding, this is incredible!" She grinned at Milla, listening to whoever was on the call. "No, I can't believe it. In an hour. Uh-huh, I—oh, you think I should?" She chewed on her lip and glanced at Diego. "Okay, yeah, yeah. I think I can swing it. How's the cruise?" Julie's eyes widened at whatever the person said, and she covered her mouth with a hand. "That's awful. Are you alright? Yeah, no, I know you were looking forward to it … oh, I hate that for you. Duval Street's so much fun. At least there's New Orleans … uh-huh … uh-huh … yeah, I'll run an inventory check … I will, promise … ok, bye, hon!" Julie grabbed her phone, rolling her shoulder and stretching out her neck. She smiled apologetically at Milla. "Sorry, that was my Upline."

"Your what line?"

"Upline," Julie explained as if that explained it, wandering down the hall and out of earshot.

"I'm going to need an explanation." Milla appealed to Diego, who had taken over re-dressing the mannequin. She checked the time on her phone, half-registering the unread text notification and a missed call. "But quickly, I need to get over to *Dr. Darkly's*"—she emphasized with a mocking tone and air quotes—"for our session."

"Not much to explain," Diego said. "It was her Upline. The woman calls her like three times a day."

"Her Upline?"

Diego ran a hand down the mannequin's arm and wandered through the racks to drop his sewing kit on the counter. "It is whoever got her into ICYMI. They have regular check-ins, a chat group; pequeña bruja, it is a whole thing that I do not have the patience for."

Milla opened her mouth to press him, whirling around when the bells over the door jangled, and a familiar voice exclaimed, "Mein Gott, what have you done to your store?"

EIGHT

THE COLD, TEUTONIC VOICE snapped Milla's spine straight. Diego spun around, took one look at the tall, imposing figure of the Morgenhexe, and promptly found somewhere else to be. Morgen tracked his retreat and pulled a blue and white gingham scarf off a rack near the door, holding it to the light. "Hideous." The scarf fluttered to the ground, disdain wafting from the witch. "Ruins the entire aesthetic."

"That's what I said," Milla exhaled. She skirted around the counter and approached her foster mother. "What are you doing here?"

Morgen's placid expression tightened. "Blessed be, Ludmilla."

"Blessed be," she mumbled to the floor, ears burning at the reprimand.

Morgen scrutinized the witch from the top of her head down to her feet. "You look well."

"Passing fair."

"I am certain the A.I.A. assigned to your demesne will report that he is pleased with your stewardship."

Milla snorted. "If he ever feels like doing his job."

"Have you not been proving yourself to C.R.O.W. as Witch of the Demesne?" Morgen arched a brow. Elegantly. Which was utterly unfair.

"No," she blurted. "I mean, yes. We meet for like an hour every day at his ridiculous pink cottage, but all he wants to talk about is how I spend my free time."

"Every day." The other eyebrow followed. "I hope you are not allowing yourself to become distracted, Ludmilla. It would not be wise to have a repeat of your time with Master Lightner."

Milla curled her hand into a fist, biting her tongue to keep from blurting out that of the two of them, Darkly was the one who kept getting *distracted*. "No."

"No?"

"No, *Jezibaba*."

"Good." Morgen gave a terse nod. "Now, where is he?"

"Where is…?"

"Your Aural Insurance Adjuster." She swept around Milla, charging past the fixture of scarves to thumb through a stack of tightly folded tunic tops on an end table. "Is he not here yet?"

"Why would he be here? I told you, he barely does his job. He just asks me inane questions over lunch."

"Dinnae ken my questions are *that* inane," Darkly snarked from the door, over-tall body filling the frame. "How else would I have learned Osprey has the best tacos in St. Augustine?"

"El Potro has the best tacos in town," Milla corrected.

"Agree to disagree."

"And what in the nine rings are you doing here?" She dropped a hip against the counter and glared at Darkly.

"What am I—" the witch blinked, bewildered. "I told you yesterday—"

"Not distracted at all," Morgen mused.

"—that I was bringing your *čarodějnice* by today." Darkly stepped into the store, revealing the young woman that had until then been hidden by his mass.

"My …" Milla slid her gaze to the borderline ethereal young woman standing in the doorway.

In black leggings and a fashionably baggy v-neck under an oversized cardigan, she exuded a social media influencer vibe that, next to Darkly's cowl-necked cardigan and unnecessary scarf, had them looking like a matched pair. Hair like spun caramel gleamed under the fluorescents, accenting tanned, dewy skin, and draping over her shoulders in long, beachy waves Milla could never in a million years manage.

If Milla were being honest with herself, which was a new thing she was trying, she had absolutely zero memory of Darkly telling her he was bringing her *čarodějnice* by today. Between his weird freak-out during their session, the morning rush to fit ICYMI into her store, and the onslaught of customers, she barely even registered it was a Friday. But sure enough, here was her apprentice, gazing up at Darkly with a look that bordered on adoration, which was the last thing the over-tall C.R.O.W. witch needed.

Her warm, honey-amber gaze drifted to Milla, and an expression of unfettered hope replaced the open adoration of Darkly. A weird flutter began in her belly, followed by a flush of warmth crawling out from the center of her chest.

Nerves, she realized with a start. She was *nervous* and, dare the witch to admit, excited.

"Milla," Darkly spoke softly. His back was straight, shoulders tense, and green eyes watching her with a closeness, reminding Milla that this was a test. All of it was a test. The sessions, the quid pro quo, her apprentice. Every moment in this Aural Insurance

Adjuster's presence was a test, and she'd been foolish to pretend otherwise, if only for a second. "This is your *čarodějnice*, Ana Maria Metresa. Ana, meet your *polednice*."

"Blessed be." Ana dipped her chin. "It is so nice to meet you." Her slight smile blossomed into a broad grin, and she grabbed Milla's hand, giving it an energetic shake and releasing it just as quickly. Her upper lip twitched—the only outward sign of what she thought of Milla's cold, clammy skin. "I'm sorry, that was so forward. I just–it's been—"

"Blessed be," Milla saved the witch from herself, nerves vanishing at Ana's endearing awkwardness. "How have you been settling in?"

"Well, I'm stuck at my grandparents' house without a car, no one delivers out to Vilano Beach, and CineNet has gotten so boring lately." Again, she smiled at Darkly, who was squinting at the new merchandise in Milla's store. "Probably would have gone crazy if it wasn't for Mr. Simmons."

The witch in question coughed into his fist, his cheeks flushing bright pink. "Darkly, please. Just Darkly."

Julie chose then to wander over, all mortal innocence and a bright, curious smile. "Hi, y'all! Welcome to Southern Gothic." She offered her hand to Morgen, who stared at the appendage with barely concealed disdain. "I'm Julie, just helping Milla out for a few days."

Morgen looked to Milla.

"Oh." *Shit.* "Um, this is my foster mother, Morgen," she gestured to the Morgenhexe, who inclined her head, "and my … therapist." Milla swept her hand at Darkly, only realizing what she'd said when his eyebrows rose, and an infuriating smirk drove a dimple into his cheek. *Double shit.* "Mr. Simmons."

A light akin to laughter sparkled in his eyes, and Darkly shook her hand. "Pleasure."

"Julie?" Diego's head popped out of the hallway. "Can you cover the register?"

"Oh!" The nurse shot the party of witches an apologetic smile and squeezed through them to slip behind the display. "On it, Diego!"

"Thanks, tío," Milla muttered under her breath. The Stitch Witch had an uncanny ability to know when she needed help, and for every day of the last year, Milla had been grateful for him.

"Tío?" Darkly asked.

"My uncle," Milla answered. "On my father's side." She tried to smile at her new *čarodějnice*, surprised when it came easily. "Sorry, I'm not really sure how all of this works. I was eight when Morgen became my *jezibaba*."

"A demonstration is traditional," said Morgen. "Shall we head to the office?"

"Uh, sure." Milla gestured for the group to follow. "Fair warning, my office is tiny. Like, really tiny." A glance back at the imposing Morgenhexe and over-tall C.R.O.W. witch had Milla frowning. "Honestly, I don't know how we're all going to fit."

"We will make do," Morgen stated.

"I don't know." The witches formed a single file line, the shortest leading the way. "It's small on a good day, but with all of Julie's inventory, we had to start using it as a stockroom."

Milla shouldered the door open, revealing a space not much bigger than a closet. ICYMI boxes filled every shelf and surface, save for the narrow folding table acting as her desk. A decrepit laptop covered in stickers lay closed on the table beside a pile of notepads and a small tray of office supplies. An antique swiveling chair with a wicker back and brass wheels sat behind the desk, accessible by a narrow, Milla-sized path between the boxes.

"Wait," Ana blurted at the reveal. "Is *all* of this ICYMI?"

"Yeah." Milla glanced back at her apprentice. "You know it?"

"Of course I do!" She squeezed around Milla and flipped up the box panel, eyes scanning the contents. "It just popped up one day. A friend back home, in Bellevue, got involved super early, and now she runs a massive downline."

"Those are … words." Darkly covered his mouth with a hand, but Milla heard the smile he tried to hide.

"Laugh all you want. One of her crosslines made enough to open a boutique in West Hattiesburg. I think it's closed now, though," she frowned ."Family illness or something."

"Really?" Milla scrunched her nose at the boxes. "Someone opened a store with this crap?"

"Really," Ana nodded. "Sells like hotcakes. You'll need to place another order soon, or you'll run out of inventory."

"Wait, what?" Milla gaped at the boxes. "How?"

"ICYMI," Ana explained as if that explained it.

"Right, well, until that happens, my office is a stockroom."

"It was already a stockroom," Morgen sniffed. "You gave the office to your employee."

"Roommate," Milla corrected.

"I thought he was your uncle," Darkly muttered.

"And he runs his tailoring out of there," Milla continued. "I didn't need the space."

"Things change, Ludmilla." The Morgenhexe disappeared behind a tower of boxes, reappearing as she settled in the swiveling chair. Milla pulled a folding chair out from between two stacks of boxes and propped it against the table. She glanced between Darkly and Ana, trying to determine the most proper way forward when the C.R.O.W. witch spared her.

"I'll stand." He shoved a stack of boxes into the hallway and stepped into the office, crowding against Ana, who bit her lip and blushed. Milla watched the pair dance around each other—Darkly trying to close the door around his large, lanky frame, and Ana, who *could* move out of his way but chose to let the preppy witch repeatedly butt and brush up against her instead.

She rolled her eyes, pulling two boxes from a stack and plopping down on top of them. "So," she said when Ana had settled in her folding chair. "You're from Hattiesburg?"

"A suburb. I live—lived," her eyes dropped as she corrected herself, "with my parents on Canebrake Lake."

"There was an incident, as we discussed," Morgen stepped in, aware that both *čarodějnice* and *polednice* were grateful for the interruption. "The Ways only opened to Ana a few years ago. Her previous mentor, Tracy, was a technomantic who trained under me at Big Torch Key." She shot a pointed look at Milla. "You may be familiar with her work; the E.R.I.E. scan functions off of her research."

Being exceedingly familiar with E.R.I.E. scans, Milla whistled. Properly known as Energy Reading Investigatory Equipment, the E.R.I.E. worked by scanning a witch's energy signature to identify their Way. Ezra had been part of the data pool when C.A.R.B. was first testing the technomancy, and to this day, his energy signature as an Obnubilari served as the data point for capturing reads on other Mind Witches. Now, every Enforcer was equipped with an E.R.I.E., using them in their unending hunt for desecrants, blackened auras, and witches Forbidden and Foule.

"That is an impressive resume," she said carefully. Three witches stared at her for a moment before Milla realized she was expected to lead the conversation. "Um, right. So …" Morgen offered absolutely zero assistance. Darkly frowned, darting bright eyes towards Ana along with the tiniest jerk of his head. "Right! Demonstration." Milla straightened on the boxes and faced her *polednice*. "Ana, would you be comfortable showing me your Way?"

The relationship between a *polednice* and *čarodějnice* was one of the few which allowed one witch to ask another their Way. Outside of this and the rude use of an E.R.I.E. scan, a Way was offered, never demanded, and a witch's Ways were unique.

Most mortal knowledge of witches came from fairy tales and films, casting the wanderers of the Ways as old women in candy huts or a threesome of Mother–Maiden–Crone waving their hands over a bubbling cauldron. To mortals, witches were occult creatures consumed by the dark arts. Necromancy, haruspicy, hexes, and curses. Blights on the land and womb, flooding of the plains and homes, all blamed on the wicked witches of human lore without any allowance for the Fine and Faire among them.

This was wrong, obviously. There was an obnoxious amount of Fine and Faire witches wandering around, Milla's present company included.

Regardless, the Ways were many and open only to those borne of a magickal maternal line.

As the daughter of a vestic, or seer, she had inherited that particular Way from her mother. Though where Quadmilla Probuditna was known for her skill in divining, Milla's sorry attempts at seeing could hardly be relied upon. Partly to blame was the true nature of her Way, but mostly, it was the childhood she spent being trained by Morgen. The focus on hand-to-hex casting had left Milla's vesticism to fritter and waste away until it was more of a burden than a skill. Now and then, when emotions were high and her stress level near its breaking point, she would see the potentials in a circumstance. Reality would fracture, showing Milla three separate truths, but the magick was nearly useless without the trained skill of a true vestic.

Still, every witch had a Way.

"Yes, please demonstrate." Morgen templed her fingers under her chin, oceanic eyes cast towards Darkly. "I am very interested in what sort of witch C.R.O.W. has sent my foster daughter."

"As am I," Darkly mumbled.

Milla twisted on her boxes. "You don't know?"

He shoved his hands into the pockets of his cardigan. "Rude to ask."

"Of course, I'll demonstrate!" Ana scooted to the edge of her chair and began picking through the office supplies next to Milla's laptop. She dumped a handful of paperclips on the table and threaded them together, talking as she worked. "It works best with inorganics and synthetics like polyester, nylon, anything with an acrylic or acetate base. Paperclips wouldn't usually work, but you've got these cheap plastic ones, so I should be able to get it to go."

"To go?" Milla slid off her boxes and hovered over Ana's shoulder. The young witch threaded two more paperclips onto the center link in her chain, splaying them out like arms.

"I know, it's weird. Tracy didn't know what to do with me." Ana looked up at Milla, smiling. "Said I kept messing up her E.R.I.E."

Milla glanced at Morgen, who was watching the girl work with a careful eye. Not a great sign.

Ana laid her paper clips out carefully, adjusting the next set of clips as though they were legs. "Can you summon some salt?"

"Can't summon." Milla dug a tiny carton of Morton's out of a crate shoved under her desk, watching closely as Ana circled the paper clips in the fine white grains. She set the tube aside, spread her hand over the paperclips, and faltered, glancing over her shoulder at the witch leaning against the door.

"It's alright," Darkly assured her. "I'm only here to observe Milla."

Taking one steadying breath, Ana pinched her brows together and splayed her fingers wide over the paperclips in their circle of salt.

The language of her intent was a surprise and a song. Dominican-accented Spanish rolled off Ana's tongue like a lullaby, rich and sweet as the fruit of the Caribbean with a bitter edge that spoke to the history of the island's people. Papers fluttered. A warm, phantom breeze pulled at Milla's hair as Ana's ritual caught, the magick finding root in the plastic clips.

A moment passed, and nothing happened. Ana exhaled, her shoulders dropping in defeat, and the paperclips sat up.

NINE

VESTIC Diviners and soothsayers. Includes alomancy, astrogalomancy, favomancy, geomancy, tasseomancy, pecthimancy.

Nae bones, entrails, blood, or teeth.

"Unique, indeed," Morgen murmured.

Milla stared at the paperclips marching across her desk, her jaw threatening to come unhinged. What she witnessed was … it was *impossible*, and yet it was *happening*. Inorganic material fed with the simulacrum of life, and the witch who had done it was beaming up at her, happy, hale, and whole.

Her palms tingled, the magick in Milla begging to be used. *This is wrong.* She flexed her fingers, curled her hands into fists. *This is impossible. I need to—*

Muted buzzing, like a bee caught in a jar, broke Milla from her stupor, saving her from herself. "How does it—"

"He'll keep going like that until I tell him to stop," Ana chirped. "Do you know what my Way is? Tracy ran all sorts of scans on me but could never figure out what magick this is. We never submitted anything to C.R.O.W. because, you know, Death Witches are supposed to be able to—"

"That's not necromancy," Milla stated the obvious. "Those paperclips are in-organic."

"Right, I know, but C.R.O.W…." Ana's eyes drifted to Darkly. Her bright smile faded at the edges, the witch suddenly wary, and wow, didn't Milla understand the feeling.

"I'm nae here to observe you," Darkly assured, though his voice was tight, eyes wide and black. He blinked, meeting Milla's gaze for half a breath before scrambling to pull his phone from a pocket. The buzzing stopped, and he shoved the device out of sight. "Ludmilla, a word?"

With less than a glance at her, the over-tall witch pulled the door open and left the room.

"I should—"

"Go, Ludmilla," Morgen tipped her head at the door. "Appease C.R.O.W."

"Right." She faltered, eyeing the paperclips and Ana. "But don't you think I should…"

"Ludmilla?" Darkly called from the hallway, snapping his fingers. "Havenae much time."

"Holy Horned God, don't you snap at me." She charged for the open door, hollering up into Darkly's face. "I'm not a *dog*."

"Outside," he replied, heading for the rear door.

"I'm not a dog!" She started after him and was stopped by Diego rushing down the hall.

"Bruja, before you storm out to what I am positive will be an epic and emotionally charged argument, Julie and I could use your help up front."

"What—" She peered past Diego. It took a beat for what she saw to translate into anything comprehensive. Bodies packed the front of the store, swarming the displays like ants on a mound, bustling in clusters and crawling around one another. The noise from the front of the store was an indecipherable hum, so Milla focused on the customers and the garish cloth clutched in their hands. "—the fuck."

"I understand you are busy with your *čarodějnice* and, um, Mr. Simmons, but if there is any way you could delay your meeting until later …"

"What's going on?" Ana joined them in the hall, looked at the women crowding Southern Gothic, and beamed. "Oh, this is fantastic." She pushed up the sleeves of her cardigan and turned a mega-watt smile on Milla. "Can I help? Please? I miss working a salesfloor, and I'm already familiar with the merchandise."

"She is?" Diego leaned back on his hips, assessing Ana with a shrewd flit of his eyes.

"Apparently," said Milla.

"Please?" Ana begged, bouncing on her feet. "If your friend—"

"Diego," he supplied.

"If your Diego," Ana smiled at him, "is alright on the register, I can help the women find what they need and familiarize myself with your store." Her gaze drifted the hall, honey-amber eyes darting over the ornate china hutch and the shelves still hosting Milla's curios. A blink was all the reaction she gave the ventriloquist's dummies, and then she was back to making her case. "I can help out as part of my apprenticeship."

"That feels like a violation of some sort of labor law," Milla said.

"Nonsense, Ludmilla." Morgen joined them in the already cramped hall. "Unpaid labor is the cornerstone of any good apprenticeship. Ana is here to learn from you as the Witch of the Demesne. Part of that education rests in observing how to tend to the mortals under your protection."

"See?" Ana clapped her hands. "Your *jezibaba* says it's okay."

"I mean, I guess," Milla hedged. Julie's voice could just be heard above the din of the customers, her usual Southern genteel now sharp and frantic. Milla fluttered her lips with a sigh, mind going a million miles a minute. "But I'll have to add you to the payroll to keep it official and file for whatever license is required for an … internship. We already have enough people claiming I'm exploiting Diego; the store doesn't need to *add* to our problem."

Darkly rapped his knuckles on the glass of the rear door, calling the attention of the gathered witches. He scowled, pointed to a nonexistent watch, and walked away. From the front of the store, Julie raised her voice to a holler. "I'm sure my colleagues will be back from their break *any minute.*"

"Bruja," Diego prompted. "She knows the merchandise."

"And I love customers," Ana added.

Milla looked from one witch to the other, skipping over Morgen entirely. She knew what her *jezibaba* would say, and right now, Morgen was anything but a mother. "Alright," she nodded. Ana squealed and clapped her hands. "But just until this rush dies out."

"You won't regret this, Milla—I mean, *polednice*! I'm going to get you *so* many sales!"

"I'm sure you will," Milla replied, but the witch was already gone, scampering down the hall and throwing her arms in the air as she greeted the first customer she reached.

"Oh. My. *Goodness*, the lilac goes so well with your ash-blonde hair!"

"Gracias, Milla." Diego squeezed her elbow and dropped his head briefly on her shoulder. "This is going to be good for you."

"Yeah," she answered. "Right."

He left her in the hall, suffering the weight of Morgen's gaze and torn between fleeing to the chaos in the front and hiding in Diego's sewing room.

"It would not be wise to ignore an agent of C.R.O.W." Morgen tipped her head to the rear door. "Even if he is a mere aural insurance adjuster."

"I know, I know." Milla tugged at the ends of her hair. "Any idea what set him off like that?"

"One would assume Mr. Simmons to be capable of answering that question, Ludmilla." Morgen sniffed and started to turn away. "If you need me, I am only a summons away."

"Wait, you're leaving?"

"Any witch trained by me is more than capable of holding her own against a horde of mortal customers."

"I meant with him." She jerked her thumb at the rear door, implying the irate witch in the alleyway.

Morgen glanced over Milla's head with a faint smile. "Perhaps you should rely on the skills taught to you by Master Lightner." Milla's fingers darted to her surgical scar, a move her foster mother tracked. Coldness stilled her features, and that whisper of a smile fled. "I will remain close by at my timeshare in Daytona. If any of this proves too much, Ludmilla, do call."

"What is your problem," Milla barked the moment she stepped into the abandoned alleyway. "Wait."

A pile of broken down boxes littered the corner where her store met a brick wall covered in near-ancient, chipping plaster. At the opposite end of the alley, the dumpster she shared with the ice cream store and torture museum hummed with flies. Besides the shadows clinging to the corner opposite the boxes, the narrow alley was empty.

She stormed out to The Court, scanning the passing crowd for an over-tall, sunburned ginger, cursed when she didn't see him, and spun around only to run face-first into his chest.

"Watch it." Darkly's hands came down on her shoulders, steadying Milla as she again cursed. "You alright?"

"Where in the nine rings were you?" She threw off his hands and rubbed her nose.

"Just beside the door." He pointed over a shoulder. "Dinnae ken how you didnae—"

"No, you weren't."

Darkly dropped his arm. "I assure you, I was standing just there."

"I would have seen you."

"Maybe you were distracted." He grinned, rolling his shoulders and lifting his chin in a way Milla assumed was intended to be distracting. In reality, it made the red-headed witch in his scarf look like a preening rooster.

"Whatever." She charged into the formerly abandoned alleyway. "What was so important that you needed to snap your fingers at me."

"I needed to speak with you," he stepped beside her, "privately."

"So you summoned me like a dog?"

"Right, well, I panicked."

Milla side-eyed him. "Panicked?"

"You try to keep steady when the Morgenhexe is glaring at you from across the room."

"She's not that scary."

"She's bloody terrifying," Darkly argued. He swept a hand through his hair, gaze going unfocused. A full-body shudder brought his attention back to Milla. "Am nae positive that young witch is the right *čarodějnice* for you."

"Oh, right to the point then." Milla crossed her arms and sneered at the witch. "And how would you even know if she's the right *čarodějnice* for me? You know nothing about me, my Way, or my demesne."

"And whose fault is that?" He countered.

"Excuse me?" Milla blustered. "I'm not the one wasting a witch's time with quid pro quo ice breakers, *Mr. Simmons*. And shouldn't you have assessed whether or not she was the right witch for me to train *before* bringing her by?"

"Isnae my job tae—"

"Yes, it is!" She threw her arms wide, voice echoing off the alley walls. "You're my Aural Insurance Adjuster, you're supposed to be investigating me—"

"Observing."

"—and determining I'm no threat to C.R.O.W. or the demesne so you can go home and leave me alone. Not asking me what my preferred form of exercise is, or where to find the best margarita in the Florida Panhandle."

"Which is?"

Milla blinked, her mind grinding to a halt at the question.

"Well?" He closed the distance, ripping that ludicrous scarf from around his neck and dropping his chin. Green eyes gleamed down at Milla, and she found herself pressed against the wall, needing to escape that over-bright gaze, having nowhere to run and wondering why she didn't mind. His closeness zeroed her focus onto Darkly and Darkly alone, dimming the rest of the alleyway into faded grays. "Fancy a drink, hen?"

He cocked his head, smirked, and Milla bit her lips to keep from whimpering. Magick thrummed around him, and her palms tingled in response. It would be so easy to reach out and steal some of that magick for herself. So Horned God-damned easy to draw him in and finish what they'd started.

Milla licked her lips, moths fluttering in her belly as his clove and clean smoke scent overshadowed the stink from the dumpster. The smirk dimpled his cheek, and her fingers twitched. Goddess, it was one thing when he flirted with her in the privacy of his cottage—if that's even what he was doing—but to do so in public, behind her store?

"This is familiar." He dropped an elbow against the wall, leaning closer. Her breath hitched, a new realization dawning as Darkly pulled his lower lip between his teeth. "About that drink? Ken I could go for one whilst mulling over what I'm to tell C.R.O.W. Unless …"

What if this *wasn't* flirting? It felt intentional, but witches were creatures of intent, C.R.O.W. employed witches more than any other, which begged the question: was he baiting the witch or urging her on?

Rely on the skills taught to you by Master Lightner.

Morgen's warning trilled, and she pressed herself deeper against the wall. Ezra had pushed Milla to her breaking point time and time again. He had rigorously trained her in the Ways, testing her on the intricacies of her magick, but he had also taught her how to survive, how to read witches and her surroundings and gain the upper hand.

Darkly's attention was too focused, too keen. His posture was tight, as though the witch were holding himself back, but from what? The quick reading of his palm that she had performed in Drake's Fire told Milla he was emotionally driven but level-headed and logical, that his sense of justice was ruled by will, and right now, Darkly was a witch at odds with his will.

"Unless?" She tried, tipping her head to the side and keeping her voice light.

"Unless you fancy explaining to me how a witch with a Way like hers"—he glanced at the door to Milla's store—"is an appropriate *čarodějnice* for a vestic like you."

"A vestic like me," Milla repeated, ice in every word. "You don't know anything about me."

"That may be, but I know enough to question why a witch capable of bringing office supplies to life is being entrusted to a seer with a demesne she shouldn't have."

"A demesne I shouldn't—" Milla slipped under his arm and backed away. "What could you *possibly* know about my demesne? You've never even seen how I tend to it, much less asked me a damn thing besides how I got it."

"Havenae invited me."

"What?" Milla straightened, her shoulders dropping in a mixture of alarm and befuddlement. "What do you mean *invited you*? It's your job to investigate me."

"Observe," he corrected, "and it felt rude to insert myself."

"It's not rude when it's your job, regardless of how terrible you are at it."

"Even so," he shot her a tightlipped grin that dripped with sarcasm, "the polite thing to do as Witch of the Demesne would be to invite me along. Show me some good intent, as it were."

"Good intent."

"A gesture of goodwill." The grin deepened into something teasing that Milla could not even begin to decipher. "From one witch to another."

"You want … an invite?"

"From you? Yes." Milla scoffed and Darkly lowered his voice. "Who wouldnae wish to feel wanted by a witch like you?"

Milla gaped bug-eyed at Darkly. When he failed to rescind his question, she snorted. "You really can't help yourself, can you?"

"Dinnae ken what you mean."

"Fine." She stormed to the door, gripping the handle and glaring at his reflection in the glass. "Tomorrow morning. You are officially invited to join me as I tend the demesne."

"Excellent. Fancy a bit of exercise, what time do you run?"

Surprise riddled through Milla at his question. She turned a narrow-eyed glare over her shoulder, assessing the witch anew. He was terrible at his job, seemed as interested in investigating her as she was in being investigated, and yet he'd managed to remember she tended to St. Augustine on her morning runs, feeding the demesne with her magick and securing the territory as hers.

It wouldn't do to have him witness that. Not yet, at least. She needed time to assess his true aims, get settled with Ana, and find a new balance to the upset caused by C.R.O.W. Then, maybe, she would let him witness how she fed the demesne. But tomorrow?

"Mm-mm." She shook her head and pulled open the door. "Not a run."

"What then?"

Spinning to face the witch, Milla shot an equally sarcastic grin back his way. "A desecrant."

Ten

"Why nae evict the skunk apes?"

Milla rolled her eyes. From the moment she'd sat down in his ludicrous, cranberry-red hybrid, Darkly had peppered her with question after question about the demesne and the cryptids, creepies, and crawlies who called it home. She answered to the best of her ability, trying not to get annoyed when he pressed for more, but a witch had her limits.

"Where would they go? They live in my demesne; it doesn't seem right to schluff them off on the Panhandle Coven."

"And you broker peace between the *xana* and *rusalka*; why?"

"Because they share the water and represent the joint cultures of the witch who stewards their demesne. Which is me. Half Czechian, half Spanish Ludmilla Probuditna." She angled toward the C.R.O.W. witch, eyeing him with a thinly disguised sneer. "Horned God, shouldn't you know this?"

"Only acting in the capacity of my role as Aural Insurance Adjuster and ensuring that you do."

Cauldron of batshit, Milla had thought. "First left after Mussallen Park," she said aloud.

Darkly did as she directed. Hunched over the steering wheel, he squinted at the narrow dirt road stretching to the horizon. Palm trees and black mangroves tunneled the lane while buttonwillow hugged the trunks of taller trees, obscuring whatever suggestions of civilization existed beyond this uncharacteristically desolate stretch of Vilano Beach.

"You sure this is it?"

"It's what her directions say." Milla frowned at her phone, annoyed with the witch and his questions. "Ana said it's all the way down, the only house on the road."

"No wonder she was so excited to work at your sto—" He slammed on the brakes as a hunched, hairy shape darted across the road, disappearing into the buttonwillow on their left with a flash of golden coat and a tawny puffball of fur at the end of its tail. "Get tae fu—"

"Ball-tailed cat." Milla pointed to the right. "Over there, I think I see a driveway."

Darkly shot her an incredulous look, turning the wheel with the heel of his palm. "Care to explain?"

"Little cat, ball on its tail, looks like something Dr. Seuss came up with," she explained. "And it's the only house down here, has to be her grandparents'."

They pulled up to the stilted structure, Darkly muttering darkly under his breath while Milla fired off a text to her *čarodějnice*, double-checking her directions.

Milla had imagined a traditional Florida coast condominium from the younger witch's descriptions. White stucco and stacked decks offset each level so they had a view of the water. A manicured lawn, maybe a pool.

Goddess, she'd kill for access to a pool.

Instead, she and Darkly peered through the windshield at an homage to Baba Yaga's hut. The stilts of the structure were reinforced at odd angles, seemingly braced against themselves and supporting a brown shingled, slope-roofed Everglades cottage, complete with dense mosquito netting surrounding the porch and deep green shutters closed firmly against the late January sun.

A minivan that had seen better days was parked in the gravel driveway beside a cluster of low, scrubby bushes. Milla spied the wooden planks of a dock disappearing into the growth and a small pagoda nestled among the trees.

Vines wound around the stilts supporting the cottage, giving them a shaggy, feral appearance. They climbed the balcony as though they sought to consume the house, budding with fat green pods due to burst into flowers at the first hint of a genuine spring day. The stairs leading to the front door folded back on themselves in a tight twist, and, at the summit, a screen door slammed shut. Ana's bootheels clunked down the warped wooden steps, her long, gleaming hair flying behind her like a molten banner as she fled the house.

Cheeks puffed and eyes bugging, the witch yanked on the car door and fell into the back seat in a cloud of floral perfume that barely masked a burnt plastic, rancid cigar, and chemical sear stench. Her hands grasped Milla's and Darkly's chairs, and she lurched forward, greeting them both with a big grin and sunny, "Hello!"

"Hi!" Darkly met her cheer with a too-broad grin of his own, eyes blown wide with surprise. "Should we call the authorities? Fetch the fire grenade? What on the Goddess's green earth is that Foule *stench*?"

Ana's smile faltered. She glanced at Milla, uncertain.

"I think he means, 'Where's the fire'?" She explained, glaring at Darkly. "You looked like you were fleeing something up there."

"Oh." The *čarodějnice* bit her lips, eyes darting up at the house, then back to Milla. "Gran just caught a snake and the smell is because it's low tide."

"Shecaughtawhat." The blood rushed from Milla's face. She gripped the handle on the door, muscles in her arm gone taut.

"Ah, well, skunk apes, *rusalka*, and a massive cat with a frou-frou tail dinnae give you pause, but a snake mucks you up?"

"Just drive," she snarled at Darkly, fighting the urge to slam her hand down on his knee and force the car into motion.

He eyed her, putting the hybrid in reverse and taking his sweet, little baby Horned God time backing out of the driveway. "Only wanting to understand. Man-eating water sprites and hairy beasties the size of professional basketball players arenae cause for a fright but a *snake*—"

"I will hex you."

"Your Aural Insurance Adjuster?" He grinned at Milla, batting his eyelashes innocently. "Doubt that." When she grumbled and wriggled lower in the seat, he danced his fingers on the steering wheel, obnoxiously proud of himself. "Now, where to?"

Fort Mose sat on the edge of a salt marsh north of St. Augustine. The site of an eighteenth-century Spanish fort, the outpost had flourished as a free black settlement, the first to be sanctioned as such in what was then Spanish Florida. Buried by time and silt, the ruins were uncovered in the late nineteen-eighties, the land elevated to state park status, and it was now a popular residence for many of the desecrants in Milla's demesne.

Such as the *leshy*.

"You have a *what?*" Darkly stutter-stepped to a halt at the edge of a pier jutting out into the many splintered fingers of the Tolomato River, eyes nearly bugging out of his head.

"A *leshy*." Milla threw a hand up over her shoulder, tugging on her galosh and dropping into the knee-high water. "*Leśnik, leśniczy, lasowik.*" She waded into the swampy murk, Ana following close behind. "He Himself, O, Honorable One of the Forest. He of the Pine Barrens, Uncle, Woodsman, or would you prefer the Polish *borowy*?"

"I am well aware of what a *leshy* is, thank you," the insurance adjuster snarked.

"So snakes don't bother you, but a *leshy* is what gets your chinos in a twist?"

Darkly sat on the pier's edge, grumbling under his breath in unintelligible Scottish as he tugged off a shoe.

Milla cupped a hand at her ear. "Sorry, what was that? I can't hear you over the sound of doing my job."

When he didn't answer, she put her back to the A.I.A. and trudged through the salt marsh. A splash let Milla know he'd decided to follow the witch and her *čarodějnice* into the shallow waters, and she mentally cursed his ability to be so Horned God-damned terrible at his job, yet determined to actually do it.

Thanks to his stupid long legs, he caught up within a few strides. His chinos were rolled up to the knee, and the boat shoes dangled from his fingers. "I said, what I cannae comprehend is *why you have one.*"

"Because he lives here." Water sloshed into her boot, dribbling down Milla's leg and drowning her socks. Ignoring the C.R.O.W. witch's continued grousing, she let Ana catch up to turn this little excursion into a lesson. "A *leshy* is a Slavic forest lord," she paused, giving the *čarodějnice* the opportunity to stop a repetitive lecture. Ana adjusted the canvas bag on her shoulder but remained silent. Attentive. So Milla continued. "He protects the woods and creatures within it, like a *woodwose* in the United Kingdom, or the *basajaun* in Basque Country."

"A *leshy* is a desecrant," Darkly corrected. "Dangerous. A thing Forbidden and Foule." He met Milla's frown with a deep, dark look. "And as Witch of the Demesne, you shouldnae be harboring a first-degree desecrant within your territory."

"I'm not *harboring* him." She rolled her eyes. "He was here before me; who am I to kick him out?"

"The Witch of the Demesne, Ludmilla!"

"Which makes me a steward, not a dictator, Darkly!" She flung her arms wide. "It's not my place to decide who or what is evil—"

"It really is."

"—and kick perfectly peaceable creatures out of their home just because C.R.O.W. has determined them to be distasteful."

"That's nae …" Darkly ran a hand through his hair, tousling the absurd pompadour, and flung it toward her, fingers splayed. "As Witch of the Demesne, it is your role to secure the territory from threats. He ought to have been banished ages ago."

"Why?" She countered, whirling in the salt marsh and thrusting her hands down on her hips. The C.R.O.W. witch was closer than expected, and she had to angle her face up to glare him in the eye. "What has he done wrong other than exist? He lives here, Darkly. This is his home, just as it is mine. The *leshy* doesn't bother me, and I don't bother him beyond dropping off little gifts now and then to keep the peace."

He clenched his jaw, working it side-to-side before trying again. "C.R.O.W. regulation states that—"

"You think I care what C.R.O.W. regulation states?" Milla scoffed. "They also say that a witch shall use no magick, whether Fine and Faire or Forbidden and Foule, to intercede, interject, or otherwise intervene in mortal affairs, and yet every demesne has a witch doing *just* that."

If possible, his eyes narrowed further. "Yet to see you travel your Way where the demesne is concerned, Ludmilla."

She tucked her chin, angling away from him. "I'm a rule follower."

He stared at her for a beat, lips pressing into a thin line, a tight little purse, and then, "HAH!"

"Oh, fuck you." She pivoted away from him, ears burning.

"Tried that," he retorted.

"You *asshole*—"

"*Polednice!*" Ana clapped her hands over her mouth.

"D'ye think I came up the Clyde on a banana boat?" The Scottish witch stormed after her.

"It's your favorite song, Tally Man," she snapped, stepping onto a sodden bank and eyeing the tracks in the mud. Long sweeps indicated something had been dragged into the copse of trees at the center of the tiny island. "You tell me."

"Milla, I mean, *polednice*, I don't think …"

"*What*, Ana?" Milla snarled at her *čarodějnice*, utterly done with this conversation.

"I—" the young witch shrank away, gripping the straps of her bag with both hands and edging closer to Darkly, who, if anything, had managed to add murderous to his disdainful glower. "Nothing."

"Great work, *polednice*," he goaded. Milla went ramrod straight; fists clenched at her sides. She tipped her head back and closed her eyes, trying to swallow her anger and get to the count of ten before she exploded.

She made it to three before she was storming across the bank, index finger extended. Darkly was still in the water, making their heights equal, and she jabbed him in the center of his chest. "By Rite of Manipulation and Invocation of the Ways, by C.R.O.W.'s laws, this *leshy* has done nothing wrong. So, should I banish him solely for existing? How fair is that? He tends the mangroves" —she jabbed him again— "he keeps the gators and the manatees from getting stuck in the weeds" —and again, half aware of the splotch of brown, aging linen her touch left behind and too angry to care— "and gives a fun little fright to the local teens looking for a make-out spot. He ensures Fort Mose remains a beautiful natural space for the residents of *my* demesne to enjoy. So, no, I won't be banishing him or exiling him or whatever other batshit C.R.O.W. would have me do."

She started to jab him a third time, and Darkly's left hand darted up lightning-quick, long fingers closing over her knuckles. He dropped his shoes on the bank and grabbed her elbow, jerking Milla forward half a step. Any more than that, and she'd tumble right off the bank into his arms.

As in the alleyway, magick seethed from the witch, rolling up Milla's arms and raising goosebumps. She gasped at the shock of his touch, her arm tensing, and a piece of his anger melted into a question, the harsh glint in his eyes easing. He slid his palm to cup the back of her arm. Milla shivered at the intimacy of that touch and the tender pressure of his fingers, too stunned to resist when he brought his face alongside hers.

"Didnae mean to startle you," he murmured in a low, rolling tone that she felt in her very bones. This close, she could smell his body wash or cologne or whatever it was that had the preppy witch smelling like a wintry bouquet of clove and clean smoke. He slipped his fingers from her hand, grazing Milla's shoulder before laying his palm flat at the nape of her neck. "But we're nae alone."

"Oh?" Thrown by the swift pivot from prying C.R.O.W. witch to whatever this was, she sucked a breath in through her teeth, struggling to keep in one piece. Dipping her chin, Milla pressed back against his hand to meet his eyes … which were pinned on something behind her. Darkly nodded, the tiniest dip of his chin, and slid the hand at her elbow across her lower back. With the slightest press of his palm, Milla, Horned God damn her, leaned into the witch.

"*Leshy?*"

"*Leshy,*" he rumbled, an impossibly cool puff of breath teasing her ear. "Doesnae look pleased to see us."

Milla twitched her face to the side, which, unfortunately, caused Darkly's lips to brush against her ear. They each gasped, drawing away from one another. He dropped his arm from her back, though the hand at her neck lingered. His fingers curled and sent an altogether different shiver down her spine before they, too, were pulled away.

"Ana," Milla's voice shook. She cleared her throat, backing away from Darkly and gesturing for the *čarodějnice* to step closer. "Ana, my bag."

"*Gran Bwa.*" The witch stared across the bank at the *leshy*, caught in the sight of two moss-bright eyes.

"Ana, look at me," Milla willed steadiness into her tone—a sense of calm. *Leshy* were unpredictable, quick to judge, and quicker to act if a threat were perceived.

"*Gran Bwa*," she repeated, nostrils flaring and the whites of her honey-amber eyes fully visible. The fingers of her casting hand danced in the air as the threat of her magick rose.

The *leshy* cocked a thorned head at Ana's voice, tightening his grip on the club in writhing vines serving as a hand. He crept to the edge of the copse of moss-draped oaks which made up the tiny island.

"That's right," Milla nodded, surprised at the connection Ana had just made. *Gran Bwa* was the Loa of the Wood, a Haitian Voodoo spirit similar in construct and regard as a *leshy*. She was briefly impressed, then remembered the young witch's chosen language of intent: a thickly accented Dominican Spanish. It made sense she would recognize the guardian spirit as a being of Hispaniola. "*Gran Bwa*, the Great Wood. Very good." Her fingers brushed the girl's arm, and Ana blinked into herself, all but throwing Milla the bag she was holding.

She clutched it to her chest, shooting a stern look at Darkly. "Stay here."

He opened his mouth to protest, gaze darting over Milla's head and saw something there that made him reconsider. He crooked his fingers at Ana, gesturing her closer. To Milla, he nodded.

Facing the *leshy*, Milla exhaled and let some of her magick feed into the ground around her, allowing the desecrant a moment to recognize her power and her place as Witch of the Demesne. He shrank with each step she took, the oak-straight posture and broad limbs of his shoulders lessening until instead of the vine, branch, and twig being glooming at her from behind a shrubbery beard, Milla stopped before an old, hunched man in tattered rags. The moss-bright eyes remained, gleaming in a face flushed purple from his godly blue blood. She lowered her eyes out of respect, spotting the shoes on his feet.

Both backward.

"Dobře, leśnik," she greeted him in Czechian, her intentional language, as an equal rather than bowing before him. "I have brought a gift."

"Přivedl jsi zloděje," vines groaned out his reply.

You have brought a thief.

Bright eyes lifted over Milla's head, and she followed his gaze, frowning when she realized he was referring to Darkly. The idiot had stepped onto the bank, placing himself between Ana and the *leshy*, though thankfully, he'd kept his distance.

"Any idea why he's calling you a thief?" she called back. The witch startled, chin tucking and eyes widening.

"Nae," he answered. Milla translated. The *leshy* rustled the leaves in every tree on the tiny island, surging his power through the roots. Milla felt the rush beneath her feet, unable to shout a warning before rope-like tendrils burst from the ground, winding up Darkly's right leg. "Get tae—"

"Ukradl jsi můj stín," the forest spirit howled. "Jsi zloděj."

"The only thing he's ever stolen is my patience," Milla thrust her hand into the canvas bag, grabbing the red scarf within and tearing it free. A wintry breeze rushed off the river, dragging at the *leshy's* trees and warping the dappled shadows. It caught on the wool in her hand, raising the offering up like a banner. "He's not a thief, but if it makes you feel better, I'll never bring him here again."

The scarf seized the spirit's attention. Moss-bright eyes trailed the vivid garment, and ancient lips parted in hunger. He shuffled near, leaning close to her offering, and his features warped and blew out—skin cragged into bark-ridden wood, the scraggly beard thickening to dense green foliage. An ancient face regarded the gift and the witch before him, humor whorling in the knots of his eyes.

"To je krásné tkaní, čarodějnice."

This is a lovely weave, witch.

"*Polednice*," she replied with a fierce grin. The *leshy* spread his lips, revealing leaves where his teeth should be. Laughter like twigs snapping beneath booted feet echoed through the copse, and a branching finger accepted her gift, looping it around a neck that was at once ancient and massive, and withered and human.

He inclined his head, and only then did Milla bow. Deeply. Straightening, she raised her casting hand, palm out. The *leshy* pressed his forehead to her palm, pinning Milla where she stood with the ever-lasting light of greenlife gleaming deep in the knots of his eyes. A papery hiss sounded from behind her, and from Darkly's choked cry she knew the roots were being withdrawn by their master. "I am satisfied."

"Until next time, friend."

He withdrew, dragging on Milla's Way as he did. She swayed, drawn to the *leshy* like a magnet, only to be stopped by a solid grip keeping her from being entirely consumed by the leshy's influence. Cradling her hand against her chest, she watched the being take up his club and lumber away, the tail of his new scarf disappearing among the trees.

Darkly pulled Milla back against him, his hold that of a man trying to reassure himself rather than ensure her well-being. "What is it I'm meant to have stolen?"

"Jeho stín," she answered. "His shadow." The truth. No need to lie, as it made no sense. That was the problem in dealing with beings quite literally old as dirt; they made no Horned God-damned sense half the time. Darkly's hand tightened on her arm, and she explained, "The *leshy* get confused, being ancient as they are. You probably look like someone that crossed him in the past."

"Probably," Darkly agreed, his eyes trained on the trees. "I've nae idea how I'm gonnae explain this to C.R.O.W."

Milla snorted, ducking out of his grip and patting the witch on his arm as she walked away. "Sounds like a you problem."

Eleven

Darkly made it fifteen minutes into their drive before starting again with his questions.

"How often do you wade out to treat with the desecrant?"

"The *leshy*." Milla ducked her head back in the window. "Take the next left."

"Why?"

"Because this traffic is ridiculous." She threw her hand at the windshield and the one-and-a-half miles between herself and the Colonial Quarter. "We can cut through the neighborhoods to Magnolia and get around the Scenic Highway traffic."

"Nae what I meant." He tapped his blinker and eased into the left lane.

"I think he means the *leshy*, *polednice*," Ana added. "I'm also curious. It seems like a lot of work to keep him happy when you could just …" She wiggled her fingers, which Milla translated as "do magicky things."

"Seriously?" She twisted in her seat. "We talked about this. He doesn't bother me; I don't bother him."

"But…he's scary!"

"So am I," Milla answered. Darkly chuckled. "What? You don't know me, I'm terrifying."

"Nae doubt." He pinched his lips to keep from smiling, pointedly watching the road and not looking at Milla.

"Right on San Marco and a left on Nelmar." She narrowed her eyes at the witch, daring him to laugh outright. "Turn right at the end of the road."

"Still havenae answered my question," Darkly managed after a moment. "How often do you treat with the *leshy*?"

"Monthly, and before you ask, I broker negotiations between the *rusalka* and *xana* quarterly."

"And charge the demesne when you run," he completed. "Why nae involve the local cultists? You could feed your Way into their rituals and have them pick up the charging of the demesne."

"Oh, that's a good idea!" Ana grabbed the back of Milla's seat and gave it a shake. "That would free up your mornings to work in the store. We could open earlier, sell more ICYMI, and—"

"Not a chance," Milla snapped. "That pack of drunks is a nightmare to work with. They wouldn't know the first thing about charging the demesne, much less using my Way to do so."

"Which, as the Witch of the Demesne," Darkly sent her a stern, jade-bright glare, "is something you are responsible for. The cultists are part of your demesne; they're attuning themselves to your Way, which is … what exactly?"

"Vesticism."

"Sure." Darkly worked his jaw and tapped the blinker arm, harder this time. "Vesticism."

There was a darkness to the how he named the Way, a menacing growl to his brogue that had every hair on Milla's arms prickling in alarm. She sat up straight, pressing against the door to create more space between herself and the witch. "I'm not giving up my morning runs."

"Then let them deal with the *leshy*. Or the skunk apes." He jerked the steering wheel, turning hard onto Magnolia. "Delegate your tasks."

"Is that a suggestion or a demand from C.R.O.W.?"

"Somehow, Ludmilla, I doubt you truly wish to hear my answer."

"No, I do, *please*," she sneered. "Tell me what the great, all-powerful C.R.O.W. thinks I should do with *my* demesne. Banish the *leshy*? Manage the *rusalka* and *xana*? You do know what they mean when they say 'manage,' right?"

Ana grabbed the shoulder of Darkly's chair. "They don't mean anything bad, do they?"

The C.R.O.W. witch clenched his jaw, knuckles blanching as he gripped the steering wheel.

"Extreme prejudice," Milla goaded him on. "Isn't that what the official grimoires state as protocol?" She raised her hands, pinching two fingers on each in air quotes. "'Desecrants Forbidden and Foule are to be treated with extreme prejudice.' C.R.O.W. would have me put them down, and we already went over this; I refuse."

"Then delegate," he barked. "Give some of your tasks to the people and witches who can manage them better than a Vestic—"

"Stop the car." Milla punched the seat buckle with her thumb, tearing the corner of her nail free from the bed as she did. Pain flashed along her finger and shot up her arm. "Stop the fucking car."

"Ludmilla—"

"C.R.O.W. says I have to show you how I tend my demesne, fine, but I don't have to sit here and listen to you belittle Vesticism and micromanage *my* demesne." Her palms tingled, the veins in her arms fizzing with a burn that threatened to escape. The cabin of his tiny hybrid was too small, full of too much plastic, nylon, and fake leather. There was nothing real in here, nothing she could spend her magick on without hurting them and letting C.R.O.W. see, and she needed to get *out*. Milla closed her eyes against an oncoming migraine. "Stop the Horned God-damned car."

"Ludmilla," he started.

"STOP THE CAR." She slammed her fist against the door, jerking forward when Darkly slammed on the brakes. His arm shot out, catching Milla before she collided with the dashboard. She snarled, yanked on the handle, and all but threw herself into the road.

"Where are you going?" Darkly hollered.

"To work!" Milla flung him a middle finger over her shoulder and slammed the door. The sound echoed a moment later, and she mentally braced herself for the over-tall witch and his obnoxious questions. Gritting her teeth, Milla charged down Magnolia Avenue, brushing her fingers over wooden fences and along the curve of tree trunks.

She hardly processed the sweep of moss-draped oaks, painting dappled shadows on the asphalt and root-broken sidewalk. St. Augustine's Oak Alley was one of her favorite stretches to run, and a part of her had been excited to show this corner of her demesne to the C.R.O.W. witch. She wanted him to see the beauty of the Ancient City and the good that she tended and nurtured in the hopes it would overwrite the unorthodox systems she had created with the desecrants.

Instead, she had let his prying push her over the edge, and now her hands burned with unused magick, her mood black enough to dim the world with shadow, and a painful stabbing prodded the backs of her eyes.

"*Polednice!*" Ana cried out instead, her hurried footsteps rushing closer. "Wait for me."

Milla slowed and stilled, finally looking back down the road. Darkly and his red hybrid remained at the end of the block, the witch now standing behind the open driver's side door. His attention on Milla was a weighted thing, shrinking the world into a narrow tunnel and running down the length of it was her apprentice.

"What are you doing, Ana?"

"Coming to work," the younger witch panted. She stopped beside Milla, her cheeks perfectly pink and hair a salon-worthy windblown. "Julie said she had to be at the hospital today, and we're late enough as it is. Diego's probably tired from running the store by himself all morning, and I—"

"Right." Milla stepped onto a sidewalk running the length of a coquina and tabby wall. She brushed her fingers over the bits of seashell reinforcing the oyster lime as they walked, relishing each sharp edge and rough patch. Bit by bit, the burn in her palms eased, the tingling in her arms lessening as she grounded herself in the demesne. "I forgot Julie wasn't helping out today."

"It's okay; you've had a lot on your mind." Ana paused at the entrance to the Fountain of Youth, St. Augustine's most well-known tourist attraction, and gazed up at the stucco arch and bold, red letters. "Did you know St. Augustine is the oldest colonized settlement in America? I did a tour the other day with my friend, and the guide said the Spanish arrived in 1565."

"And the Timucuan People were here before that," Milla answered, walking right past the front gates to the park. "They matched the midden findings to the shell mounds just north of Daytona."

"How do you know that?' Ana scurried to keep up, her eyes still on the Fountain of Youth as Milla led them down Magnolia Avenue.

"My foster mother has a timeshare down there, spent a lot of my spring breaks hiking in Tomoka State Park with her nephew."

"Oh." Ana went quiet, long enough that Milla started cursing herself for being a poor teacher. It was hard enough to concentrate on easing her Way into the demesne without giving herself away, much less attempt to give a brief history of the Floridian peninsula while she was at it. "ICYMI is having their Spring Sales Kickoff in a few weeks."

The non sequitur threw Milla and she stopped, facing her *čarodějnice*. "What?"

"They announced it would be in St. Augustine a week ago." Ana picked at a shell mortared into the wall. "At the Fountain of Youth." She tipped her head at the wall and the grounds behind it.

"And?"

"And I thought, maybe, we—I mean, Southern Gothic should try to go as attendees."

"Horned God, Ana, *why*," Milla goggled at her. "The city is gonna be overrun with a thousand bleach-haired Karens, and you want to *go*?"

"Diego thought it was a good idea."

"Of course he did." Milla dropped her head back, swallowing a groan as she pinched her eyes closed.

"If we order more inventory by the end of the week and Julie grows her downline, it should boost her standing with the company enough to earn a badge."

"I have no idea what half of that means."

A peal of laughter bubbled free from the younger witch. "That's why you have me, *polednice*! I know ICYMI like you know your demesne, inside *and* out."

"Thank the Goddess for that," Milla muttered.

"Leave it to me." Ana beamed back at her, eyes gleaming in the dappled light. "I'm here to help."

A cloud of floral perfume billowed out of Southern Gothic's front door, accosting Milla and setting off a minute-long sneezing and coughing fit.

"What," she wheezed, "in the Horned God—"

"My flowers!" Ana shrieked, clapping her hands and slipping around Milla. "Oh, they're so beautiful!"

"You do not think they are too much?" Diego's voice was muffled by the massive bouquet of gerbera daisies, carnations, roses, and marigolds in his arms.

"Not at all! Put them on the end table, next to the tunic dresses."

"Why do we have flowers?" Milla asked. She kicked a wooden wedge under the door to prop it open and clear the air.

"Did she remember the lilies?"

"Si, Ana." Diego set the vase down and sneezed into his elbow. "And the candles, though I wonder, do they also have to be scented?"

"Of course!" The young witch hurried to the rear of the store, and another squeal announced the discovery of, Milla assumed, more flowers.

"Why do we have flowers?" she asked again. Diego sighed and pulled off his glasses, taking his time to clean the lenses before answering.

"Your *čarodějnice* claimed the store needed 'brightening up,' and Morgen approved the purchase as you were in the throes of an argument with your aural insurance adjuster."

"Morgen approved …" Milla gaped at her store; the brightly colored dresses and leggings, the flowers covering any free, flat surface, and enough lit candles that *surely* this was a fire hazard. "And you let her?"

"She said it would be good for you to delegate some tasks."

Milla bristled at those words, too close to what Darkly had suggested in the car. St. Augustine was her demesne. *Hers.* Not Morgen's, not C.R.O.W.'s to determine how it should be tended. It belonged to Milla and whether or not she even wanted the damned territory, she wasn't about to let some trumped-up Scottish witch waltz in and tell her how to care for a demesne he'd only spent a whopping seven days getting to know.

Diego replaced his glasses, blind to Milla's rising anger, and frowned at the sunshine-yellow blooms. "Though I think the flowers and the candles are to disguise the awful scent of the clothes."

"It's normal." Julie marched through the door and dumped two over-loaded bags from a home goods store on the counter. "The clothes get made and immediately sealed in plastic and shoved on a boat. Sometimes they pick up the smell of whatever else is in the crate."

Diego scrunched his nose and gestured to the tunic dresses. "And what was in the crate with these, two tons of *jamon* left out at low tide?"

"It's not that bad." She pulled a glass jar from the bag and unscrewed the lid. A wave of vanilla and honeysuckle crashed over Milla, and she covered her nose with a hand, backing away from the counter.

"I thought you had work today."

Julie stared blankly back at her, blinked, and shook her head. "I do; came over on my lunch break to get these set up." She dropped a bundle of reeds into the jar, fiddling with the sticks until she was happy with how they splayed. Her hand went back into the bag, retrieving another reed diffuser that she arranged near the door on her way out to the beat-up sedan idling on Hypolita Street.

"Horned God, that's strong." Milla took the reed diffuser and tucked it under the counter. Then dropped a plastic bag over it for good measure. "At least it's not stopping the tourists from buying any of this crap."

"Tss, Milla. It is not crap if it sells." Diego tipped his head at a cluster of women picking over piles of ruffle-strap tops. "Unlike your … stuff."

"Hey, I've made sales." Which was true. Technically. None of the larger pieces had moved, but the women who bought the leggings also bought bangles, earrings, early twentieth-century beaded headdresses, dreamcatchers, brooches, and cameos.

"No, I know. It's very exciting …" Julie wandered back in, phone pinched between her ear and shoulder, her arms laden with more bags. "Uh-huh, it's just that … well, I'm still paying off my credit card from everything I had to order just to get started." She mouthed "sorry" at Milla and dumped the bags on the floor behind the register. Glass jars clinked together, and another cloud of floral perfume wafted into the air. "I could, but I don't know if I have the …" She dug in the bag, retrieving an air freshener, and plugged it into the powerstrip velcroed to the display case. "You really think it will?"

Milla sent a look to Diego, mentally trying to convey that, *apparently* there was a limit to the number of oil diffusers one could purchase.

"Yeah … no, the store has plenty of space, I-wow, that fast? You think I should?" She paused, thoughtful, and then headed down the hallway. "No, it'd be nice to have a better rank, and the conference is right down the street. I'll bring it up with my, um, crossline."

Milla unplugged the air freshener and dumped it in the trash, one eye on Julie shouldering open the door to the stockroom-turned-office-turned-stockroom. When the mortal was out of earshot, she asked Diego, "What was that about her credit cards?"

He never had the chance to answer. Julie came skipping out from the stockroom with Ana at her heels, broad smiles on both faces.

"I have great news!"

"Ooh, tell." Diego propped his elbow on the counter, chin in his hand.

"My Upline, that's who was on the phone, can set me up with a discount *and* expedited shipping if I double our next order and add on accessories." She followed this with a high-pitched squeal and bounced on her toes, clapping her hands.

"Accessories?" Milla side-eyed the growing display of plastic bangles beside her register and the unopened box in her arms.

"Like bags, totes, clutches." Julie shrugged. "You know, accessories."

"Think of how much more we could sell with refreshed inventory," Ana pressed. "*In-season* inventory! With accessories!"

"I don't know—" Milla started. Diego moved behind Julie and Ana, shaking his head and drawing a line across his throat. "—what the upfront is?"

"It's not bad. I think I have enough to cover it. I mean, I should after my next paycheck."

"Julie," Milla started again, and this time Diego didn't stop her. Julie did.

"It will be worth it. Ana thinks I just need to get a few girls in my downline to start generating residual income, and then it all practically pays for itself."

It still didn't feel right, but who was Milla to say? Julie was a grown woman. She'd never given Milla cause to think that she was financially irresponsible. "Alright, I guess." Ana squeaked, and Diego smiled fondly at Milla. His hard-won approval bolstered something deep within her, and she nodded more fervently. "Yeah, sure. It'll help the store, right?"

"Yes!" Ana clapped and bounced on the balls of her feet. "Ohmygosh, Julie, we have so much to do!" She grabbed the nurse's hands, and they both started jumping in place, vibrating with excitement. "We have to place the order *immediately* and then start mapping out the new footprint of the store."

"I'll call out of work the rest of the day!" Julie squealed.

"Wait," Milla grabbed Julie's shoulder, attempting to ground the woman. "Are you sure that's a good idea? Diego and I can handle—"

"We should build dressing rooms!" Ana blurted. "If customers can try on the clothes in the store, they'll buy more."

"That is not a bad idea." Diego pulled Milla's hand away and guided her back behind the register. "You promised," he murmured.

"Yeah," she tripped her gaze over her store, scrunching her nose at the slow creep of ICYMI strangling her curios like pastel kudzu. "Yeah, I did."

And that was the bitch of it.

TWELVE

XANA A desecrant water spirit of northwestern Iberia (see: Asturias); similar in nature to the lorelei, rusalka, and sirens. Creature Forbidden and Foule (see: changeling habits; xaninos).

MILLA STEPPED WIDE OVER the creaky floorboard halfway down her hall, casting a quick glance at the snoring redhead on her couch.

Diego had ushered in an exhausted Julie well past midnight. The pair and Ana had spent the last few days placing orders, further rearranging the furniture and curios, and building a pair of PVC and curtain dressing rooms between rounds of customers swarming into Milla's store like ants to a picnic.

Ana had sufficiently fitted herself into the pulse of Southern Gothic as if the store had never existed without her. She used her Way to affect the shop—the ballerina in the music box now twirled to "Bad Romance" by Lady Gaga instead of "Danse Macabre", the broken Berthoud chronometer ticked happily along, and a Tiffany lamp with no light bulb turned itself on when the sun set—and kept the vases filled with flowers, the oil diffusers full of oppressively perfumed oil, and the customers happy.

In the afternoons, she joined Milla on her tasks around the demesne, befriending the *xana* in the retaining pond, braiding flower crowns for the skunk apes in Twelve Mile Swamp, and going so far as to set up a minor altar in Milla's office.

"My grandparents don't practice," she had explained. "Every time I set up an altar, Gran steals the candle and tosses out my incense."

Having seen the dreary, wardless cottage where her grandparents lived, absent any intentional touches that marked a house as a witch's home, Milla understood her *čarodějnice*'s hesitance to practice in a place designed to stifle creativity.

Even so, the flurry of activity, Ana's effervescent excitement matched with Julie's ongoing chatter, and the constant crush of *people* was exhausting. Every day had ended with Milla falling into a deep, deathlike sleep and waking with a hangover from drinks she hadn't had. The only saving grace to the introverted nightmare of her life was that Darkly had remained absent.

Not a text, call, or surprise appearance to gripe at her for not reaching out. And why would she?

It was his job to investigate her, not *her* job to seek out the obnoxiously tall witch. If radio silence and suspicious absence were how he chose to conduct his affairs, who was she to question his tactics?

When the new inventory arrived on Tuesday afternoon, Milla begged off early, grabbing a hunk of paper-wrapped pork loin from Diego's minifridge and informing her roommate and *čarodějnice* that the demesne called.

"Do you want me to come with you?" Ana eyed the package and cast a woebegone look at the maze of boxes filling Southern Gothic. "As your *čarodějnice*?"

"No!" Milla blurted too forcefully. But if Ana came along, the whole task would take twice as long, and there was a bed in Milla's immediate future. "No, it's fine. The raw-head is senior level, and I think your skills are better used here."

The relief on the young witch's face had been comical. She recovered quickly, a trademark Ana grin showing off perfect white teeth. "Okay! We're really close; you won't even recognize the store when you come in tomorrow."

"No doubt," Milla muttered through a pasted-on smile before scurrying out the door, eager to feed the raw-head and get home to her mostly empty duplex. No customers, no aural insurance adjusters, no endless supply of air fresheners, diffusers, and flowers that rotted at a concerning rate. Just Milla, her bed, and the not-ghost of Ezra lingering in the periphery.

She hadn't been surprised when Diego's weary voice and Julie's footfalls echoed in the hallway only hours before dawn, and in an effort not to wake the nurse, she now tip-toed to the door. The hinges groaned as she pulled it open, unavoidable in an old house in an old city with a witch like her living inside, and slipped out onto the porch, closing the door as gently as possible. Adjusting the baseball hat on her head, she spun around to skip down the stairs.

"Mornin'," Darkly greeted her.

"Holy Horned God!" Milla slammed her back against the door, dropping the hat in her hand.

"Careful." He smirked at her from the front walkway, dressed in a technical shirt and running shorts that would have been a decent length on any normal-sized person but on him landed on the distracting side of short. His legs were leanly muscled, just like the rest of the witch, and the curious arc of a scar followed the inner curve of his right knee. "Didnae mean to frighten you."

"Sure you didn't," Milla grumbled. She swept her hat from the porch and shoved it on her head, which deepened Darkly's smirk, his eyes crinkling. "What."

"Orlando Magic?" He gestured to Milla's baseball hat. "Are you joking?"

"I like basketball." She jogged down the steps, brushing past him. "What do you want?"

"Thought I would join you for a run," he answered. "It's how you tend the demesne, aye?"

"Yes." Milla narrowed her eyes. "Don't you have some weird hangup about being invited places?"

"Aye."

"What happened to that?"

"Didnae return any of my calls," he shrugged. "I thought it prudent to check in."

"When did you call me?" Milla pulled her phone from the pocket of her shorts. "All I have are a bunch of missed ones from…Unknown Caller."

Darkly's grin widened. "As I said."

"Horned God." Milla shoved her phone away and took off at an easy jog. The witch easily caught up, his long stride covering twice as far as her much shorter legs could manage.

"It's a little on the nose, don't you think?"

"What?" She whipped her head up, scowling, obviously.

"Your hat. Orlando Magic," he clarified. "Seems a mite direct."

"Is that a bad thing?" Checking for traffic, Milla darted across the road and continued toward the San Sebastian River.

"Nae," Darkly huffed. "Only surprising." He jogged in place, waiting for a break in the traffic before darting across Riberia Street to run on the sidewalk. Milla frowned when he pointed them south toward Eddie Vickers Park. The park she ran regularly. She glanced at the witch, his face set and eyes hidden behind a pair of deep, black sunglasses.

It shouldn't have been surprising that he knew her route. *It's probably in my file*, she reasoned, and he had been in town long enough to become acquainted with the habits of St Augustine's inhabitants, witch or not.

"Why is liking the Magic so surprising?" she pressed, needing the C.R.O.W. witch distracted as she worked an easy sigil with her right hand. Magick pooled in her palm, and she swept fingers over slats in a white picket fence running the length of the St. Augustine Distillery's patio. It bled from her bones and veins, a tingle of energy surging through her skin to feed the demesne—a quiet little ritual performed with half a thought and good intent.

Darkly spun and jogged backward. His eyes dropped to her hand, now closed in a light fist as she jogged, before flitting up to meet hers. "Because not much about you is straightforward, Ludmilla." That irritating grin flashed, and he spun back around, startlingly quick on his feet. "Did you just do something?"

"Just my job," Milla answered.

"Tell me about it."

"About what?"

"Your job, the demesne." He slowed his jog for her to catch up. "You."

"This game again?"

"You do your job, I'll do mine."

"Fine." She gestured for him to turn left into Eddie Vickers Park. "But you just got that I like basketball for free. It's your turn to tell me something."

"Awright."

And he did. For the next few mornings in a row, at eight o'clock sharp. Some days, she chose the route, and other days, he did. No discussion, no stunted posturing of "after you" at the first intersection. It just happened. Either she would lead, or he did, holding pace side by side until their breathing aligned and their footfalls were synchronous.

Darkly asked questions about the demesne, the cryptids, and the desecrants that called it home, and Milla learned that he hated the rain and cold. "Too dark and dreary," Darkly explained, thus he took a job in Florida. His favorite food had been kebab, but Mexican was now top of the list. The scar on his right knee was from an old ACL injury he'd never fully recovered from—thus the pivot from soccer to boxing—and he had attended university in Edinburgh and Exeter, where he read classics and studied clinical counseling.

"So you wanted to be a therapist?"

"Paranormal Psychiatrist."

"Well, shit," Milla replied. "How in the nine rings did you end up an aural insurance adjuster?"

He shrugged, offering nothing in the way of explanation. "And you?"

"Spanish and European history."

"Here I thought Spain was a part of Europe."

"Har har," Milla turned them onto Ponce de Leon Boulevard. "Spanish, as in the language and history with a focus on Colonial Spanish History in the New World."

"Ah," he grinned, chortling, "I see."

"What's so funny?"

"I *si*." He glanced at her, looking far too pleased with his terrible joke.

"That's awful." Milla increased her pace so he wouldn't see her smile.

"Why Colonial Spanish history?" Darkly asked once he'd caught up.

"Always thought it was interesting. Terrible, but interesting." A half-truth. Milla was the daughter of a Czechian vestic and a Spanish advoccultant who had cut his teeth as an Enforcer. She had been undecided about her degree when starting at Flagler, but after a disagreement with her mother, she had chosen to study her father's culture instead.

"Elaborate."

"Elaborate?"

"Tell me something interesting," he demanded.

Milla glanced at him. Darkly smiled, and she shook her head. "We did a section on Voodoo culture and how the African diaspora adapted their religions to the New World."

"Is Voodoo prevalent in Florida?"

"Not really," Milla admitted. "Ezra wanted me to take the course. He thought it would be good for me to know more about the culture and Way."

"Why?"

Milla stumbled, biting her tongue in the process. It was enough that she was tied to Ezra as her mentor and was implicated in the ritual that led to his being Gone, but she didn't know how much C.R.O.W. knew about the entire affair. The last thing she needed was to admit her part in the ritual and their aim to a witch sent here to investigate her.

She directed Darkly to turn, running them around the retaining pond and mentioning in an attempt to change the subject that this was where the *xana* dwelled. After a minute of running in silence, Darkly stated, "All I know about Voodoo I learned from a James Bond film."

"That is the least surprising thing you have ever told me," Milla replied, relieved he had moved off the topic of Ezra. "And it's all wrong. For one, Voodoo is a religion as much as it's a Way, but they're two completely different things, and two, the Baron doesn't come flying up out of a grave. There is a horse, a vessel, to host the Loa."

"Loa?"

"Spirits who appeal to the great Bondye on behalf of the devotees." She put up a hand, telling Darkly to wait, and bent at the waist, gripping her knees as she caught her breath.

"Alright?"

"Jus' needa minute," Milla wheezed. Though she ran the demesne almost daily, she did so alone. Talking this much while trying to maintain pace was hard. "Hoo — okay. So there are two priests, right?"

"As in the film."

"Sure, fine. Just like in the historically accurate, impeccably researched Roger Moore cinematic masterpiece." Milla rolled her eyes and continued. "Two priests, or witches, representative of two particular Ways."

"Which ones?"

"Shouldn't you know this?"

"My education was different than yours," he shrugged.

"Well, my—that is, Ezra told me the original *oungan* and *mambo*, the Voodoo witches who performed the ritual, were historically a Dark Witch and a Death Witch. It's part of what led to their extermination."

Darkly made a thoughtful noise. "That, at least, I knew."

Milla nodded. It was a large part of Witchstory: the hunting and extermination of all things Forbidden and Foule, of which those two Ways were at the top of the list. Death Witches, the necromantics of nightmares, still popped up from time to time and were put down just as quickly. Dark Witches, on the other hand, had long ago been shoved into the realm of children's stories and cautionary tales, painting the image of a witch that could steal your Shade, leaving you a mindless, emotionless husk to be commanded as the Dark Witch willed.

"Anyways, the priests or the witches call the Loa and invite him or her to mount the horse."

"Sounds exciting."

"If a tonic-clonic seizure is your idea of a grand mal time," Milla snorted.

An odd little half-smile quirked the corner of his mouth. "You're awful."

"Milla," a voice whispered her name, quiet and kind in a way that felt like a lie.

"Mrghgrnfl." She buried her face deeper in her arms, too exhausted to lift her head and address whoever it was interrupting her nap.

"Milla, wake up."

"No."

The door to her office creaked wider, letting a cloud of floral perfume into the tiny, cramped space. Milla clenched her eyes tight, willing herself back to sleep.

"It's time to wake up, Millapet." A finger brushed down her face, the lightest touch from temple to cheekbone to jaw. "You need to wake up."

She jolted upright, heart pounding wildly and eyes overwide. Every nerve in her body alight with magick begging to be released. A fizzing that became a burning all too fast. "Where is he?"

"Where is who?" Julie was close; her hand outstretched as if ready to jostle the witch awake. But close as she was, the mortal was too far away to have brushed a finger along the side of her face and too new in Milla's life to have known how she would respond to that touch, much less know that nickname.

Millapet.

She tripped her gaze over the boxes, knowing he wouldn't be there and feeling his presence just out of sight, hovering over her shoulder as a phantom that would disappear the moment she turned around.

"Milla, are you alright?"

"Huh?" She forced herself to look away from the shadows and see the living and breathing nurse right in front of her. "Yeah. Yes. I'm fine." She stared at Julie, grounding herself in the steady nature of the nurse. Dark shadows clung under her eyes, and her pinkish, freckled face was unusually sallow. "What are you doing here?"

"I came to get tape for the label maker," she explained. "Diego said he sent you back here for it an hour ago."

"No," Milla shook her head and the last bit of terror away. "I mean here, in the store. Don't you have work today?"

"Oh, I traded shifts with another nurse." Julie's eyes flitted to somewhere above Milla's head. "She wanted to work days to spend more time with her kids, and my daughter lives with her dad, and Ana said y'all needed the help so—"

"When will you sleep?"

"I'll bunk at the hospital before my shift," the nurse shrugged. "And Diego said I could crash on y'all's couch in the mornings until we open up."

Milla straightened, her lower back protesting the movement. "Julie, that's not sustainable."

"Well, neither is how this store is being run," she snapped. "They need help out there, and you're back here sleeping."

"Excuse me?" Milla pushed to her feet, muscles groaning from the effort. "I ran six miles this morning with Darkly, who is more stork than man. I'm tired."

"Right," Julie simpered. "Tired from running with your therapist every day. Don't you think that's a little inappropriate?"

"Don't you think that's none of—"

"Julie," Ana's figure filled the doorway, "did you find the tape—oh, Milla! You're up. Do you know where the tape is for the label maker?"

"Yeah, it's right up"—an eye-watering yawn erupted, cutting her off. Milla covered her mouth with one hand, popping onto her toes and reaching for the shelf over her desk. Again, her muscles creaked, ensuring she felt the repercussions of each extra mile she'd run that morning—"here. Wow."

"And you're worried about my sleep?" Julie snarked.

"Thank you!" Ana plucked the tape from Milla's hands, facing Julie before the witch could respond to her friend's sass. "Did you get more flowers?"

Julie blinked, and in that nanosecond, her entire demeanor shifted. Gone was the contempt and exhaustion, her face swept clean of negativity as a bright smile burst, tugging the mortal from pissy to pleasing. "I did! And more of those yellow candles. I thought we could float them in little coupe glasses for the window display?"

"That is the cutest idea!" Ana clapped her hands, and the pair started down the hall. Milla edged around her card table and followed them to the front of Southern Gothic. "Oh, I love it! Milla, don't you love it?"

"Sure, but why do we need more flowers?"

"The ones we had already died," Julie explained. Milla halted, her still-tingling arms flaring as if to punctuate the explanation. "I suggested getting satin flowers, but Ana and Diego agreed that fresh was best."

"No, Diego said fake flowers were tacky, and an affront to whichever god you believe in," the Stitch Witch commented. "Ana demanded the fresh flowers." He shot Milla a concerned look before rushing up close to fix her hair. Lower lip thrust out, he re-tied the knot securing a flannel around her waist and whispered, "I cannot keep blaming the dead flowers on our air conditioning and pest control, Milla. Have you ordered your tea yet?"

"Shit," she sighed and cast her hand at the store. "No, with all this going on, I keep forgetting."

"It is a lot," Diego nodded. He took her hand and cupped it in both of his own, eyeing the scars and looking at her over the rim of his glasses. "If you place the order today, how long will it take to get here?"

"Three days if I rush. And if the dispensary has all of the ingredients." She took her hand back and held it to her chest. "I have everything we need at home; I'll make a brew tonight."

"No, bruja," Diego hissed. "It is too strong when you make it. Place the order, si? No more distractions."

"No more distractions," she agreed.

"Milla?" Ana called. "Could you cover the register while Julie and I set out these flowers?"

"Sure thing, Ana!" Diego scoffed, and Milla waggled her phone at him. "I'm placing the order right now, tío."

Thirteen

THREE SHARP RAPS ON the window had Milla snorting awake. The shadows in her room were long, crawling across the floor and clinging to corners, creating the suggestion of a presence, a figure haunting the periphery where there was no one and nothing. Because there couldn't be, because he was Gone and on the other side of the glass was Darkly, standing in her backyard with a frown on his face and phone in hand, pointing to the screen like she could read it from that far away.

"What?" Milla snapped as if he could hear her.

He lowered the phone, his eyes followed, and then he straightened, flushing a bright pink that would have been endearing had Milla not looked down and seen what caused him to blush.

Her comforter was a crumpled mass at the foot of the bed, revealing the flimsy cotton bra barely covering her breasts and the boy-cut undies she had slept in. Shrieking, Milla scrambled for the comforter as Darkly vanished from view.

She kicked out of bed, wriggling into a pair of compression tights and grabbing her sports bra and a running shirt. It was only half past the hour; Darkly wouldn't have been waiting too long, though it would have been better had he not been waiting at all. The damn A.I.A. was determined to observe her tending the demesne, no doubt hoping she would slip up and reveal herself to be what C.R.O.W. must suspect.

Why else would he keep showing up?

"—eral Vermont Heights women were hospitalized last night after being found unconscious in their homes." A newscaster's voice echoed from the front room, the volume raised above the sound of breakfast being cooked. "Officials are reporting a spate of carbon monoxide poisonings. Residents of Coquina Crossing are urged to perform routine checks of their fire and carbon monoxide detectors. Please contact the St. John's County Fire Rescue if you are experiencing any dizziness or confusion, shortness of breath, headaches—"

"Can you turn that down?" Milla hollered over the grating mid-Atlantic accent reading the morning news.

Diego startled, dropping the bowl he'd been whisking. He swept the remote from the counter and aimed it at the television, muting the news while taking in Milla's running clothes. "The door."

"I know he's at the door." She rolled her eyes. "He snuck into the backyard."

Diego widened his. "Who?"

"Darkly."

"Darkly was in our backyard?"

"Yes?"

"When?" Diego peered out the kitchen window. "There is no one there."

"I know, he left." On cue, a fist beat at the front door. Hinges in need of oiling creaked, and the door swung open. Milla and

Diego turned in tandem to face the witch in their doorway, fist raised and a look of surprise on his face.

"Shouldnae leave your doors unlocked," Darkly advised.

Diego smacked her shoulder. "That is what I was going to say before you mentioned the witch haunting our backyard."

"Could've sworn I closed that last night." She walked the hallway, aware Darkly was watching her and far too distracted by the door to care. "I'm sure I locked the deadbolt when I got home."

"Where were you?" He crossed the threshold, glancing at the ward affixed to the doorframe as he did.

"Not that you're privy to my private life, but we worked late at the store, and then I took Ana to handle an issue with the skunk apes. I vividly remember closing the door; look." She pointed to mud-spattered boots shoved behind the door with her socks and pants. "Wait."

Darkly peered over her head. "Why are your pants in the hallway?"

"I left them there?" She took in the stern jaw, the hard edge to his voice, and the quiet little flicker of laughter in his eyes. "I do that."

"I can confirm," Diego called from the end of the hall. "That is a thing she does."

Darkly angled his face at Diego, who scampered back to the kitchen. When he looked down at Milla, all traces of humor were gone, replaced by what she thought was anger. It was hard to tell with him, as bemused sarcasm seemed to be the go-to.

"Had I known your door was unlocked," he rumbled in a low voice, "I would've gone straight to your bedroom."

Alright, so that is decidedly not anger.

Milla's mouth went dry. "To do what?"

Darkly grinned, her toes curled, and he knew it. His gaze dropped from her face to her chest, and the humor dancing in his eyes kindled brighter. "St. Augustine Hot Mama Cocoa Run?"

"I got a free cup of hot chocolate at the finish line."

"Ludmilla," he practically purred her name, tongue curling around the last syllable as though he savored the taste, "that shirt is pink."

"So?" She glared at him out of self-preservation. Stomach fluttering, she twisted around his over-tall body and skipped down the steps. His nearness, that *look*, and how he'd crooned her name … Horned God, she needed to put distance between them before magick burst from her skin, ready to devour Darkly, the house, the demesne.

The demesne. She broke into a jog, not bothering to check if he followed. *Run it out, Millapet.* Ezra's voice rang crystal clear in her skull. *Burn it off so they don't see.*

Sunlight crawled through the window, striking the mirror and needling through her closed lids. She groaned and rolled over, groping the bedside table for her phone. Notifications filled the lock screen: missed calls, news blasts, and text messages. She squinted, read the time, and bolted upright.

Nine. Shitshitshit.

The store opened in an hour, and she had promised to help process the new inventory. Because there was always new inventory. ICYMI boxes were being delivered by the day. Leggings, dresses, headbands, bangles, purses. All of it hideous and all of it selling while working Milla, Diego, and Julie to the bone. Only Ana seemed immune to the strain. Her smile beamed brighter by the day while Julie, working night shifts at the hospital and refusing to take the days off, had begun complaining of headaches and adopted a wan transparency, as if the nurse had been half-scrubbed out by a gummy eraser.

The wise thing would be to shower, dress, and high-tail it to the Colonial Quarter. Play the part of the good boss and work alongside her employees to ensure the day ran as smoothly as possible. But her fingertips tingled, the flowers kept dying, and last night Diego had pulled her aside to mention yet another rat in the trap.

Milla glanced again at the clock. If she left now, there would be just enough time to tend the demesne, burning off whatever magick she could, and head straight to Southern Gothic. Diego kept spare clothes in his sewing room, she could get by with a quick wash in the bathroom sink and keep her distance from the customers.

"How in the nine rings did I oversleep?" She grumbled, struggling into her running clothes and scrolling through missed messages from Unknown Caller:

> Outside, ready when you are x

> Wakey wakey gonnae run the lakey

> Plz ignore that message

> have i missed you?

> u alive

She re-read the first message, focusing on that lingering "x," which refused to explain itself. Rather than read too much into what was obviously a typo, she charged down the hall and out the door.

An hour later than Milla usually ran, St. Augustine was already well into its day. The morning traffic had subsided, welcoming the first wave of tourists driving in for the weekend. She caught every red light, impatiently jogging in place and unable to shake the feeling that she was being chased. A flicker in the corner of her eye, a shadow cast at an odd angle, a prickling at the back of her neck. She glanced over her shoulder more than once, half expecting to see Ezra keeping stride. His rich khaki skin flushed darker from exertion, sweat clinging to his shirtless torso as the sun and shadows worked in concert to show off the body he was so proud of. Some days, he would smile when she glanced back, lifting his chin and lengthening his stride to put on a show just for her.

On other days he would scowl.

"Faster, Milla." He always held to the belief that she could be better. Faster. Something more than she was. "You have to be faster."

They hit the end of The Bridge of Lions, legs churning and arms dropping as the sidewalk spilled them onto Anastasia Island. Milla bent double, hands on her knees, and sucked in deep, ragged breaths.

"Again." Ezra jogged in place beside her, frowning.

"I ... need ... a minute." She pinched the cramp at her side, walking in a circle. Her thighs were screaming, there was a worrying pinch behind her left kneecap, and she was beyond thirsty. "Can I have some water?"

"There's no water where we're going, Milla."

"But there's water in your hand." She reached for the bottle, and Ezra stepped away. "Ez, please."

His eyes were hard, and Milla noticed with some small measure of satisfaction that he was breathing heavily, his chest pumping and nostrils flaring as he tried to regain control. It was always about control with him, never allowing the slightest hint of weakness, though she saw the strain of effort in every line of his body. Sweat beaded at his brow, glistening on brown skin as evidence he'd had to work to keep up with her. But he was Ezra Lightner who could never admit to defeat. Ezra Lightner who always won, even when he lost.

"You want water? Rest?" he hissed in her face. "Then earn it." Ezra flicked the fingers of his casting hand at Milla. She staggered back at the burst of pain between her eyes, and by the time she opened them, he had a solid lead on the bridge. Milla took off at a sprint, scimitar sharp hands carving the air and intent burning in the muscles of her legs. She was going to earn that water, dammit, to prove she was strong, to prove him wrong. To make him proud of her.

She caught Ezra paces away from the St. Augustine end of the bridge, smacking the flat of her palm against his elbow on the backswing. Panting and dizzy, she braced herself against a palm tree as he stumbled to a halt, sweat running down her back. He blinked at her and then stalked forward, drawing her hand away from the tree to kiss the heart line on her palm.

"That's my girl."

Milla tripped over her own feet, staggering along the shore of Maria Sanchez Lake until she bent double, gasping and sobbing with her hands on her knees.

She couldn't breathe, her bra was too tight, the sun was too hot, she was drowning on dry land, and Ezra was right. She wasn't fast enough, not when it mattered. She'd needed to be fast, needed to be better. If she had been, he would still be here, but he wasn't. He was Gone, and it was her fault.

Fire erupted along her arms and legs, a pain beyond cramps. She whimpered, gritting her teeth against the magick and scanning the ground for anything solid to latch onto. Anything real to keep from falling back into her memories. Churned grass and loose soil, goose droppings, empty beer cans, and, half-hidden by a low shrub, the body of a seagull.

The diversion of a dead bird was a Triple Goddess-sent blessing, a focal point in the madly spinning world that she could cling to. A thing that was real and ready for Milla to spend her magick on.

So she cataloged the gruesome scene, applying what she noted and what she knew to be true of her demesne and its residents; all too willing to fall back on the skills Ezra had taught her.

At first glance, the seagull looked to have been the victim of a neighborhood dog. The bird's neck was bent at an angle, teeth marks visible in the sodden down. The open cavity of its body swarmed with flies and ants, though there was little in the way of coagulated or pooled blood. Large-ish canid pawprints surrounded the corpse, half-erased by curious swipes through the dirt that could be from either a tail or a lame foot. An empty wine bottle and a bottle of malt liquor lay nearby, still in the brown paper bag it was purchased in.

So, not a dog. Likely a coyote—*although, the blood thing*.

Milla covered her mouth to stifle a gag at the stench, bile rising as she eyed the ground, fairly certain there was a *dip* trotting about her demesne. Her spit gobbed in the dirt, thick and acrid, her nausea worsening at the implication of a Catalonian hellhound in S. Augustine.

They were easy enough to handle. A jar of pig's blood and a banishing hex would do the trick. As far as the corpse was concerned, the bait shack at the lake's southern end would have paper towels and trash bags, so there was no need to step into her Way. It was more what the *dip* represented that worried her: a witch out of control, her magick leaking into the world and summoning desecrants to her demesne.

She straightened, already forming a plan, turned, and smacked into a hard body smelling of sweat, clove, and rain. A strong grip closed over her elbows, steadying Milla before she could stumble backward and fall into the lake.

"Careful," Darkly warned, spinning her around and away from the bird.

"Are you following me?" Milla snapped.

"Nae." He ducked his head to look her in the eye. "Are you alright?"

"Yes."

No.

"I saw you bent double ..."

The forced calm she had been barely managing ruptured at Darkly's presence. Heat flooded her veins, and a white-hot prickling stung the corners of her eyes. She wriggled, trying to free her arms from his grip, and the witch relented. "What are you doing here?"

"Went for a run," he said. "Same as you."

"This late?"

"Aye," he grinned, eyes bright and hard as gems. The jovial expression looked pasted on. A mask worn to deflect from what Darkly was truly thinking. "Was meant to run with a friend, but she was late."

"A friend."

Darkly stared at her. The corner of his mouth twitched, and he raised a hand, summoning the deep black sunglasses and sliding them on. "I saw you turning onto the lake, thought perhaps we could finish the run together."

"So you were following me."

"What were you looking at?" He deferred.

"A dead bird." Milla gestured to the shrubbery. Darkly twisted at the waist, scanning the ground. "Why were you following me?"

"What dead bird?"

"What?" She edged around him. "The seagull, under the bush, right—" The ground was messed and matted where the bird had lain. The paw prints and odd scuffs remained, but the corpse was gone. "Oh, no."

Darkly stepped beside her, casting Milla in a cool shadow. "You're sure there was a bird?"

"Yes!" She rushed to the bush. "It was right there. A *dip*, a-a desecrant must have gotten it. There was no blood, but the paw prints and the—"

"Drink this." He forced a water bottle into her hand that most definitely had not been on his person a moment ago. It was cold. Ice cold. "Take a deep breath to calm down."

"I *am* calm. There was a bird." She thrust her finger at the bush. "It was *right there*, and where in the nine rings did you get *ice water*."

"Dinnae doubt you saw something that alerted you to a desecrant in the area, Ludmilla, but there's nothing there." Lean fingers circled her wrist, lowering her arm and applying gentle pressure to turn Milla to face him. Her skin felt too tight, too thin to contain the way her magick surged at his touch. "No bird, no blood, no…" He dropped her arm, and the sunglasses vanished, revealing green eyes swirling with a deep, gray smoke. Milla startled, choking on a cry of surprise. "Holy Horned God."

"What is it?" Milla twisted around and immediately wished she hadn't.

A few paces off, a seagull marched industriously along the lakeshore, nipping mites and crumbs from the grass. Darkly blinked, his throat bobbing as he glanced at the bush, the mess in the dirt, to Milla, then back to the seagull.

The same seagull. Milla was certain it was the same seagull because its head dangled at an unnatural angle, and the interior of its body cavity was on full display.

"Triple Goddess's tits," Darkly cursed.

The seagull squawked, and Milla ran.

FOURTEEN

MILLA BURST THROUGH THE door, tearing down the hall of her duplex, chanting, "Whereisitwhereisitwhereisitwhereisit?"

She dropped to her knees, digging under the bed for a box wrapped in silk. How long had it been, two weeks? Three? Triple Goddess, how had she lost track of the time and let it get this bad?

You're better than this, Millapet, Ezra chided. The ghost of his presence filled her back, blanketing the room in disdain. *I taught you better than this.*

"Go away." She pulled the box free and tore the ribbon away. "You're not here."

But you want me to be. A phantom finger caressed her face, from temple to cheekbone to jaw. Milla jerked away from the touch of a witch who was Gone, wrenched the lid off of the box, and sobbed.

Empty. Emptyemptyempty.

She stared into the box as if she could make herself a conjurer and refill its contents. But her cupboards were empty, her jars mislabeled, she'd never placed that order from Savannah, and her heart was about to pound out of her chest.

She took a shaking Big Girl Breath.

Another.

And she got to work.

Panicked words became an incantation powered by intent. Like the magick it was, her need was manifested as a forgotten pile of dried herbs on top of the refrigerator, a jar of dried juniper berries rolling in the back of a drawer, a film of ash clinging to the rim of her mortar, and a patch of dandelion in the corner of their yard. She harvested the hellebore with her bare hands and chewed the hawthorn twig, grimacing at the taste while grinding the rest of the ingredients into a muddled paste.

The kettle began to whistle, and her phone *zzz-zzz-zzz*-ed across the bedside table, bumping into the plate holding her candle—black, obviously.

She ignored it. It was either Darkly or Diego, the latter wondering why she hadn't shown up to work, and the former probably worried because the Horned God-damned insurance adjuster had to go and be a decent person. Following her and trying to help when she needed him to leave her alone, thank you kindly.

The demesne was fine, ticking along like clockwork under Milla's stewardship, and Milla was fine. She had her store, she had Diego, an apprentice, and her tea. She didn't need Darkly distracting her from the Way leaking out of her body and into the demesne. She couldn't have him learning what she was and ruining everything she'd worked so hard to hide.

"Not today, chucklefuck."

Using the rounded head of the pestle, she scraped her concoction from the mortar into a reusable twenty-ounce coffee mug and, steaming kettle in one hand, held the trembling fingers of the other over the opening. Starting was the hardest part. She had to be certain of her intent. Any doubt, any weakness, and it wouldn't work. She would be found out. He would put together the meaning behind the bird and the witch, Milla would lose the demesne, and it would all be over.

The end.

Zzz-zz-zz-zzz-zzz

The cadence of buzzing from her phone shifted from incoming texts to a call. Milla set the kettle down and rose, careful not to disturb her circle and sigils of ash and bone. Unknown Caller gleamed at her from the screen.

Don't answer that, Millapet.

She held her breath, for once agreeing with Ezra's not-ghost. The phone switched to her chosen wallpaper, and Milla exhaled when no voicemail notification appeared. She knelt in the ritual circle, popping the lid on her kettle to check the temperature. The water inside was just under boiling, thanks to the modern marvel of double-walled engineering that had amused Diego for days.

Diego. Right.

Milla grabbed her phone and typed a message to her roommate. It would be cryptic nonsense to anyone else, but he would know what to do.

Finally, she knelt and took one last meditative breath before slamming her fingers over the top of the mug, focusing her intent, and fighting off a scream when near-boiling water poured over her left hand. She once thought she would get used to the pain, but a ritual demanded three things and always took more than the witch expected.

Intent: a witch must believe, clear-headed and wholeheartedly, in her aim.

Desire: a witch must want, above all else, the thing for which she is appealing to the Triple Goddess.

Sacrifice: well, this one was obvious. Nothing in this world was free.

Her hissed scream faded to a whimper, and the stench of rot hit her nose. Though chewing hawthorn numbed her tongue, it wouldn't spare her from tasting the liquid death she was about to pour down her throat.

Milla fought back a gag, stirring her tea with the hawthorn twig thirteen times counter-clockwise, whispering her incantation of "hellebore, hemlock, hawthorn and clove", but in Czech because it sounded far cooler than in English, and before her intent could waver, she chugged the scalding tea.

In two swallows, it was down.

She gripped the edge of the mattress, hauling herself from the floor. It was easier for Diego if she got to the couch or bed, though the latter was much preferred. Milla would have performed the ritual in her bed to spare him the effort, but she hadn't figured out how to successfully construct an occult circle on her down comforter; so the floor it was, in easy reach of her bed, a plug to keep her phone charged, and a trash can for what came next.

Oh shit. Trashcan.

Milla spun, and the world spun with her, curling her gut into knots. She clamped a hand over her mouth. Too soon, it was too soon; she needed to keep it down until the magick took root. Attempting another step, her knee buckled, and Milla hit the floor. A bright flash of pain had her seeing stars, and salt and metal flooded her mouth, her tongue throbbing. The room dimmed, her vision tunneling as the first of the cramps hit. She curled in on herself, grunting and hissing through her teeth as the first wave passed. Clinging to her last shreds of focus, she clawed up the bedside table and hit send on the prepared text to Diego.

And then she was screaming, sobbing, writhing, and dying inside for hours, days, weeks, eternity. Aware of every minor ache, the throbbing in her jaw, the searing burn on her hand, and the dying tingle in her palms. The intent behind the magick took root, speeding through her veins like a black snake, strangling and suffocating her Way.

Minutes, hours, days, no way to tell, and then Diego was there, dragging her limp form upright and pulling hair away from her face.

"Did you make it yourself?" His palm was cool against her fevered cheek, and her head lolled forward when he removed it. "Maldita sea, pequeña bruja, you know it is too strong that way." She felt herself mumbling, trying to explain, but the words wouldn't form properly. Scuffing sounds, a vacuum, frantic Iberian cursing, and then he was back, looping his arms under hers and trying to drag Milla from the floor. "You couldn't get yourself in the bed first? Mi diosa, Milla, we've been over this." He set her against the bed, and Milla slumped to the side. Her head thunked against the bedside table, and there she stayed, unable to move because she was dead inside. "Was it so bad?"

And then he was gone, running down their hall in response to a slamming noise deeper in the duplex. The light winked out, her room going pitch black, and Milla was flying—no—falling in the dark.

"Nae." A shadow passed before her door, there and gone again. "Nothing, not even with a—aye, ken that, but you dinnae understa—"

Milla blinked, her eyes dry and crusty. Burning. She blindly groped her bedside table, finding the familiar shape of allergy eye drops. Relief was near immediate and Milla curled into a ball beneath her covers, letting the artificial tears run down her cheek.

"Black." The shadow passed again, this time not bothering to stop. "Dinnae ken, it's plain black on a china plate that says 'Life is Fucking Relentless.'" Darkly's voice dropped low as he moved down the hallway. "Aye, there's a crab smoking a cigarette on it." A pause. "Pinched in the crab's claw." A longer pause. "Her grimoire, college textbooks, a rock, a locket, and some origami."

"Buenos dias." Diego filled in the doorway wearing rumpled harem pants in gold and a deeply plunged, now wrinkled, v-neck shirt. The jacket he favored for the outfit was absent, as was his assortment of rings; his only embellishment was the glass vial with its bit of bone hung around his neck. He swept a hand through disheveled hair, glanced down the hallway, and stepped quickly to the bedside. "Before you get angry, Milla, he just showed up at the store. He said you ran off, and he did not know what to do, so he came to find me."

"What?" Words tasted like grave dirt in her mouth.

"Honestly, it is probably good he followed me here; I could not get you into the bed by myself."

"Diego," she croaked. Her throat was raw and likely blistered from the scalding tea, and her brain struggled to keep up with what her roommate was implying. "What happened?"

"Which answer are you wanting for that question?" Diego knelt beside the bed, his voice low. "The 'you tried to poison yourself again' answer, or the 'Deus ex Machina in the shape of an overly tall, unfairly attractive Scotsman' answer?" Milla closed her eyes, and Diego squeezed her hand. "What happened, neteř?

Because he is asking questions I either do not have the answer to or really, really do not want to answer."

"There was a seagull," she explained. "On my run."

"Si, that clears things up."

"Diego, it was dead." Milla silently pleaded with the one person who understood.

Diego rose and swept hair away from her face. "And it is safe to assume your Aural Insurance Adjuster witnessed the previously dead seagull?"

"I don't know what happened."

"I understand, pequeña bruja." He pressed a gentle kiss on her forehead. "Let me go get some lotion for your hand. You rest, tío Diego will take care of you."

He left. There was an argument in clashing accents, a door opened and slammed, and then silence. Milla thought she slept. Her eyes were closed at least, and sleep made sense because dreams only happened when you were asleep, and Ezra was Gone. So it had to mean she was asleep and dreaming. That was the only way to explain why Ezra was, in fact, not Gone and instead sitting in her wingback chair by the window.

"You're Gone," she whispered.

"For now." His mouth, those plush lips she knew so well, curved into a smile.

"You can't be here." Ezra's smile faded, just a bit. Sliding from the one that thrilled her to her bones to the one that made Milla choose her words carefully.

"But you want me to be," he whispered in her ear.

FIFTEEN

MILLA SHAMBLED INTO THE kitchen, hesitating when she found Julie asleep at the table. Not wanting to wake the nurse but unable to ignore the summons of coffee and breakfast, she shoved a few necessities in the pocket of her hoodie, gathered the grinder and coffee in her arms, and, using a combination of elbows and hips to open the storm door, stepped onto the back porch.

The shrubs at the far end of her backyard rustled at the whirr of the grinder, and a little head of straw poked out.

"Mornin'," she greeted the *polevik*. The tiny desecrant shook his head, beady black eyes conveying more disapproval than a bundle of hay ought to be capable. She dug in her pocket, retrieved a tiny liquor bottle, and tossed it into the bushes. The *polevik* blinked, rustled his thanks, and disappeared into the shrub.

"Hey." Milla jumped at Julie's tired voice. Her hair was pulled into a messy bun, curling wisps frizzing from her temples. If she had looked tired a few days before, the nurse was now exhausted, her skin paper-thin and eyes dull. "How are you feeling?"

"Less like death." She offered Julie a weak smile. "Sorry if I woke you." Her friend gave a weak shrug and waved the apology away. "What are you doing here?"

"Diego asked me to bring you to the store." Julie lifted her gaze over Milla's head. "Well, actually, he told me to take a nap"—she paused for a breath—"because I was useless to him if I kept passing out at the register, and that I wasn't allowed to come back"—and another—"until I'd gotten some sleep and you had woken up to come field questions from a particular customer with a smile on your face, no matter how painful it may be."

Milla blinked, working through Julie's words to find the unspoken meaning behind them: people, specifically, tall, green-eyed people who were terrible at their jobs, were asking questions, and Milla needed to appear as if everything were normal. She picked up the grinder and bag of beans. "Has it been busy?"

"Yeah." Julie held the door wide. "I don't know how Ana does it. I can barely keep my eyes open, even with coffee." She shook her head, wandering into the kitchen and taking two cups from the cupboard. "The more customers we have, the more chipper she gets."

"Extroverts are weird."

Julie huffed in agreement, shaking her head at Milla. Her tiny smile faltered. "I'm sorry for yelling at you the other day." She rubbed her breastbone. "I shouldn't have snapped, not after you brought Ana to help with the store and have been so flexible with everything."

Milla waved her off. "I shouldn't be sleeping while on the clock, not when this whole thing is my fault in the first place." She poured the grinds into the coffee filter and set the pot to brew. "We should probably get to the store, then. I'm sure Diego needs a break."

"He certainly deserves one." Julie wandered to the front room, returning with a small glass jar and a first aid kit from her shoulder bag. "Especially after the last two days." Milla looked down, counting her toes and the tiles on the floor. "Oh for … Milla, I know you went through something terrible, and you know what I went through." Her words took on a breathless quality, like the mortal was speaking too fast for her lungs to keep up. "There's no reason to be embarrassed or ashamed. You're taking the right steps, having Diego move in and seeing this new therapist, even if it is weird that you run with him daily." She sent Milla a stern look. "Hiccups are to be expected; just don't forget you have people who love you." Julie stepped close, unscrewing the jar. "We're here for you, just a phone call away, alright?"

"Alright," Milla whispered, unable to correct the lies that Julie had been sold.

Julie lingered on the sidewalk, covering a yawn as Milla picked her way down the flagstones. The sun was too bright, too … buttery, its warm yellow glow casting the world in a soft filter. She paused at the end of her walk, unease churning in her gut.

Or maybe it was guilt.

If she'd kept her cool when Darkly surprised her at the lake, or ordered the tea when Diego first reminded her or been smart enough not to attempt that stupid ritual with Ezra, none of this would have happened.

But it had, and it did. Milla had made this mess herself, and it was time to clean it up. She stepped onto the sidewalk, swaying under the bright sun. Her legs were wobbly, lacking the solidity of connection she usually felt with the demesne. Nothing a few days wouldn't fix. A demesne was a demanding thing, and Milla had left St. Augustine to its own devices for too long.

By the end of the block, her breathing was heavy, and the faint headache she had woken with felt more like iron pins being driven into her temples.

"You coming?" Julie called from across the street, not-so-subtly checking her watch.

"We'd get there faster if we drove," Milla panted back.

Julie's answering yawn shut that idea right down.

Tourists wandered the Colonial Quarter with cups of coffee, lining up in front of the donut shops and breakfast joints along Treasury, sweat dotting brows and dampening cotton as the morning sun turned the narrow streets into an unseasonable furnace. Milla regretted her choice of boots and skinny jeans. The crystal and dream-catcher necklace around her neck felt like an anchor and a net all at once, making it hard to breathe. She shrugged out of her oversized cardigan, bare shoulders on display, and clutched it to her chest.

Pausing at the corner of St. George Street, she leaned against a gaslamp and tugged at her necklace. Goddess, it was hot. Was February always this hot? Steps away, Julie waited with her eyes glazed and half closed, and further on, Agatha looked up from her crystal cart and squinted at Milla. Instead of yelling, the old woman came shuffling over with a handkerchief.

"It will be alright, dear." She smiled, sharp blue eyes gazing fondly at Milla. "We can fix this." With a handkerchief as a barrier between their hands, Agatha pressed an amethyst shard into her palm. Warmth bled from the charged crystal, trickling into the fine bones of her hand.

"Thank you," Milla rasped.

"Just give it some time, hm?"

Milla nodded, feigning understanding as she started down the street, the crystal clutched in her hand. It was best to humor

Agatha, and what was the harm in accepting a gift from a kind old woman? Milla was a witch, but she wasn't rude. Not to other witches—or, at least, those who were actually good at their jobs.

A memory gnawed; the echo of Darkly's voice in her hall, his stopping to check on her. Diego had said he'd run to the store and followed him home, but since being ushered from the duplex, there hadn't been a single call, text, or surprise appearance on her stoop. True, she could have responded to any of the messages he'd sent while she concocted her potion. Probably should have, considering they ran the full gamut of "r u ok?" to "Ludmilla, please answer your phone," to "I'm starting to get worried," followed by "I'm coming over," and finally "Don't do anything you'll regret."

Too late, Milla thought, tightening her grip on the amethyst as she approached Southern Gothic.

"You're late," Ana snapped from the door. "You were supposed to be here an hour ago."

"Sorry, Ana," Julie mumbled, shuffling into the store.

The young witch glared after the nurse, her face twisted in a mean scowl. She turned her eyes on Milla, and the scowl vanished instantly, replaced by a sweet smile. "Oh, *polednice*, you didn't have to come all this way." Ana lay a petal-soft palm on Milla's forearm, drawing her in for a hug. Her cloying floral perfume had Milla stifling a gag as she pulled away.

"It's my store." She wavered a smile, needing to look strong for her apprentice. It was bad enough that Darkly witnessed what she—what the tea had done. Whatever the aural insurance adjuster would tell C.R.O.W., she could at least ensure her failure as a *polednice* wasn't in his report. "Figured I should be here to help."

"How are you feeling?" Ana ushered her inside.

"Tired," Milla answered truthfully.

"You need to take it easy."

"No, I need to be here, helping you, Diego, and the demesne."

Ana pursed her lips. "We have Julie; why don't you go home and get some more sleep?"

"Julie's about to keel over," Milla argued.

"I can't stay, anyway," Julie added. "I traded shifts at the hospital to have tomorrow night off. Just wanted to make sure Milla got in okay," she yawned, jaw cracking, "and to get my car."

"Are you going to be good to drive?"

"Hm?" Julie blinked, shook her head, and pasted on a weak smile for Milla's sake. "Oh, yeah, if I leave now, I can grab a quick nap in the parking lot and sleep off this headache."

"Jules …"

"You're leaving?" Ana whisper-hissed, honey-amber eyes darting to a nearby customer and back. "You can't leave. I need you here, working the register."

"It's my POS," said Milla. "I can work the register just fine."

"No, but, *polednice*, she's—"

"Exhausted and has a real job that isn't working in my store," Milla snapped. "Why don't you go help the customers, Ana?"

The younger witch opened her mouth, but only the tiniest little squeak escaped. Her hair fanned out as she spun around, the floral scent of her shampoo, conditioner, or whatever slapped Milla in the face. She pressed her lips together, willing away a wave of nausea, and turned to Julie. "You sure you're alright to drive?"

"It's only fifteen minutes," Julie nodded. "I'll call you when I get there."

"Call me when you start your shift; grab that car nap first."

"Will do." The mortal hugged Milla briefly, shivering at the contact with her bare skin. "Put a sweater on, Milla," she chastised, pulling away. "You're cold as death."

✻

The rest of the day passed in a blur. Milla worked the register, Diego helped customers, disappearing mid-afternoon only to return with salads from the Italian restaurant around the corner. Ana flitted from customer to customer, plying them with her bright smile and easy charm.

At six o'clock, Diego all but threw himself at the door, twisting the lock and flopping his back against the glass. "Finalmente."

"We did it." Milla pumped her fist in the air. "And we cleared the last of the boxes from my office."

"Just in time, too." Ana flopped into a rococo chair beside the register, only to be shooed from her seat by Diego, who slid onto the upholstery and lounged. "There's a delivery coming tomorrow; I was about to ask if we could use the sewing room."

"The what?" Diego straightened.

"*More?*" Milla goggled at her *čarodějnice*. "How much more of this … stuff are we going to sell?"

"Julie isn't at the executive level she needs to be to start recruiting a profitable downline, and with the convention coming to town, we need to—"

"Convention?" Milla swallowed, relishing the sight of empty stands and tables, the remnants of gaudy ICYMI merch revealing hints of the store beneath like a fast fashion, archeological dig.

"Yes, convention." Ana tipped her head to the side. "What did you think all of this was for?"

"I assumed it was to repair our social media standing."

"And what better way than to attend the ICYMI Spring Sales Kick-off as a Diamond Qualifying Vendor?"

Recognition sparked at those words in that particular order, shoving the image of a heavily made-up, middle-aged mom to the forefront of Milla's memory. "Ugh, Goddess, the Karen was a Diamond Qualifying—"

"The Kayleigh," Diego cut her off. "The woman who got us into the mess that Ana and Julie are getting us out of."

"Whatever."

"Did I mess up?" Ana fisted and pressed her hands to her chin, making doe-eyes at Milla. "I noticed we were going to run out of inventory, and Julie is so close to being a Diamond Qualifying Executive. With the convention coming up, I thought we should capitalize—"

"No, it's fine." Milla sighed and dropped her head, pinching between her eyes. Her headache from that morning had come roaring back, slipping the edges of her vision out of focus, one of the risks of drinking her tea too often or making it herself. The potion dulled parts of Milla, allowing others to rise to the surface. "Goddess, I thought we were almost done with this," she muttered. "Tell me about the convention?"

"It's biennial," Ana started.

"They do it *twice* a year?"

"No, bruja," said Diego. "Once every other year."

She shot a dark look at her roommate. "You can't figure out how to swipe right on Humpr, but you know what 'biennial' means?"

He shrugged.

"It was in New Orleans two years ago," Ana added.

"I thought ICYMI had only been around for two years?"

"Something like that, but after the convention, it started popping up all over the southeast," she explained. "My friend and I went, made a whole weekend out of it. We went to the French Quarter, watched Mardi Gras parades, and then the convention …" She clasped her hands and sighed. "New Orleans is so magical, don't you think?"

"No," said Milla. "Nothing about New Orleans is"—she crooked her fingers in the air and mocked Ana's wistful tone—"magical."

"Beg to differ," Darkly's brogue rolled from the gloom of the hallway, startling the trio of witches. "I've heard the food is to die for."

"Holy Horned God!" Milla pressed a hand to her chest, heart pounding. "How did you get in here?"

He hooked a thumb over his shoulder. "Back door was open."

"Well, we're closed," she snapped. "What are you doing here?

"How are you feeling?" Darkly countered.

Milla went still. Of course, he would have questions. Of *course*, he would worry because he was a nice witch despite being shit at his job whenever he bothered to do it. Or maybe that was the ploy. Pretend to be shitty, pretend to care, and catch the witch off guard.

He greeted Diego and Ana with a terse nod before his bright, green-eyed gaze landed on Milla. She expected anger or condemnation, a dark glower, and stern mien, but the witch looming in her hallway was anything but. The shadow of a beard clung to his jaw, and his normally styled hair was tousled, curling slightly in the humidity. The khakis he wore cuffed at the ankle were rumpled, and his shirt was untucked, which was nothing compared to his weary expression. The witch looked as exhausted as she felt.

"I locked that door." Diego broke the tense silence, squeezing around Darkly and skittering down the hall.

"It was open," Darkly repeated. The fingers on his left hand twitched, and a coin appeared pinched between his thumb and forefinger. He danced it across his knuckles and back again, not looking away from Milla. "How else would I get in?"

"Why are you here?"

"You didnae return my calls."

"I've been busy," she replied, asking for a third time, "What are you doing here?"

Darkly blinked, his shoulders dropping. "I was worried about you." His gaze darted over the store, taking in the florals and pastels before returning to the witch dressed in black standing at the center. "Came to see if you were alright."

"As you can see, I'm fine." She crossed her arms, ignoring how his admission made her heart do a little flip. *He's just doing his job, poorly as that may be.* "We're all fine. Did you need anything else?"

"Aye." His eyes narrowed, his nostrils flared, and Milla was struck by how anger looked … interesting on him. Not out of place, everyone was capable of anger, but where Ezra's anger poisoned the air in the room, and Milla's was a black, spitting thing, Darkly's was borne from a place of caring. "Dinnae suppose you can join me for dinner?"

"Not hungry."

"A walk, then."

"Why?"

Darkly opened his mouth, shut it, and huffed an aggravated sigh. "We need tae talk about what happened."

"Nothing happened." Milla glanced at Ana, who made herself scarce. "I had a bad run. I got heatstroke."

"You call that heatstroke?" He strode across the store, stopping an arm's length from Milla. The fingers on his left hand twitched, and he shoved them into a pocket. "Milla, you were bloody well comatose."

"I'm fine."

"You're nae *fine*. What happened?" A wisp of something trailed over his iris, fogging the bright green, there and gone again. Milla blinked, startled by whatever that was, as much as by his nearness and the worry in his voice.

This isn't real, a little voice that sounded all too much like Ezra whispered. *This is an act; he wants to catch you off guard. Think, Milla.*

Morgen's voice followed, that last warning before she wandered off to Daytona. *Perhaps you should rely on the skills taught to you by Master Lightner.*

She swallowed her gut reply, throat thick and tongue dry, and took in what she knew of the witch and his needs. C.R.O.W. had sent him here to observe her. He'd witnessed Milla at her weakest without knowing it was her strongest. No one could know because if they knew, she would lose everything. She needed to divert his attention away from what he had seen, away from the memory of her comatose and ragdoll limp on the floor. Needed his interest pointed elsewhere, but what else had he witnessed that she could—

"The *dip*," Milla blurted, surprising herself. "I still need to deal with the *dip*."

"The *dip*." The Spanish word was soft on his tongue, just as her name had been.

"Isn't that why you're here? To make sure I'm well enough to tend my demesne?"

"Milla—"

"So come with me to tend the demesne." She spun, grabbing her sweater off the counter. "You've seen how I treat with the *leshy*; now witness how I handle a *dip*."

Sixteen

"Come…on you…pieceofshit fence." Milla threw all her muscle into the wirecutters, cursing at the fence made from kryptonite or adamantium, whichever impenetrable metal constantly foiled superheroes. She let go with a groan and eyed the hole. If she removed her jacket and had enough of a head start, it would work, even if she preferred an extra inch or two of clearance. "Vibranium?" Grass rustled, and Milla spied a tuft of straw-tied hay sticking up amongst the green. "What is Captain America's shield made of?"

The *polevik* shrugged, shushing like wheat stalks in a breeze. A twinkle of light glinted off of black eyes hidden in the straw.

"Big help you are." The *polevik* chattered his annoyance, and Milla rolled her eyes, digging in her jacket pocket for a one-ounce bottle of vodka. "Here." She tossed it into the shrub. "Drink that when we get home. I don't need this thing getting distracted."

"Mnohokrát děkuji," the *polevik* thanked her, saluting Milla with a sheaf of wheat. He toddled through the grass, disappearing behind a cluster of jelly palms hugging the rear wall of the St. Augustine Distillery.

"No problem." Milla set aside her wire cutters, grabbed the carton at her feet, and poured a liberal amount of salt beneath the hole and beyond. "That oughta do." The empty field tilted when she stood, and she braced herself against the fence, careful not to disturb the wards she had drawn. "Whoooo," she giggled, "whoopsie."

Tucked at the end of Cedar Street, right behind the St. Augustine Distillery, the field and unfinished harbor occupied a chunk of prime real estate in a quickly gentrifying corner of the Ancient City. With its proximity to the distillery and the fact it was walking distance from Milla's duplex, the field was the perfect place to hunt a *dip*.

Fog purled off the San Sebastian River and crawled across the field. High humidity had raised the dew point, and Milla shivered as she eyed the water, dreading where this little endeavor would lead. But the *dip* needed to be dealt with, and Darkly needed to see that she was capable.

"Nothin' to it but to do it." She stumbled across the field and onto the abandoned dock of the San Sebastian Inland Harbor, faltering when she spied Ana and Darkly huddled together under the only working light on the dock. They were a matched set, looking like they had stepped out of a Vineyard Vines ad. Her apprentice wore a soft purple, belted button-down jumpsuit, pewter gray chunky cardigan, and bright white sneakers, while Darkly still wore his rumpled Yacht Bro Elite uniform, now with the addition of a quarter-zip pastel sweater.

"Gonna nae do that," Darkly grumbled at something Ana said, scowling at the younger witch.

"Come onnnnn," her *čarodějnice* goaded. "It's after hours, and she's had a really bad couple of days. Look—" Milla snorted as Ana thrust her arm at the sky, swaying in her sneakers. Darkly shot out a hand, grabbing her by the shoulder to keep the young witch from teetering off the edge of the dock. "Moon's up, bottom's up."

"She cannae be serious." He released her, keeping his hand out, ready to grab the *čarodějnice* if she teetered towards the water again.

"C'mon, Darkly." Milla stepped into the pool of light and dropped her eyes to the bottle in his hand. "You gotta drink up, or this won't work. Also, issit adamantiminimum or vibraniuminum that can't be cut?"

"Are you oot yer nut?" Darkly's voice rose in pitch, which caused both Milla and Ana to snort.

"What'd he just say?" Ana giggled, summoning a champagne flute from nowhere. She clinked the base against the bottle in Darkly's hand.

Milla sent him what she hoped was a stern look. "I have no idea."

"Are you drunk." He glowered at her.

"Very." She shot fingers guns at him.

"How did you get *this* steamin' in an hour?"

"With heated effort," Milla answered. "Which izzit?"

"Which is what?"

"Adam-adamanti—ugh, which metal." Ana swatted his arm, withdrawing her hand with a hiss and shaking out the fingers. "Oh, Goddess, you're hard."

"Am nae."

"Oh, Horned God." Milla giggled and pressed her fingers to her mouth.

"Did you just giggle?" Darkly's eyebrows flew up his forehead, the witch looking so affronted that it dragged another giggle out of her. Disturbed, he raised the bottle he held to his mouth.

"Is that Seagram's?" Milla gaped at the bright blue liquid within, and her giggling became a full-on cackle.

Darkly lowered his bottle. "And if it is?"

"Holy Horned God, you are, like, a whole deal." She brushed past him, aiming for the bag she'd tucked beside a pylon. "Drink up; we needta get to work."

"Doing what."

"Huntin'." She worked the leather strap free of its clasp. "*Dip*."

"I've nae come out here to be insulted."

"A *dip* is a Catalonian desecrant." Milla dropped the wire cutters into her bag. "My Arabic's terrible, but if it were any good, I'd call it a *dhibb*."

Darkly blinked, angling his face at Ana. "Does this mean anything to you?"

"I'm jus' an apprennice." She raised the champagne flute to her lips and tilted her head back, pouting when she realized it was empty. Darkly sighed and spun his wrist in the air, summoning a small bottle of Prosecco.

Milla wrinkled her nose, eyeing the bubbles and the over-tall witch. "Did you just have that ready?"

"And if I did?" He arched a brow.

"You fancy." Ana snatched the bottle and read the label.

"Isnae mine," he muttered.

"Then whose is it?" The younger witch gazed up at Darkly with wide doe-eyes. "It's cold. Do you have any beer where this came from?"

"Beer?" Darkly snatched the Prosecco back. "In a champagne flute?"

"It's cute." Ana beamed at him, trailing her finger up his forearm. "I like cute things."

If anything, Darkly looked worried.

"Did you at least bring booze, like I asked?" Milla pulled a mason jar out of her bag, thick, deep crimson liquid schlorping inside. She held it by the lid and circled her wrist, sending viscous red legs dribbling down the sides. Darkly shrank back, clutching his bottle of fruity malt liquor. "This'll only work if we're *proper steamin'.*" She rolled her r's, trying on a Scottish accent for size.

"Aye, I brought gin." He gestured to a black plastic bag at his feet. Milla spied the red screw cap of a bottle of Beefeater next to a six-pack of her favorite IPA. "Dinnae ken if this is a good—"

"The *dip* hunts drunks," Milla cut him off, narrowing her eyes at the gin. "They make easy prey in the Catalonian foothills and vineyards. It likes to stalk them through fields 'n' drains 'em of their blood."

"Ewww." Ana slid closer to Darkly as if he could defend her from what Milla had just said. He frowned and eased a step away. "Please tell me we're going to kill it once we catch it."

"What?" Milla rose to her feet, wobbling off balance. Darkly reached out, ready to catch her, and she teetered in the opposite direction, clutching the jar of pig's blood in both hands. "Horned God, Ana, *no.* I'm not a murderer."

"Then how, pray tell, do you propose to secure the demesne?"

Milla angled her upper body at Darkly, sending him a broad, drunken grin. "I'ma use myself as bait."

All six feet and change of aural insurance adjuster sized up the witch and, from the sour expression on his face, found her lacking. "That is a terrible plan."

"And you guys, too."

"Even worse."

"Got a better one?"

"Likely."

"Hardly." Diego sauntered beside Milla, looping his arm through hers. She grinned, then squealed in delight as he held up a bottle of port-finished bourbon from the distillery. "Did I miss the fun?"

"Gimme, gimme." She made grabby hands at the bottle, pushing the jar of blood at Diego. It was bad enough that she had to catch a *dip* only a few days after drinking her tea, but doing it with only gin in her system would have been terrible.

"What is he doing here?" Darkly gestured to the Stitch Witch and took a bracing swig of his Calypso Colada.

"*He* has not seen a *dip* in years," Diego started. Milla elbowed him in the side. "And he would like to witness the undoubtedly hilarious performance of our Witch of the Demesne as she attempts to capture the pobre perro del infierno."

"How often do you get *dip* in St. Augustine?" Darkly asked. Before Milla could reply, he pointed his bottle at her. "Better question, how often does an American demesne find itself home to Catalonian desecrants?"

"We're Spanish," she lisped. Not on purpose, but Diego smacked her arm anyway. "Obviously." Swigging a mouthful of bourbon, she circled her finger in the neck of the bottle and dabbed liquor on either side of her throat. "The *dip* is here for the same reason there's a *polevik* in my backyard."

Darkly's jaw dropped, his gaze drifting across the empty lot toward Milla's duplex two blocks away. "A what now."

"Cryptids"—she turned her back on the C.R.O.W. witch to address Ana—"are native to an area. Like the Jersey Devil, or Mothman, or snassquatch. In Florida, we've got skunk apes, which is our snassquatch—"

"Sasquatch," Diego corrected.

"Thass what I said." She pointed the bottle at him. "The snassquatch, wampus cat, and hog kong—"

"Gaun an' shut yer' gob." Darkly finished his bright blue alco-pop and tossed it over his shoulder … where it promptly disappeared. "Now you're just making things up."

"Oh, like Nessie isn't real."

"Ne'er said that."

"Goddess, you two bicker," Ana tittered, pulling the tab on a beer and pouring it into her glass. Milla and Darkly jerked their faces at the young witch, snapping, "No, we don't/dinnae."

"O, por diosa." Diego wrapped his hand around Milla's, and thus the neck of her bourbon bottle, forcing her to walk away from the aural insurance adjuster. "To the point, pequeña bruja, while the night is still young."

"Right, so, cryptids, yeah?" She eyed both Darkly and Ana. When neither of them interrupted, she pressed on. "They belong to the area, the general popular belief, but desecrants follow the witch. It's why we've got a raw-head under the Bridge of Lions. A Cornish witch settled here at some point 'n' brought one with 'em, and belief in the thing spread. The Spanish colonized this whole area, an' it's protected by a half-Spanish, half-Czechian witch."

"Do you often have *dip*?" Darkly asked.

"…no," Milla admitted. "This is the first one, at least since I've been Witch of the Demesne."

"Odd, that." A new bottle of Seagram's appeared in his hand, this one bright orange. "If you've nae had one before, how are you so certain a *dip* is what we're dealing with?"

Milla stared at him, her drunken mind slogging through a reply that would satisfy C.R.O.W. She landed on, "Asking in a professional capacity, I assume?"

"Always." The ghost of a smile curled his lips. He twisted the cap off his bottle and took a long swallow.

"The seagull." Milla shrugged out of her moto jacket, and the cold crawled up her arms. She shivered, rubbing at goosebumps, when she noticed Darkly staring expectantly. "Yes?"

"D'ye mind elaborating?"

"Yes." She toed off her shoes, peeled off her socks, and started on the buttons of her jeans when he circled her wrist with his fingers.

"Elaborate." His voice was low, edged with a dangerous note she couldn't place. It warbled down her spine like a finger dipped in wine and circled around the rim of a glass. Heat bloomed low in her belly, settling as a deep, troubling ache that had Milla leaning forward. Darkly hissed a breath through his teeth and released his gentle grip on her arm, finger by finger by finger, stepping out of her space and softening his features into a carefully calm expression. "Please."

"The seagull." She shook her head, clearing her mind of whatever in the nine rings *that* had just been. "On my run the other day, before"—she darted her gaze to Diego. His knuckles were blanched around the jar of pig's blood, but he nodded in silent support of whatever she was about to say—"before I made my tea. It was drained of blood, and the tracks on the trail were from a large dog, but one that appeared to be lame."

"Whoa," Ana breathed. She glanced between Milla and Darkly, who was downing his malt beverage like his life depended on it. "She's like a detective."

"Witch of the Demesne." Milla shrugged, quietly packing away the compliment.

"But why do you have to handle it?" Her *čarodějnice* pressed. "Can't we call C.R.O.W.?"

"C.R.O.W. is here," Darkly slurred, his accent thicker and tongue lazier. He tossed the now-empty bottle over his shoulder and summoned yet another to hand, tipping it in Milla's direction. "An' she's the Witch of the Demesne."

"S'part of the job," Milla clarified. "I gotta take care of all the creepies, crawlies, and cryptids. I keep the demesne strong, an' the demesne keeps me strong." She wiggled her fingers. "With maaagick."

It was more than that, obviously. The demesne was a part of Milla. The map of the Ancient City's streets was engraved on her bones. The music of her riverfronts and beaches underscored every thought of every day. Milla was the Witch of the Demesne, and the demesne made her more. It was a reservoir, an anchor, and a burden all at once.

Ana peered at Milla over her champagne flute, honey-amber eyes glowing in the low light. "You can pull magick from the demesne whenever you want?"

"S'long as I tend it regularly," Milla slurred and nodded, proud of the younger witch for putting that together. "Probably why I'm so tired. Didn't get to charge it yesterday like I usually do."

"Oh, probably." Ana chewed her lip, thinking, then shrugged and downed her glass.

"Am still hoora curious how a vestic secured St. Augustine," Darkly mused.

"Still wondering why you got benched," Milla countered.

He looked away, cheeks flushing. "So how do we manage this *dip*, Madame Vestic? Fortune tell it to death?"

"Already told you," she grabbed her bourbon, raising it in cheers. "By getting absolutely steamin' drunk."

✳

"Jus'a'li'l bit more." Milla edged forward, and the horizon tilted forty-five degrees. Swinging her leg out, she wide-stepped and overcorrected, shouldering into Darkly, who stumbled back, tripped, and went down in a heap of arm and leg.

"Aye, watch it, ye dafty," he slurred, rolling onto his back and sitting up in the grass. Dried blades clung to his hair and down the length of one arm. He blinked and beamed up at Milla. "Ye alright, hen?"

"Hen?"

"Ugh, stop flirtingggg," Ana whined from a few feet away. "It's embarrassing."

"Deberías verla cuando realmente lo intenta," Diego muttered from the opposite direction.

Milla gasped, sweeping her arm to smack the Stitch Witch. He was too far away, and she stumbled forward to keep on her feet. "Esscuse me, señor, you have never once seen me try."

"¡No!" Diego gasped, "¿En serio?" This time, Milla managed to swipe at his arm, and the witch danced away, cackling.

"Erryone drink more." She swung her bottle at the group and her head swam, gut curling uncomfortably. "We gotta get this thing tonight or, or, or—"

"Or?" Darkly's voice came from somewhere to her left.

"Or Imma … Imma…" She pressed the back of her hand to her mouth, tasting sour, hot spit. "Oh, Horned God, Imma be sick—" The bourbon fell from her hand, and she hurked into the grass.

"I told you to stick with beer," Diego sang in the break between heaves, his shape obscured by the fog. It had grown thicker as they wandered the field, swallowing their knees, blurring the buildings, and shrouding the empty lot in a fae guise.

"Doesn't work fassenough," Milla groaned. The grass rustled, and someone sidled close, the heat of their body blanketing her bare legs.

"I ken the need for alcohol, the desecrant bein' what it is an' all." Darkly voice was low, his words careful on a tongue made thick from sugary, malted adult beverages. He placed the flat of his hand at the base of Milla's spine. "Dinnae ken why this endeavor requires the removal of your pants." His fingers curled, nails tickling her skin, and then, "Not that I mind."

Goosebumps crawled up her legs, and Milla stared at her feet, just visible beneath the fog, telling herself it was from the cold and *not* his touch. She dug her nails into the skin above her knees, needing the pain to sober her thoughts. The entire point of bringing him along was to prove her demesne was secure despite what he'd seen. Not for him to witness Milla throwing up after getting five minutes away from blackout drunk, or to find an excuse to touch her bare skin, and definitely *not* for her to like when he did.

Her head ached, the migraine that had been threatening all day needling deeper into her eyes. She squinted across the lot, ready to admit defeat, and spied two red pricks of light. "Give it a minute."

"Aye?"

She swayed, closing her eyes long enough to work a little piece of magick so she could think clearly; drilling down into herself for the quietest, tiny thread she could reach of a Way she'd drowned. Her palms warmed as she hauled that fragment of her Way to the surface and cleared her head.

Darkly slid his hand to her hip, tugging Milla closer. "Did you just—"

"I need you to listen to me, Darkly, and do exactly what I tell you."

"What're you—"

"Can you do that?" She angled her face up at him, noting the flicker of a scowl. He opened his mouth to retort, and she cut him off. "Can you do that?" Darkly closed his mouth, pulled his hand away, and nodded. "Good." She straightened, keeping one eye on those red pricks of light, closer now, having moved silently through the fog. "Now run."

Milla bolted, heartened by the grunt and curse from the Scotsman she left standing in the grass. His stride being longer, Darkly hauled beside her within a few footfalls, shouting, "Explain?"

"*Dip*," she panted. "*Dip, dip, dip*, Diego, Ana, get outta the way!" Her fingers grazed Diego's arm as she passed him. Another piece of quiet magick, one she hoped would be obscured by the proximity they held to a desecrant.

A desecrant that was now tearing after them.

The field wasn't large. Goddess, from where she'd thrown up, it was barely a tenth of a mile to the water. But Milla was drunk, her feet clumsy, a Horned God-damned *dip* was on her tail, and her plan, admittedly, wasn't the best.

For one, it depended on Milla outrunning Darkly. Which she could do sober, lost in her traumatic memories, and desperate to prove she was capable. But right now, Milla was none of those things. She was terrified, drunk beyond belief, and wearing little more than slip-on tennis shoes, boy-cut undies, and a tank top.

She stumbled, tripping over her own feet. A hand gripped her arm, keeping Milla from falling, and she yelped as a foreign magick surged against her skin. The firm grip released, and cold pressed against her lower back, urging Milla faster. She let her legs obey that subtle prompt, churning her feet through the overgrown grass.

Jaws snapped at her heel, and panic had Milla glancing over a shoulder, where a wolfhound-sized creature loped unevenly less than a foot behind. A long snout, lips peeled back to reveal knife-sharp teeth in a frothing mouth, and two red eyes burning with a fury that spoke to rabid hunger buried in a face coated in fur so dark it was almost swallowed by the night. Her only saving grace was the lame foot every *dip* was cursed with. The sole hope for the drunkard's survival: outracing a creature with only three good legs.

She had enough clarity of thought to form one sassy remark. *Well, game fucking on.*

"What's your plan?" Darkly hollered again. Milla ignored him, scanning the fog and searching for the fenceline. She thought she was on target. Thought she'd planned this well enough. That she'd kept the exit point in mind as they wandered the field. It was a fool's hope; she recognized that now. She ought to have invested in some glow sticks, a lantern, or a flashlight, but no. Like Ezra, she'd let ego determine her actions, and now she was running blindly through a fogged-over field searching for a one-and-a-half-foot by two-foot hole cut into a fence she couldn't even Horned God-damned see.

Her heel came down on something hard in the grass. Hard and round. It skidded out from under her, and Milla was airborne, staring at a swathe of stars visible through a seam in the overcast sky before her back hit the ground, the wind rushing from her lungs.

"Fu-u-u-u-ck," she gasped in the instant before the *dip* would be on her. She threw her hands up over her face and heard Diego yell. Heard a wet splash in the grass. Heat and dank and fetid swamp lurched over her, bypassing the witch altogether as the *dip* followed the scent of blood on the air, a diversion tossed by Diego to gain the witch time. She rolled onto her side, pressing the heel of a palm against the earth. The grass rustled, and she looked up to see the *polevik* staring back at her, black eyes glimmering in a straw face.

At his feet lay an empty, one-ounce bottle of Ketel One, the plastic cracked from Milla's weight coming down on it. The little field sprite raised his arm to point over her shoulder, jabbering in raspy, dry Czech, "Hloupá čarodějnice, beze mě bys to nikdy nenašla."

She followed his gesture, eyes widening at the twisted points of a chain link fence barely visible in the fog. "Thank you," Milla wheezed, "Děkuji."

"Přines mi ještě vodku."

"Yes," she agreed. She rose to her knees, hands clasped in thanks. "All the vodka. However much you want."

He chirped his pleasure and sprinted through the grass. Milla gained a foot, pushing against her knee to rise. Two hands grasped her by the shoulders, lifting the witch and turning her around.

"Plan?" Darkly asked, his face unbearably close to hers. An alarming roll of magick seethed off of the A.I.A., and her belly fluttered at his nearness.

"Same plan." She wriggled out of his grasp, and the brand of his hands echoed in her bones. Snatching the cracked bottle of vodka from the ground, Milla scanned the field, spotting the *dip*. She hurtled the bottle at its shoulder and shot a feral grin at Darkly. "Run."

"Hate this," he snapped but fell in stride beside her as the hellhound gave chase, yowling, yipping, and nipping at their heels. Milla kept her eyes on the ground, following the tamped-down path her *polevik* had made through the grass. In half a dozen strides, the fence was visible. After another half dozen, she could discern the hole she'd cut and the black nothing of the San Sebastian River on the other side.

"Veer left!" She shouted at Darkly.

"What?"

"Fence!" Milla ducked. "Veer left!" She tightened her core and bent a leg beneath her as she dropped into a slide. Cut metal scraped her thigh and her shoulder. The salt stung as she passed over, under, and through it, but the *dip* followed, and that was all that mattered. She heard the shrill yip of fright and saw the bursts of neon purple in the instant before she splashed down in the San Sebastian River. The salt and banishing wards she'd applied to the fence had worked, sending the desecrant far, far away from her demesne.

Milla burst through the surface with a deep breath and disbelieving chuckle. She swam to the river's edge, where Diego lay on his stomach, an arm extended. Grabbing his hand, she reached for the bank with the other, only to have Darkly seize her wrist and haul her from the water.

He settled Milla on solid ground, patting down her arms before gripping her hips, a broad grin stretched across his face. "So that's why you werenae wearing any pants."

SEVENTEEN

GODDESS, THE SUN WAS the worst, mocking Milla with its cheerful glow and flittery, fluttery, flowery warmth. It baked the Colonial Quarter cobbles, making the air in the furnace-like streets steamy and thick, making it nearly impossible to take a full, satisfying breath. She threw her body against the door of Southern Gothic, and the bells jangled, drilling into her already aching head. Tossing her bag on the counter, Milla threw herself onto the vinyl bar stool, dropping her elbows and cradling her head.

"Good morning, *polednice*!" Ana chirped.

"No," she groaned, dropping her forehead against the chilled glass. "How are you so awake?"

"I didn't drink half a bottle of bourbon and go for a swim in the river," her *čarodějnice* sagely replied.

"Rude."

Ana tittered, set a can of sparkling water on the counter, and skipped off to help a customer. A steady trickle of tourists and a few locals Milla half-recognized wandered in over the next few hours. Compared to the last few weeks, the store was quiet. A blessing considering Milla's current state. Diego was no better.

Ana had already shooed him from the PVC and shower curtain dressing room, telling him if he needed a nap that badly to go to his sewing room where no one would see him. Diego responded by collapsing dramatically into the antique rococo chair he had won in a fierce online bidding war.

Thank the Goddess for Ana. The young witch was her usual bright and sunny self, easily winning over their customers. So much so that no one complained when dealing with the hungover, cranky witch at the register.

The noon lull arrived, marked by a slowing trickle of customers. Milla rang up the last one, folded her arms on the counter, and dropped her head. Sun glinted off the windshields of cars parked in Toques Place, baking the front of Milla's store. A sticky sweat had broken out along her shoulders, and no matter how hard she closed her eyes, the sun *hurt*.

She was half asleep when a cool shadow draped over the counter and the witch. She sighed, relief dripping along her temples and easing the headache, only to tense when their new customer spoke.

"Dinnae ken you'd fancy a lunch?"

"Ugh," she groaned, rubbing her face in the crook of her arms and dragging bleary eyes up to Darkly. He'd forgone his preppy casual uniform, opting for a black v-neck and joggers, his hair perfectly tousled. "What are you doing here?"

He stepped back from the counter, affronted, and took the shade with him. "Thought that would be obvious from my asking you to lunch."

"Right." Milla rubbed her temples. "Sorry. Hangover." Darkly nodded. From the bags under his eyes and waxen complexion, Milla felt it safe to assume he felt about as awful as she did.

"Usually, I'd say yes, but it's just us today." She waved a hand at Diego, slouched on his throne.

Ana flounced into the room, her arms full of pink carnations and red roses, a welcome change from the yellow daisies, daffodils, and tulips she favored. She stopped short when she saw Darkly and freed a hand to flip a thick curl of hair over her shoulder. "Hi, Darkly!"

Darkly stared blandly back at her, then re-settled his gaze on Milla. "Just you?"

"And Ana," Milla amended. "Sorry you wasted your time coming all the way down here."

"Wouldnae have been a waste if you'd answered your phone."

"It was on silent," she argued. He frowned. "We're closing early tonight—"

"I have plans with Julie," Ana interjected, "and these two are hopeless without me."

"—can we do dinner?" Milla finished.

"Ehm." A flush crawled onto his face. "Cannae tonight, I've also … got plans. Up in Jacksonville."

"Coffee after a morning run?" She tried.

Darkly fidgeted, his gaze drifting over her head. "Might nae be free tomorrow morning."

"Oh." Milla slouched, realization struck, and she went ramrod straight, nearly slipping off the stool. "Oh! Okay, um …"

"Oh, my Goddess, you two are so awkward." Ana swept over, dumping her flowers and guiding Milla from the stool. Sweet floral perfume wafted from the witch, turning Milla's stomach. "She would love to have lunch with you. Diego and I can manage the store."

"Are you sure?"

"Positive," she nodded. "Take all the time you need; just be back before five."

"Right, fine. Let's go, then." Milla charged past Darkly and out of the store, faltering at the oppressive humidity.

"Call me if you're going to be late!" Ana hollered.

Milla patted her back pocket and stopped when she did not feel her phone. "Shit." She whirled and ran face-first into a chest full of Darkly. "Double shit."

His arm shot out, keeping Milla from stumbling with a hand flat against her lower back. She tried not to notice the heat of him or the crisp and smoky, intoxicating incense of *him*. Failing miserably, she mumbled into his chest, "Forgot my phone."

"Ken you might need that." His voice was a low rumble, the words for her and her alone. Milla caught the wistful expression he wore, only for it to harden as he jerked his face up and away. Jaw set, Darkly stared out over Toques Place. His hand, however, lingered, fingers curling at the base of her spine, their touch tingling through to her bones.

He dropped his arm away, and Milla scuttled back into the store, fuming mad at herself for caring that he, *apparently*, had a date tonight. So what if he had a date? He was a good-looking man with a stupid accent and an even dumber smile, and she was just a job.

Darkly marched them directly to Ancient City Pork 'n' Butts, which was quite possibly the worst bar-b-que restaurant in the Southeast. They had a decent covered patio, which Darkly ignored, heading for the wrought iron tables in full sunlight. Milla sat with her back to Toques Place, the sun beating down on her shoulders, while Darkly reclined in his seat, comfortable behind his sunglasses. Of course, she'd forgotten to bring her hat. Or sunglasses. Just like she'd forgotten her phone, Goddess, this hangover was the *worst*.

"You couldn't pick a spot in the shade?"

"Nae," Darkly grabbed a menu, waggling his fingers at Milla. "Summon your hat."

"I can't summon hats."

That earned a glance, mild surprise raising his eyebrows over the frames of his sunglasses before he returned his attention to the menu. "I think I'll have the burnt ends," he said. "I've heard they're good."

"They'd have to be," she muttered, snagging her menu and using it to shield her from the sun, "since everything here is burnt."

A woman cleared her throat, and Milla finally noticed the waitress in the restaurant's unfortunate uniform hovering beside their table. The dark green shirt stretched tight across her chest, distorting the words "I Like Big Butts" written in Comic Sans. Beneath the ill-advised motto was the obscene graphic of a potbelly pig given anthropomorphic pouting lips and blue eyes with lashes. The back of the shirt was worse, showing the same pig with the addition of an excessively aggrandized posterior.

"You know what you want, hon?"

"Soup and salad." Milla hadn't even glanced at her menu. Every restaurant like Pork 'n' Butts had soup and salad on their menu. Some even tried to be cute and listed the item as a Super Salad, which Milla just hated.

"Ranch, bleu cheese, balsamic, Italian, Thousand Island, Russian, poppyseed, lemon poppyseed, oil and vinegar, buffalo ranch, chipotle ranch, buttermilk ranch, parmesan ranch—"

"Dry." She closed her eyes and tilted her head back.

"Chicken nood, French onion, tomato bisque, chili, vegan chili, turkey chili, chowder, clam chowder, cod chowder, corn chowder—"

"Tomato."

"Please," Darkly added. Milla glared at him. "And I'll have the burnt ends with cornbread, beans, and hush puppies." A pause. "Kim."

"That'll just be a few," Kim replied, her tone far warmer with him than it had been toward Milla.

When Kim was well out of earshot, Darkly nudged her foot with his shoe. "Soup and salad at a bar-b-que restaurant? I hear they revoke your Southern Charm for that."

"I don't eat meat," Milla replied.

Darkly straightened in his chair, coughing into a fist. "Sorry, I didnae ken—"

"How would you?" She cut him off, not wanting to have this conversation. Not wanting to care that he was embarrassed for bringing a vegetarian to a restaurant known for its poorly smoked meats. "I never told you."

"I could have asked," he retorted. Milla braced herself for a snide remark, inferring it was her fault he didn't know. His sunglasses were still on, so she couldn't see his eyes, but his mouth frowned, and he squirmed under her scrutiny. "I should have asked, I'm sorry."

"You're sorry?"

"Aye." He scratched at his collarbone. The silence stretched, growing fraught with a tension Milla had absolutely zero desire to name as it began with "Darkly's going on a," and ended with "date". She shouldn't even care. She was his task. His job. Just as she had been Ezra's job.

"This is her?" Ezra took in Milla with a glance, keen eyes assessing, judging, and discarding her instantly.

"Yes." Morgen crossed her legs, reclining in the wingback chair across from Milla.

"What am I supposed to do with this?" He turned his back on her, and Milla silently fumed on the sofa. His insufferable tone held a note of disappointment, as though he'd hyped himself up for a sweet job only to be handed a bitter pill.

"You train it."

"I am not an it," Milla hissed. Ezra's mouth twitched in an amused smile.

"Then behave like a witch," Morgen replied, her voice bland.

"What does it do?" Ezra still would not look at her for more than a flick of his eyes, a habit that was beginning to royally piss her off.

"It does this." Milla stood, reaching for his shoulder. Ready to show the pompous obnubilari what she was capable of when a bright light flared behind Morgen. A warning.

"Ludmilla!" She snapped, still poised in the chair. Milla froze, and Ezra trained his eyes on the palm of her hand, reading the lines. Another twitch of his lips, and he met her gaze.

"Interesting."

"Indeed," said Morgen. "And what else do you see, young Lightner?"

He faced Milla, the haughty demeanor vanishing behind stoic calm. "May I?"

"May you what?" she asked, then froze under the full brunt of his stare like a deer in headlights. Teal fizzed and sparked to life deep in an intoxicating amber. Dancing and leaping, dragging Milla under his spell. A light flared in her eyes, startling her back a step, and it took a moment to realize that the Morganhexe had not cast her illusion a second time. This was not a sun bright burst filling the room; this light was focused entirely in her mind. It grew brighter and brighter, searing *and scouring, and then dimmed until the pain behind her eyes receded. She blinked, starblind, and Ezra Lightner's mocking voice filled her head.*

"Oh, yes. I do believe I can do something with this."

"Where did you go just now?"

Milla startled into the present, her vision blurry as pain prickled behind her eyes. She sank in her chair, shaken by the unwanted memory. Slowly, the world slid back into focus, the three Darkly's in front of her collapsing into one. "Nowhere."

"Fine," he grumbled, insult, or maybe disappointment, flashing over his face as he reached for his phone.

"I was thinking of when I met Ezra," she blurted. His hand froze above his phone. "The day Morgen brought him by the duplex and our first, um, lesson."

"I had wondered about that."

"Oh?"

He nodded, settling back in his chair. "Most of C.R.O.W. has, for a long time."

"I figured as much," she snarked. "Why else would C.R.O.W. send an A.I.A. to investigate me?"

A muscle twitched in his cheek. "Am nae here to investigate you, Milla." He swept his glasses away, and they vanished. Bright eyes stared at her from across the table, hard and determined. Again, there was a waft of something gray and smokelike, there and gone again, that darkened the green. "I'm here to help you, but I need you to help me."

"I know …" she hesitated, uncertain how much C.R.O.W. knew about her and Ezra, the ritual. "I know I'm not the … easiest person to be around." She sighed. "Things were the way I liked them. Quiet, stable."

"Predictable?" He asked. She nodded. "Beginning to see how a vestic could manage the demesne."

Milla flinched at the lie he was slowly coming to believe. She lowered her eyes, trailing the shadows painted on the sidewalk and her legs from the sun burning through gaps in braided strands of iron. A cloud must have drifted in front of the sun because the shadows belled and bled together, stretching from under Darkly's chair as a mass of cooling gray reaching for her feet. She drew them underneath her chair, and the shadows receded as the cloud moved away.

"Why didnae you use magick to deal with the *dip*?" he asked, voice lowered in a whisper.

"Banishing wards are magick."

"You know what I'm asking, Milla." His voice was weary, resigned, as though he already knew she wouldn't give him the answer he wanted.

What is your Way?

"I didn't need to." She grabbed the salt from the table, spilling some into her palm and looking everywhere but at him. The waitress returned with Milla's soup and dry salad; the greens wilted, and the grape tomatoes shriveled. Tomato bisque sloshed over the side of the bowl as the woman all but tossed the food down. Darkly's meat platter was set before him with more care, the burnt ends glistening gray in the sunlight, and his quiet mutter of thanks earned a smile from good ol' Kim.

When she left, after offering him no less than six different kinds of sauce, Darkly cleared his throat. "I need to tell C.R.O.W. something, Milla. After what I saw with the seagull and in your home—" His voice faltered, and at that, she finally met his eye. "They're asking me questions I cannae answer. They want to …"

He coughed into his fist, and more smoke drifted over his eyes. "C.R.O.W. wants to call me back."

Those words pinned Milla to the uncomfortable chair. "Why?"

"They arenae pleased with my lack of progress in assessing the security of the demesne and how a witch of your Way became its steward." She opened her mouth to argue, but he raised two fingers, halting her. "I've filed my protest asking for an extension."

"Why would you do that?"

"Because I see you every day, I see the work you've put into yourself, the store, and guiding Ana. Because another witch might be too rash in their assessment and care of the desecrants calling St. Augustine home." Milla straightened at what almost sounded like praise, only to slump when he finished bitterly with, "But C.R.O.W.'s word is our law."

A headache built in her temples, prodding at the back of her eyes. The sun, the awful salad, the conversation. Milla pinched the bridge of her nose, eyes closed, trying to stave off the inevitable.

Darkly prodded his burnt ends with a compostable fork and popped one in his mouth. After two solid attempts at chewing, he discreetly spit it out into a napkin. "I needed you to talk to me, Milla."

"Not this again."

"Yes, this again." He summoned his sunglasses and put them on. "I have a job to do—"

"Me."

"Yes, my job is you. To assess your ability to secure the demesne and determine the state of your aura." His tone was flat, the words sounding recited rather than believed. "To mitigate risk and help prepare you to be the *polednice* and eventual *jezibaba* that Morgen and C.R.O.W. believe you have the potential to be."

"Don't talk to me of potential," she snapped. White stars danced as the migraine began in earnest. "Why can't C.R.O.W. just leave me alone? Let me run my store and live quietly until I am gone and forgotten?"

"Is that what you want? To sell the hideous clothes Julie keeps scrounging up from Goddess knows where at a steep mark-up to tourists?"

"Yes," she grumped.

"I dinnae believe you. Not for one second do I believe that is what Ludmilla Probuditna actually wants."

"How would you know?'

"I wouldnae," he snapped. "And that's exactly why C.R.O.W. wants to send me home." Milla looked away, blinking into the sun. It wasn't fair that C.R.O.W. sought her out, thrust Darkly at her, and then decided on a whim to take him away just because she wasn't ready. What in the nine rings did they expect? That she would fawn over a handsome man with jade green eyes and an accent that rolled along her bones and then share her entire life's history? They should have known better. What happened two years ago happened, and she should have seen it coming, but she didn't, and now Ezra was Gone, and Milla had come back here to rot.

Alone.

"Well, it was nice getting to know you." Milla shot Darkly a curt nod and whirled from the table, stopping at the sight of Diego, pale and wide-eyed, holding his phone out to Milla.

"You did not answer your phone," he said.

"She never does," Darkly snarled.

Diego's brows rose over his frames, looking between them. "Sorry not sorry to interrupt whatever is happening here, but Milla, you must take this." He gripped the glass vial on his necklace with one hand, holding out his phone with the other. The call had been running for a few minutes, and the area code was local, though she didn't recognize the number.

"Who is it?" She searched her roommate's face for a hint, a clue, and found nothing to prepare her for what he said next.

"It's Julie."

EIGHTEEN

"WHAT DO YOU MEAN she isn't here?"

"Exactly that," the nurse at the desk snapped. Her foul mood wasn't necessarily aimed at Milla. The lobby was full-to-bursting with mortals. Children sat in the aisles, crying or zoning out on tablets, while their fathers checked phones or stared at nothing, eyes glazed in the way of panicked retreat. "She's not here." She tapped on her keyboard, picked up the receiver to mutter something to someone beyond the waiting room, and looked past Milla and Darkly. "Mr. Aguilar?"

Darkly pulled her out of the way as a harried middle-aged man rushed to the desk. Just like he'd ushered her to his little red hybrid and escorted her to Flagler Hospital.

"I don't understand," she mumbled. "They said they found her in her car."

The voice on the phone had been hushed, as if the nurse who'd called was doing so in secret. "She never clocked in for her shift, God, if we'd only known …"

If they'd only known that Julie had made it to the hospital. That she'd passed out in her car and missed her shift. She'd needed help, and it was only by the grace of whichever god looked out for the nurse that her car didn't have air conditioning, and she drove with the windows down.

"… saw her on the way to my car and remembered you two were close …"

Milla only half listened. Her body vibrated from panic, and the world kept slipping in and out of focus. The phone was pulled from her hand, the sun blocked by Darkly's long, cool shadow, and then the witch pulled her into a hug and asked, "What do you need?"

And she'd asked for a ride.

The headache she'd been fighting all day worsened as they neared Flagler Hospital. Slicing and pricking the space between her eyes with white hot needles. Sunlight strobing behind the palm trees had her dropping her head between her knees and groaning as a sticky, cold sweat burst along her neck and back. Darkly muttered an apology, and cool darkness blanketed Milla, shielding her from the sun and the migraine until the charge nurse told them Julie wasn't there.

"This is my fault," she mumbled.

"How is this your fault, Milla?" Darkly guided her to an empty corner of the lobby.

"I should have checked in on her; I should have known that she was—" her breath quickened, the knife-sharp pain in her temples sharpening an agony beyond a throb. "And she was so tired, she said she would call, but she never called—"

"Breathe, Milla." Darkly set her against the wall, urging her with a gentle push to bend her knees. To sit. She dropped her head between her knees, trying to catch her breath and keep the world from slipping out of focus. Flashes of her last visit to the hospital came and went with every breath. The flourescents in the lobby became strobing lights on an ambulance, making her head spin. Diego sobbed into her phone in Spanish so thick that Milla could only catch, "Como estoy aqui? No entiendo como estoy aqui."

Over and over and over again.

And there was a red-headed nurse yelling that she couldn't find a vein. They worked without local anesthetic; she was too dehydrated. The numbing gel was not an option; there was too much blood. Milla remembered the stitches. Every pinch, drag, prod, and pull. Twenty-seven on her right and forty-two on the left, and when she woke, restrained to the bed with a mouth as dry as the Tortugas, Julie was there with a clipboard, a name tag, and a careful smile. Milla's palms were stained yellow from the iodine for weeks, and when the stitches had been absorbed, and her hands unwrapped, she was a witch with no lifeline.

"—confused and dizzy. Poor thing filled a trashcan before her ride came, didn't even know where she was—"

Darkly was talking with a nurse when Milla blinked back to herself, rubbing her back with the flat of his palm. Cold bled from his touch, soothing her panic with every gentle press. Without a word, he took her hand, drawing attention to the raised web of skin on her palm. The scars itched and throbbed, pulsing with the memory of what she had done. Belatedly, Milla realized she'd been scratching at her palm, her nails irritating the flesh until it was red and raw.

"I didn't mean to scare you with my call." The new nurse was looking at her. Darkly, as well.

"Milla?" He ran his thumb over her knuckles.

"There's something I forgot to do today," she answered, numb. Darkly watched her for a moment before returning his attention to the nurse.

"Do you know where she is?"

"Home." The nurse crouched to be at eye level with Milla. "She wouldn't let us admit her; said something about her ex-husband?" Milla nodded, and the nurse frowned. "God, he's such an asshole." She lowered her voice further. "Her cousin took her home, but he said he had to get back to the office and couldn't stay. I don't think she should be left alone, but if we admit her, then the court—"

"I'll go," Milla said.

"I'll take you," Darkly rumbled.

"You have your date later," Milla protested. "I'll call an OverAuto."

He cut her off with a squeeze of his hand and gently pulled Milla to her feet. "I'll take you."

Milla bounced her knees and drummed her fingers, pent-up panic jarring every nerve. She fiddled with the air vents, hoping the air conditioning would soothe her headache. Then she got too cold and slammed her palm over the roller, aiming the air away. Nauseous again, she spent minutes readjusting the vents. Darkly drove carefully, likely remembering how she'd thrown up in an empty field, Goddess, last night, but even he had limits.

His hand dropped to her knee, giving a gentle squeeze, and he left it there, running his thumb back and forth on the outside of her leg in soothing strokes. Milla tensed, caught between not wanting him to touch her and wanting him to touch her more. He squeezed her leg again and drummed his fingers along the inside of her knee.

"Hard enough to drive on the wrong side of the road without your legs causing a distraction." His hand slid just a touch further up her thigh. She might have moved her leg so it would be easy for him to do so, though no one could definitively prove it. "Is there anything I should know before we get there?" Darkly asked, slowing the car at a stoplight.

"What you don't know could fill a—"

"Milla." He locked his gaze on hers. A ribbon of black wafted across his iris like smoke in a gentle breeze until it was gone entirely and the green bored into her. "Please. I need you to tell me *something*."

"Julie is a nurse," Milla began, pulling her legs out of Darkly's reach. She laced her fingers together, trying to find the words, the breath, to give him something that would paint enough of a picture to satisfy the witch, and C.R.O.W. "We met when I … when they brought me in after I … after everything with Ezra, and I—"

"You dinnae have to—"

"Isn't this what you want?" she croaked. "For me to explain to C.R.O.W., through you, how I earned the demesne?" Darkly didn't move, save for the tiniest twitch of a muscle in his jaw telling her she was right. Milla hated that she knew his face, knew his quirks and his mannerisms well enough by now to notice.

Unable to bear it, *him*, she looked down at her scarred hands and took a breath, calming herself to get through just this piece of her story. That much she could give before C.R.O.W. stole him back.

"After everything with Ezra, when I came back to St. Augustine, I did something stupid and desperate that I couldn't take back. Diego was there to call nine-one-one, but what I did—the power fueling the ritual was enough to earn me the demesne." He drew in a quick hiss, intent on the witch sharing a private piece of her Soul. An explanation she hadn't given anyone else, even if it was only half of the story. "I was out of it when they brought me in; I barely remember the procedure," she lay her hands palm up, feeling the heavy weight of Darkly's gaze on her scars, "and when I woke up, there was Julie."

Darkly put his eyes on the road, easing the car across the intersection, his knuckles bone white as he gripped the steering wheel.

"She used to be married to a real piece of shit, and when she tried to leave him, he put her in the hospital. My insurance had Ezra as the contact, but he was already Gone, and they misunderstood my state, m-my Way and the cost it takes, my injuries … It doesn't make sense to these mortal physicians, and they assumed—Julie assumed—even though he'd been Gone for a year—" Milla's voice hitched and she rubbed her eye. The headache had retreated enough for her to function, but it lingered on the edges of her mind, waiting.

"C.R.O.W. assumed," Darkly whispered.

"I figured as much." Milla pulled her feet up, wrapping her arms around her knees. "Ezra pushed me where my Way was concerned, but he only wanted me to be the best at what I did. Can you blame somebody for wanting their partner to be the best? Have the best?" Darkly shook his head. "His tactics as a teacher could be cruel, but as a-a partner, he was anything but. Any bruises and cuts I wore when I was wheeled into this hospital were by my own hand."

What he thought of that, Milla had no idea. She closed her eyes and focused on breathing, filling her lungs entirely for what felt like the first time since this witch had sat beside her in the bar. They rode in silence, Darkly following his rental car's GPS. After a few minutes, he cleared his throat and brushed his fingers against her arm.

"Thank you, for that," he said. "But I was thinking more along the lines of, 'does your mortal friend know we are witches'?"

Milla blinked, surprised that was all he had to say. "Oh, no. She still thinks you're my therapist."

"*Still?*" The car swerved, and his eyes bugged. She nodded, biting her lower lip, and the witch sputtered a laugh. "Bampot."

Nineteen

SYLVAN GROVE APARTMENTS WAS a rundown complex shoved behind a gas station and a discount movie theater. Pushing fifty, the apartments suffered from five decades of misguided efforts by property managers who had determined a fresh coat of stucco or paint, but never stucco *and* paint, was the proper way to entice future residents to stop by the leasing office.

For all that it was shabby and a bit "hackit", to use Darkly's term, the lawns were green and trimmed, and children played unsupervised in a tot-lot in the center of the complex. Julie had moved in a few years prior, upsizing from a one-bedroom, one-bath condo less than a quarter mile from the hospital to a two-bedroom, one-bath apartment within walking distance of an elementary school.

Milla knew the second bedroom had been intended for her daughter to have a space of her own over long weekends and holidays. Milla also knew the bed in that room had never been slept in. Julie never said anything, but that was Julie. She wasn't one to put others out for her needs, which was why Milla was here.

The doorbell had been broken since before Julie moved in, so Milla stepped up to the door and knocked. A moment passed with no movement from inside, and she knocked again.

"She might be sleeping," Darkly offered. He peered through the open blinds. "Doesnae have any lights on. I can go talk with the property manager to see if they'll let us in."

"I don't want to involve them." She shook her head. "Her neighbor complained about a leak after the last hurricane, and they evicted her for deterioration of the property."

Darkly's jaw dropped. "Americans."

"I know, right?" Milla agreed.

For whatever reason, that had him looking utterly baffled.

When a third attempt at knocking failed to produce Julie, Milla pressed her palm against the door. Even without having drunk her tea, steel was hard to work with. One of the many reasons Milla preferred her old duplex near the Colonial Quarter over commercial apartments was the sheer amount of wood. Compared to metal, wood had life, a Soul to which intention could call, though she had to admit living in a complex with a pool would be nice.

She called to her Way, willing it to a semblance of life. There was the faintest stirring of *something* deep within her. A whisper, a dying breath, and she pulled on that with all her strength. "*Otevři.*"

Open up.

Darkly snapped straight, his keen gaze landing on her palm against the door. Without looking away, he slid his phone from a pocket, pressing a button on the side before tucking it away.

Milla's attention wavered from her intent, and the weak grasp on her Way slipped. She scowled, pinning her eyes on the steel door and putting more of herself into the words. Feeding intent with desire with every bubbling consonant as she sang her plea, all too willing to pay the sacrifice the ritual demanded.

"*Otevři.*" Open the door. "*Prosím, otevřete.*" Please open the door.

Because if this worked, if she managed to hold onto that gasping thread of her Way, he would see, and C.R.O.W. would know.

"*Otevři.*"

A quiet calm descended at her back, Darkly's palm pressed against the door, and a soft baritone joined her intent with a voice that looped and coiled like a Celtic knot. "*Oscail. Le do thoil, oscail suas.*"

She did not recognize his language of intent, but there was a sense of knowing and seeking, of gaining and … smug pride.

The deadbolt slid free, and Darkly stepped away, leaving Milla bewildered and a little bit breathless. Rather than address any one of the numerous questions rattling in her head, she turned the handle, opening the door a foot before it butted against something heavy. She threw her shoulder against the steel, wedging it another inch, and then the smell hit. A rotten flower and burnt plastic stink with a chemical bite, like a soldering iron gone haywire.

"Oh, Goddess." She slammed a hand over her nose and mouth, stifling a gag.

"Horned God, what is that boggin' reek?" Darkly shoved the door wider, pushing over a stack of boxes. He shouldered past Milla, darting for the window and wasting no time raising the shades and sliding the pane aside.

Milla held in the doorway, stuck there by dread and the interior of Julie's apartment. Stacks of boxes were shoved against the walls, piled on the dining room table, and filled the living room. Her stomach dropped, witchy intuition from her mother's side telling her what this was, how *bad* it was, but Milla didn't want to believe it.

"There another window?" Darkly asked. Milla pointed to the sliding glass door hidden behind a cardboard wall. He cursed under his breath and maneuvered through the stacks. A moment later, sunlight flooded the room, wholly revealing the awful.

"ICYMI," Milla breathed, dropping her hand, eyes watering from whatever that Horned God-awful stink was. "It's all ICYMI."

"The stench?" Darkly's head popped up over a stack.

"No, the boxes." She gestured to the logo on the side of a box. Milla stepped into the apartment and staggered at the full assault of the stink and gloom—the *wrongness* in the space. An immediate weakness crawled up her legs like she'd been stung by a jellyfish bloom. She leaned heavily against a stack of boxes that swayed with her weight. Darkly rushed through the narrow pass, reaching for Milla and halting at a quiet moan.

Both witches swung their heads around at the sound. Milla peered through a crack in the boxes, finally spotting the pale nurse on the couch, fast asleep—dear *Goddess*, she hoped she was asleep—under a ratty flannel blanket.

"Goddess, Jules." Milla shoved off the boxes, bracing a hand on the cardboard to keep steady. The tingling subsided with every step, but the *wrongness* persisted. A greasy, sticky sensation, as though she'd coated herself in lotion, wriggled into latex, and run a mile in eighty-five percent humidity.

Milla crouched and lay her hand over Julie's forehead, driven by a need to know, to protect. To *fix*. She was all too aware of Darkly watching and not caring what he might think. The nurse whimpered but did not wake. Her lips were thin and cracked, ashen against sallow skin as dry and coarse as tea leaves. Closing her eyes, Milla chanted her intent, and a faint pulse of magick belled out from her hand. She felt the tired beat of Julie's heart, the weak thrum of her pulse. Heard the sluggish flow of blood in the nurse's veins and beneath it all—the promise of life.

Milla pulled her hand away, head spinning and the taste of dirt in her mouth. She risked a terrified glance at Darkly, hovering at the edge of the boxes. Twice now, she'd called on her Way, called on the magick she and Ezra and Morgen had worked so hard to hide.

Her aural insurance adjuster wore an expression that was equal parts amazed and alarmed. His eyes fogged in that funny way of theirs, and the fingers of his left hand danced against his thigh. They regarded one another in a moment that stretched until something in the room *dinged*.

The rotten stench bloomed anew, snapping the moment. Milla whirled, eyes dancing over the room, the just-visible corner of the kitchen counter, the Horned God-damned boxes; nothing out of sorts, save for the fucking *boxes*. The smell faded, or Milla's offended nose had desensitized itself to the stink. She opened her mouth to tell Darkly that Julie was okay. She was alright, and thank you for the ride, but could he please—

Ding.

And it was back, a pulse of rancid perfume accosting the senses.

Milla rose, pushing around Darkly to check the outlets, sniff along the walls, and trail her fingers over a window sill.

Nothing.

No smoke, no sparks, no clutch of birds bursting ominously from a tree.

Ding.

Scrunching her nose, she crawled along the front of the sofa like a dog hunting truffles. Cardboard shuffled as Darkly worked his way nearer. "What are you doing?"

Ding.

"Did you hear that?" Milla glanced over her shoulder at the witch, almost missing the faint, white glow lighting up the underside of the couch. Worming her hand into the narrow space between couch and carpet, Milla's fingers grazed hard plastic—Julie's tablet. She worked it free, sliding the device out from under the couch as another *ding* lit up the screen.

A group chat flared and faded, emojis that meant nothing to Milla beyond modern hieroglyphics. Then the tablet dinged again and again, the group chat gaining speed as a conversation played out.

She didn't mean to snoop, but then she caught Julie's name in a flare of text, and before she could think too hard about what she was doing, Milla used poor, sweet, comatose Julie's finger to unlock the screen.

"Milla!" Darkly whisper-shouted. She ignored him, scrolling through the chat history.

It was innocent enough, an ICYMI sales group. The messages focused on event planning, new inventory, and sharing inane inspographics with tired text like "BossBabes get shit done ;)" and "Mompreneur is a full-time job!" scrawled in frivolous fonts over high contrast, over-saturated beach scenes.

Milla stopped on the text that mentioned Julie from a woman named McKenzie Miller, asking if anyone had heard from her.

"We were supposed to run a live event tonight. I'm so ragged these days I really can't field this by myself. Does anyone know where she is?"

The tablet dinged with a new message, and Milla scrolled down, this time reading the responses, all of them an attack on Julie, which, considering she was currently passed out on a couch, felt rude.

> I can't believe she would leave you hanging like that! @JulieKettler wtf?

> Hun, srsly, let me in you crosslin. I would NEVER

> Has anyone flagged her upline?? @KayleighMasterson

Milla chewed her lips, scrolling and tapping, paying attention to the profile pictures of the women. Some of the faces were familiar, though she couldn't quite place them. Annoying but not surprising. St. Augustine was a city of less than eighteen thousand people. Small enough that family trees should probably be referenced before marriages were allowed between locals.

Another ding filled the screen with thumbs up and applause reactions. Milla dragged her finger to see what she had missed, finding a message from Kayleigh Masterson berating Julie for being, in her words, "the worst." Milla narrowed her eyes, wondering why that name sounded so familiar.

"Hannah, hun, THANK YOU for alerting me to Julie's failure to check in; this is absolutely unacceptable! It is Not. Okay. Every ICYMI rep must be responsive, and as your Upline, I am so so so embarrassed that she has left you hanging."

Milla had to re-read the message twice before it made any sense. She tapped on Kayleigh's profile picture, navigating to her personal page, and a hundred tiny little pieces clicked into place.

"What the fuck."

It was the Karen. The Executive Bitch Queen who had tried to buy the Pinkerton. The same awful woman who wrote that awful Yap! Review: same hair, same contoured cheeks, same shimmery cheekbones, and self-satisfied, self-righteous smile.

The air around Milla suddenly felt very, very thin. Like she'd been launched to the stratosphere and her only lifeline was the tablet in her hands. She tapped on the woman's profile and opened the album. The most recent pictures were of Kayleigh in New Orleans' French Quarter, adorned in beads with a cocktail. Her grinning in front of Cafe du Monde, fingers and lips artfully dusted in powdered sugar from the beignet in her hand. Kayleigh on a cruise ship, Kayleigh on a white sand beach, Kayleigh strolling down St. Augustine's Oak Alley, and Kayleigh—

"Oh, Goddess." The tablet fell from Milla's hands. She snapped her eyes to Julie, the blood rushing from her face and leaving her dizzy.

"Milla?" Darkly crouched beside her, bracing a hand against the arm of the couch, which had his arm all but draped across her shoulders.

The warmth of him pulled Milla into herself. She scanned Julie's face, seeking a hint, a clue, an answer to the why and the—"How?"

The nurse sighed in her sleep, eyes darting beneath thin, veined lids.

"Horned God, is that—?"

Milla snatched the tablet before Darkly could pick it up, showing him the picture of Kayleigh and Julie in St. Augustine's most famous tourist trap: Ponce de Leon's Fountain of Youth. They were smiling and hugging, laughing like old friends, and there were more. Julie and Kayleigh chatting over coffee. Julie and Kayleigh waving at whoever was taking their photo *in front of Milla's store.*

I took the day off to meet a friend from out of town, the nurse had said, and Milla … *Milla* had planted the idea.

Taking her to the Fountain of Youth? She had asked because that was what you did with visitors from out of town. It was where you took them, but she didn't mean … she couldn't have known—

Coffee first, then after that, maybe. I'm not sure what she wants to get up to, Julie had said. *She got in town yesterday.*

It was all right there, right under Milla's nose. If she had only gotten over herself long enough to see that Julie was hurting, that she needed help, that she'd been taken advantage of, and this woman, this Kayleigh, was the cause.

The tablet dinged, that rancid, burnt metal-and-plastic stench flared, and Milla jolted to the present, reading the most recent message.

"Gals, you think the B at SG would give us Julie's inventory for tonight?"

It took her a moment. Another. Then, someone shared an animated image of Wednesday Addams attempting to smile, and Milla was enraged again. She jumped to her feet and charged through the stacks of boxes. "Time to go."

"Milla," Darkly barked, twisting and wedging his over-tall mass through the narrow passage. "What are you doing?"

"Hun hunting." Milla marched out the front door, ready to storm down the stairs and sniff out this Kayleigh Masterson. Let her see what a real witch could do.

"You cannae—" Darkly reached for the tablet. Milla pulled it away, forgetting that Darkly claimed to be a boxer. His free hand swept up, almost snatching the device from her fingers;

good Goddess, was he fast. Milla clutched it to her chest, dipped, and spun, only to be wrapped in Darkly stupid-long arms and squashed in a back-to-chest bear hug. They wrestled in place; she attempted to wriggle out of his grip, and Darkly snatched the tablet, dancing away.

"You cannae steal a comatose woman's tablet!" he hollered.

"Give it to me, Horned God-dammit!"

"Milla?" Julie's voice, weak and breathy, froze both witches where they stood—Milla grabbing for the tablet and Darkly with his arm held up in the air to keep it out of her reach. In the daylight, Julie's skin had a grayish, corpse-like hue. She huddled in the doorway, the ratty flannel blanket clutched tight around her shoulders. "What is your therapist doing here?"

"He … gave me a ride over."

"Why does he have my tablet?"

"I—" Darkly's eyes went wide, pleading with Milla. It was tempting to let him try to come up with a lie and likely fail, but Milla needed his help. Or at least, she needed him not to tell C.R.O.W. anything.

"I wanted to let your friends know you were okay," Milla lied. "Didn't want to wake you up, so I brought it outside."

"Oh." Julie frowned, her brow wrinkling as her gaze darted from Darkly to Milla to her tablet. "Okay."

That was … odd. Julie wasn't normally one to back down from such an obvious lie. "How are you feeling?"

"Tired." And there it was, one word that told Milla volumes. Normal Julie was not a taciturn, one-word-answer person. Normal Julie would ramble about how her day was so busy, and there was a new recipe she wanted to try, so she had to go to the grocery store, but they didn't have the limes she needed, so she went to another store before heading home. Then she got caught

in traffic and realized she needed to get new shoes for work, and
then it was ten o'clock, and she had forgotten to eat dinner. That
was Julie, who told a story to say she got home late and was tired.
"Tired" was what a poor imitation of Julie would say. "Come in,
if you want."

She picked her way through the entryway, walking with the
slow shuffle of the sick and elderly. Something deep in Milla's
chest threatened to fracture as she watched her friend maneuver
around stacks of boxes and stand in the middle of her living room,
looking small and alone.

Her unfocused gaze dragged over the boxes, and Julie's face
crumpled. "I don't know what I'm going to do."

"Do?"

"With all this shit," she spat. "I don't know what I was thinking.
Ana thinks we can sell it, but I'm so *tired*, and Kayleigh said, she
said—" Julie pressed her fingertips to her temples, taking a shaky
breath.

"Jules, what happened?" She took her friend's elbow, guiding
her to the couch. "Your friend at the hospital said you fell asleep
in your car?"

"I don't even remember the drive." Her admission was hushed.
Hesitant. "I was dizzy when I left your store, and I've had this
headache for days. I closed my eyes for a minute, and the next
thing I knew, I—" Julie shivered and pulled the blanket tighter
around her shoulders. "There was a note from management
on the door when I got home." Milla glanced at Darkly, who
had maneuvered to the kitchen counter. He held up a piece of
letterhead, face grim. "They're saying that running a business
from the premises is illegal." Tears welled, and her voice quivered.
"They're threatening to evict me. I maxed out my credit cards,

and I don't know what I'm going to do. There's no way we can sell it all before … before …"

"They wouldnae evict a sick woman," Darkly balked. "That's inhumane."

Milla and Julie stared back at him.

"It's cute that you believe that," Milla stated. She peered in a nearby box, open on the coffee table. Garish tie-dye glared back at her. "We'll think of something, Jules."

"I only wanted to help you and Diego," Julie blubbered. "I messed up. I'm going to lose my apartment, and then I'll lose visitation."

"No." Milla slapped the box closed, putting what she could of her Way into the word. "We'll sell it at a discount if we have to. I'll take off the consignment percentage the store takes, and we'll go over your credit cards." Milla paced the narrow walkway between the boxes. "The other half of the duplex is a two-bedroom; if the worst happens and you're evicted, I'll call my landlady and act as a reference."

"But what about ICYMI?"

"What about it? It was fun or something, but you need to quit while you're ahead…ish."

Julie reared back as if Milla had just suggested they drown kittens in the retaining pond behind the complex. "I can't quit."

"Why not? It's just a job, one that's run you into severe debt and exhaustion. We'll sell what's here, and that will be it."

"You don't understand. I still owe Kayleigh money, and she's my Upline; she depends on me, Milla. *Me.*"

"Why should Kayleigh care? And how do you even *know* her?"

"Nursing school and—ugh! You don't understand." Julie crumpled to the couch. "If I don't sell, my Upline doesn't get her percentage, and then *her* Upline doesn't get paid." The tablet dinged, and Milla's head ached from the stench.

"What is that?"

"What is what?"

"That smell." She wafted a hand in front of her nose. "Do you have one of those oil diffusers burning? Or an iron plugged in?'

"I don't ...." Julie glanced around her living room, her attention lingering on the television, confusion wrinkling her forehead. Milla followed her gaze to the dried bouquet and the champagne glass on a shelf above the television. A yellowish residue colored the bottom of the glass, and beside it was a picture of Julie and Ana in Southern Gothic and another of those Horned God-damned oil diffusers. "This is all my fault."

"What?" She flinched. "No, Jules."

"Yes, it is." Julie dropped her face into her hands. "I asked her to back off of your store. She said if I joined her downline and followed her advice, she'd take down her post."

"Wait, I'm sorry, Kayleigh bullied you into this, *and* she gets a percentage of your sales?" Milla ran the numbers in her head. The store took a twenty-percent commission fee, so it was safe to assume Kayleigh was taking something similar. Still, that left sixty percent of the sales to Julie, so what was her take home after adjusting for the cost of the clothes themselves?

"Sounds like a pyramid scheme." Darkly had wandered near, his phone in hand and a worried look on his face.

"It's *not* a pyramid scheme." Venom laced Julie's words, and the vehemence of her retort sapped the last of her energy. She sank against the couch, taking a shaky breath. "Sorry, I-I'm sorry."

"It's alright," Darkly assured her, brushing his fingers against Milla's arm. A tingle bled over her skin in the wake of his touch. "Milla, can we talk outside for a moment?"

"I…" She glanced at Julie, whose eyes had already drifted closed. "Yeah, sure." She followed Darkly through the stacks and out onto the stoop. "What's up?"

He hesitated, opening his mouth and closing it twice before speaking. "I hate to do this, but I need tae—"

"Oh, shit, that's right," Milla cut him off. "Your date, or—Jacksonville or whatever."

"Nae that, I—"

"No, it's fine," she waved him off. "I mean, thank you. For the ride out here and to the hospital."

Smoke clouded his eyes, and Darkly dropped to the topmost step to bring his face level with hers. "I can cancel my, ehm, date. Only, I have to"—he held out his phone, the screen blank—"C.R.O.W., ehm, the Panhandle Coven …"

"I know! I know. I'm just a job, and you have to tell C.R.O.W. something about me and the tea and the *dip*, I get it, go. I need to stay with Julie, so I don't really care what you tell them." She turned to go, and he grabbed her hand, fingers pressing gently yet firmly against her scars. The gentlest tug had Milla turning, coming face-to-face with Darkly.

"You're nae 'just a job,'" he rumbled, voice low. His eyes dropped to Milla's mouth for a breath, barely long enough to notice. "I can cancel my plans and come back here. I'll bring dinner, and maybe we can—"

"No, thank you." She pulled her hand free, flexing her fingers to keep from cradling the warmth of his touch against her chest. Did she imagine he frowned when she pulled away? "We'll be fine. She's just going to sleep, anyway. I'll order some OverEats and let Diego and Ana know where I am." With that, Milla turned and headed for the door, stopping when he called her name.

"Milla." He gripped the rail, knuckles blanching, and his face held a wistful, wanting expression. Those arresting eyes bright fixed on her. "Stay in tonight, aye?"

"We literally just addressed that I would."

"Aye." Darkly frowned. "We did." He rapped his knuckles against the railing and turned, jogging down the steps. Milla had just begun trying to puzzle out that last request when he stopped on the landing. "Milla?"

"What?" She whirled, glaring down at him. Darkly sent her a tiny smile.

"Happy Valentine's Day."

Twenty

AUDIOMANTIC Sound witches and secret keepers.

Julie was deep asleep by the time Milla recovered from Darkly's parting blow. She lay a blanket over the nurse, opened the window in her bedroom, and quietly closed the door. Tiptoeing through the boxes, she fired off a few text messages—one to Diego, letting him know where she was, what had happened, and apologizing profusely for leaving him to close the store by himself, and one to an audiomantic witch she knew with a van— and then she got to work.

The windows were opened to air out the apartment, the rotten flowers and oil diffuser thrown away, and the champagne glass set to soak in the sink. She shoved the boxes out the door and was taking a sort of inventory when the audiomantic showed up. Together, they loaded the ICYMI boxes into the van he used to carry sound equipment from venue to venue in the greater Jacksonville area.

"Just take it to the store?" he asked, wrinkling his nose at the stench.

"Yeah, Diego will meet you in the back to offload."

"Smells like shit."

"It really does." Milla huffed a laugh. "Something about how they pack it at the warehouse. I'll shoot you some money for trucking it over."

He lightly cuffed her on the shoulder. "Call it a favor, kid." She started to protest, and he waved her off. "Always wise to have the Witch of Demesne owe you a favor!" Paul grinned and hopped into the van, waving as he drove away.

She fidgeted on the sidewalk, uncomfortable with the exchange and unsure why. She was the Witch of the Demesne. She *could* call in these favors from her fellow witches, so why did it feel like a new weight had been placed on her shoulders?

The question nagged as she cleaned the rest of the apartment, half listening to the television she'd turned on for some level of noise outside her head.

"Good evening, and Happy Valentine's Day! It is Tuesday, February fourteenth, and this is the evening report. Tonight, the Jacksonville Icemen face the Florida Everblades in a ..."

Milla dug through Julie's cupboards, the newscaster's trained Mid-Atlantic accent little more than background noise to her work. She pulled out a heavily used, chipped green enamel Dutch oven and set it on the stove, rescued an apple from the bottom of the produce drawer, and scrounged Julie's spice rack, selecting cloves and cinnamon sticks. After a moment's deliberation, she grabbed the rosemary for good measure. On the back patio were several terra-cotta pots half filled with rain from the last storm. Milla carried them inside, one by one, filling the Dutch oven and placing the rest of the ingredients into the simmer pot with intent.

"Light the grill, fill the cauldron, wait for the water to boil, and try not to think too hard about the fact you're now a caricature of a Shakespearean witch."

Ezra's voice filled her head. She swayed, struck by the memory. Her vision blurred, the cinnamon stick in her hand becoming three.

"Double, double," Milla waggled fingers over her Dutch oven, cackling like a mad woman.

Ezra stared at her blandly from the grill, spatula in one hand, a plate of raw steak in the other. "I see acting lessons weren't part of the Morgenhexe's endeavors."

"She said I wasn't worth the toil and trouble."

He rolled his eyes, bland expression twisting up into a wicked grin. "The trouble I agree with, sugar. The toil, however, I am becoming increasingly fond of."

Milla gripped the counter as the cinnamon stick rolled across the Formica. She closed her eyes tight, focusing on her breathing, the bubbling of the rainwater in her simmer pot, the sleeping woman in the other room; forcing herself not to search the apartment for any hint of his not-ghost. Her right arm twinged, the surgical scar prickling, and then nothing. She took a deep, intentional breath and exhaled.

Focus the intent.

Focus.

"Focus, Milla." Ezra tapped her temple. Gentle, demanding. *"And then gather your ingredients with intent in hand."*

Cinnamon for healing and protection, clove for defense against negative energy, and rosemary for peace, all bound with intent and desire. Without knowing what truly plagued her friend, this was the best she could come up with: protection, care, defense, and peace. It was a simple ritual, one of the first all witches learned. The hardest part was remembering to keep the cauldron from boiling dry.

With nothing left to do but wait, Milla sat on the couch and attempted to embrace a sense of calm to match the intent of her simmer pot.

"Breaking news from St. Augustine Shores where residents are in shock after a suspected carbon monoxide leak hospitalized several women in the Refugio Cove Condominiums. Jaime Olivera is live on the scene. Jaime?"

Zzz.

"Thanks, Pat," the Hispanic reporter wore a suitably somber expression. "The scene in St. Augustine Shores is grim this Valentine's Day. Witnesses to the scene report that what began as an innocent gathering of friends to celebrate 'Galentine's Day' ended in tragedy."

Zzz.

"Five women have been hospitalized for carbon monoxide poisoning, while others on-site report dizziness and shortness of breath. Residents are being asked to vacate the property for the time being until the St. John's County Fire Rescue has cleared the premises."

Zzz.

Unable to ignore the alerts, Milla grabbed her phone from the charger. The ICYMI group chat was going bananas, with messages flying at a breakneck pace. She scrolled up through the chat because, of course, she had used Julie's account to add herself to the group. What was she, stupid?

McKenzie had posted an hour prior, a group photo of women in garish ICYMI leggings, tunics, and dresses huddled around a kitchen island, drinks in hand. Comments on the photo were a mix of hearts, happy faces, and clapping hands emojis, various iterations of "You go girl!" and "#bossbabe," followed by a second comment from McKenzie, which read, "The girls and I decided to take a night off of ICYMI and celebrate ourselves instead! Didn't need @JulieKettler after all ;)"

"Rude," Milla scoffed and scrolled, stopping on a post from Kayleigh Masterson.

"Hey babes, don't forget to boost your channels for the spring sales initiative. Remember, each territory's top-selling Diamond Qualifying Executive will receive a complimentary pass to the Spring Sales Kick-off in St. Augustine FL where my Upline is giving the keynote!"

A slew of likes and hearts had attached themselves to the post, and then, almost as an afterthought, Kayleigh had posted again.

"Keep McKenzie in your thoughts and prayers, huns."

Milla narrowed her eyes at the screen. "What happened to McKenzie?"

She scrolled up to the group photo, scanning the women huddled together with wine and cocktails, smiling in their bold print clothing. The photo had been taken an hour earlier at whatever event McKenzie had been supposed to host with Julie, so what could have happened to—

"-ified as McKenzie Miller." Milla ripped her eyes from the phone, staring in disbelief at the television screen. Jaime Olivera addressed the camera beside the super-imposed photograph of a middle-aged woman wearing a floral blouse and white leggings, smiling broadly as the sun set behind her. She glanced at the picture on her phone, immediately identifying the same woman. "If you are experiencing confusion, dizziness, chest pain, or chronic headaches, medical authorities urge you to leave your home and seek treatment."

And then the group chat *exploded*.

> Oh my GOD how terrible. Thought and prayers xoxo

The news is saying it was carbon monoxide @JennaMorales doesn't your ex live in that complex?

I'm praying for them!

Should we set up a food train?

@Kayleighmasterson didn't your old crossline die of carbon monoxide poisoning?

So terrible

Oh wow I went to a birthday party there once

I think she did, or at least it shut down her store. Shame, I loved stopping in whenever I drove through Hattiesburg

ohmigod. Oh. My. God. you guys, my cousin is a nurse at Flagler and they JUST brought Mckenzie in

Does anyone have a recommendation for a dog groomer in JAX?

"Posh Pooch," Milla muttered. She chewed her thumbnail, scrolling up, up, up in the thread on a hunch. Ana had mentioned a boutique in Hattiesburg, one run by a friend. She knew it was specious; she *knew* it was the weakest of weak links, but ICYMI, Hattiesburg, and Kayleigh Masterson being mentioned in the same breath was *too* convenient.

Zzz. Zzz-zzz-zzz. Zzz. Zz-Zzz.

"Fuck." Milla mis-swiped, catching a notification, and the entire chat scrolled to the most recent messages. More thoughts and prayers, a debate about salon groomers versus home groomers, and Kayleigh Masterson wrangling her huns.

"Ladies, this is a chat for ICYMI Qualifying Executives, sales initiatives, and crossline management. It is unfortunate what happened in Hattiesburg. My Upline Annalisa is still trying to recover from the trauma she experienced when Jennifer passed. I can't imagine how she feels knowing more of our gals are involved in the tragedy in St. Augustine, but we all need to remain focused on our Spring Sales! Love y'all, don't forget to post to your socials!"

Milla waited … and waited, but not a single woman added to the chat. Their "thoughts and prayers" and friendly discussion shut down in one fell swoop.

What do you see? Ezra's voice prickled in the back of her mind. *Read the scene Millapet; what have you learned?*

Kayleigh is involved.

She knew it like she knew her name and her Way and the demesne she never wanted. Kayleigh was at the top of this sick pyramid, and the women beneath her were dropping like flies.

Of carbon monoxide poisoning.

Milla's gaze drifted to the bedroom door, her mind careening to the woman on the other side. One death was a tragedy. Two were a coincidence, and witches did not believe in coincidences.

Confusion, dizziness, chest pain, or chronic headaches.

Julie knew Kayleigh; Kayleigh was from Hattiesburg. Something had *happened* in Hattiesburg, and now she had a name—Jennifer.

Think, Millapet. The whisper of a finger brushed from her temple to cheekbone to jaw, lighting up Milla's right side with goosebumps. She shivered, jerking away from the ghost of a touch that wasn't there.

She evacuated, or something, Julie had said. *Haven't you watched the news today?*

Sick curiosity had her clicking on Kayleigh's profile picture once more. She scrolled through the posts, tapping on one that led to a photo dump.

Because she was curious.

Obviously.

The pictures were almost identical, save for slight changes in angle and location, documenting the solo vacation of a woman trying to present as happy. Backing out of the album, she scrolled further, stopping when she saw her store. The display in the window told her this was from January when Kayleigh had come in, and the date of the post confirmed it.

"Huns, I need your help! This trashy little store has no business operating in St. Augustine. I can't believe how rude the owner was. She should go back to Transylvania and leave Florida to people who like the sun."

Milla sat back, far more offended than she should have been. "Czechia, and RUDE."

Stay focused, Millapet.

She expanded the comments, scanning the replies and savoring each and every damning word. Jenna Morales and McKenzie Miller were there, promising to leave their own reviews along with faces Milla knew had never graced her store … but they were each in the group chat. This woman, this *Kayleigh* had set her Huns after Milla's store and bullied Julie into being a part of their awful pyramid scheme. She was from Hattiesburg, a woman named Jennifer had died, Julie was sick and somehow … *somehow* she was responsible for the women at Refugio Cove.

She grabbed her phone and opened the Yap! app to check their reviews. They had earned back one of their lost stars, which was good, but the bad reviews remained front and center. Diego, Ana, and Milla had spent hours on the phone with Yap! Customer Service trying to get them removed. They had flagged and replied, explained, and waited on hold like the diligent shopowners they were.

Now, staring at her screen and relishing the red-hot rise of righteous anger, Milla was happy those reviews still existed on a public platform. Along with the group chat, it was proof they were ICYMI representatives under the sway of Kayleigh Masterson, Diamond Qualifying Executive Bitch Queen.

Riding the high of victory, Milla took screenshots of the reviews on her phone, Kayleigh's initial post, and the participants list of the ICYMI chat group, sending them off in a series of rapid-fire texts to Unknown Caller.

She sent a fourth text that read, "GUESS WHAT?" staring at her phone for far longer than she cared to admit, waiting for a reply.

"—reporting that two of the women caught in this unfortunate incident have been pronounced dead on the scene, while others remain in critical care."

Lights flashed on the television, strobing Julie's living room in red and blue. Milla set her phone face down, bouncing her legs as jittery energy flooded her limbs. Jaime Olivera was still reporting from the Refugio Cove parking lot, sweating in his polo and windbreaker as paramedics loaded a stretcher into an ambulance. Over his shoulder, and only noticeable to a witch who knew what to look for, was a group of officials in black on black on black. A woman stood at their center, white blonde hair reflecting the emergency lights, thrusting her finger at the chest of a tall, broad-shouldered man while a thicker-set, darker-skinned man looked on.

"Shit." Milla jumped to her feet, pacing the worn carpet, her fingers trembling. "Shit, shit, shit." She stopped and stared at the screen—the male witch the woman had been berating had vanished, and now the blonde witch was rubbing her temples with her fingers. Because of *course* they were witches.

They were C.R.O.W.

Enforcers. Witch hunters on the scene of what was being hailed as a tragic accident in *her* demesne.

The demesne she hadn't tended in with her Way in … days. "Double shit."

The jittery energy in her legs became a burn, an itch in the back of her mind of a task left undone. She wrenched open a closet door, pulling out an overnight bag left in anticipation of the inevitable movie night, where she drank too much and needed to sleep it off on the couch.

Before she could second guess or weigh the consequences of what she was about to do, because Horned *God* would there be consequences if those Enforcers even suspected for a minute who, or what, she was, Milla was lacing up an old, worn pair of running shoes.

It was only three miles to the Colonial Quarter. She could charge the demesne by running its width, ease that nagging prickle in her mind, and check in with Diego. She would be back in an hour. Two, at the most. Those Enforcers would likely be busy at Refugio Cove for hours before hauling themselves up to Jacksonville. It was going to be fine. The Panhandle Coven didn't know about Milla's relationship with ICYMI, or that the Huns had doxxed her store, or that she'd pissed off a top-tier Karen.

They didn't know that she'd neglected her duties as Witch of the Demesne.

It was going to be fine.

Twenty One

RUNNING ALONG STATE ROUTE 207 was never a treat. The sidewalk was overgrown in places, the cars couldn't be trusted not to run stoplights, and the crematory always made her feel like she was being watched. Add to that the drag in her legs from panic and exhaustion and the incessant prickle in her mind, and Milla's run went from a necessary distraction to self-flagellating punishment. A thick, sticky sweat slogged down her spine by the time she turned onto Ponce de Leon Boulevard, but she powered through, slogging step after heavy step into the heart of her demesne.

Towering clouds of pink, purple, and dazzling gold drifted across the sky, the fading light pressing the palm trees into cookie-cutter silhouettes. It was idyllic, the perfect night for strolling the Colonial Quarter hand-in-hand with a lover. For sharing sweet words over wine and charcuterie. For driving to Jacksonville for a date with an unknown woman.

Milla pushed her pace up Cordova, sticking to the perimeter of the Colonial Quarter to avoid the worst of the Valentine's crowd. With Enforcers in her demesne and a Way already clawing free from the effects of her tea, it was better to be cautious. Better to be careful of drawing unwanted attention. Better to tend her demesne and the thoughts of Kayleigh and her Attack Squad, of Julie lying limp and sallow, of something she forgot to do, and of Darkly.

Darkly pushing her for answers she didn't want to give.

Darkly taking her hand in the hospital and on the stairs.

Darkly's arm across her shoulders like a brace against the breaking storm

Darkly on a date.

The road split into three, the lamppost blurred in triplicate, and the earth tilted beneath Milla's feet. She staggered to a halt, catching herself on a low stucco wall. Air sawed through her lungs as she shook her head once, twice, trying to settle the world back into itself.

Goddess, it had come on her without warning. No prickles behind her eyes, no migraine, nothing to tell Milla she was risking an attack like *this*.

Really?

"Horned God," she gagged, bodily rejecting that derisive, bourbon-slick voice in her head.

Focus, Milla. Think. Ezra's voice snapped, berating her as he always did. *I trained you better than this.*

She'd had a headache all day, but she'd been hungover. Panicked and *scared*, and now—

"No. Nonono." She pushed herself from the wall, staggering past the Old City Gates. "Not doing this today."

Castillo de San Marcos rose in her fractured vision, a looming monolith against a lilac sky. A car horn blared as Milla stumbled onto the road. Someone shouted, but she couldn't stop. She had to keep going, had to outrun her mother's Way, and that voice taunting her every step.

It's your own fault, Ezra chided, which he couldn't do because he was Gone. *Only Gone because you failed me, Millapet.*

"Don't call me that," she wheezed. The sidewalk swelled and split only to surge back into one straight line while the seawall heaved on her left. Again and again, pulsing with the beat of potential. Milla's stomach churned, her eyes ached, and heat sped through her veins.

Use it, Milla.

"No."

Use it!

"*Fine*," she snarled, swept her palm over the paw of a Medici Lion, and charged onto the bridge. Her legs churned over asphalt and concrete, her body bleeding the wild energy that was too large to contain, that was—

"*—too much, Ez. This city is too much; I can feel it under my skin, in my head, I can't … I can't—*" she sobbed.

He stroked her arms, her hair. "It's alright, sugar; tell me what you need."

"*I need it out.*" Milla blinked, staring at the howling face on his shirt. "*I need to get it out; it burns.*"

"*Do we need to go to a Range? One of the cemeteries?*"

She shook her head, wrapping her arms around him and listening to his heartbeat. Letting the life of him quell the rising tide of energy in her. The energy she couldn't redirect, couldn't control. Ezra's fingers tunneled in her hair, gripping Milla's head and tilting it back to look her in the eye.

"*Show me,*" he ordered. And she did. Ezra fractured into three; she scanned the possibilities, the potentials, gasping at what could be. What she hadn't thought to be an option, but oh, had a part of her hoped. The Ezra on the left broke away, lips swollen and eyelids heavy, and smiled. "Now, Millapet, choose whichever seems the most fun."

And she did.

Milla sobbed as the bridge spilled her onto Anastasia Island, raw from the memory of that first time and everything that had come after. Had she not failed, had Ezra been *here*, he could have handled this. He would have drawn Milla up the stairs and into their bed, spending her Way in the way only he could, and then she'd be safe. Secret. Unknown. Not a Witch of the Demesne, a polednice, or under investigation. She would just be Milla, and he would be Ezra, and they would be together, and everything would be different.

Better, he added.

"No," she gasped.

Intent filled the air on Anastasia Island. A heady perfume of want, desire, and need. That accidental magick even mortals could practice. Tables spilled out on the sidewalk, cafe lights and firepits dancing wildly as her vision continued to blur into three and back to one. The quiet laughter of men and men and women and women and men and women, doe-eyed and blushing, drowned out Ezra's voice as Milla ran through the haze, shortening her breaths to prevent the intent from taking hold in her mind. There was enough noise in there already, along with that needling feeling she'd forgotten to do something. Something vital.

A quick loop through one of the wealthier neighborhoods led her back to the riverside park where the Bridge of Lions loomed. Orange-yellow light from the street lamps reflected over the water like fractured will-o-wisps, casting the perfect backdrop to the enchantment of Valentine's Day. The sun had set in full, the streets emptied as lovers wandered home.

Her feet hit the grass, and Milla hit the proverbial wall, crashing against the barrier of exhaustion she'd been chasing for miles.

Thighs screaming and lungs burning, she slowed to a walk as the last dregs of nervous energy were siphoned away by a hungry demesne, and, finally, the erratic pulsing of the world ceased.

One bridge, one voice in her head, and one vision replacing her fractured sight.

Milla paced in a slow, sore circle, her thoughts a jumble of water, shower, food, and bed, but first—get to the store, check in with Diego, and call an OverAuto to drive her back to Julie's. She took a measured breath, setting off slowly for the bridge. Her eyes skimmed the road ahead and the wrought iron streetlamps. She let herself get lost in the nothing of a weary mind, gazing out over the water, and a shadow grabbed her by the foot.

"No, no, no—" Milla slammed to the ground, pebbles shredding the heel of one palm and her knees. Rolling onto her side with a groan, she pushed into a seated position. Blood beaded on her kneecaps, black in the dim light and distorted by the flickering orange glow from the street lamps.

"And I was having such a nice run." She glanced around for broken concrete, a rock, a twig, anything that might have caused her fall, but the sidewalk was clear and even. "Huh."

Tired, she told herself. *I'm tired and tripped over my own feet.*

Still didn't stop her from glancing around at the shadows. Tired as she may be, she could have sworn she saw those shadows move. A flicker out of the corner of her eye had Milla twisting where she sat, arm held out, and fingers crooked in a hand-to-hex offensive sigil.

Nothing.

"Hello?"

A truck rumbled by, followed by a taxi blaring house music. Water lapped against the bridge's pylons, Milla's breathing rasped, and nothing moved.

Not a shadow, not a flicker of light.

"Stop being a stupid witch," Milla grumbled. There was a first aid kit in the bathroom of Southern Gothic. She could clean up and keep Diego company while he worked in his sewing room. They could get pizza and take it back to Julie's. Her stomach growled, liking the idea, and Milla took off again at a trudge.

The metal grating of the drawbridge clanged under her feet, a shadow twitched, and Milla skidded to a halt. Old habit had her fingers bending and dancing, drawing a sigil in the air to pull energy into her hand. The magick she called was thin and weak, no more tangible than spider silk. She quietly cursed, eyes scanning the dark. Her mother's Way was useless in situations like this, and her own Way was too tea-drunk to be of any help, so of course, some creepy-crawlie would choose *now* to attack the Witch of the Demesne.

Blood trickled down her shins and into her socks. She ignored the uncomfortable squishing, swiveling on the balls of her feet to check the sidewalk behind her, jaw clenched so tight her teeth ached. The street lamps at the end of the bridge pulsed, flickered, and went dark. The next pair followed, and the next. One by one by one, leaving a black void between Milla and the intoxicating call of Anastasia Island. Her gut clenched, and the fine hairs on her neck prickled in alarm.

Because she was; alarmed, that is. All things considered, Milla decided that she had every right to be. She was a witch Forbidden and Foule, standing over running water on a night charged with magick Fine and Faire. She was vulnerable and tired, and she couldn't shake the feeling she had forgotten something.

She took a step away from the oncoming darkness, and then another. Blood dripped from her injured palm, landing on the metal gates with a faint *hiss* drawing a deep, hungry growl from the raw-head who lived beneath.

"Pretty little witchling."

"Oh, shit," Milla hissed, finally remembering what it was she'd forgotten to do.

Tuesday night was Feed the Raw-head Night.

Double shit.

She allowed herself one second to be pants-shittingly terrified, berating herself through the nine rings of the Inferno and back, and then she ran.

The raw-head slithered out from under the bridge, flayed skin slapping against weeping-puss shoulders. It jerked after her, inhumanly fast, and Milla had just about had enough of the shitstorm that was *today*.

She needed to get off the bridge, back onto land and the safety of her demesne. There was a chunk of raw meat waiting in Diego's mini-fridge. She could grab that, sprint back, lob the chuck roast as hard as she could at the river, and pray to the Triple Goddess the raw-head forgave her for her oversight.

Easy.

Except her heart was screaming, and the lions protecting St. Augustine were a quarter of a mile away.

Be faster, Milla.

She pressed her speed as Ezra's not-ghost yelled in her ear, admonishing her for not being fast enough, good enough. For not taking his training seriously. For forgetting to feed that Horned God-damned raw-head.

You have to be faster. I need you to be faster, Milla.

"Bad words, bad deeds," the raw-head slathered in her ear, and Milla shrieked, throwing her arms over her head and ducking low. Gore and fetid juices splattered on her arms and legs as it stumbled past, too-long limbs flailing on an emaciated frame.

"Oh, Horned God," she gagged. She was allowed; it was utterly disgusting.

Lurching for the barrier separating the sidewalk from the road, Milla gripped the pale green rail and launched herself up and over, landing hard on the asphalt. An SUV swerved around her, catching blood-and-gore-stained Milla in its headlights. The driver over-corrected, tires screeching as the vehicle swerved in the other direction and slammed on its brakes. Burnt rubber filled the air, someone yelled out, and Milla panicked, running down the middle of the road in the opposite direction.

The wrong direction.

"Fuck!" She dropped low to half-skid, half-turn, mostly duck a swipe of the raw-head's arm. Its nearness tainted the air with the reek of low tide, overpowering the pleasant enchantment of the evening with the acrid burn of a lit match, muddled spice, and nauseating vanilla too close to sweet rot to be pleasant. It blanketed her body and filled her nose, like calling to like, a sensory summons of her Way that left Milla dizzy, her palms tickling. "Fuckfuckfuck."

She pressed on, looking back once to put eyes on the raw-head. Something cold and smooth grabbed her by the ankle as she did, holding firm and yanking her to the ground.

"Come the fuck on!" She hit the asphalt, passingly fascinated that the ground had a slight give to it, cradling her fall enough so she could gain her feet. She scrabbled at the road, gagging at the wet *slapflapslapflapslapflap* of the desecrant's flayed skin rushing past.

"Bad words, bad deeds," the raw-head burbled through bleeding gums, careening around on too-long legs and grabbing for her. "Unpunished!"

"It was *one* time." Milla jumped back, holding up her middle finger and thrusting it at the disgusting creature. "One time, I forgot to feed you."

The raw-head responded by lurching at her; teeth snapping, skin flaps … flapping. Altogether a disgusting experience. Zero out of five stars. Would not recommend.

She used the creature's momentum to her benefit, ducking under the desecrant and breaking into a hunched, hobbled run with her right arm cradled against her chest. Her shoulder stung, her hip throbbed from the impact of her fall, the raw-head was gaining, and she was thoroughly, entirely annoyed.

Bobbing lanterns on boats harbored at the municipal marina grew larger by the footfall. Solid ground was close, so close that Milla felt hope kindle, which … she really should have known how foolish that was.

Claws scraped the back of her shirt, extra-knuckled fingers gripping her ponytail. The stench of mottled flesh, muscle, and fat gone to decay overtook the heady vanilla burn. Milla gagged in earnest as she was yanked back. She spat up into the desecrant's face, and the raw-head screeched, releasing Milla to swipe her acid spit away—a fun little perk of being a witch. She spun around, uninjured arm held out before her, struggling to hold a warding sigil with the fingers of her left hand.

"Do *not*," she warned. Her pinky trembled. The sigil she formed was weak, but the raw-head had no way of knowing. Weak as it was, it would have to be enough. Goddess, she hoped it was enough. She slid her foot out behind her, feeling for any bump or crack in the road that might trip her and finding none.

Keeping the raw-head in her sigil, Milla took a step back, and then another and another, into the inky black of the bridge. "Do not make me use my Way."

The lions were right there, her demesne was *right there*. Only a few more feet and she'd be back on solid ground, safely in her demesne and out of the raw-head's territory. It would go slithering back under the bridge where it belonged, and Milla could stagger to the store, fetch that Horned God-damned hunk of chuck roast, and feed the damn thing.

The raw-head had other plans.

It skittered forward, skin flapping, rags flying, launching at Milla. Before she could spit or call intent to her hand, it had her by the shoulders, and they hit the ground together. The air whooshed from her lungs, and she shuddered at the wet-velvet feel of flayed skin tickling her shoulders, her chest and neck as they rolled together. Grass tickled her bare arms, wet earth rising to mingle with the stench of the desecrant.

"Bad words and bad deeds," it fizzed and burbled.

Goddess, it smelled even worse up close. Raw meat left in the sun too long, the exposed river bottom at low tide, and the cloying, overpowering vanilla of sweet rot.

Milla managed to pinch her lips before a soggy hand with jagged, cracked nails pawed at her mouth and her throat. Digging and clawing at the behest of the singular drive in its wretched existence: to flay her skin from her body piece by bloody, unpunished piece, twisting Milla into a miserable, desecrant creature just like itself.

"Such bad deeds," the raw-head shivered with sick arousal at the scent of her wickedness. A pointed knee dug bruisingly into her thigh. Pressing its weight against her torso, the raw-head snaked an arm across her throat. Milla writhed and kicked beneath it, unable to scream. Her heart skittered madly, her lungs fighting for air beneath the press of that rancid body. She scratched at gore-damp skin, unable to draw the coal-kindling attention of the desecrant's eyes away from her face, her lips, her mouth.

It trailed a rusted razor blade of a thumbnail across her lower lip, tearing the flesh and trying to force its way in. Milla jerked her head away, and the raw-head tore at her throat instead, leaning close and running a tongue like seaweed over her mouth.

"Delicious, wicked little bad words."

Milla whimpered, jerking her face away. Lights flickered in the distance, dancing in the corners of her eyes. She couldn't tell if it was the street lamps, the SUV flashing its headlights, or the stars in her eyes. She would have to breathe soon. The raw-head would let her. It would wait until she had choked enough to open her mouth for one last gasp, and then its hands would be there, and it would tear and rend and ruin.

Unless ...

Goddess, this was a bad idea—the worst. Just truly terrible, but Milla needed to breathe. She pressed a hand against the grass, feeling the roil of her demesne beneath her palm. A reservoir of power she often fed and rarely touched, always a hair's breadth away and so out of reach.

Please. Milla closed her eyes, retreating to the last safe space in her mind where Ezra could never find her. *I don't ask for much. I'm sorry I forgot to feed it. I'm sorry I haven't tended to you; you* know *who I am. You know* what *I am.*

Her chest caved under the pressure of rising anger, her heart sped, and her skin tingled. The earth beneath her hand surged, then settled.

Please, she begged. *Julie needs me, those women need me*, you *need me*.

The raw-head pressed its arm against her throat. Her lungs were burning, and someone was screaming as the world blurred, not into three but into nothing.

Please.

Her demesne agreed on a sigh of wind through palm fronds high, high overhead. The ground beneath her palm surged again, and this time, magick slammed into Milla and ribboned up her arm. Hot and fast, burning as it sought an exit, needing to be used, and her Way rose to meet it. A door deep within Milla that had long ago been bricked and barred opened wide, demanding she step through.

Above her, the raw-head's eyes rolled in the red meat ruin of its face, reveling in her fight and fear. It shuddered a breath, ready to flay her skin. "You invite grief, little witch." Its voice was husky and dark, the hunger insatiable, and Milla knew it was time.

I'm sorry, she thought at the raw-head. *You don't really deserve this.*

It couldn't hear her; it couldn't know how sorry she was, but the words needed to be said before she did what had to be done because Darkly was right, even though she'd absolutely never tell him that to his face. Milla had put work into her store, into herself. She had put the work in, and disappearing didn't mean dying, Horned God-dammit. If she had to step into her Way, just a little, just enough, to avoid that wretched fate, then so-fucking-be-it. Because as much as the raw-head wanted to strip her skin from her bones, Milla wanted to live more.

Wherever her body touched the ground, she drew from the demesne, magick speeding through her veins as a burning ecstasy that Milla had to admit she'd missed. She wriggled her arm free, clawing her fingers and jamming them into the raw-head's emaciated waist. It jerked at the jolt of her Way and glanced down to where her nails pressed into its hollowed side. A low keening began in its throat when the creature realized who she was—*what* she was.

"Bad, bad, bad, bad," the raw-head writhed, unable to escape. Its arm slithered away from her throat, fingers that had been ready to flay now pawing uselessly at Milla's wrist.

She snatched its upper arm and pinned the desecrant to her in a death grip, hissing a long overdue breath and chanting her intent into that fleshless face without a thought or care for the consequences of what she was doing. And, oh, would there be consequences. That Milla knew beyond a shadow of a doubt, but in this moment, drunk on her Way and determined to erase the raw-head from her demesne, Milla decided she wanted to live and damn the consequences.

"*Návrat, návrat, návrat. Spát spánek mrtvých.*" The raw-head jerked and writhed against her. Clawing now, its nails tearing her skin as it tried to scramble away. "*Návrat, návrat, návrat. Spát spánek mrtvých.*"

Return, return, return. She used the innocent chant to hide her true malicious intent, calling on every lesson from Ezra and the Morgenhexe combined. *Sleep. Sleep like the dead.*

"*Návrat, návrat, návrat. Spát spánek mrtvých.*" Ash spewed with every word. The raw-head wriggled with one last burst of frantic energy, and Milla doubled her intent, rolling onto her knees and pinning the weakened desecrant beneath her. Hissing into its flayed face until the keening died to a whimper, a shudder, a gasp, and then the raw-head was nothing more than a pile of dust.

She stood, staggering back a step, two, three, and ran into the welcoming dark.

Amethysts blazed bright and purple as Milla stumbled past Agatha at her crystal cart. She raised a hand to shield herself from their flare, staggering down Charlotte Street and practically falling through the rear door of Southern Gothic.

The lights were blazing, and the nauseating floral perfume from the oil diffusers clouded the air. Milla followed Diego's voice to the front of the store, wincing with each step. She brushed her fingers over a basket of flowers that wilted as she passed, knowing her hand looked like a tool of death.

"Oh my god," a woman gasped, covering her mouth with an orchid-printed scarf. Diego turned from the register where he had been in the middle of a transaction, nearly falling over at the sight of Milla haunting the hallway.

Tears finally began to pool and gather, and she blinked at their customer, garbling out, "Please don't put this on Yap."

Twenty Two

Just as every ritual demands a sacrifice, the use of one's Way has a cost, a payment required of the witch relative to their Way.

"Did you get a good look at him, honey?"

"Him?" Milla rasped. Her tongue felt thick, fat, and useless, and her throat was as dry as a tomb.

"Whoever attacked you." The woman pulled a fresh baby wipe free from the package and dabbed at Millla's lip.

"Pequeña bruja?" Diego reached out with trembling fingers and took her hand, squeezing tight.

"I…" Her eyes burned at the restrained display of his fear, at the weight of what she had just done with Enforcers in her demesne. "I'm so sorry."

"No, sweety, no. It's not your fault, honey, okay?" Their customer squeezed her elbow, oblivious to the silent conversation happening between the two witches. "Did you get a good look?"

"I was tackled from behind," she choked out, shuddering. "An SUV stopped, and someone got out. He ran off."

"Good Lord. I'm glad you're alright, sweetie. Maybe don't drink so much next time, hm?" She waved a finger from Milla to Diego and back. "Do you two…?

"I'm her roommate," said Diego. "I'll take care of her." He offered the woman a discount as he ushered her away, leaving Milla sitting against the wall.

"Oh, I couldn't."

"I insist," he pressed. "A discount, or buy one get one free."

"Well, I suppose." The woman was quiet for a beat and then, "Do you have any leggings with the logo?"

"The … the ICYMI logo?" Diego sounded startled. "I am not sure; I can look."

"I know it's silly, but I'm a sucker for a good logo." The woman gestured to the stack of boxes beside the register. "It's cute, don't you think? With the Y being a coupe glass? It really stands out." Milla squinted at the boldly printed letters and the unfurled petals dotting each *i*, clear even to her bleary vision. Her attention snagged on the Y which, sure enough, was a champagne glass. "But without being *too* noticeable, you know?" The woman continued. "Like the golden arches, we all know they mean McDonald's, but it's not obvious; it's just there."

"Huh." Diego squinted at the logo. "I suppose that makes sense. I do not even remember the first time I saw the logo."

Milla blinked at his words, a half-formed image flaring and fading, an idea just out of her reach.

Focus, Milla.

It was the weakest of links, but it tied together the disparate pieces of her puzzle—ICYMI and Kayleigh, Hattiesburg, and a woman named Jennifer, because Milla remembered *exactly* where she'd first seen that logo.

Diego threw the lock the moment their customer left. Sliding down the wall, he sat beside Milla and inspected the torn, blackened nails. "Bruja…"

"I'm sorry," she repeated. "I used my Way; I didn't know what else to do."

"And you managed this after your tea?" Diego patted her hand. "What was it?"

"The raw-head," she croaked, her mouth dry. "Diego, I—he's gone and there's … Goddess, I fucked up."

"Ssh, ssh, pequeña bruja, it will be okay."

"It won't," she wailed. "It won't be okay. I used my Way, and they'll … they'll …" Milla's stomach heaved. The world had taken on a hazy tint as the last dregs of magick pumped through her veins, and now she was hit by the full cost of her Way. Unfazed, Diego pulled over a trash can, redoing her ponytail and rubbing her lower back as Milla emptied her stomach. When she could speak, Milla turned her head to gauge his reaction to her next words. "They're here."

"Who, neteř?"

"Enforcers."

Diego ushered her home, forcing Milla into bed and urging her to sleep. "There is nothing we can do tonight. Sleep, bruja, and we can fix this in the morning."

But sleep never came. Every time she closed her eyes, she felt that velvet-wet slip of skin against her neck and smelled the pungent rotting vanilla stench too sweet to be pleasant. So she sat up against her pillows, bloodied knees drawn to her chest as she scrolled back back back in the ICYMI group chat and waited for dawn.

With the first rays of sunlight, the group chat flared to life with tired inspographics, a stream of "Good morning, huns!" and a gross misuse of emojis. She kept an eye on the group while applying fresh band-aids and struggling into skinny jeans with holes at the knees. Stepping into a pair of Birkenstock cork sandals with thick leather straps, a gift from Morgen, Milla pulled on a black tank top and a Buffalo plaid flannel, cuffing the sleeves at her elbows.

She twisted her hair into two messy buns at the nape of her neck and scowled in the mirror at her swollen, cut lip and the scrapes starting to scab on her cheekbone. Her neck was mottled purple and yellow, but the flannel hid the bruising on her arms. Having done what she could not to appear *horrifying*, Milla shoved on a pair of oversized sunglasses, texted Diego, letting him know her plans and her suspicions, and set off, stopping only to lock the door behind her.

It wasn't until she stood at the base of those three white stairs, listening to the pleasant *tink tink tink* of a seashell sigil swaying in the breeze, that Milla stopped to think about what she was doing.

Bruised, still bloodied, and tired beyond belief, she'd run to the witch tasked with investigating her at the crack of dawn.

Absolutely unhinged behavior.

She pinched the bridge of her nose, breathing in and out, in and out. He was an Aurual Insurance Adjuster; he was here to observe and determine the security of her demesne. But he was also C.R.O.W. If she could explain, get him to understand the *why* behind what she'd done, maybe he would … help.

Help with what? Covering up the fact you used your Way to handle a raw-head?

Okay, so maybe expecting Darkly to help with *that* was a stretch, but he'd ask questions about last night, regardless. It was her demesne, and five women had been hurt by *something* that called Enforcers to the scene. This wasn't just about the raw-head;

it was about doing her job well and keeping C.R.O.W. out of her business. This was about Kayleigh Masterson doxxing Milla and her store; about Kayleigh pressing Julie into buying more than she could sell. This was about ICYMI and all the arrows pointing toward Kayleigh *not* being just a pushy, middle-aged bully.

Obviously.

Milla had spent the night unable to shake the feeling something else was happening behind the scenes. It was all too coincidental, and witches didn't believe in coincidences. Fate, yes, but never coincidences, and whenever Kayleigh popped up, so did ICYMI and Hattiesburg, and now she had proof. She just needed someone else to look at it and assure her she wasn't coming unhinged.

Because blaming all of your woes on leggings was *definitely* unhinged behavior.

That sobering thought had Milla hesitating on the flagstones. What if he didn't believe her? What if this "proof" she had wasn't any proof at all? What if she just hated what Kayleigh had done to her and Julie, and this was the attempt of a frazzled mind to make sense of a bad twist of fate? What if she wasn't here for help but had come to Darkly for … comfort.

"Oh. Oh, no." Milla turned her back on the cottage, deciding her time was more prudently spent grabbing a coffee at the cat café and ignoring the ill-advised feelings she was *apparently* developing for her freaking Aural Insurance Adjuster. The insurance adjuster she'd propositioned in a bar and had nearly fucked in an alleyway. The witch who had canceled their run because he assumed he would be spending the night in Jacksonville. "There. Problem solved. He's not home; I don't even know why I'm here."

And that was when she noticed the silver Land Rover parked in the driveway behind Darkly's red hybrid.

She was still working through this when a lilting voice called, "Can I help you?"

The woman on the porch could only be described as luminescent, even while wearing one of Darkly's shirts and nothing else. White-blonde hair dusted her shoulders in a stylish bob, framing dewy pale skin, achingly perfect cheekbones, and the largest blue-green eyes Milla had ever seen. Something about her tracked as vaguely familiar, but her whole ethereal fae vibe was oppressive enough to keep Milla from placing where she'd seen this Goddess of a woman before. No wonder Darkly easily shrugged off Ana's advances if *this* was his girlfriend.

She cocked her head, scanning Milla in all her bruised, swollen-lipped glory, and a pitying smile played at her pink lips. "Miss?"

"No, no. I'm sorry." Milla raised a hand to cover her mouth, spinning around with every intent to crawl into the earth and die.

"Are you one of Darkly's claimants?"

That word burned into Milla as if the woman's soft voice had branded her skin. *Claimant.* She hitched her shoulders and fisted her hands, urging her feet to move, but they wouldn't, and it was a betrayal of the highest sort. *Stupid feet.*

The screen door slammed closed. She took a deep breath and managed a step before it opened again, spice and smoke swirling in the air.

"Milla?"

She couldn't turn around. Couldn't look at him. Her ears were red and burning, heat crawled up her neck, and her body ached. Why was she even here?

The steps creaked under his weight, and Darkly dropped a hand on her shoulder. "Did you need something?"

She flinched, ducking out of his touch. He had chosen the bruised and scratched shoulder, but how could he have known? Darkly backed away, taking in Milla with a look of horror so genuine she almost believed he cared. "Milla, Goddess, what happened?"

"The raw-head," she croaked, staring at a point on his chest and shrugging as if it had been a non-issue. "Caught me on a run, but I handled it. I just-I came here to tell you so you could tell C.R.O.W. I handled the raw-head. It's gone. He won't bother anyone anymore, so St. Augustine is safe. Okay?"

When Darkly said nothing, she looked up and, by the Goddess, he was terrified. His forehead wrinkled, and his pupils constricted, eyes scanning her mouth, cheek, and neck. He licked his lower lip and reached out, hesitating at the collar of her flannel before dropping his arm. "Milla—"

"I'm sorry I interrupted your, um, morning."

"Didnae interrupt a thing." Darkly pulled at the collar of his v-neck and she finally registered that he was sheened in sweat, cheeks flushed, and standing barefoot in gym shorts and a shirt he'd likely pulled on as he ran out the door. It was hitched at the side, showing the cut muscle of his torso. She swallowed, forcing herself to look at the sky, the palm trees swaying overhead. *Oh, look, a bird.*

"I'll go," she managed. "Sorry. For this."

"Milla, please." Darkly stopped her with a brush of his hand against her arm, fingers trailing down to her wrist. "Talk to me. What do you need?"

"Nothing."

"Liar."

"Not technically," she countered.

He stared at her, hard, and the briefest twitch of a smile quirked the corner of his mouth. "Come, sit. Dinnae walk away." His fingers curled over her palm, and he gave the gentlest of tugs. "Please."

And how could she say no to *that?*

Milla let him lead her up the stairs, settling in a wicker chair, the seashells swaying over her head. She stared at the protective warding hidden in their design and felt a sudden rush of clarity. There was little witches did without intent. It was trained into their bones and inscribed on their Souls to act with intent in all things. The wrong wayward thought or a stray emotion too strong could unleash chaos and magick deemed Forbidden and Foule. Whether accidental or intentional, the practitioners of the Forbidden and Foule had been weeded out through the centuries until magick was regulated and choked in the firm grip of C.R.O.W. The very coven that sent Darkly, who sat her under a sigil of protection crackling with magickal energy so potent it made the hair along her arms stand on end.

Milla wondered who he was protecting.

The opening strains of a movie score sampling Belafonte's "Banana Boat" trickled through the windows of his cottage, followed by the sound of the shower running. Darkly glowered, the piano and horns began in earnest, and Milla watched with quiet amusement as his glower turned to something positively deadly.

"I asked you not to go out," he finally grumbled.

"What?"

"Last night, I asked you not to go out, and you went for a run." His tone was low and even. Dangerous.

"Yes?" Milla angled her face at him. "I needed to tend the demesne, and my thoughts kept spiraling, so I went out rather than sit at Julie's and do nothing."

He nodded, eyes distant. "Where was Diego?"

"At the store."

"Ana?"

"She had plans with some friends." Milla took a deep breath, throwing all caution and potentially unhinged behavior to the wind. "Look, I know this sounds insane, but I noticed something last night in the ICYMI chat, and I wanted to get your—"

"Where?"

"I … in the group chat Julie is in. There's this woman, Jennifer, and she—"

"Where was Ana? Didn't she have plans with Julie?" He interrupted her again, rocking forward and placing a hand on Milla's knee. She froze, eyes dropping to his knuckles, red and raw. "Was she at Refugio Cove?"

"How in the nine rings would I know?" She jerked her knee away. "I was at Julie's."

"Until you weren't."

"Are you implying that I—"

"Nae!" Darkly barked, flinched, then lowered his voice. "Am nae implying anything Milla, it's only…" He glanced over his shoulder with something like fear in his eyes. "C.R.O.W."

And it hit.

He was supposed to be in Jacksonville last night, and this morning, he'd left Julie's apartment in a rush to, Milla assumed, go to Jacksonville. But he was here. Home. With a woman who looked like she'd stepped off of a Victoria's Secret runway, a woman with white-blonde hair that would easily reflect lights from an ambulance or police car, and he was terrified.

"Oh my Horned fucking God." Milla lurched forward, gripping the arms of her chair. "You fucked an Enforcer?"

"What?" Darkly whipped his head around, skin gone terribly pale. "Nae, it's not-I mean…"

"Holy shit, dude." She shook her head slowly. "I knew you were C.R.O.W., but sleeping with an Enforcer is a whole 'nother level of crazy."

"Am nae sleeping with her," he snapped.

"Oh, yeah, sure. She's just at your house, in one of *your* shirts, at the ass-crack of dawn."

Darkly's face went an amusing shade of red; then his embarrassment settled into a deep, dark glower. Smoke swirled in his eyes, and a chill grew between them, prickling her skin. Shadows crawled where before there had been sunlight, curling into his lap like a familiar come home to its master. Intrigued, Milla looked up into a face gone hard and dark. "Am nae sleeping with her, and I asked you to stay in last night." Coal-black eyes burned into her. "Why did you go out?"

"Why did you ask me to stay in?" She countered, unphased by whatever *this* was. Milla had faced her fair share of creepies and crawlies and witches with Ways that were weird. Still, she had to admit there was a certain appeal to this hard, wicked Darkly, and a secret part of her was thrilled.

He blinked, the black siphoned away, and his expression softened. "Enforcers," Darkly whispered. He brushed her knee with his fingers, face somber as if whatever *that* was had never happened. "She messaged they were coming down, responding to some surge of magick, and I didnae want you to take any risks."

"I'm fine; nothing happened."

His fingers danced on the armrest, one leg bouncing. "You were attacked by a raw-head, Milla."

"I'm *fine*." She waved it off. "I fell on the bridge." His knee stilled, but the fingers kept up their percussive *tap-tap-tapping* on the wicker. "Tripped over a crack in the sidewalk or my own feet. I don't know, but I forgot to feed the raw-head; it must have been drawn to the scent of my blood."

Tap tap tap tap tap. "How did you handle it?"

"A chronomantic hex."

"A chrono-hex?" Darkly stilled. "Didnae ken you knew those."

"Studied under the Morgenhexe, remember? She taught me all manner of hand-to-hex." As a Morning Witch, Morgen had a broad understanding of chronomancy. The particular chrono-hex Milla referred to was a favorite of many chronomantics in the field, capable of turning back the literal clock and returning a creature to its most basic carbon form. In the raw head's case, a pile of carbon-rich dried mud. Ashes to ashes, dust to dust, and all.

Darkly turned over his phone, drummed his fingers on a knee, and tapped the screen before vanishing it back into wherever he summoned things. "How hurt are you?"

It was less a question and more a demand, so Milla shrugged the shoulders of her flannel down, showing him the bruises and abrasions on her arm. His eyes tracked the wounds, lingering on her throat and the hideous tartan the Raw-head had made of her skin. He swallowed, looking sick to his stomach, and rose to stand beside her chair. She let him inspect her lip and shivered when he tilted her chin up, knuckles brushing her cheekbone and tucking a strand of hair behind her ear. She imagined that he lingered longer than necessary before stooping to check the band-aids on her scraped knees.

"Minnie Mouse?" He raised an eyebrow at her.

"It was all we had."

Darkly snorted, taking her left hand in his own with such gentleness that Milla almost jerked it away. "And somehow, through all of this, you found the time to paint your nails?" He glanced up from the black nail polish hiding blackened nails to smirk at her.

"Diego got bored."

He ran his thumb over her knuckles, watching Milla closely. "You said you found something?"

"I … oh, yeah." She pulled her phone free, opening it to the ICYMI chat. Darkly watched, quiet, as she scrolled and scrolled and scrolled, growing frustrated at the amount of useless chatter. "Hold on, I had it up before walking over."

"Take your time," he murmured, again sweeping a feather-soft touch across her knuckles. All at once, Milla felt ridiculous. Perched on the edge of a wicker rocking chair, bruised and bloodied, with an over-tall witch on his knees in front of her. Not that she didn't *like* him on his knees in front of her or the tender way he held her hand, but this was hardly the time, and he was hardly the witch. Heat crawled up her neck, and she squeezed Darkly's hand before pulling away.

"A woman in the store last night said something about the logo," Milla began. "About how it was distinctive, even when you didn't really notice it, and I remembered—the first time I saw it was in the bar."

"The bar?"

"When we met. Here, look." She handed him her phone and pointed to the post she'd found. "Jennifer Sanderson posted this four weeks ago."

The post was short, so short Milla had almost discounted it entirely until she read the reply.

"I'm so tired of being tired and dizzy all the time." Jennifer had written in reply to a general post asking how the group was doing. "The grind is exhausting. I feel like I can't breathe, and these headaches have been killing me. I think I need to take a break."

Kayleigh had replied, "Hey gurl, my Upline and I want to chat with you offline, check ur dms", followed by a heart, a broken heart, and a kissy face. The next post about Jennifer Sanderson was from Kayleigh, informing the group she had died of carbon monoxide poisoning.

Milla tapped on Jennifer Sanderson's picture, loading her profile to show him a series of testimonials in memoriam and animated images of glittery floral arrangements. Jennifer was a school teacher of thirty years, taught beginner's ballet at a local dance studio, ran a Paint Night at a wine bar, and was a frequenter of a local craft store. She was normal. A mother, a wife, a member of the community.

And she was dead over some tacky leggings.

"Milla," Darkly murmured, bringing his face closer to hers. "Why are you showing me the social media page of a pleasant-looking, middle-aged woman?"

"A *dead*, pleasant-looking middle-aged woman," she corrected. He stiffened, but she pressed on. "Four weeks ago, Jennifer Sanderson was found dead in her home. It was the story on the news when we met."

"The news?"

Milla shook her head. "You wouldn't have seen it; there was a vampire slayer killing monsters in a cheerleading skirt on your screen."

"Sorry, what?" Darkly blinked rapidly. "Why would the monsters be in skirts?"

"No, the vampire slayer, and I only saw it because I was trying to ignore you. Don't give me that face." Because he was giving her an infuriatingly adorable mock-insulted face. "Look, she posts this, talks to Kayleigh and whoever her Upline is outside of the chat, and then she *dies*."

"Milla."

"Of *carbon monoxide poisoning*. I know how it sounds, but just … just hear me out, okay?" She opened the images folder on her phone, showing Darkly the screenshots of the women in the group chat, Kayleigh's initial call to action to her horde of huns, the Yap! reviews, and finally, the photo of the women from Refugio Cove. "It's all related to ICYMI. These women—Kayleigh gets them to join, they go all in, exhausting themselves, and then she does … something. I haven't worked that out yet, but it's *her*."

"Milla."

"I'm not crazy," she snapped, lurching from the rocking chair, which sent Darkly sprawling back. Pacing the porch, she tried to verbalize what she *knew*. It all made sense in her head; she just needed him to understand. "ICYMI shows up in Hattiesburg two years ago. Ana said it herself; it just popped up at some convention in New Orleans. She said she knew a woman who opened a boutique that closed due to family illness." She poked her screen, returning to Jennifer Sanderson's page. And again to open the "About" section before thrusting her phone at Darkly, still sprawled on the porch. "Here. Look."

And he did, sitting up, scrolling the profile, and reading what Milla had. His brows pulled together, green eyes narrowing as his mouth pulled into a tight line.

"Two years ago, Jennifer Sanderson got involved with ICYMI. She opened a boutique to sell the clothes, and four weeks ago, she posted that she wanted out. Kayleigh pulls her aside for a chat, and Jennifer winds up dead. Of *carbon monoxide poisoning*."

"You dinnae ken that."

"Don't I?" Milla stole her phone back, opened the browser, and held the screen towards Darkly as the news report she'd seen weeks ago in Drake's Fire played.

"Breaking news out of Hattiesburg: a woman identified as Jennifer Sanderson was found dead in her home. Medical authorities are attributing the death to carbon monoxide poisoning while family members cry foul play. Our local affiliate has the details." The news anchor cut out, and a wet-sounding voice started speaking. "They said it was carbon monoxide, but my sister and my daddy was in the house. They're just fine, and that don't make any sense. None of it makes any sense. She was hardworking, you know? Worked two jobs, *two* to make sure we was comfortable, and then just collapses from poisoning none of us got. I-I just can't believe she's gone, what are we going to do with all of this sh—"

"Darkly," the blonde woman called from the door. Her accent, Milla now recognized, was Irish because, of course, this dewy blonde was interesting and foreign. Darkly paused the news report and popped to his feet. "I need to head north. Are you free later this week?"

Milla pinned her eyes on the seashells, watching them sway and *tink* together in the breeze coming off the river. The patio creaked under Darkly's feet, the screen door bounced closed, and—Milla must just hate herself because she had to look—Darkly kissed the woman on the cheek. She was even more devastating in clothes than she'd been in one of his shirts. Fitted light gray ponte pants, heels that stretched her legs a mile long, a short-sleeved pink pastel cashmere top that made her hair glow, and just the barest dusting of makeup. Milla closed her eyes, but nothing could have drowned out the husky tone as she said, "Thanks again for last night."

"I'll message you later."

The woman smiled at Milla, triumphant, which just seemed rude, and flitted down the steps towards her expensive Land Rover to drive to her fancy job as an Enforcer.

Darkly slid down in the wicker rocker, dropping his head against the backrest and staring at the haint blue ceiling as he rocked back and forth. Milla waited it out, whatever this passing storm was. What could she say? "Hope the sex was great?" "Sorry, my horrid appearance scared her off?"

After a few moments, he rose and stomped inside. The movie cut off at one of Milla's favorite parts, where the ghosts tried to scare the new owners out of their home. Darkly stormed back out, the screen door slamming behind him.

"In the back of that video," he began. "Those boxes in the garage."

Milla sighed, sinking into her chair as relief flooded her body. He saw it. He knew exactly what the last piece was that had brought Milla to his front stoop. The itching, niggling little image that had been hiding in plain sight. "Yes."

"Those were all ICYMI."

She nodded. "All of it. Every box behind that woman in the news report is ICYMI."

"And those women last night, at Refugio Cove …"

"McKenzie Miller was supposed to host that event with Julie. My guess is it was to get more people in their downline."

Darkly's face fluttered as though the witch had quickly tried to understand what she'd just said and disregarded it as unnecessary. "And Kayleigh is at the top?"

"Kayleigh is at the top." *That I know of.* "Or if not the top, she's close to it. I have an—"

"Inkling?" He finished for her. Milla nodded, knowing how ridiculous it sounded.

Darkly sighed, paced in a circle, and dropped his head to pinch the bridge of his nose. "Mam always said nae to doubt a vestic," he muttered. The witch inhaled three times, steadying himself, before raising his head and looking Milla dead in the eye. "What do you need?"

"I need to go to Hattiesburg."

Another sigh, only this time he dropped his head back to stare at the haint blue ceiling. "How'd I ken ye'd say that?"

TWENTY THREE

"Si, okay," Diego nodded. Then shook his head. "Sorry, I am not following. You think the Karen—"

"Kayleigh," Milla corrected.

"The Kayleigh is responsible for the deaths?"

"Yes. Well, no." She grabbed the stone and origami tiger from her bookshelf, packing the latter in a small wooden box and shoving both in her bag. "But she's involved somehow."

He stared at her for a long beat, brown eyes intent and hard. Then shrugged. "Okay."

"Okay?"

"Okay," Diego nodded. "So you go to Hattiesburg, seek out Kayleigh, and qué? Ask her to please stop killing mortals over ugly leggings?"

"Sort of." Milla wrapped a locket in a wad of underwear. Darkly wanted to shower before they left, so she had trudged home, belatedly texting to ask if he'd pick up Julie and drive her over. He'd agreed, of course, because the witch was, for *some reason*, following her shaky lead.

Later, she would have to figure out why. Right now, she needed to pack and bring Diego up to speed. "I want to speak to that woman from the news report, Jennifer Sanderson's daughter."

"Why?" He dug through Milla's dresser, selecting shirts and scrutinizing each before placing it in the duffel bag or returning it to the drawer.

"To find out where it started. All of Kayleigh's downlines pay her a percentage, but she mentioned having an Upline of her own. Jennifer Sanderson was her crossline; I think the word is. I need you to contact her daughter, Sarah. Tell her we're ICYMI vendors or something. I don't know."

"And a call will not suffice?"

"I want to check out the house myself." Milla dropped to her knees, scrounging under her bed for running shoes. "See if there's anything Forbidden and Foule going on. A wayward curse or a hex."

Diego chuckled, smiling fondly at Milla when she stood. "Sometimes I forget you were raised by the Morgenhexe."

"Through no lack of trying, I'm sure."

He shook his head, the smile fading to a somber line. "Hattiesburg is in the Delta, Milla."

"It is."

"Are you certain you should be going there? What if she—"

"I'm not going to be anywhere near New Orleans. She won't even know I'm in the territory," Milla cut him off. "It's eight hours to Hattiesburg, so that should give you time to—"

"Only eight hours?" He pinched a cropped My Chemical Romance t-shirt between two fingers, nodding before setting it in the duffel. "I will never get used to how fast it is to travel these days. And how are you getting there?"

"Darkly's giving me a ride."

He shoved the t-shirt back into the drawer, selecting Milla's black-and-white striped a-line halter instead. "I bet he is."

"Diego!" Milla's neck heated. She grabbed the halter. "Horned God, I'm gathering *facts*, not going on a date."

"Are you arguing clothing with a Stitch Witch?"

Footsteps in the hall spared Milla from answering, and Darkly popped his head into the room. He'd changed into cream-colored slacks cuffed at the ankle, boat shoes, and a fitted short-sleeved button-down covered in palm fronds. Not what Milla would have chosen for a long drive, but the witch was irritatingly committed to his casual nautical aesthetic. "Julie's on the couch; she could barely keep awake on the drive over." His eyes landed on Milla and the halter in her hands. "That's a nice top; you should bring it along."

Diego batted Milla's arm. "I told you."

Exhaustion caught her before they hit Jacksonville. It started as a tiny yawn in the drive-thru coffee line, then quickly devolved into jaw-cracking, eye-watering yawns as Darkly's little red hybrid chugged up I-95.

"Close your eyes, Milla," Darkly chided. "You didnae sleep last night."

"Don't wanna be rude," she grumbled, slouching against the door.

"Fancy a long drive." He reached over, patting her knee and leaving his hand right there. "You Americans have the straightest roads."

Milla snorted, a protest that she was Czechian, not American, dying on her tongue. The rumble of the road, the cozy clove and smoke scent of Darkly, and the idle circles he drew on her knee were too tempting to resist, and before they entered the city limits, Milla closed her eyes.

She woke to an argument.

"—knew you'd argue," Darkly hissed into his phone, eyes narrowed and trained on the highway. The voice on the other end of the call was irate, their muted yelling just loud enough for Milla to hear but not discern their words. "After last night, do you honestly believe I would—" He slammed the heel of his palm against the steering wheel. Milla took that as a hint to mind her own business, checking the notifications on her phone and trying desperately not to listen in on what was a fascinating one-sided conversation.

"This isnae like the Netherlands, and I'll thank you nae to mention it again." A pause. "Aye." A longer pause. The voice on the other end had quieted, Milla noted. Not that she was listening. She read through Diego's messages, checked the address he'd sent, and put it into the map application to estimate their arrival time. *Not* eavesdropping on the witch holding a very emotional conversation in the seat next to her. "You promised, Big Yin." This was quieter, pleading, and Milla snuck a quick glance.

Darkly's face was pale, his eyes swirling with that odd smoke as he chewed his lower lip, listening intently. "A day or two. It's a long drive." He must have felt Milla watching because his eyes darted her way. He blinked, shoulders tensing, and the bright green was back. "Aye hen, you too."

He hung up, dropping his phone in the cupholder and gripping the steering wheel tightly. The muscles in his arms tensed, triceps bulging beneath lightly tanned, freckled skin.

"Sorry I slept so long," she tried.

"You were tired." Darkly dropped a hand to the gear shift. "I'm glad you slept."

"Yeah, but for six hours?" Milla gaped at him. He looked exhausted, pale, and worn around the edges. "Do you want me to drive the last bit?"

He opened his mouth, closed it, and shook his head. "Nae."

The Mississippi state line rushed by, marked by a sign reading HATTIESBURG 73. Milla coughed, setting her phone in a cupholder and lacing her fingers together. "That's, like, what? One hundred and twenty kilometers?" Darkly huffed, his grip on the steering wheel eased, and he nodded. After a few more miles of quiet, Milla tried again. "Soooo, what happened in the Netherlands?"

"Dinnae."

"Is it what got you benched?" His eyes widened, telling Milla her teasing was on the right track. She tapped a finger to her lips, flinching at the flare of pain from the raw-head's cut, then pointed at Darkly with a gasp. "Wait. Don't tell me. You got caught by a … a rogue corpomantic." He raised an eyebrow. "No? Okay, a Dark Witch, then." That earned a second eyebrow, and Darkly shuffled in his seat. "They were attracted to your name and wanted to enthrall your Shade for wicked and evil deeds forevermore."

"Wicked and evil deeds?"

"Like voting for Brexit," Milla nodded sagely. That earned her an outright laugh and the smile that drove a dimple into his cheek.

"Bampot." He rubbed a knuckle under his eye. "Sorry you had to overhear that."

"It's fine," she stated. "Everything alright?"

"Aye," he exhaled. "That was my—ehm, Fiona."

"Fiona." Milla's stomach dropped. She affected a light tone, attempting to draw Darkly out of his mood for the last of their drive. "She's probably wondering what was dire enough to whisk you away for a romantic overnight in Hattiesburg."

"Something like that."

He stopped at a rest area so Milla could use the bathroom, and the next hour passed in near silence. Darkly chewing on his fight with Fiona, and Milla trying not to address how she felt about the ethereal Enforcer having a name. It made her real in a way she didn't like, filling the backseat of his car with the Shade of her.

Finally, he turned the hybrid onto a tree-lined street in West Hattiesburg. Cracked concrete driveways pulled away from the road leading to houses set back on brown grass lawns. The world was cast in gray clouds promising rain, and Milla wriggled her toes in her cork sandals, wishing she hadn't left her boots in Julie's apartment.

"Anything I should know before going in there?" Darkly parked in front of a split-level ranch house. A metal post at the center of a mound of freshly churned dirt held prominence in the yard, and a newer model minivan occupied the driveway. The garage door was open, displaying the wall of ICYMI boxes like a hideous blemish on an otherwise pleasant face.

Milla pulled out her phone and opened her text messages. "Diego says she agreed to meet with us by selling her a version of the truth."

"Aye?"

Milla frowned at her phone. "I'm an ICYMI representative interested in purchasing her inventory." Darkly snorted. "Don't laugh too hard, you're my husband."

She stalked up the driveway to the sound of his snickering. He leaned in close as she knocked on the door, rolling that infuriating accent in her ear. "Gaunnae gies a smourich?"

"What?" Milla jerked her face to his, tracking the inane grin. He grinned wider, the door creaked open, and too late, she noticed the windchime sigil of protection hanging over his shoulder. "... the fuck."

"My thoughts exactly," the witch in the doorway snapped. Her sharp gaze landed on Darkly. "You're not the man I spoke to on the phone."

"You're a witch," Milla blurted.

"Hedgewitch." The woman sent her a flat stare. "And you're not ICYMI."

Darkly slung an arm around Milla's shoulders, pulling her close. "What my dear wife means is, we are sorry for your loss, Mrs.—"

"Ms."

"Ms. Sanderson, our sincerest condolences."

Sarah Sanderson studied Darkly, his arm draped over Milla, and she huffed. "At least your friend on the phone weren't lyin' about that." She frowned and waved them into the house. "Come on in."

"I don't know what I find more insulting," Milla muttered. "That I'm not believable as an ICYMI rep or that she believes we're married."

Sarah sat them in a breakfast nook with cups of scalding coffee and an assortment of sugar-laden creamers. She perched on a barstool at the center island, watching Darkly curl his lip at the off-tan color of Milla's coffee when she'd finished adding the proper amount of caramel mocha creamer.

Piles of mail and unopened carbon monoxide alarms covered one end of the counter, while the other hosted a swath of red cloth and a glass dish shaped like a butterfly. A whittling knife, the nub of a red candle, a tree cutting, and a pipe sat on the dish. The Sanderson family had taped a worn-edged, wrinkled picture of Saint Joseph to the wall, and beneath it was a small, lumpy doll with mismatched button eyes boring into Milla.

"You're not ICYMI," Sarah finally broke the tense silence. "Why are you here?"

"I wanted to ask you about your mother," Milla started.

"Stepmother," Sarah interjected.

"Sorry, your stepmother. She died of carbon monoxide poisoning?" Sarah snorted, anger flushing her face a deeper brown. She straightened on her stool. "There have been similar instances in St. Augustine," Milla rushed out. "Three women were hospitalized last night for carbon monoxide poisoning; two died, but there were other people at the same party who were unaffected."

"So y'all drove to Hattiesburg?"

"You said in that news report your dad and sister were in the house, but only your stepmom got sick?" Sarah nodded, waiting for Milla to continue. "I'm trying to figure out where it all started."

Sarah stirred her coffee, watching Milla from the corner of her eye. "You came here under false pretenses, sayin' you was with ICYMI."

"We're truly sorry, ma'am, for the lie—" Darkly began.

"Then I think you already know where this all started." Sarah slid off her stool and began rummaging in a drawer. "You the one that runs Southern Gothic?"

"I—" Milla blinked and shared a look with Darkly. "Yes, how did you know?"

"Internet. You can find out everything about anyone in no time." She pulled out a smartphone. "They gave me access to my stepmom's social media accounts when she passed; the ICYMI gals came down hard on you a few weeks back. Never liked that Kayleigh woman, not since Jennifer met her at that MLM convention down in New Orleans." She looked from Milla to Darkly and back. "You say you want to know where this all began. I say you need to get down to the Crescent."

Scalding coffee splattered on her fingers and the table. Milla cursed, dabbing uselessly at the puddle with her sleeve. Her eyes drifted to the button-eyed doll, and her heart skittered to a halt. Goddess, she could almost see Ezra glaring at her from across the room, telling her with a look to hold it together. Not to give anything away. Darkly brushed her arm away, pressing a wad of paper towels he summoned from *somewhere* in her mess. A hand swept across Milla's lower back, and then Ezra was beside her, whispering in her ear that everything was fine, that she needed to—

Believe in me, Millapet.

"Milla?" Darkly slid his palm up her spine in a soothing motion. "All good?"

"I, uh, yes." She blinked rapidly, dispensing with the not-ghost of Ezra and offering a wan smile to the witch who was there. "Phone buzzed. Startled me."

Sarah and Darkly looked at her silent phone on the table, splattered with drops of coffee. She grabbed it, wiped the liquid off on her pants, and shoved it under her thigh.

"Riiight," Sarah drew out the word. "Anyways, I went through Jennifer's old messages, wanting to let people know what had happened, see if I could source any more information, or get rid of all those shitty leggings." She pinned them both with a sharp glare. "Ever notice how they feel slimy?" Milla nodded, and Sarah hummed, satisfied. "Best I can figure is a glamour of sorts."

"Cannae be," Darkly breathed. "If the Fair Folk in the Isles were involved, C.R.O.W. would know."

"Fair Folk?" Milla angled her face at him.

"Faeries," he answered. She snorted.

"I don't know about faeries and the Isles, but the damn tights are painted in glamour. Those women never stood a chance." Sarah slid the phone across the table. "Here. Found a bunch of private messages from Kayleigh. My stepmom was her crossline."

"Meaning they worked together, but she didn't receive a percentage of Kayleigh's sales, correct?" Milla asked, wanting clarification. Sarah nodded.

"And what's an MLM?" Darkly cut in.

"Multi-level marketing." Sarah twisted her mouth into a disgusted frown. "Fancy name for a pyramid scheme. Jennifer and my Dad were always looking for a way to make a quick buck. She worked two jobs, Dad's a long haul trucker, but it never seemed to be enough. I did what I could, but …" A shrug. "The district life insurance my stepmom had is barely going to cover the mortgage on the house. I'm trying to convince my dad to move."

Darkly tapped a finger against his mug, the coffee untouched. "Why not sell the ICYMI inventory?"

"With the Spring Sales Convention coming up, none of the women in the group think they can move it into their sales. Some offered to 'take it off of my hands,' but they ghost me when I mention what I want for the trash." She yanked the freezer door open, withdrawing a plastic Tupperware of ice. It *thunked* on the table, and Milla stared down at the handful of credit cards frozen in their own glacier. "Did that two years ago when she maxed out the first credit card opening that damn store. Wish I'd known she had the number saved on the ICYMI website."

Darkly whistled, long and low. Milla just stared and stared. Julie popped into her head, red-eyed and blubbery over maxed-out credit cards, and the nameless women in McKenzie Miller's photograph, now hospitalized or dead. How many more had been caught up in Kayleigh's scheme? How many more women were going to suffer? She needed to end this. She needed to be certain the rot festering in her corner of the world was, at the least, ending with Julie.

The phone on the counter buzzed, followed by Milla's, and all three witches wrinkled their noses at the onslaught of a burnt plastic stink.

Sarah jerked her chin at Milla. "You notice it too, huh?"

"What?"

"Technomancy." She smiled, a cruel gnashing of teeth that had nothing to do with Milla and Darkly and everything to do with their phones and the stench, which, Milla just realized, flashed following activity in the chat groups. She grabbed her phone and tapped into the group.

"Oh, Goddess." Her hand rushed to her mouth, and she hissed at the flash of pain from her lip.

"What is it?" Darkly leaned close, his pleasant spiced scent overpowering the burn of foul intent. They scanned the chat group while Sarah scrolled through the same on her stepmother's phone.

"There's been another one," Milla turned the screen towards him, "in Vilano Beach, they haven't released the name."

"Vilano Beach? Isnae that where—"

"Ana." Milla darted from the breakfast nook, slamming her hip against the table as she frantically dialed her *čarodějnice*'s number. "Ow, fuck. Come on, come on, come on …"

"Hello?" Ana's voice, uncharacteristically somber, came over the line.

"Ana! Oh, my Goddess, are you alright?" Milla paced in the Sanderson's dining room, her breath coming in short, unsatisfying bursts. "Is everything okay? Where are you?"

"Where are you?" Ana retorted. "Diego said you left, that it was just him and me today, and there are *so many people*." She lowered her voice to a stage whisper, and Milla could almost see the young witch ducking behind the mannequin. "Where's Julie?"

"She's sick."

"And where are *you*?"

"Hattiesburg." Milla tracked Darkly filling the doorway, his mass blocking the light streaming through the kitchen. "I wanted to talk to Sarah Sanderson about—"

"You went to Hattiesburg, and you didn't take me?" Ana gasped. "Do you even know what I went through last night?"

"I …" That drew Milla up short. A faint prickle began behind her eyes, and she pinched them closed, swaying as Ana told her what she already knew. Because of course, of *course*—

"One minute she was fine," she sniffled. "They were all *fine*, and then McKenzie collapsed, and Ashley, she … she …"

She was there. She had plans with Julie; she was there at Refugio Cove with the women who spent a day belittling Julie. With women that were supposed to be Julie's *friends*.

"Ana," Milla breathed. "Oh, Goddess, are you—"

"She *died* before they even got her to the hospital. And then Jenna and the *police*—where *were* you?"

"You weren't in the picture," Milla blurted. "I-I didn't know, and you weren't in the picture, I thought—" Her fingers had gone numb, her scar itched, and the prickling behind her eyes grew to a needle-sharp stabbing.

"What?"

"In McKenzie's picture, you weren't in it."

"Obviously," she sniffed, her voice congested from tears. "Who do you think took it."

"Oh, Goddess." The world narrowed to a very fine point, the only warning before it fractured into three. She slammed a hand over her eyes, keeping them closed and counting her breaths. In, two, three, four. Out, two, three. In two-three—Goddess, it wasn't working.

Focus, Millapet.

In two-three …

"She alright?" Sarah asked. Ana's sobbing and blubbering drowned Darkly's reply, and Milla was going to be sick. Her *čarodějnice* was supposed to be cared for. She was supposed to be *safe*. She was Milla's responsibility; she had failed her like she'd failed Julie, the demesne, and Ezra.

Focus, he snapped. *I trained you better than this.*

The phone fell from her hand, thudding to the floor, and she rushed from the room. Limping, muscles screaming, she didn't know where she was going, only that she couldn't be here in this house with that button-eyed poppet glaring at her from across the room.

Darkly caught her at the door, strong arms wrapping around Milla's waist and tugging her against him. Gentle hands moved to her shoulders, and in a low, soft voice, he told her to breathe, to count what she could see, touch, feel, taste, and smell. To name three things she saw; and all she saw was Ezra, Gone. Julie unconscious and Ana in a condo of dead and dying women.

"I have to go. I have to go. I have to go." She couldn't catch her breath, couldn't swallow, couldn't *think*, and he was holding her too tight, and she needed to go. To Ana, To her *čarodějnice*, her student, her friend, her responsibility. "She was there; she was in that condo; she's my apprentice."

Darkly went tense, sucking in a sharp breath. "She was where?"

"I need to get back. I need to get home."

"I know." He palmed the back of her head and held her to his chest, making her listen to the steady beat of his heart until her breathing calmed and her pulse stopped jumping frantically. "I'll get you back, but think, Milla. Think for a moment." His fingers curled in her hair, and cold ebbed from his touch, spreading over her skull as though Milla had dipped her head into a cold, glacial pool. "We're eight hours away; where is Ana now?"

"At the store," she mumbled into his shirt, inhaling his wintry scent. "She's at the store."

"With?"

"With Diego." Two fingers pressed at the base of her skull until Milla looked up at him. For the briefest moment, three Darklys gazed down. One scowling with hatred in his eyes, one with the soft, wistful expression she'd caught in the corner of her eye, and one shrouded in shadows.

She blinked, the three collapsed to one and Darkly pressed a kiss to her forehead. "There she is."

Milla wrapped her arms around him, feeling his steadiness, his surety. Enjoying the press of his hand against the back of her head and not wanting to leave the safety of *him*. It would be so easy to let someone else take care of her. Let someone else clean up her mess.

But Milla was no longer that witch, happy to hide behind Ezra and do as she was bid. So she took a Big Girl Breath and stepped away.

Twenty Four

"How did your stepmom and Kayleigh meet?" Milla charged into the kitchen and grabbed her coffee cup for something to do with her hands.

"At the convention in New Orleans, like I said." Sarah Sanderson settled at the nook. "Complete strangers, and they carpooled home."

"Economic of them." Darkly wandered back in, Milla's phone in hand

Sarah snorted, a derisive sound Milla was beginning to think came as second nature to the woman. "Sure, if you call roping my stepmom into shilling crap leggings to unsuspecting housewives 'economic'."

"And Jennifer was thinking about quitting as a rep?"

"Not thinking, she did." Sarah tapped the screen twice and slid the phone across the table, showing them a private chat. Milla compared the timestamp to Jennifer's last comment in the group chat. They were dated within minutes of one another, and the private chat involved Kayleigh, Jennifer, and a third name Milla hadn't yet seen. Sarah grunted, tapping the phone screen. "This was the last conversation my stepmom had with anyone before she died. She told Kayleigh she was tired of the hustle and was going to close the store when her lease ran out."

"And who is this …" Milla squinted at the members of the private chat. "Annalisa?"

"Ugh," Sarah rolled her eyes. "Their Upline, some woman they met in New Orleans. She was constantly texting my mom about buying more of that crap."

"Why would she do that?" Darkly dropped a hip against the island, setting Milla's phone down.

"Kayleigh and Mom were crosslines," Sarah stated.

"And that means?"

"They were crosslines. They worked together, and a percentage of their sales went to Annalisa, but *their* sales and those of the women in their separate downlines didn't directly impact each other." Darkly nodded, eyebrows lifted, and Milla was hit with the sudden clarity that he hadn't followed Sarah's explanation at all.

"So the more people in your stepmom, or Kayleigh's, downline…" she started.

"The more money trickled up to Annalisa at the top of the pyramid," Sarah confirmed. "Jennifer would work with Kayleigh to set up events, though I have no idea why Kayleigh didn't open the boutique herself. Lord knows she did far better at selling the tacky shit. Then Jennifer told Kayleigh she was quitting and offered her the sponsorship of her downline. Kayleigh accepted, which is why she's all over the chat group."

"She knew she was going to get all of the sales percentages from the other women," Milla said, her voice flat. Again, her gaze drifted to the button-eyed poppet. "And they met Annalisa in New Orleans?"

Sarah nodded. "Told you where you need to go."

Milla wiped a clammy palm against her thigh and swallowed. For every new piece of information floating among the scattered corkboard in her mind, there was a city-shaped piece making her increasingly uncomfortable. For not the first time, Milla cursed her inability to use her fractured Way on objects. Her mother could scry information from a scrap of cloth, suss out intention, and divine where the wearer was heading and what they'd been thinking. Her mother could have slapped her hand on any of the leggings in the Sanderson's garage and given Milla a heading—a tangible lead.

All Milla could do was attempt to read broken potentials with no way of knowing which was the truth … unless she chose.

"Did you ever meet Annalisa Pighah?" Darkly gestured to the phone and the conversation between Jennifer, Kayleigh, and their Upline.

"Never." Sarah tapped on the image. It opened to a locked-down profile showing tired inspographics and random posts about merchandise. The only picture in the profile album was of blonde curls brushing artfully over the "ICYMI4LIFE" badge on a paisley blouse. "And that's the only conversation I found with Annalisa involved. Everything else came through Kayleigh."

Milla propped her elbows on the island, massaging her temples. "That woman is going to be the death of me."

"Not if she kills me first," Sarah grumbled.

"I don't suppose you have her address?" Milla peered hopefully at the hedgewitch.

"Her new one?" She barked a laugh, waving a hand in the air. "That's rich, you think she'd want to keep in touch with *us* after her move?"

"Move?"

"Out your way, around four weeks back." Sarah tapped on the phone, opened Kayleigh's profile, and scrolled further back than Milla had gone. She stopped on a photograph of the irritating woman beside a 'SOLD' sign. "She was waiting on the divorce to finalize before selling. Last I heard, she was moving in with her parents somewhere south of Jacksonville."

"Oh, my Horned God." Milla dragged her hands at her eyes. "She's in my *demesne?*"

"Alright," Darkly rubbed his palms together. "So, we find Kayleigh, figure out who this Annalisa woman is, and—" Their phones dinged before he could finish his thought. The acrid stench flared again, and he lost his composure. "Figure out what the feck that stench is."

"Tried to tell you earlier; it's some sort of technomancy. The stink happens whenever someone in the group chat triggers"—Sarah waggled her fingers—"something."

"What do you mean?" Milla asked.

"Broadcast," a thin, watery voice came through the speaker on Milla's phone. Two witches and a hedgewitch blinked at each other, then dropped their eyes to the phone and the ongoing call.

"Ana?" Milla gaped.

"Hi, yeah, I'm still here," her *čarodějnice* sighed. "Did you forget about me? *Again?*"

"Ana, I'm—"

"Could have sworn I hung that up," Darkly muttered. "What was that about broadcast?"

"Broadcast?" Sarah sneered. "Like television?"

"*No,*" Ana huffed. "Broad Cast. Casting through technology to affect a wider range of people. Tracy, my former *polednice*, was working on it."

"Tracy Johnson?" Sarah startled. "The C.R.O.W. witch up from New Orleans?"

"Mother fucker." Milla slapped the counter and stomped in an angry circle. "Why is it always Horned God-damned New Orleans?"

"What do you have against New Orleans?" Darkly asked.

Milla looked at Sarah, and Sarah looked at Milla. They both glanced at the button-eyed poppet perched on the stack of mail.

"I … just don't like it." Milla edged around the island, putting distance between herself and the doll. Sarah snorted. "Ana, can you tell us more about Broad Cast?"

"There's not much more to tell." Her voice had gained strength. Surety. "It's a means of casting through social media to influence the hive mind. Like when everyone on Blather teamed up to cancel that one actress."

"Or when the idiots on Sayit tracked down the marathon bomber," Sarah added.

"Exactly! Tracy was testing the efficiency of casting intent across different social media platforms."

"Like in a chat group," Milla said.

"Yes!" Ana agreed. "Ugh, you're so smart, *polednice*. But it does something weird to the mortal tech, so you get the stink."

"The sacrifice." Milla nodded, eyes darting back and forth as she picked apart the theory of the ritual. "The intent is the rallying cry, the desire to spread a specific message, using hashtags or … or re-shares. So the sacrifice has to come from somewhere."

"The phone itself, or the mortal on the receiving end of the casting," Darkly caught on.

"Hashtags as ritual." She leaned against the counter. "It's clever, have to hand it to the witch at fault."

"Think of the possibilities," Sarah murmured. "The internet as a demesne. Good Lord, this could topple governments."

"Just as easily as it could promote goodwill," Milla argued. "Two sides to every Way."

"So we're after a rogue technomantic with a vendetta against housewives." Darkly scratched his cheek, unconvinced.

"It's about the energy." Milla chewed her lip, winced, and chewed her cheek instead, weighing what she knew about rituals and transference of power. "The potential gain and the actual loss. Whoever is doing this, Kayleigh, Annalisa, or whoever is drawing from the women in the downline."

"Elaborate." He crossed his arms and dropped a hip against the counter next to Milla. The warmth of his body was like a blanket, wrapping around the witch and bracing her against the chilling realization of what they were facing … and what she needed to do.

"They're using the women in the downline to gain energy, feeding off of their affirmations. Look," she grabbed Jennifer Sanderson's phone and found her final post in the group chat. "Her last message was about wanting to quit, and then she talked to Kayleigh and Annalisa about just that. But all of *these* women were in Jennifer's downline. Removing her created a dam in the energy flow, cutting off whoever is at the top from their source."

"So clever," Ana gushed from the speaker.

Darkly unfolded one arm to raise a finger. "One comment in a chat group isnae enough evidence to jump to conclusions."

"You saw Julie yesterday. She was terrified of quitting and letting Kayleigh down—"

"Sounds familiar," Sarah muttered.

"—just like any other mortal would be with a witch forcing their intent on the weaker-willed."

"And that's an unfounded argument." He stepped close, becoming a wall between Milla, Sarah, and the phone. "Correlation isnae causation, Milla."

"So we talk to Tracy," she slipped around him, "and we find Kayleigh. Allure her to tell us what's going on."

"That might be harder than you think, *polednice*," said Ana. "When Tracy got sick, they—C.R.O.W. sent her back to her home demesne." Milla stilled beside the butterfly dish and its odd assortment of items, taking in the pipe and the knife. The tree cutting and the portrait of Saint Joseph, finally seeing them for what they were. "She's in New Orleans."

The scar on her arm prickled. Milla gripped the counter, closing her eyes for one solid Big Girl Breath and opening them to glare at the little poppet peering at her from behind a flour canister. When she spoke, her voice was deadly calm. "No one in the group wanted your stepmom's merchandise?"

"No," Sarah scoffed, voice sour with disdain. "Fine bunch of women. Super supportive. Really."

"I'll buy it." She faced the hedgewitch. "All of it. At cost, at a markup. Name your price."

"Milla, can you cover that?"

"Ezra didn't leave me destitute, Darkly." That shut him up. He crossed his arms, glaring at the ceiling.

"I appreciate your offer," Sarah side-eyed them both, "but it's thousands of dollars; I can't in good conscience accept your money."

"We'll sell it at the store on consignment if it makes you feel better. But I can't in good conscience leave you saddled with all that hideous shit when I could be helping instead." She glanced at Darkly, startled by the soft, admiring expression that overtook his glower, and told herself she didn't care. This wasn't for him.

It wasn't even for her. It was for Sarah and her stepmother, it was for Julie and Ana and any other woman who had been roped into this scheme. "I'll cover the shipping costs as well."

Sarah opened her mouth, shut it, and glanced at Darkly.

"He has no say in this," Milla cut her off before an appeal could be made to the man in the room. "It's my store, my money, my deal." Sarah's gaze flickered over Milla, and she nodded, witch to witch.

"Milla, are you sure—"

"I need you to take inventory of the ICYMI in the garage." She threw her hand up, cutting Darkly off. "Sarah and I need to talk logistics."

He didn't argue, thank the Goddess, but the glower returned. Sarah waited until he was out of earshot, watching Milla scrawl a name, number, and address at the bottom of a shopping list. "Gonna be a long ride back to Florida with all those boxes in that hybrid you rolled up in."

"I think you and I both know we aren't heading back to Florida," Milla sighed.

Sarah's eyes widened, flicking to the hallway Darkly had skulked down and back to Milla. "You sure it's wise to take a witch like him down there?"

"C.R.O.W. has witches in the Crescent." Milla tore the bottom of the list free and pressed it into Sarah's hand. "He'll fit right in. Call this number and tell Diego what's going on. He'll manage the funds transfer and arrange for someone to pick up all of that ICYMI." For a fleeting instant, Sarah looked pained. Regretful. Milla swept the poppet from the counter, set it beside the butterfly dish, and gestured to the contents. "Rada Nation?"

Sarah nodded. "Loko."

"I was never very good with the Rada," Milla admitted. "Better with the Gede."

"I remember."

Milla snapped her eyes to the hedgewitch, thinking back through the fog of memory. Her heart echoed the beat of drums, and the whisper of a chant rose in her ears. "You were there?"

"She called me down from Picayune," the hedgewitch lowered her voice. "Summoned all us unaffiliated hedgewitches from 'round the Delta."

The panic Milla had managed to tamp down came roaring back, rushing the blood from her face and fingers. The drumbeat rose in tempo, fear lapping at the witch like water against the shore. "Will you tell her I was here?"

"The Madam has eyes and ears all over the Delta." Sarah nodded to the poppet. "You'd best be hittin' the road if you hope to get there before sundown. She'll be wantin' to speak with you."

"Yeah, no shit."

Dread tailed her down the driveway, stalking Milla like a predator in the woods. Darkly pressed a hand to her lower back when she stumbled over a crack in the concrete. "There's a hotel nearby," he murmured. "I called ahead and grabbed us a room."

"No!" she blurted, too sharp, too frightened, but how could she explain? Goddess, the walls were closing in. No, not walls. *Jaws.* An angry, gory maw of teeth. A trap Milla had walked right into, and now the Madam knew where she was, where she'd been. For two long years, Milla had avoided facing her failure, avoided facing *her*, and now she had no choice.

No way around it now, Millapet. Ezra appeared beside her, taunting Milla with amber-bright eyes sparking teal. *You'll have to explain. You'll have to take him with you. How will you manage, I wonder, when he knows what you are? What you did?*

Darkly's hand fell away, and it took Milla two steps to notice he'd fallen still, waiting for her to explain. She shouldered her fears, hiding them beneath a veil of sarcasm. "Knowing you, it'd turn into a one-bed-trope situation, and no offense, but I'd rather not."

"Nae sure how I'm not to take offense to that," he scoffed. "A few weeks back you couldnae wait to get into a hotel room with me."

"Goddess." She threw an arm in his direction, fingers splayed. "You really can't help yourself, can you?"

He folded his arms across his chest, staring at her in challenge. "Suppose I didnae want to."

Milla opened her mouth with every intention of yelling at the witch; of cutting him down and drawing a deep, impassable trench in the figurative sand between them, but the lie wouldn't form. The challenge ebbed from his face, his hard glare softening with something resembling hope, so Milla spoke the only truth she could. "You're my aural insurance adjuster."

His shoulders dropped. "Aye, that I am." He slid both hands into his pockets and brushed past her. "So if not a hotel, where to?"

Milla frowned and kicked the driveway. "New Orleans."

Darkly stared at her, his green-eyed gaze darkening with every passing second. "Of course."

Twenty Five

"You almost ready?"

Milla's reflection froze in the mirror, liquid liner held at the corner of her eye. Ezra stood over her shoulder, fiddling with the half-skull mask in his hand. A feline smile curled his lips in the way that made her stomach flutter. She straightened and pouted. "Just about."

"Took you long enough, Millapet." His grin widened, and he reached over her shoulder with a gloved hand, adjusting the fall of the glass vial worn on a chain around her neck.

Beads clacked and rustled when she spun, throwing her arms around his shoulders. She squealed with delight as Ezra buried his face against her neck, nipping at the patch of skin beneath her ear. Milla melted flush against him, reveling in his scent, his strength. Like bourbon and cedar, utterly intoxicating and wholly capable of driving her mad.

"We'd better hurry," he rumbled, low and wicked against her skin. "She hates when we're late."

"What's a few minutes when compared to eternity?" Milla ran her hands along the crushed velvet of his lapels, laying them flat against his chest. Hands at her waist, he pushed her away so they could take in each other's costumes.

As a son of the city, Ezra had dressed to honor his heritage by wearing most of a slim-cut suit with coat and tails. The trousers were a charcoal pinstripe that clung to the muscle of his thighs and made Milla's mouth water when he turned around, and the coat was a glorious piece of tailoring. An eighteenth-century style open-front frock with a high, black velvet stacked collar that brushed Ezra's jaw. It was cut from the deepest, richest purple cloth Milla had ever seen, and the wide tails billowed when he walked, lending the witch even more of a mysterious air. The open front allowed him to show off the muscled planes of his chest beneath a tailored emerald green vest. Gold thread bordered the cuffs, and the jacket and vest featured gold buttons cast as skulls.

Milla thrilled as he rolled a feather-and-bone warded top hat along his shoulders and into his hand. Ezra took a deep bow, sweeping his arms wide, then dropped to a knee, plopping the hat on his head at a jaunty angle and gesturing for her foot.

"You'll never get these laces done in that sinful corset." He winked at her, and Milla's breath caught in a way that had little to do with how tightly laced she was into her costume.

Being a daughter of Český-Krumlov, hers was an ode to the strzyga diviners that had earned their reputations in the halls of Aragon and Burgundy. A bustled skirt flared out from a gold and black striped corset in alternating deep green, brassed gold, and stygian black layers. Lace gloves ran the length of her forearms, the seam of the right covering her scar. Silk stockings the same purple as Ezra's coat clung to her legs, held in place by garters and revealed by the pin of her skirt. Her knee-high boots were an anachronistic touch with their comfortable stacked heel and an absurd amount of eyelets. Worth it for the way Ezra ran his hand up her calf and along her thigh.

She smacked it away.

"You keep doing that, and it won't be my fault we're late," she chided. Ezra gripped her leg, pulling Milla off balance, sliding his casting hand

under her skirt, and pulling her hips closer to his mouth. He nipped the inside of her thigh, chuckling when she wriggled in his grip.

"The sooner we go, the sooner we can come back here," he murmured, voice low and rumbling against her core. "The sooner I can unwrap this lovely birthday gift."

She shivered at the promise in those words, and Ezra pulled his hands away, rising slowly.

"Come along, Millapet. I want to show you off."

Mardi Gras was in full swing and the Quarter ribald with celebrations. Milla caught sight of the floats parading down Bourbon Street as they traversed the length of Dauphine hand-in-hand. Banners and beads hung from windows, and on every street, joyous cries of "Laissez les bon temps roulez!" sounded before more beads or plastic vials of alcohol rained down.

Ezra swept his hat off to a bevy of women on a balcony, appealing to them for tokens they happily threw. He screwed the cap off of a tossed vial, and Milla tilted her head back, drinking the spiced cinnamon rum and shaking her legs like a can-can dancer. Ezra broke into a brief Charleston after drinking his own, and the women howled with laughter, shaking their legs and asses, all in bold print matching leggings.

The city was alive, the earth heaving with energy, and the night's potential was staggering. Milla was thankful for the alcohol and Ezra's steady presence as he drew her deeper into the Quarter. She held his hand, perhaps a little too tightly, but he didn't seem to mind. Ezra had prepared her for this—for the cavalcade of life and death that filled the air, the heady intoxication that breathed from every bar and balcony. He had trained her well. He had made her strong.

Strong enough to do what was asked of her.

What they had planned.

They crossed Ursulines Avenue, and Ezra turned them onto Governor Nicholls, rattling off last-minute instructions.

"And you're certain you can run in that thing?"

"The front unclasps." Milla scratched her corset, fingers catching on the enclosures. "I practiced doing it one-handed."

"That's my girl. Now, remember, don't hold back; your Way is welcome here."

"I know."

"Do you?" He stopped in front of her, gripping Milla's fingers and kissing the knuckles. "Millapet, we don't have to hide among this crowd. You can be you without fear of repercussion."

"Ez," she laughed. "You've told me this a thousand times!" It would be a relief not to have to hide. To not have to stay three steps ahead of another witch, constantly trying to figure a way to spin her magick into something else. "I'm looking forward to it."

He beamed and kissed Milla's cheek. "Fix your mask; we must appear as a pair."

"Maman Brigitte and her Baron." Milla trilled in a poor French accent, adjusting her half-skull mask over her eyes. "How exciting." Ezra's eyes sparkled teal beneath his mask, and Milla blew him a kiss.

The LaLaurie Mansion loomed in the heady night, presiding over the corner of Royal Street and Governor Nicholls like a grande dame at the start of a season. Ezra led the way, marching into the carriage yard and alighting the steps as if he had done so a thousand times. Milla supposed that, being a son of the city, he likely had. The doors opened to reveal a party in full swing, spilling laughter, music, and the kaleidoscopic scent of magick out into the yard. Milla closed her eyes, inhaling deeply of the energy-saturated air, and let herself be led inside by the hand.

A tall, strawberry-blonde woman in a trim uniform greeted them with a tray of champagne, silvery eyes shining behind a nondescript black mask. Ezra grabbed two flutes, eyes lingering on the woman before tipping a glass against Milla's lips.

Black licorice and bubbles danced on her tongue, her head swam, and Ezra snatched another glass, placing this one in her hand as he sipped from his own. They wound through the mansion, their progress marked in her memory as a series of vignettes:

She brushed her hand against a bouquet of dead flowers presented by a woman with startling blue-green eyes, her face hidden behind a mask of the sun, and a man whose face was a blur. The flowers returned to the full bloom of life, followed by a polite smattering of applause. Ezra whispered in the woman's ear, and she shook her head, gesturing to the Blurred Man.

A brunette woman with her face covered by the moon burst into loud laughter at a touch from Ezra's finger against her brow. Beside her, a blonde woman dressed as the dawn smiled as though she held a scintillating secret all to herself.

A man in a crown and a crimson half-skeleton mask stood behind a woman in a blood-red domino. The man gripped the woman by the wrists, dancing her hands over a white-sided container on a table. Ezra drew Milla closer, laughing at the dead mice waltzing within.

More absinthe-capped champagne found its way into her hand, and a rum infused with fiery peppers was poured into her glass. They fed each other beignets, and Milla used her Way on a table of shrimp cocktails. The shellfish began writhing in their martini glasses, and the woman in the sun mask sang, "Daaaaaaay-oh!"

Flowers bloomed and withered beneath her hand, wood greened, and Shades were given a voice for a brief moment. It felt like coming alive, like discovering she could breathe underwater, and the potential was more intoxicating than the alcohol.

Ezra kept close, whispering encouraging words and holding her hand when she doubted, until at last they found themselves in the hall of the Voodoo Queen.

"This is her?" She spoke to Ezra, but her ageless eyes never left Milla. Poised and appraising, she filled the room with her presence while remaining perched upon her throne. "This is the girl you have chosen as your consort?"

"The Witch." Ezra bowed, voice bursting with pride. For Milla.

"She's white."

"So was your second husband," he replied with a snake-oil smile.

The Voodoo Queen pursed her lips, shallow eyes sparkling with laughter as she drank in all that was Milla. "And she can perform to our standards?"

"She can," Milla announced. "And what's more, she does so willingly."

Ezra's fingers trailed down her arm, tracing the twin to his own scar and drifting across the unbroken lines of her palm. Their fingers laced, he stood beside Milla and faced Madame Marie Laveau, the Voodoo Queen of New Orleans.

"Isn't she incredible?"

Marie cocked her head, eyes dancing between Ezra and Milla, and the corner of her impeccably made-up lips twitched in a smile.

"Indeed." Her hands moved so fast that Milla thought she must have blinked. A sharp clap sounded, and the hall fell silent. "The witching hour is upon us," Marie announced, rising from her throne to descend the stairs. She lowered her voice, speaking directly to Milla as she brushed by. "I hope you ate, girl; this is going to be one hell of a night."

They were caught up in a crowd buzzing with excitement. Ezra gripped her hand, tugging Milla into a short hallway. She opened her mouth to ask what he was doing, and then his tongue was on hers, the full length of him pressing Milla against the wall. His hands gripped her waist, her arms, fingers burrowing in her hair and tilting her head back so he might taste her more deeply. When he finally pulled away, she was breathless, breasts heaving in the corset as she tried to gather herself.

"You trust me, Milla?" he murmured against her mouth, kissing her again. This time, the sweep of his tongue was deep and probing, pouring heat into her belly.

Milla's head swam from the alcohol. From him. She arched into his touch, running her hands up his back and returning his kiss. Losing herself in him and him in her. When he pulled away again, Ezra ran a finger from her temple to her cheekbone and along the line of her jaw.

"You trust me?"

"I do," she breathed. Ezra glanced down the hallway, eyeing the steady stream of people leaving the mansion.

"Do you believe in me?"

"I do." Milla cocked her head, simmering bubbles of fear replacing the heat in her veins. "Ez?"

He looked back at her, a frown haunting his expression. "You're my favorite thing in this whole world, Millapet."

Skyscrapers and red-brick buildings bled together, fading into nothing and reforming as wrought iron balconies, pastel walls, and dark green shuttered windows. The French Quarter's architecture slid by her window, distorted from the rain beading on the glass. Darkly was silent; had been since the fourth failed attempt to get Milla to talk to him as they crossed Lake Pontchartrain. It wasn't intentional, and when she couldn't bear the angry, hurt glances any longer, she managed to mumble, "Migraine."

That pacified him, and Darkly let her mope.

"In five hundred meters, turn right onto Dauphine Street."

Milla grabbed her phone from the console and turned off the navigation.

"Reckon I might need that."

"Mm-mm," Milla shook her head. "She always gets the next turn wrong." Darkly chewed his cheek, glancing at Milla. He turned the car onto Dauphine, and Milla pointed at an alleyway to the right. "Turn there, after the newsstand."

"I'm impressed you could find a hotel with vacancy." Darkly tapped the blinker and slowed the car, waiting for a clutch of women in shorts, tank tops, and an egregious amount of beads to jog by. "And with two beds, no less."

Milla huffed a laugh, offering nothing by way of explanation. He would know the truth soon enough. She dropped her forehead against the window instead, enjoying the soothing cool of the glass. She felt fevered and sticky, but whether it was from the migraine or the result of being in this city again, she didn't know.

The alleyway was a narrow afterthought carved between buildings, a mere shadow of its past life as a former carriage lane. It widened into a modest yard, and Milla pointed at an empty parking spot. Darkly parked and pressed himself against the steering wheel, craning his neck to read the words painted on the wall. "Says we need a parking permit."

Milla dug in her backpack, withdrawing her wallet and handing over a narrow, neon pink strip. Darkly raised his brows but said nothing as he shoved the permit between the windshield and the dash.

Rain fell in heavy sheets, obscuring the notice on the wall as soon as the wipers were shut off. "If I wanted rain, I ne'er would've left Scotland." Darkly grumbled. He pulled an umbrella out of nowhere and opened it above the door as he stepped out. Milla tracked him in the mirror, disappearing into her blind spot and reappearing to open her door. "My sister loves the rain. Cannae fathom why."

The entrance to the building was hidden behind a double-shuttered door on Dauphine Street. She pressed a number into the keypad, flinching at the *kerthunk* of the automated deadbolt and pulling the shutter open to reveal a narrow hallway with a flight of stairs at the rear. If Darkly said anything, Milla didn't hear him. She was entirely focused on not losing herself to the memory of this place. To the last night spent here in Ezra's arms and the six months after.

"I never wanted to come back here," Milla muttered. She climbed the stairs and stalked along the narrow hallway. The key in her hand burned, edges biting into the flesh of her fingers. It slid into the lock as it always did, and the tumblers shuddered into place as if they had been freshly greased.

Someone had been by to empty the trashcan and remove perishable items from the refrigerator and cupboards, but everything else was the same. The throw pillows on the couch were disturbed from the last night she had slept there; the crocheted blanket still lay in a pile where she'd left it. The crime novel she had been reading was face down on the kitchen table beside a notebook and one of her favorite pens. Milla picked up the book and scanned the page, glancing over the binding at Darkly. "The movie was better."

Darkly put down the heart-shaped glasses he'd picked up from the table, eyeing a notepad with scrawled directions, a takeout menu, and a stack of junk mail addressed to one Mrs. Ludmilla Lightner.

One of the chairs was slightly pulled out as if the last person to sit there had just left, and a pair of men's running shoes had been kicked off under the table. Milla frowned at them, her gaze drawn down the hallway to where the edge of the bed was just visible.

She dropped her keys, missing the table entirely. Her backpack slid free, the damp moto-jacket followed, and then she was staring down at Ezra's suitcase, right where he'd left it on the trunk at the foot of the bed. The lid was opened, his clothing half-packed for a trip he would never take. Someone had made the bed, closed the curtains, and draped a purple scarf over the lampshade. A small stuffed doll, the sort used to teach little girls how to sew, sat beside the antique alarm clock on the bedside table, mismatched button eyes watching the witch.

A Shade lingered in the room, a remnant of tangled emotion. She could almost hear her gasps and Ezra's murmured adulations—whispers of how proud she made him, how she was his favorite thing in the whole world.

"The whole world," Milla murmured, and the bed fractured into three.

She staggered back, raising a hand to shield herself from the visions, but it was too late. These were memories, not Seeings, and memories lingered behind your eyelids.

On the right, they were making love. Ezra thrusting deep inside her as she cried his name to the Triple Goddess. In the middle, Milla was curled in a ball on her side, sobbing into her hands as Ezra trailed a finger from her temple to her cheekbone to her jaw. Tender, careful, concerned. And on the left was Milla clutching her shattered arm to her chest, still wearing that ludicrous costume. The half mask was gone, her hair tangled and knotted, and her makeup smeared in black and green streaks.

Blood stained her skin, and she screamed at the windows while red, white, and blue flashes of light distorted her features.

Milla forced her way out of the Soul and Shade of memory and emotion, bumping into someone tall and steady. Someone who smelled liked the finest incense and held her shoulders in a careful grip.

"Milla, what is this place?"

She turned and met Darkly's eyes for the first time in what felt like days. Movement behind him snagged her attention, and she watched as the shadows on the wall fanned out and curled at the edges like a wave rushing to consume their source. She forced herself to look away, to look at the bed. "This was a home."

Ezra was there, curled around Milla as she sobbed into her hands. "You're my favorite thing in this old world." He angled his face to smile at the two other witches in the room. "My Millapet."

Milla staggered away, nails digging into Darkly's arm and dragging him from the room.

"I need a drink."

TWENTY SIX

THE SUN DIPPED BELOW the horizon as they crossed the threshold of the oldest operating bar in the French Quarter. A colonial-style pitched-roofed, plaster-walled house turned blacksmith shop turned Bourbon Street favorite, Lafitte's held a Soul and a Shade all its own. But where so many structures in New Orleans held on to their ghosts, the terrible and the horrific or the painful and sad, Lafitte's held onto the laughter and meetings of friends compounded over its three hundred years of existence.

A great fireplace filled the wall behind the bar, and different kinds of bourbon, gin, and vodka were displayed on the stone mantelpiece. High-backed stools lined the L-shaped bar, and low-backed, inviting chairs in leather and velvet were placed in half circles around the main room. A barn door on the southern wall led to a side yard hosting wrought iron chairs, Biergarten tables, and televisions.

Milla stepped up onto a stool at the crook of the bar, hooking her heel on the rail of the one next to her and pushing it out for Darkly.

"Do you know what you want?" She raised her hand to the Mix Witch behind the bar, Jean, who had been tracking her from the moment she set foot on the front stoop.

"Something stiff," Darkly answered, "that preferably works quickly."

"That can be arranged." She faced Jean, addressing the witch directly and with intent. "Nos salutations à la Madam." The bartender nodded, waiting. "Et un sazerac et un vaudou, s'il vous plaît."

His dark eyes flitted over Milla and Darkly before he wandered away to make their drinks. Her stomach twisted with nerves. Were she the Milla of two years ago, the Milla who hadn't failed, she would have marched up to the doors of the Madam's home and demanded entry. But she wasn't, and she did, so she paid the tithe like any other witch—with a show of faith.

Darkly took in the bar and the bottles, toying with a napkin before facing Milla. "You speak French?"

"Only enough to order drinks, and only from Jean."

"Ah." He started to follow that up, biting his tongue as a clutch of tourists trickled through the front door and hurried to the side yard. Lafitte's had that effect on mortals, a built-in look-away hex that had only grown stronger over its many years. A witch could always find a seat at the bar, while mortals would find themselves compelled to scurry to the garden or hover near the chairs at the safe, warded corners of the building.

Jean returned with a Sazerac smelling sharply of black licorice and a purple slushie drink in glass cups rather than the plastic and styrofoam favored by French Quarter bars.

"Compliments de la Madame." With a wink at Milla, he snapped his fingers, and the candle on the bar flared to life. She and Darkly both sat up, inhaling deeply the nutty, floral scent of sweet cicely and primrose, with just a bite of fennel to tickle their noses. Her stomach twisted again, this time not unpleasantly, and she found herself glancing at Darkly who averted his gaze to pointedly study his purple slushie.

"Veuillez vous amuser," Jean hummed, wandering to the other end of the bar.

Music blared from the street, and a parade streamed by the open doors. The first line beat out a rapid tattoo before the horns joined in, joyous and celebrant. New Orleans Jazz was a magick of its own, the knowledge a tightly held secret among its practitioners. Darkly watched the parade, his green eyes sparkling at the music's rise and fall and the tuba's blasts.

While he was distracted, Milla slid from her stool, taking her Sazerac along to the restroom. Her head was fuzzy and belly warm when she returned, and the glass from her tumbler had sliced a small cut along her thumb; her tithe to the city paid. She wrapped her finger in a few squares of toilet paper, reminding herself to toss it into the fireplace before she left. Horned God knew the Madam already had enough over Milla.

Darkly watched her approach with a bittersweet twist to his mouth. She sent him a question in a glance, and his expression turned rueful. "Forbid a fool a thing, and that he will do."

"Pardon?"

Darkly raised the purple slushie to his lips. "Just thinking about the past."

"Oh?"

"Bonny lass at a bar, wayward witch just blown into town." He winked. *Winked.* And that was all it took for Milla to blush like an idiot.

"That's right, it was the first time you lied to me." Milla tried to keep her tone light, pretending she hadn't heard him call her bonny, which she thought meant pretty, which meant he thought of her at all.

"Me, lie? Never." He took a sip of his drink and promptly choked. Pressing the pad of his thumb over the straw, he withdrew it, moved his thumb, and watched the purple slush slog back into the cup with a look of amused disgust. "What is this, frozen petrol?"

"House specialty," Milla laughed. "Jean calls it a Voodoo." Darkly immediately took another deep slurp, and her eyes wandered to Jean at the end of the bar. The Mix Witch wasn't even trying to hide that he was eavesdropping, not that Milla could blame him. Darkly reeked of C.R.O.W., and Milla was, well, Milla and her glass was gone. "Grape juice, bourbon, vodka, and a little Mix Witch magick." She wiggled her fingers over his drink and Darkly yanked it out of her reach.

"Well, I did ask for something strong that would work fast."

Milla smiled, her lips drawn tight. She propped her elbows on the table. "I know you have questions."

"I do." Darkly conceded, staring at the bottles lining the mantelpiece.

Milla waited, surprised to find that she wanted to talk. About the apartment, Ezra, New Orleans. So much so that it hurt when he kept silent. Moments passed, he drank his slushie, and Jean slid a fresh Sazerac in front of Milla. A Mix Witch always knew what you needed, only this time he got part of it wrong. Milla pushed the glass across the bar with her toilet paper-wrapped thumb. "In a go-cup, please."

He nodded, approving, and dumped the cocktail into a short plastic cup. They had made their offering and performed the requisite show of faith to the city's keepers. Whatever game Jean played in giving her glass, Milla could only guess. A warning, maybe? He was a witch at the end of the day, and witches tended to look out for their own. But Jean was also very, very old.

Darkly didn't speak until his Voodoo was finished, and a go-cup of Royal Navy rum sat before him. "Now that I've taken the edge off, I am gonnae ask you a question and would truly appreciate the truth."

"Alright?"

"What is your name?"

"My name?" She leaned away from the witch. "Why does my name matter?"

"Pretend, for a moment, that it matters quite a bit." He dipped his chin. "To me."

Her body tensed at the insinuation behind those words. She clenched her jaw and ground out, "Ludmilla Saxana Probuditna Lightner. Legally."

"Legally?"

"As far as the mortals are concerned, yes." She chewed her lip, sober enough to notice the ache from the raw-head had lessened. Magick tingled in her fingers and her palms, and she was just drunk enough not to care. "Does C.R.O.W. not …?"

"Nae." He shook his head. "Your file is missing a lot of key details. When did you two …" he circled his hand in the air, "you know."

"Four years ago." She broke away from his stare and took a sip of her Sazerac. "Almost to the day. We were starting to make plans and thought it prudent to arrange life insurance policies."

"Ezra didnae leave you destitute." Darkly leaned away, understanding.

"That he did not." Milla sighed. "It took a year to receive anything. I was under observation by the police and the insurance company for the first six months, then shuttled out to

Český-Krumlov when I was no longer a person of interest. When the payout came, I bought a one-way ticket to St. Augustine and opened my store."

Darkly studied the fireplace, his throat bobbing. The low dancing flames turned his eyes an opaline gold, and Milla allowed herself the pleasure of looking at him. Darkly deep in thought, clever eyes darting as he thought through a problem. Absent the sunglasses and the lazy smile, absent the mask of a self-assured aural insurance adjuster, he really was handsome, and that was the problem.

The candle burned between them, its buoyant flame twisting, bobbing, and curling, sending up a single plume of smoke that tickled her nose and made her want to scoot her stool just that much closer to his.

"We never bound ourselves before the Triple Goddess," she said, unprompted. Darkly blinked, still staring at the fireplace, so she continued. "Maybe we would have, had he not … but we didn't, and I've come to be grateful for that. I loved him, then, and I know he loved me, but Ezra wasn't-he didn't …" She pursed her lips, trying to find the words. "It wasn't the healthiest relationship. In the end, we wanted different things out of life. I wasn't willing to go with him where he wanted to go."

"And where did he go?"

"Somewhere dark," Milla murmured the truth into her cup. "Beyond the shadows where he can't be reached."

Darkly sat up at that, drinking down his rum and coughing.

"You alright?"

"Brilliant," he wheezed. "Feel like telling me about the apartment?"

"Not remotely." She smiled at him. His face was hard, determined, but something like mirth flickered the green in his eyes to black and back. "It was Ezra's. Well, his family's, as I understand it. A Lightner has lived there for longer than I could gather from the deed." She took a drink. "I suppose it's mine now.

"That would explain why you have the keys." Darkly sent her a fleeting smile, blinked, and then blurted, "It was a mistake, ye ken."

She sat up, facing him again. "What was?"

"That day at the bar." Surprise flickered over his face as if his words had caught him off guard. "Didnae ken who you were. Truthfully, didnae even know a woman had been sitting there. Only saw an empty stool next to a half-drunk pint. Thought it was a bloke's, if I'm being honest." He pulled a fist to his mouth, coughing. "I was excited, jet-lagged; it was my first night in America. I was gonnae get pleasantly drunk and watch the sun set behind the palm trees."

"Sounds lovely," Milla smiled. "Did you?"

"Eventually." He ducked his chin, cheeks flushing, and a wavy auburn curl brushed his forehead. "Did you know the green here is different?" He didn't pause long enough for her to answer; just kept rolling through his thoughts as if he'd been stumbling over them for a while, only now able to give them a voice. "Aye, the Highlands are green; moss and kelly and forest. But here you've honeydew and tea and palm and brilliant fern. There are brightly painted houses, and everyone is tanned, wearing pinks and purples, blues and bright whites. Nary a stitch of cable knit on a body. I spent an hour walking the Colonial Quarter, taking pictures and sending them to my sister." Milla propped her chin in her hand, enjoying this rambling and verbose Darkly. "Your demesne is lovely, Milla. There's an aura, a Soul and Shade bound to the place." He smiled at her, a true smile that crinkled his eyes before it turned sad. "And then there's you."

"There's me?"

"Sunshine, palm trees, and a feisty little witch in sharp relief." He spun his cup, staring at the tornado the motion made of the dregs. "Felt like I'd died and gone to heaven." Darkly's voice was an awed whisper, sending a chill up Milla's arms. She leaned closer, nudging his shoulder with hers, and Milla could have sworn the shadows drew close and deepened his eyes to black. "Shouldnae have asked your name." He shook his head. "Almost didnae, almost let that be a bit of fun in an alley, and then you—" Darkly dropped his head, shaking it slowly. "You made the loveliest little sound, and I wanted to know your name."

"Oh," she gasped. Soft and low.

"Aye, that's the one." Darkly crowded her with his broad shoulders. The corner of his mouth curled wickedly, and he fractured into three.

Oh, Horned God. She startled back, eyes dancing from one Darkly to the next. She wasn't expecting it, hadn't felt any warning signs. If she had, she would have tried to stave it off. No good ever came of those images that split and multiplied before her. Seeing had gotten her in Ezra's bed, and Seeing was the reason he was Gone.

She ought to close her eyes and look away. Wait this out until the three Darklys settled into one, and yet … all three were staring at her with a hungry, pained expression. As though the witch was holding himself back, afraid of reaching out. She remembered his palm, logic ruled by will, and the bow of a heart line that spoke of someone wanting affection but afraid to ask for it.

And here were three Darklys wanting Milla, with absinthe on her tongue and a head full of candlesmoke, waiting for her to accept the invitation he couldn't put a voice to, and *Goddess,* hadn't been asking in his way? With each odd session and run and with his hand on her knee, and now she was Seeing him with her fractured Way, an artifact of magick passed down by her mother: three Darklys, three potentials to explore. Milla didn't know which was more unnerving: the identical nature of the triplicate Seeing or that she knew immediately which potential she wanted to explore.

The middle Darkly knew. He spread his lips in a wicked, blade-sharp grin that curled her toes. A dark magick calling to a kindred spirit. The left and right Darklys kept silent, their hungry stares fixed on her face, green eyes swirling with smoke. The middle one leaned closer, toying with a strand of her hair and giving it a sharp tug before tucking it behind her ear.

"Please," Left-hand Darkly entreated, offering his hand.

And she took it.

TWENTY SEVEN

MILLA HALF FORGOT WHY they had come to New Orleans by the time they left the second bar. The French Quarter smelled of licorice and the sweetly spiced incense of the witch holding her hand, beckoning them deeper into her streets. What did she care about tights and mortal women when she felt giddy in a way she hadn't in years? Light and free, her laughter came easily, bubbling out of her belly at the most inane things. She wouldn't say she was drunk, because no self-respecting witch would ever admit to being drunk, but neither was this the fatuous giggling of a non-bourbon-addled brain.

The part of her mind that Ezra had trained, the part she kept behind iron-clad walls where no one could reach, flagged the behavior as Other. It raised a minor alarm, prodding Milla and asking her to *stop! Think for a minute.* She would, noting then the ever-present stench of spilled alcohol and bodily fluids on Bourbon Street, recoiling from the sugary drink she held, and then—

A match was struck, a candle lit.

Sweetly scented smoke tickled her nose, and a new drink found its way to her hand. The first taste blossomed as nutmeg and clove, overriding Reason and Logic with the inimitable strength of Want and Desire.

Darkly paused every so often, blinking out of the haze with smoke drifting in his eyes. Then he found Milla, and his smile bloomed, and they were on their way. Happily ambling through the gridded streets of the Quarter spinning quietly into a labyrinth for two.

They got better as Milla and Darkly kept on. Milla knew it was a They and had thought herself prepared for Them, but no one ever was. New Orleans was their city, their playground, and They manipulated every aspect of the demesne at the behest of Her. Milla could almost feel the strings of the compulsion, almost grab hold of the intent in their spell, but then They would change their tactics. Swapping a hex for a potion, a potion for an urge, an urge for a whisper and then it was too late.

The sugary drinks became bourbon or beer as They remembered her tastes; conversation came easy and free, and no amount of warning from the alarmed part of her could stop Milla now.

That was how good They were. They knew her, knew what she had done, and knew who she had sacrificed in the doing.

A match was struck, a candle lit, and Darkly reached across a green table, swiping his thumb against her sugar-dusted lip and popping it into his mouth. Milla ordered chicory coffee in a vain attempt to break free, but *They* ran Cafe du Monde, and the coffee tasted of spice, and it was too late. So she stole their napkins, spilled water on the table, and stashed their used cups in her bag or tore them to shreds and flushed them down the toilet. She tried to keep track, but They were good and Darkly had his arm around her shoulders, and Milla was only one witch.

Cardamom tingled on her tongue even when she had no drink, and Milla wondered if Darkly would taste of the spice if they kissed. From how his gaze dropped to her mouth, she was almost certain he was wondering the same. So she pulled him through the Colonnade and into the French Market and made him eat fried alligator, dipping the pieces in garlic-heavy remoulade and popping them into his mouth. He hated them, but he liked her and liked her fingers near his mouth, so he allowed it, and then they were on the patio of Pat O'Briens.

Darkly slouched in his seat, a foot propped on the edge of Milla's chair and a long leg stretched out beside her, boxing her in and keeping her right where he wanted her, which was near him. He had summoned a black coin to hand, dancing it over his knuckles with his eyes closed and a lazy, infuriating smile on his face that made him look like a lizard on a rock. Happy, content, and woefully out of control of the situation.

Milla idly trailed her fingers along his calf, sipping her Hurricane and trying to figure out a way to destroy the plastic cup. She knew she looked just as stupid-happy drunk as he did, with her lazy smile and heart-shaped sunglasses. She was well aware of that piece of her mind yelling at her to go back to the apartment and perform a cleansing ritual, but she didn't care, so she ignored it.

A waitress wound through the wrought iron tables, strawberry blonde hair piled high atop her head. She dropped a candle on their table and withdrew a book of matches from her apron. Darkly opened his eyes and, without a word, flipped the candle upside down.

"It's dark out," she tried to explain, but Darkly shook his head and stared at her until she wandered away.

"What was that about?" Milla cocked her head.

"The candles're givin' me a headache," he slurred. "Gettin' hard to keep my thoughts straight."

"I think I know what you mean." She moved her hand from his leg, but he nudged his foot against her thigh.

"Dinnae," he murmured.

"Dinnae?"

"Dinnae stop." He dropped his head back. "S'nice." Milla chuckled, resuming trailing her fingers along his shin and calf, tracing idle circles and half-thought allures onto the fabric of his pants. "Thought Mardi Gras would be busier."

"Not for the last few years." She shook her head, happy when the patio didn't blur. The garlic in the remoulade was helping. She would need to get them pizza or a po-boy, something to clear the fog from their heads. She should probably warn Darkly, but that part of her brain hadn't quite re-awakened yet. Milla felt a twinge of guilt at the realization that maybe she didn't want it to. Maybe she could have this. Have him. Maybe They were doing her a favor, which she knew was a lie the moment the thought gathered form, only to fritter away when Darkly hooked his foot around the leg of her chair, pulling her closer.

"Mm." Darkly took a long draw from the straw in his cup. Smacking his lips, he eyed the ruby-red cocktail. "The terrorist attack at the lake probably didnae help."

He didn't look at her when he said it, but Milla felt the blame, the accusation. C.R.O.W. knew like *They* knew, and They were still upset with her.

"No," she whispered.

"You were here, aye? With Lightner?"

"Yes." Milla pulled her hand away, lacing her fingers in her lap. She had wondered when he would ask; wondered when he would piece the dates together. She had hoped it wouldn't be under the influence of alcohol and candlesmoke, but Milla's luck had never been that good.

"Had to be terrifying." He dropped his foot to the ground, sitting up in the chair. "The attack, and then Ezra—"

A match was struck, and the waitress returned, hovering three umbrellas away. For a heartbeat, Milla thought this was it, Their summons, but she only lit the candle in her hand, set it at the edge of the table, and walked away. Anise drifted their way on a faint breeze. Darkly scrunched his nose and looked to the source of the scent, a frown pulling the corners of his mouth down. Milla waved a hand before her face and tried not to breathe.

"What are we doing?" He asked, eyes fixed on the candle.

"I don't know," Milla replied, a little sad that he had asked. A little mad at herself that she was even sad. Darkly dragged his gaze to meet hers, and they stared at each other, breaths ragged and uneven. Smoke drifted in his eyes, and Milla glimpsed a shadow of the Dark Darkly that had been teased time and time again. The one with a magick that called to her own, stirring the energy in her veins to urge her closer, to connect.

He felt it; he must have because his hand was on her knee. The weight of his palm sent a thrill up her leg and into her hips as they leaned toward each other. The safe, aware part of her hammered against its walls, telling Milla to stop, leave, run to the apartment, burn the contents of her backpack, and scour her skin of Their effect. The rest of her mind was focused on his irises gone dark and the press of his palm against her leg. How he slid his hand up her thigh and the fact her apartment had a bed and shower big enough for two.

Darkly halted a hand-span from Milla, forcing out a thought and sparing them both. "Quid pro quo?"

"You want to play games?" She exhaled, her words low and breathy. "Now? "

He wetted his lips, pulling that plush lower lip through his teeth. "I find it best to seek answers when one's tongue is loosened by alcohol."

Goddess, he wasn't looking away. Milla needed him to look away if she was going to maintain control of the situation. "My tongue isn't that loose," she replied, and, Horned God damn him, he smirked.

"I'd be interested in testing that theory." He winked. *Winked.* Jarring her enough to lean back and only then did the witch notice the circle of candles surrounding them.

Shit.

They had been busy while Milla was distracted. She reached for her drink, not wanting to forget her cup.

It was gone.

Double shit.

Darkly was saying something and she spun around to see him thank the waitress and place his cup on her tray. Milla blinked, her mind still catching up to the utter disaster she had led them into, and then the waitress was gone.

"Triple shit." Milla grabbed him by the wrist, hauling his inebriated lank upright. "We need to go."

"Go where?"

"Anywhere," she gritted through her teeth, dragging him through the maze of chairs and murmuring apologies when her overstuffed backpack nudged a tourist in the back of the head. The cups, plates, and napkins within crinkled, and Milla cursed herself. She'd been so careful, keeping track of or destroying everything they touched and anything they had drunk from, keeping Darkly *safe* only to stop paying attention at the wrong time. They had already paid their tithe, a formality not even the Madam would abuse, but now she had their cups with their spit and fingerprints. Milla needed to get them *out* before the Madam used what was now rightfully hers.

She ran through the hallway separating the courtyard from Bourbon Street, spinning in place as she tried to pull a mental map of the French Quarter into her inebriated mind. Toulouse was to the left, St. Peter to the right, which meant Jackson Square was at her back and—"Oh, Goddess."

They were in the heart of New Orleans with heads full of candlesmoke, and Ezra's not-ghost was leaning against a lamppost, his Shade as much a part of the French Quarter as Milla's was not.

Think, Millapet.

Step One: they needed to get out of the French Quarter. Get some food in their bellies.

Step Two:

Milla tripped over her feet, blushing at thoughts of Step Two.

Step Two involved far less clothing, and they definitely needed garlic-full food before they even attempted a scouring ritual on each other. Something told her Darkly knew what she was thinking and where her mind had wandered because he wrapped his arms around her waist, pulling Milla back against him. His hand splayed across her stomach, rough callouses scraping along her midriff, and her heart skittered as a dangerous warmth pooled beneath his touch.

"What're we doing, Milla?" His accent rolled and roiled in her ear, shivering down her spine. She wriggled around, her chest pressed against him, and for all the world, they looked like any other drunken, amorous couple. A decent disguise, she realized.

One look at Darkly's face told her this was no feint, and she had to admit she went a little weak-kneed at the intent in his gaze.

"We need beads," she managed.

Darkly chuckled. "Odd place to start, but I'm game if—"

"Loose strands," Milla sputtered, gaping at him. "And we need to leave the Quarter."

"To go where, Milla?" He entreated. "Tell me."

"I'm trying to," she whimpered. His fingers were kneading her back, his scent cloying and intoxicating, and someone lit a match nearby. Movement in a shop door turned both of their heads, and Milla scoffed in disbelief when she read the sign. Dropping her face to Darkly's chest, she curled her fingers in the fabric of his shirt, inhaling deeply of him and the damn incense drifting out of Marie Laveau's House of Voodoo.

"We are so fucked," she laugh-sobbed.

"Why do I know that name?" Darkly asked, mystified. His chest rose and fell against her cheek in a deep bellows, and Milla panicked.

"Don't breathe, Darkly." She slammed her hand over his mouth and nose, drawing him away from the store and the cloud of candlesmoke that enveloped them. She felt him smile against her palm. Saw the gleam in eyes gone black. He placed his hand over hers, pressing her palm to his lips and kissing her scars with such tenderness that Milla almost lost her composure on the corner of Bourbon Street and St. Ann. It took every wit remaining in that safe corner of her mind to grind out, "Keep your shit together, Simmons."

She positioned them over a sewer grate, gagging at the stench, and slid a hand in his pocket to steal his phone. Her thoughts were wandering, distracting, just like Darkly's hands. He must have gotten a full lungful of the candlesmoke and kept trying to pull her into the shadows and hold her close. She grabbed his hand, giving in to the urge to place a finger to her lips, to nip the pad, and then press it on his phone.

"Beads," Darkly mumbled, pulling her into a souvenir shop. He grabbed beads by the handful while Milla ignored a series of unread messages and opened the OverAuto app. She shoved away the stab of guilt at what she'd been doing for the last few hours. Apologies could come later if they made it out of the Quarter.

Beads clacked around their necks and wrists as they tumbled inside the black sedan, and Darkly barked an address at the driver. Milla recognized the name: another bar, a safe bar. A dark, quiet place clear across the city. As far as one could get from the French Quarter without leaving New Orleans.

She wondered how he knew it, how he knew they wouldn't be allowed to leave the Quarter without a destination firm in mind.

"Oh, Goddess, I cannae…" He hunched over his legs, muttering to his knees. "She gonnae kill me, cannae believe we were so daft…"

"I'm sorry." Her heart was pounding, her skin buzzing with how deep in the spider's web of the Quarter they had spiraled. "There was no other way. Can't really go knocking on the front door in the middle of the day." A mad giggle escaped as a laugh, threatening to become a sob. "It's not like anyone will answer!" She tipped her head against the glass, only to have Darkly grab her by the hand and pull her close. "I'm sorry."

"Nae, Milla, that wasnae your fault."

"It was," she rasped, "it really, truly was." The weight of his arm around her shoulders was reassuring, and Milla let herself enjoy their closeness. For just a moment. They crossed Canal Street, and the grip of compulsion lessened. Both witches exhaled long, smoke-tainted breaths. Milla's vision unclouded, and with a light head, she leaned into Darkly, took a Big Girl Breath, and said, "I didn't think they would bring you into it."

"Into what?"

"My punishment."

"I need to know, Milla." Darkly tensed, his fingernails lightly grazed her arm. "C.R.O.W. is gonnae ask why we're here, and I need to know."

"Darkly—"

"Quid pro quo?"

Her breath caught, but she nodded. The witch had been so patient, so *kind*. Humoring her wild ideas and weak theories, driving her ten hours across the panhandle only for Milla to get them caught in candlesmoke. She dropped her head, resolving to answer him honestly, no matter the question. Her Way, the ritual on Lake Pontchartrain, where Ezra had gone … she owed the witch that much. "Okay."

"What was your plan back there?"

"That is one hundred percent not the question I thought you were going to ask." She massaged her temples, the beads on her arms rattling. "I needed to make it known that I was here. They don't answer the phone, and before you ask, I have tried. Multiple times. They demand tribute, an act of faith, and then They come to you when They are ready."

"And you decided a pub crawl was the best way to gain Their attention?"

"I decided going right to Jean and having him tell Them I was here was the best way to gain Their attention," she explained. "We drank from glassware, we willingly gave up our spit and our skin, and I destroyed the rest." She nudged the backpack at her feet, paper, plastic, and styrofoam crinkling. "Or kept it out of their hands."

Darkly made a noise in his throat. "So the pub crawl was an attempt to get me pleasantly drunk enough to make a potentially poor decision?"

"The pub crawl was an effect of the candles and the compulsion on our drinks," Milla grumbled. "I really should have been more prepared for that." Darkly chuckled, and his previous question struck a different chord. "A poor decision?"

"Potentially." She could hear the grin, and the OverAuto driver chuckled. "That came out wrong."

"No, no, that's fair." Milla returned his phone. "You have messages. Fiona?"

"Aye." Darkly nodded, staring at the screen, his brows dropped low in thought, and then he slid the phone into a pocket. "Trust me when I say she is the last person I want to talk to right now." Milla didn't say anything. What was there to say? She stared at a point on the back of the driver's headrest, wondering when Darkly would push her away. If anything, he held her closer. "Gonnae ask me a question?"

Later, she would blame the alcohol for what she asked him, but right then, with the weight of his arm around her and his spiced incense overwhelming the candlesmoke stink of the Quarter, she asked, "Am I really a poor decision?"

"A misguided one." His lips pressed against the back of her head. "A dangerous one. A decision that I could find myself completely lost in." She frowned. "But not a poor one."

"I think I'm alright with that."

The scrape of a matchhead had both witches jerking their attention to the driver. Clove and cardamom filled the car, paired with a new, wheaty scent that Milla hadn't noticed in the candlesmoke. Their driver puffed on a cigarillo and rolled the car to a stop. Flashing technicolor lights from a Christmas wreath illuminated his profile in alternating greens, blues, and reds.

"Snake and Jake's, madame et monsieur." The driver tapped his steering wheel, dragging on the cigarillo and blowing smoke out of his nose like a bloodthirsty dragon. He grinned out of the corner of his mouth, exhaling a cloud of purple smoke into the backseat. Milla caught the flash of a pointed incisor and yelped, scrabbling for the handle. "The Madame invites you to wait. Bonne nuit."

"Bonne nuit," Milla hissed, all but rolling out of the car. Darkly coughed, waving a hand cloaked in shadow to dispel the smoke. "Darkly, come on."

"I need—" Darkly didn't move, and she held her breath, diving back in to grab his arm and yanking on the witch. He looked panicked, glancing between her and the vampire, his eyes swirling midnight black. "Milla, I need to—"

"Get out of the car, Darkly. Now." She tugged with all her strength, but the idiot didn't move. Cigarillo smoke filled the car, and Milla, head clear enough for survival instincts to kick in, knew a ritual censer when she smelled it—a ritual for *what*, however, was the question.

She put all of her strength and a little bit of fingernail into dragging Darkly from the car. They tumbled out together, Milla tripping backward over her feet and the curb. Darkly stumbled upright and grabbed her around the waist, holding her tight against him. The driver laughed, blowing one last stream of tinted smoke out of his window and flooring the gas, tires squealing as the car pulled away.

"Fanger stole my bag!" Milla spat, lurching to run after the car, but Darkly kept his hold.

"Beginning to think this city doesn't like witches," he grumbled, eyes fixed on Milla, who was throwing a vulgar gesture at the rapidly vanishing OverAuto.

"What was your first hint?" She looked up at him, startled at the blown-out pupils. "Goddess, are you alright?"

"Yeah." He seemed to realize how tightly he was holding her and let go, stepping away and running a hand through his hair as he gazed up at the Christmas wreath and the blinking lights hung over the bar door. A smile twitched at the dented and warped tin roof and the faded beer ad decorating a hasty addition to the building, taking it from shotgun shack to jaunty lean-to. "Please tell me this place is warded?"

"By some of the best." Milla grabbed his hand and led him into the last safe bastion in New Orleans.

Twenty Eight

THEY PAUSED AT THE threshold, letting their eyes adjust to the dim interior. Lit only by strands of colored Christmas lights, Snake and Jake's was a crush of bodies and an assortment of mismatched chairs and couches. The bar itself was a Cub Scout grade construction of plywood, corrugated steel, and two-by-fours, and, as at Lafitte's, a witch could always find a seat. Ezra had brought her here years earlier, on Milla's first visit to New Orleans.

"This is a warded space, safe from the Madam and safe from C.R.O.W." He'd led her to the bar, just as she did with Darkly now. "Staid, witch, and desecrant alike can drink here without fear."

She sat them at the far end of the bar, not speaking, not even looking at one another, which was fine by Milla. Her head throbbed from the vampire's cigarillo smoke, and she unwound the messy buns, shaking out her hair and massaging her skull as she tried to suss out Their plan.

Because Their plan would have been *Her* plan.

The clove and the licorice, which she was fairly certain had been Sweet Cicely and *not* anise in the candles and her Sazerac, were herbs of attraction, often infused into wine and cider as an aphrodisiac, which was weird enough on its own before she added the wheat-y, cereal burn of the vampire's cigarillo to her mental recipe. Wheat was commonly used in fertility rituals and potions, a thought which made Milla slightly nauseous. Was their plan to get her pregnant? If so, *HornedGodwhy,* when they could have pursued that route years ago?

No, she decided. It was too unsubtle. Too crass for the vampires to attempt. Similar nastiness had lost witches their foothold in New Orleans in the first place, setting the stage for the vampires to swoop in. Considering the individuals involved, she doubted that she would be anywhere near their first choice if they were to attempt such a thing.

There were less cantankerous witches they could choose.

Like, literally any other witch.

So if not wheat, then sweet grass … or straw? One was used to call to the spirits, whereas the other was for the induction of magick. Rye was another attractant but for fidelity and self-control.

A glance at Darkly, who was intently watching the television behind the bar and wandering a hand up her thigh, told Milla self-control was absolutely out of the cards for him. Judging by how she adjusted her seat, allowing him better access to her leg, neither was it a concern for her.

Still, the lingering scent was maddening, and warning prickled behind her eyes. She rubbed her nose, thinking thinking thinking through her herblore. She had to consider the Quarter, her past in New Orleans, and the witch sitting beside her. The witch whose Way she didn't know. The witch with smoke dancing in his eyes and a shadow with a mind of its own.

"Amaranth," Milla muttered, an idea twitching at the back of her mind like a lost childhood memory. A fairy tale about the witches who had brought about the Inquisition. A lost Way that no longer existed. She dismissed it, her Way tickling in annoyance, and puzzled over the ritual censer.

No. Not a ritual censer. A summoning censer.

She sat up straight, scalp tingling. Sweet Cicely was British myrrh, which her mother burned as incense when conducting seances. It was used to attract the dearly departed. Pair that with cloves to comfort the bereaved, amaranth to summon spirits … *Oh, Goddess. No.*

There was only one person the Madam would want her to contact, and he wasn't dead; he was Gone.

"What'd you say?" Darkly drummed fingers on her thigh as the bartender placed two pints of Schlitz and two shots of Jagermeister in front of them.

"Nothing." Milla gestured to their drinks, happy for the distraction. "What in the nine rings is this?"

"Had a friend who loved this place." Darkly grinned, the one with the dimples, and slid a beer closer to Milla. "He told me to get here if I ever found myself in New Orleans."

"And he told you, Tiki Drink Darkly, to order beer and Jagermeister?"

"He also told me to order two dozen oysters and feed them to a beautiful woman, but you don't eat meat."

"Well," Milla huffed, a little more breathless than she would have liked. She didn't complain after that or balk at the modest challenge she was presented. After the Quarter and having her bag stolen, she needed a stiff drink or four without the cloying, lingering musk of nutmeg.

"It's showtime." Darkly took up his drinks, clinked glasses with Milla, dropped his shot in the beer, and chugged. She didn't have the time to be surprised before he was gagging and coughing, pounding a fist against his chest as his eyes watered. "Pure gie'in' me the boak."

"The fuck does *that* mean?"

Darkly coughed into his fist and looked expectantly at her. "Well?"

"*L'Chaim.*" She raised her glass, dropped the shot, and knocked it back with about ninety percent less drama than the over-tall witch had managed.

Two drinks later, they were still shoulder to shoulder, sipping whiskey and rum in contented silence. Darkly watched the denizens of the Christmas bar while his fingers kept finding her arm, her leg—a series of rapid-fire brief touches as if he were making up for lost time.

In a way, she supposed he was. A line had been crossed, a line she had led him across by the hand. She regretted it took candlesmoke and cocktails to get her there, but now that they were, Milla didn't want to step back across. Her head swam pleasantly from the beer and liqueur, the whiskey was a decent twelve year, and she edged closer to him on her stool.

"You got a faceful of candlesmoke," she said after a time. "Are you feeling better?"

"Oh, I'm wrecked," he sent her a rueful smirk, "but my head's cleared from the worst of it." His little finger traced the back of her hand, a tentative request easily ignored if it was a step too far. She rolled her wrist, revealing the scarred palm of her left hand, and could have sworn Darkly sighed at the invitation. He trailed a finger down her palm, reading the ruin of her head and heart.

Of her life. Toying with the beads wrapped around her wrist, he asked, "How are you faring?"

"Passing fair," she replied.

He laced his fingers through hers and nodded at her whiskey. "Dinnae ken how anyone drinks that shite."

"It's an acquired taste," Milla laughed at him. "Like a certain witch I know."

He dropped his glass on the bar and tapped her nose with a finger. "No accounting for taste, is there?"

"Did you just boop my nose?" Milla stared at him, bewildered.

"And I'll do it again, hen." He reached out, and Milla tore her hand free, covering her nose and leaning away. Darkly chuckled, a warm, tender sound usually reserved for puppies or bunnies, which was moderately offensive. She was a witch, after all. "Your file says you inherited your mother's vesticism, though the term they use is … 'fractured'?" Milla nodded, uncertain where he was going with this non sequitur. "Is that what you did to get us out of the Quarter?"

"Not exactly," she exhaled, relief dropping her shoulders. "No. That was pure improvisation."

"Then what do they mean by 'fractured'?"

"I see, mm, not the future but … potentials in anything with a pulse. I'm nowhere near as good as my mother. Couldn't get a read on a napkin or an article of clothing to save my life, but a person? They'll fracture when I look at them; that's why C.R.O.W. uses that term, and I'm presented with possibilities. Potentials. Ez had been teaching me to control what I Saw, how to avoid enacting a potentiality on accident."

"Enacting?"

"When I was little, I made a game of it—birthdays, Samhain, on a trip to the store. I'd let my vision fracture on purpose and choose the one I liked the best. Got a lot of ice cream and toys that way."

"You don't divine the future," Darkly straightened on his stool, understanding dawning. "You see the threads of fate." He gave a low whistle, bright eyes burning orange in the Christmas lights. "No wonder a vestic earned a place as Witch of the Demesne. I imagine that would be more of a burden than a boon." Surprise shivered through Milla. Most witches were awed when they learned of her fractured Seeing; he only seemed … sad. At her silence, he shrugged lightly. "Ken a thing or two about an unusual Way. I imagine most witches would see yours as an opportunity."

"One of the many reasons my dad sent me to train with Morgen. He wanted me to learn to protect myself from being taken advantage of."

"And the chrono-hex?" He glanced askance at her.

"The what?"

"The chrono-hex you used on the raw-head."

The blood rushed from Milla's cheeks, shock widening her eyes. Horned God, this witch was clever. Get her talking about the Way C.R.O.W. knew, lull her into a sense of security, and call out her lie when trapped in a corner. "I—"

"Ne'er mind." He shook his head sharply. "Dinnae fancy any answer that puts a look like that on your face." He frowned, chewing on his lip for a moment. "Have you Seen me?"

"Twice."

"When?"

"In Hattiesburg, briefly," Milla whispered. "And again at Lafitte's. The first time you were looking at me." She waved her hand in front of her face, fingers splayed. "Angry and sad, and your face was nothing but shadow." He coughed into a fist, staring at her over his knuckles. "And the second time, you held out your hand."

"All of me?"

Please.

"The left-hand Darkly." Her eyes fell to his left hand. The one that was constantly dancing and twitching. The one that summoned cards and coins and sunglasses. "Your casting hand." She met his intent stare, dark smoke swirling over green bottle-glass eyes. "You said please."

"Magic words." A match was struck, a candle lit. Clove and amaranth wafted from behind the bar and Darkly kissed her.

A brief brush, little more than a question before he withdrew to look her in the eyes. Enough for her to see the smoke wafting in front of the green, and then his hands leaped to the side of her face—tender and tentative. Milla had the fleeting thought that he wanted to hold her there, hold her still, but any walls she had built between herself and the witch crumbled to ash at that first feather-soft, fleeting brush of his lips.

Milla didn't give him time to doubt, closing the subtle distance to answer his question. Where their first kiss had been two strangers colliding for a minute, a moment, this was something more. This was weeks of pent-up frustration. Weeks of dancing around what was so blatantly obvious to everyone around them. This was the hours of getting to know the witch, arguing her demesne and finding that he understood. On some unknown, vestigial level, he *understood.*

Mouth to mouth, teeth to teeth, bones to bones. Lean fingers tunneled through her thick, black waves, angling Milla's head to kiss her more deeply. His scent filled her head: spice and smoke and the decadent incense she wanted to burn for days on end. He curled his hand into a fist and tugged, drawing the sweetest gasp of pleasured pain.

"There's that wee sound." His voice was a deep growl, raising goosebumps down her spine. He thrust his tongue deeper, groaning into Milla's mouth when she arched against him, and then she was off the stool, her back against a wall, and his hands at her hips, holding her to him with the threat that he would never let go.

Any remaining hesitation was drawn into the night the moment Milla's ass hit the leather seats of a car, which someone must have called. Was it her? No, the vampire had stolen her bag, her phone. Why was she even thinking about her phone?

The driver turned up the radio, punching in the address Milla managed to gasp out, and then Darkly's mouth was on hers, their bodies rolling with every turn.

He had her pressed in the crook between the seat and the door, the seatbelt digging into her back as his fingers dug into her thighs. The veil of the French Quarter parted, welcoming Milla and her witch into the heart of the demesne. Had she been in her right mind and not utterly focused on the brush of Darkly's fingers down her throat and the tease of his thumb across her breast, she might have paused. Might have looked at the passing buildings and noted the darkened windows and empty streets. Might have noticed Them watching and thought about what she was doing and with whom and where.

But what did Milla care when Darkly was whispering her name against her lips and moaning into her mouth when she cupped his groin?

The driver cleared his throat, tapping a sign taped to the back of his headrest that read, "This is a Pants Mandatory OverAuto."

Darkly tipped his forehead to Milla's and they laughed at each other, the driver, the world that had thrown them together. He drew Milla into his lap and sent an appropriately chagrined nod of apology to the driver as he wrapped his arms around her waist. The innocence and sweetness in the gesture threatened to melt her into a useless puddle. She placed her hand on his cheek, stubble tickling the scars on her palm, and kissed the tip of his nose.

"Boop," Milla whispered. He tightened his arms, and she grinned, thinking she'd won the upper hand. And *then* his hand slid between her legs, and Milla knew she was lost.

Somehow, they tumbled from the car. Somehow, she got them in the hallway to retrieve the extra key she had hidden years before. Darkly caught her wrist on the stairs, spinning Milla around and dragging her to him. His hands cupped her ass, her legs were around his waist, and her tongue was in his mouth. He carried her to the landing and pressed her against the wall, crushing her with his weight.

"So much wasted time," Darkly murmured, fingers digging into the meat of her thighs, asking her to unhook her ankles and slide down. She did, reveling in the press of their bodies and the swell of him against her thighs, her stomach.

"Not wasted." She kissed his chest, rising on tiptoes to press her lips against his jaw as she cupped his length.

Darkly groaned, bracing himself against the wall with a hand fisted above her head, pressing into her caress. "Ask me in?"

It was a plea, strained and soft. Milla recognized it for what it was: the permission he was asking for. A door slammed somewhere in the building, a matchhead scraped to life, and Darkly wound his fingers in her hair, tilting Milla's head back. "Please?"

"No," she gasped. He jerked against her, body going as taut as a bowstring. Milla ran her palm along the length of him again, enjoying how he shuddered at her touch. "No asking, telling." She scanned the waiting shadows and looked up into his eyes. "I want you."

"Thank the Horned God." Darkly hoisted her into his arms and wrapped her legs around his waist, striding into the apartment and kicking the door closed. He powered down the hall, pulling the flannel from her shoulders and drowning the not-ghost in his shadows until it was only Milla and Darkly in the dark.

Her back hit the bed, and he crawled over her. Teeth grazed her ear and her neck. Clever fingers tugged at her tanktop, pulling it over her head and giving Milla half a moment to breathe before he devoured her mouth, working her legs apart with a knee. Settling between her thighs, Darkly thrust his hips, grinding against her in salacious promise.

A thrill warbled through her core, and Milla groaned. Hooking her heels behind his thighs, she drew Darkly onto her, wanting the weight of him pressing her into the sheets. He dragged his teeth along her lower lip, and a bright flash of pain had her gasping, eyes flying wide. Then he pulled the cup of her bra away, tongue flicking her nipple and replacing the pain with a curdling wave of pleasure. Lips sucking, tongue teasing, teeth biting again and again and again. Pain and pleasure muddling together in endless waves of sensation.

She could live in that moment, she decided, in that space between the bitter and the sweet.

Tugging at his shirt, she drew it over his back, scaling her nails along the muscle. He writhed at her touch, ticklish, which only made her do it again and again until he grew annoyed.

Pulling away, Darkly ripped his shirt over his head with a snarl, buttons flying. He eyed her like the predator she suspected he was, sighting the flush of her cheeks, her swollen lips, and how she arched her back at his touch when he trailed a finger over the swell of her breast, teasing her nipple.

He placed that finger on her lips, holding utterly still.

Another request.

A question she was all too willing to answer.

Milla kissed the tip of his finger, parting her lips to take it into her mouth and down to the knuckle while holding his smoky-eyed stare. He hissed, hips rolling at what she was telling him with the sweep of her tongue, a grazing of teeth, and gentle sucking as she lowered her head against the bed.

Darkly's green eyes drank in the ragged rise and fall of her chest, reveling in the effect of his touch as he trailed that finger across her collarbones, swooping the hollow of her throat. A wicked smile curled his lips, and Milla whimpered at the sight of that subtle darkness.

"Dinnae move." He leaned close enough to kiss her. "You move, and I stop." His breath crashed over her lips, eyes flashing when she gasped at the utter command in his voice. "Understood?" Milla only lifted her chin, giving him access to what she didn't know, but a wicked part of her thrilled at his quiet hum of approval. He ran his thumb along her jaw, fingers teasing the nape of her neck.

The next kiss was a butterfly brush of his lips as his free hand undid the button of her jeans and tugged at the zipper. The softest pressure teased, a there-and-gone-again touch where she needed him most. Milla whimpered, raising her hips to his hand, and his kiss deepened, that wicked finger continuing down, down, down the center of her body until she was trembling from the searing pinpoint of his touch.

With both hands, Darkly ripped her jeans away, letting them catch at her knees. She wriggled one leg free as he toyed with the band of her underwear, and he went still. "Dinnae move," he murmured, eyes flitting to Milla's face and back to her underwear, an eyebrow raised at the black cotton briefs dotted with pentagrams. Hooking his finger in the band, Darkly mused, "A little on the nose, int it, no?" and slid them away.

He didn't give her a chance to answer.

Turning his hand, Darkly cupped her for a brief second before dragging his finger through her folds, threatening to shatter her to pieces. He lingered his touch at her clit, circling the bud until her breaths came in quick, frantic bursts. She clutched the comforter and writhed her hips, wanting that wicked, clever finger deeper, harder.

"Milla, Milla," he sighed, tormenting her with the sweep of his finger, his words, and his breath hot against her breasts. "Always running." His voice was low and rumbling against her breastbone. "Always just out of reach."

Teeth grazed a nipple, and she whimpered. Every fiber of her wanted more: more touch, more teasing, more *him*. He saw it in her halted breaths, the faint tremble of her arms. Her only warning was a flash of teeth before Darkly plunged that cruel finger inside of her, earning half a groan before withdrawing. He used her arousal to taunt Milla more and more and more, circling her clit until magick tingled to life in her veins. It called out to him, wanting to be spent and *needing* to be spent on him.

She reached for Darkly, wanting to draw the witch into her to quell that rising burn, and he plunged his finger again, holding painfully still. His lips brushed against hers in the tease of a kiss. "I already warned you, Ludmilla."

"Please," she panted, trying not to buck her hips and utterly failing. Darkly chuckled against her skin, flesh pebbling as he grazed her nipple with his teeth, sweeping it with his tongue and finally crooking that Horned God *damned* finger. And again. And again. A squeak escaped, and Milla fought to remain still.

His lips trailed her ribs and waist, and that fiendish finger slid away. She reached for him again, a greedy, selfish thing, and Darkly grabbed her wrist, setting it against the mattress and caging it in one hand as he gripped her thigh with the other. "It took me weeks to get you here, Milla," he all but snarled. "Don't. Move."

"Controlling little wi—ah!" He nipped her inner thigh and licked the crease where her leg met her hips, flicking that smoke-stained gaze to her face.

"*Now watch me,*" he ordered in a resonant *voice* full of demand.

Milla obeyed, helpless against whatever intent he'd stoked in those words. The moment she met his eyes, that wicked tongue was on her, in her, driving between her legs and drawing a deep, breathy moan. Lizard lazy strokes delved and savored the taste of her as if he had all the time in the world. The hand at her wrist slid away, and Milla gasped, arching like a bridge when that damnable finger found its home.

"Horned God," she managed, release building and driving her magick to dangerous heights she didn't think she could control. It coiled tight in her belly and her core, writhing and wriggling as a living thing until she thought she would explode from the sheer ecstasy of expectation.

He slid a second finger in and Milla panted his name, driving her hips against him and watching him work her into a frenzy. Shadows drowned out the light until there was only the black-eyed witch between her legs, his hands, his mouth, and his magick calling to hers.

A match was struck, a candle lit.

Milla thought she saw the stuffed doll on her bedside table move out of the corner of her eye, and Darkly hauled her leg over his shoulder. He yanked her closer, tongue laving against her as he cupped her breast, rolling the bud between his fingers and wringing his name from her lips.

"Goddess, Darkly."

His fingers crooked, brushing the place they had been working towards. Again, again, again, deeper and harder. Pushing her higher and higher until her skin was too small to contain the sensation. Milla thrust her hands into his hair, holding him between her legs as she screamed his name.

Her hips left the bed, and she tumbled in a freefall as release powered through her. Ecstasy reached to the tips of her toes, and rolled her eyes back in her skull. It was all she could do not to send her Way careening out into the world, so she held onto something alive to keep them both sane.

Her vision threatened to fracture as he looked up at her, withdrawing his fingers and cupping her knee with a hand. His tongue lapped at her in long, lazy strokes until she unleashed a quivering whimper, and he pulled away.

"God," Darkly bit his lower lip, tasting the remnants of Milla. He sighed and, in a chowder thick, Eastern Seaboard accent, said, "You taste even better than he dreamed you would."

Twenty Nine

Darkly blinked, the black eyes flicking to green, and the shadows in the room vanished. She scurried back like a crab, hitting the edge of the bed and falling in a mostly naked heap. Scrabbling at the hardwood, Milla yanked her underwear up shaking legs as the remnants of ecstasy sharpened to fright. Her right hand formed a ward of protection, magick pooled in her palm, and before she could think better of it, she raised it between them.

"Milla?" Darkly knelt on the bed, reaching for her. He sounded and looked terrified. So much so that she almost lowered her hand. "Milla, please, I—"

"*Nehýbejte se.*"

Don't move.

She flicked her fingers, hitting Darkly with a halting hex and buying time to scamper down the hallway. She had one leg in her jeans and her back to the front door when he came stumbling down the hall, struggling to button his pants over a fading erection. Flickering light from the gas lamps on Dauphine Street crept through the windows, casting him in a ghostly pallor, and a sigil flashed on his chest, a whirling triskelion gleaming bioluminescent against his skin. She pooled more magick in her palm and thrust her hand out.

"Milla, wait!"

"*Nehýbejte se!*" She hexed him again; extra intent spun into her casting. Crouching with her foot half in the leg of her jeans, she waited with a hand outstretched. When he didn't move or speak, she hissed, "Who are you?"

A vein in Darkly's neck bulged. Milla pinched between her eyes, muttering, "*Můžete mluvit.*"

You can talk.

"It's me, I'm me. Darkly. Darkly Simmons," he rushed out in the proper accent as if trying to convince himself. "It's me now, Milla. Would you please just let me—" The faintest brush at her ankle had her screeching. Intent on watching the obvious threat in the room, Milla hadn't noticed the shadows pooling at his feet and reaching across the floor.

She scrabbled at the door handle, yanking it open while kicking a socked foot at the coiling shadows now pawing at her knees. "You're a witch!"

"Obviously!" Darkly snapped back. He dispelled her halting hex, showing Milla with the splaying of the fingers on his left hand just how strong of a witch he was. "Is that the best you could come up with?"

Milla ran, bare feet skidding on the hardwood. She caught herself against the banister, gripping it tight and spinning onto the stairs. Her feet hardly touched the steps, and it was a miracle she didn't fall. Blood rushing in her ears and heart threatening to burst from her chest, she slammed into the shuttered door, yanking the deadbolt free and charging onto a street beside time.

Raindrops hung in the air like fairy lights, catching the flicker of gas lamps and fracturing the light into prisms, distorting the

French Quarter into a scene from Milla's worst nightmares. Her ragged breath and the deafening thud of her heart were the only living sounds as time ceased, save for Milla and the woman in a yellow silk tignon.

"Ludmilla," the Madam's voice was rich and resonant, her accent cutting through the humid air. "Have you brought me a gift?"

No. Nononono.

She pooled energy in her palms, ready to damn herself and use her Way. Would it even work against Them? Ezra had never answered that question, and now he was Gone, and it was Milla's fault.

"What do you want from me?"

"What I am owed," the Madam replied. The shallow pools of her eyes settled over Milla's shoulder. She whirled around, a sob escaping as Darkly staggered onto the street in only his pants and one sock.

"Milla?" He froze, green eyes tracking Milla, assuring himself she was alright before sliding his gaze over her head. Stumbling back a step, he knocked a curtain of raindrops aside and formed a banishing ward with his fingers.

Horned God, he looked so afraid, so lost, and it was killing her a little.

"Darkly, get inside."

He locked his gaze to hers, reaching out with his non-warded hand. Beads rattled on his wrist as he crooked his fingers, beckoning her near.

"No." Milla shook her head, letting the magick fizzle in her palms.

"Milla, please," he begged, the shadows on the walls surging for the witch.

"Et quel cadeau il est," the Madam trilled.

Darkly hollered something, his voice crashing into Milla like a Celtic wind. He lunged, arms drafting up from his sides like a swimmer breaking free from the water, and drew a pitch-black wall of shadow in their rise.

"Darkly, no!" She threw herself in the path of his magick as he thrust his arms forward, palms out. The wall of shadow slammed into Milla, knocking her back and enveloping her in a sea of stygian black. She spun, shadow-blind, and her head exploded in a red flash of pain.

Her lip throbbed. Milla clung to the ache like a drowning woman clings to driftwood. Pain was good. Pain was real. Pain meant she hadn't been drained dry and forced into an immortal life of servitude to a woman who hated her.

Because, honestly, that would suck.

Heh.

Fabric rustled, followed by the quiet *tink* of a glass being set down. Milla opened one eye, then the other, and immediately wished she'd remained unconscious.

The last time she stood in this hall, Ezra had been at her side—a steadying presence, so confident and sure. Now, absent the heat and sweat of a party in full swing, there was only Milla, bound to a—she wriggled in her chair, rattling the legs and flexing her arms to test the bindings. Wood creaked, gold brocade winked, and the smell of ancient upholstery had her sneezing.

"Baroque?" Milla raised an eyebrow at the Voodoo Queen, perched on a dais at the far end of the room. "Really?"

Marie smiled at her from a nineteenth-century European throne hewn from ash and hawthorne and imbued with wards for protection and wisdom. A witch's throne adorned with bones and feathers dangling from the finials and boasting armrests wide enough to hold a belled hurricane glass.

"I won it in an online auction after a fierce bidding war," Marie trilled. "I was, unfortunately, outbid on the Hapsburg Rococo I desired." She cocked her head to the side, tapping a manicured fingernail against her plush lower lip. "Though, as I understand, that delicious piece of furniture now resides in … St. Augustine, is it?"

Milla straightened, her blood cooling by an uneasy degree. Marie closed her eyes, nostrils flaring as the smile on her lips widened into something feral, showing the stiletto point of incisors and the modest gap between two front teeth. "The smell of fear suits you, Ludmilla."

"I'm not afraid of you, Marie." Milla wriggled against her bonds again, trying to gather magick, only for her palms to itch and go cold. She tried again, gasping as her head spun from the effort. "Ague root?" she gritted out, tremoring her head to dispel the vertigo.

"And willow," Marie affirmed, eyes flicking to something over Milla's head. She craned her neck, trying to set eyes on whatever Marie was looking at, but all she saw was the glow of stage lights in the far corner of the grand hall. "Not taking any chances with you slithering away again."

"I'm flattered?"

Marie tipped her head back and laughed. A throaty, seductive outburst that had Milla leaning forward in the chair against the better judgment of everything but her basest animal nature. A curl of dark hair escaped Marie's pale yellow tignon, coiling beside the delicate crow's feet at the corner of her eye. "Your impropriety, as always, is a treat to endure. To what do I owe the honor of this visit to my demesne?"

"Oh, you know," Milla shrugged, willow biting into her wrists. She pressed her toes against the floor, rocking the chair back on two legs as far as she could, hoping it looked nonchalant and nothing at all like an attempt to tilt it over and, ideally, fracture the four-hundred-year-old wood. "Thought I'd stop by. Show my friend around."

Unable to gain leverage, she dropped her heels and jerked forward. Marie winced as the chair legs screeched against the marble floor. Milla did it again, and Marie snarled. The chair was too heavy to keep this up, and she was too tightly bound, but the vampire was annoyed, and a win was a win. Milla glanced around in an exaggerated arc, unable to put eyes on the room's rear. "Don't suppose you've seen him? Tall guy. Talks too much."

Again, Marie's attention flicked over her head. Milla didn't bother trying to follow the shallow gaze; she had a pretty solid guess at this point and could only hope Darkly was bound as she was and nothing else.

"Yes, your *friend*." Marie rose from her throne, graceful and fluid as a cat. She descended the dais, amulets, and bangles tinkling and rustling against the black velvet of her wrap dress. "Are you certain, little Ludmilla, that he is nothing more? A new partner? A schemer like you? A lover?" She gripped the finial above Milla's head, leaning close and inhaling deeply. Milla bit her tongue, but the heat in her cheeks told Marie everything. The vampire lowered her voice, bringing her lips to Milla's ear. "What would Ezra think?"

She jerked in the chair, snapping her teeth at Marie. The Voodoo Queen laughed, flashing her fangs and spinning away with arms outstretched. Laughter peeled from the walls, cackling and fizzing in cruel mockery that only made Milla redden further.

"You've given us quite a bit of entertainment, Ludmilla. Clever of you to keep track of your cups, but you forgot …" A flick of her finger had Milla's backpack plopping out of thin air, clunking beside the Voodoo Queen's throne. "I am New Orleans, and I am not bound within the confines of the Quarter."

Milla glared at her bag, thinking thinking thinking, and trying not to freak out. "Why not take your pound of flesh and be done with me?"

Marie's smile faltered. "Who said this was about you?"

Well.

Milla had no witty retort to that, so for once in her life, she stayed quiet.

"Two witches up to trouble in my demesne. Tell me, *belle-fille*, was the need to fulfill the yearnings of the flesh dire enough to risk breaking C.R.O.W. protocol?"

"We didn't do anything." Milla jerked the chair again, gaining another inch. "I only came here to talk. With you."

Marie's upper body went statue still, her velvet skirt spilling to the marble floor like a waterfall of ink pooling at her feet. "Do you not"—she cocked her head and crooked a finger—"have a phone?"

On cue came the loud *slap* of plastic colliding with marble. Milla groaned, watching her phone hit the corner of a dais step before clattering on its back, the screen a spider web of cracks. She dropped her head against the backrest. "I had almost paid that off."

Marie twisted her wrist and glided to the dais steps—up the dais steps—alighting her throne in a smooth, unsettling motion.

Something tugged at Milla's ankle, and she flinched, straining against her bindings to see what fresh horror had been unleashed by that twist of the vampire's wrist. The tugging doubled in its urgency, and the feel of cotton balls being rubbed together ran up her leg. Her breaths shortened to panicked bursts, and she let out an indecorous "eep" when the misshapen head of a doll popped over her knee and clambered up her thigh.

Identical to the poppet in the Sanderson home, rough linen stumps stitched with mortician's thread clung to her shirt, tangling in the leather thong of her necklace and scratching her against her breastbone. A second doll climbed into her lap, and Milla shrieked, jerking wildly and upsetting the chair.

Even she had her limits, and two horrid little button-eyed poppets climbing her legs just happened to be it.

The dolls clung to her chest and leg, their crudely stuffed and stitched bodies rustling as the chair rocked back, hanging for a moment in precarious balance before crashing down onto all four feet. The doll clinging to her front scrambled onto her shoulder. Milla let out another brief squawk of terror as the stench of a mausoleum accosted her senses. Clamping stump hands to its cheeks and straining against the stitching of its lips, the doll opened its mouth as wide as it could, screaming at Milla with a sound like velcro being torn apart.

"Hornedgodhornedgodhornedgod," Milla chanted, wriggling where she sat as a third stitched horror began ascending her legs. The awful little dreadful in her face jabbered like buttons rattled in a jar and shook its head, laughing at her. She clenched her teeth, trying not to cry when the doll stroked its scratchy stump hand down the side of her face, from temple to cheekbone to jaw.

A tear fell. She couldn't stop it; the touch was so intimate, so cruel.

Crude stitching caught her sorrow, and the voodoo doll leaped from her shoulder, running on uneven legs as her bindings fell away.

"Ewewewew." Milla jumped to her feet, wiping away the feel of the horrid little things. Her scalp pinched, and a sound like a sack of wet cloth hitting the ground had Milla spinning around to find Darkly in the furthest corner of the hall beneath what looked like three sound stages' worth of lights.

He sagged forward as far as he could, held upright in a chair by binds of willow looping his mouth, neck, arms, and ankles in thirteen coils. Bright purple hedge nettle petals were scattered at his feet, on his shoulders, and dumped unceremoniously on his head, and the shadows quivered beneath his seat, unable or unwilling to bleed beyond the safety of his person.

Every thought of Voodoo dolls and vampires bled from Milla's head. There was no thinking, no stopping to assess the why behind her bindings being removed when two decades of hand-to-hex training with the Morgenhexe kicked in.

Which, in retrospect, was not wise.

She lurched for Darkly, and Marie clapped her hands.

Milla slammed against a wall, bouncing back and sprawling ass over teakettle, head hitting the marble and nose throbbing. The vampires laughed again, and Milla had to admit, yeah, that probably looked pretty funny.

She groaned, pushing into a sitting position. The third doll had come along for the ride and was perched on her lap, stumpy hands clutching the sides of its head. Milla daubed the heel of her palm against her nose to see if she was bleeding before scooping the doll into her hand and clambering to her feet, toeing the empty floor in front of her.

Now that she was standing, one glance at her surroundings told Milla all she needed to know: the center of the hall was a circular panel of bulletproof glass set over a circle of salt inlaid with barrier sigils and wards.

Unbreakable.

She let out a little cry, and Darkly looked up, eyes widening as he spotted Milla. He struggled against the willow, causing it to tighten around his neck, and the voodoo doll clutched its throat, making a sound like rasping tulle. Milla glared at the thing in her palm and whirled her rage on Marie. "What did you do to him?"

One of the dolls on her armrest held three strands of dark hair between its stumpy hands as the Voodoo Queen wound them around her finger. "To the Dark Witch?"

Milla startled back. "The *what* witch?"

"The Dark Witch." Marie favored Darkly with a doting smile. "Such a lovely gift, Ludmilla. It almost makes up for everything you've done. Almost."

"He isn't for you."

Marie plucked the hurricane glass from the table and took a long, indulgent slurp of thick red liquid. Milla gagged, pressing the back of her hand to her mouth.

"Oh, calm yourself. It's pig's blood." Marie swirled her drink. "We've moved on beyond Hollywood stereotypes. I own every meat packing plant and pig yard in the Delta."

Milla shuddered, looking back to Darkly. Even bound and slightly strangled, he was still a more pleasant sight than a Voodoo Vampire Queen slurping blood in a cocktail glass.

His eyes, wide and green and terrified, were pinned on Milla, and he shook his head. A tiny, fleeting movement as if trying to tell her not to believe anything. Her gaze fell to his quivering shadows, and she remembered the feel of those silken brushes against her legs. Remembered the *leshy's* riddle of an accusation and how shadows followed the witch wherever he went.

Dark Witch.

They weren't real. Every little witchling knew that. Dark Witches were the things of fairy tales and bedtime stories. They, along with Death Witches, had caused the Inquisition and been all but eradicated by the Tribunal during a three-hundred and fifty-year literal witch hunt. Dark Witches didn't work for C.R.O.W.

Dark Witches *didn't exist.*

But then again, neither did witches like Milla.

Mortician's thread and burlap scratched and scraped as the poppet shimmied up to her shoulder. Milla tensed, afraid Marie would take her anger out on someone she cared about if any harm befell the little dreadful.

Even if he were a deceitful liar with a tongue as wicked as he was.

"Jean notified me immediately," Marie announced when she felt Milla had had enough time to be shocked at the grand reveal. "We had planned to grab you there, but then you went and performed a Seeing right in Lafitte's." Marie *tsked* and shook her head. The dolls on her armrest waved a stumpy hand each at Milla. "You are not a witch wanted in New Orleans, Ludmilla. Your Ways are not welcomed here, not anymore. You had to have known an unsanctioned Seeing would spark the wrong sort of interest."

"I don't—" Milla swallowed, her throat raw. "It was an accident."

"And the summoning?"

Milla shut her mouth, fighting the urge to look back at Darkly. She couldn't recall the witch summoning anything while they were in the Quarter, and Milla couldn't summon *things* at all. But there was that moment, that hideous instant when her skin burned in ecstasy and the shadows in the room had swelled…

"A Dark Witch in the heart of my demesne." Marie leveled her gaze at Milla, judgment and approval mingling together. "Is he a gift, *ma cherie*? A means of making amends?"

"He's my aural insurance adjuster," Milla mumbled.

The vampires exploded in laughter again, and Marie wiped a not-tear from the corner of her eye. "So quick-witted." When Milla didn't snap back, Marie sat forward. "Oh, you're serious?" Her attention switched to Darkly, and she cocked her head in a manner that Milla disliked. Greatly.

"Eyes on the prize, Laveau."

Marie narrowed the gaze of an apex predator on a witch bound in salt. She ran the finger wrapped in Milla's hair across her lips in warning. "Oh, believe me, they are." She rose and did the creepy glide thing down the stairs, drifting to a halt at the edge of Milla's cage. "A Dark Witch, the perfect vessel, and you with your particular Way. Do you know what you both can do?" She whispered, curious. "Together?"

Milla pinched her lips, imagining they were sewn with mortician's thread like the doll on her shoulder.

"No," Marie pouted, shaking her head and gliding around the circle's edge. "No, I do not believe that you do. A pity neither of you is fully adept. Had I any idea what a specimen you had brought me, we would have been more aggressive with our tactics."

Tactics.

A summoning.

"It was amaranth!" Milla blurted as a piece clicked into place. "Clove to gain what is sought, sweet cicely for contact, amaranth to summon and—" Her eyes flicked to Marie's, full understanding sinking her stomach with dread. "Horned God."

"Yesss," Marie hissed, a cruel, sharp-edged smile peeling back her lips. Goddess, it had never been about her, she had been a tool, she had only ever been a tool. For Ezra and Marie and every witch that had filled this hall on that Horned God-damned night.

She pressed fists against the side of her head, willing the memories and the guilt away long enough to escape the hall of the Voodoo Queen. Marie tittered from her left, far too close. Milla jerked her face to the vampire, and the doll on her shoulder shoved its stumpy hand down her throat, sweeping the rough linen appendage and slicing the roof of Milla's mouth with splinters of mortician's thread. She gagged, grabbing the wriggling horror and tearing it away. The doll hit the floor with a wet-laundry *squelch,* and Milla hunched over, stomach heaving at the taste of rot and decay on her tongue. She spat a gob of blood-tainted saliva into her hand and cursed.

Marie Laveau, the Voodoo Queen, had her spit, blood, hair, and sorrow, and Milla was fucked.

"This is so fucked," she hissed.

Darkly's metal chair screeched, his yells muffled by willow until a wet thud silenced them, followed by a groan. Milla stared down the Voodoo Queen and called death into her eyes. It would be a near thing. Though her bindings were removed, the circle was a void of magick, the Ways all but closed. This would take everything that Milla was, forcing her to cross a line she had only ever tiptoed, and worse—Darkly would see. He would *know.* Milla could only hope saving him from a vampire's den would persuade him not to tell C.R.O.W.

She took a breath, intent ashen on the tip of her tongue. "He's not for you."

Marie ripped Milla's hair from her finger, running it along the saliva and blood on the doll's stump and slapping it against her throat.

"Speak." Marie rose from her throne.

"Get fucked," Milla spoke.

Marie rolled her eyes. "My time, as unbelievable as it may sound, is limited." She pointed at Milla, twirling her finger in the air between them. "Speak," she repeated, voice resonating through the marrow of Milla's bones and tingling along her teeth and tongue. "Why are you here."

Not a question because the Voodoo Queen was a demanding mistress.

Milla spoke, unable to hold her tongue, unable to craft a lie, unable to ignore how Marie's face paled further at what she said.

She spoke of Kayleigh and the bad reviews. Of Darkly's arrival, her *čarodějnice*, and Julie. The leggings and the glamour, the dead and dying women, and the Sanderson family. Marie absorbed it all, her haughty demeanor shifting to thoughtful. Milla finished with, "My *čarodějnice's* first *polednice* was a technomantic from your demesne. Tracy Johnson. She was testing a theory with Broad Cast, and I think—"

"It is not a technomantic," Marie interrupted, "and I can assure you Tracy is not at fault."

"How do you know?" Milla pressed.

"Because Tracy is dead," Marie stated, going preternaturally still. Not a twitch, not a quirk of the lips. The hall became a sepulcher while Milla stood before the Vampire Queen of New Orleans, her mind running at a million miles a minute. If not a technomantic stoking a ritual, if *not* Tracy, what sort of creature could feed off of the energy of its downline? What sort of magick would demand a cost as high as that the women had paid? She glanced around the hall at the bodies clinging to the corners and alcoves and the Voodoo Queen on her throne. "Horned God, it's not a new type of vampire, is it?"

Marie's eyebrows raised, and the compulsion to speak vanished with a flick of her finger. "Pray, do elaborate."

"An, um, energy vampire?"

The hall exploded in laughter, rattling blown glass windows and bouncing around the ceiling, coalescing as a spotlight on Milla.

Marie wiped a not-tear away and leveled her gaze on Milla. "Oh, you were serious?" The vampires laughed again, and Milla plopped down in the Baroque chair, arms crossed. Marie waved her hand in dismissal. "Those only exist in cable television shows. I should know, they filmed it in one of my Garden District homes."

"So there's no such—"

"Never has been. Never will be. There is only one sort of Vampire in this world: we are born mortal, we excel in our mortal life, and we receive an invitation to the Grander Scheme." Marie spread her arms, and the vampires lining the walls echoed, "The Grander Scheme."

"Is that necessary?" Milla said to the walls.

The walls hissed.

Marie rose, gliding down the steps. She swept a manicured hand through the air, and the press of the binding circle crashed down. Milla slumped in the chair, dizzy from the rush of magick to her person, and the vampire was on her in a whisper, bending low to leer in Milla's face.

"The Gede and Rada who remain loyal have eyes and ears far beyond my bend of the Mississippi. They whisper secrets as I slumber." Milla risked a nod to show she understood the implication, the threat, and the aid in those words. The Gede and the Rada were two of the voodoo nations of Loa. Beings Milla had zero desire to treat with.

Not anymore.

"Things long kept from this world slipped through when you failed," Marie continued. "One of them has grown enterprising. Tracy Johnson had been gathering reports of women being admitted for exhaustion across the Delta; she followed those rumors to Hattiesburg, suspecting those incidents were related to *your* failure."

"How did she die?"

Marie flitted her shallow-eyed gaze over Milla; all mirth and mockery vanished. "An attack in Hattiesburg. She was admitted to Ursulines"—the Voodoo Queen named the convent-turned-magickal hospital—"and snuck down to Des Allemands, where she was killed. One of my colony recovered her belongings and the body." She ran a fingernail along Milla's arm, stilling at the crook of her elbow. "Her notes echo your story." Marie's knife-sharp nail pressed into the apex of Milla's scar, digging into the flesh until a ruby-red droplet of blood appeared. "You summoned a Shade in my city."

"I didn't—"

"You conducted a felonious Seeing in *my* demesne. You, Ludmilla Probuditna, apprentice of Ezra Lightner, a Son of this City, you who were recently raised to *polednice* of C.R.O.W., who shields her aura so that none may see the Foule thing she truly is." The nail twisted, and Milla hissed, blinking to stave off tears. "I should report you to C.A.R.B. and use your downfall to raise myself into their better graces."

"I can't give you what you want." A tear fell from the corner of Milla's eye, one of pain rather than sorrow. Infinitely more powerful. Marie tracked its progress down her cheek, shallow eyes gleaming. "I can't bring him back, not like that." The tear dangled from Milla's chin. The witch and the vampire held their breath, and then it fell to be absorbed by her jeans. "He's Gone."

"Nevertheless," Marie's voice was low. Deadly. "Your failure brought this curse into our world, Ludmilla Probuditna, and I am owed twice over. End what plagues your demesne and mine. Clear the Delta of the rot you have introduced. Do that, and I shall do my best to forget what you are and what you have done. For now."

The power of her words coiled around Milla's lungs, stunting her breath. Pleased with her new toy, Marie splayed an open palm to the corner of the room where Darkly was held. A knife rasped through willow, and six feet and change of witch crumpled to the floor, drawing in a ragged breath.

Marie ripped her nail away, flicking Milla's blood from her fingers. Red splattered across her chest and neck, and she had had just about enough of this abuse. She jumped to her feet, knocking the chair over for good measure and ripping the beads at her wrist free. Marie reeled, eyes wide and rolling in her head as she tracked the purple plastic balls flying through the air and clattering like a tacky rain to the marble.

"You dare!" She hissed and dropped to her knees, gathering the beads and muttering, "*Une, deux, trois, quatre, cinq …*"

Darkly rushed over and grabbed Milla's arm, clamping his palm over the bleeding wound as he led her away. Milla kept her attention on the Voodoo Queen, scrabbling on the ground. The vampires at the fringes of the room rushed forward at a shriek from their Madam, gathering the beads and placing them in rows of five.

"Did she hurt you?" Darkly pulled his hand away to eye the cut.

Dumb question, considering Milla was currently bleeding.

"No." She wrenched her arm free. "We need to leave before they finish counting."

"I wondered what the beads were for."

Milla grabbed his hand and charged from the hall, retreading a path from one of her worst memories. She stormed through the LaLaurie Mansion with Darkly in tow. Around a corner, down a flight of stairs, purposefully ignoring a narrow hallway jutting off to the bowels of the manse. Marie called from the top of the stairs as she reached for the front door, black hair free from the tignon and coiling like snakes, dress askew, and chest heaving as she hissed her farewells.

"I look forward to seeing you again, Dark Witch!"

Darkly whirled at the address, pulling shadow into his hands. The surge of his magick left the witch like a burst of wintry air, and Milla gaped at the manifestation of his Way. Terrified. Thrilled. Worryingly curious.

"Would prefer you forgot my face." Darkly shook his hands empty and pulled the door open. Late afternoon sun filled the foyer, and Milla and Darkly raised hands to their eyes, blinking against the harsh light of day. He gestured for her to go first, a kindness she didn't deserve.

"One last question, Ludmilla." The Voodoo Queen smiled, running a finger along the hair glued to her throat by saliva and blood. "Who is BiminiBikini1513?"

Milla scoffed. "Still bitter about losing that rococo chair auction, Marie?"

"Speak," Marie hissed.

Milla choked and straightened, managing one panicked glance at Darkly before her tongue spilled out, "Diego Gregorio de Bimini." She clamped her hands over her mouth, shaking her head in a silent plea to the Voodoo Queen.

"How is it fair that a vampire is also a witch," Darkly complained.

"The full truth, *belle-fille*."

"My roommate and ancestor," Milla bit her tongue, but it was useless, "the Conquistador Diego Gregorio de Bimini, raised by my own hand."

Darkly jerked his face at Milla, and the vampire purred, "*Veuillez vous amuser.*"

Milla snagged the beads on his wrist, wrenching them free and flinging them across the room. "Suck a dick, Marie."

"Oh, God dammit," Marie cursed, all but falling down the stairs to count the rolling beads, and Milla dragged Darkly out into the sun.

Thirty

"What the fuck did you do, Milla?" Darkly stalked down the stairs, arms thrown wide. The door slammed at her back, and Milla wondered if the vampires were a kinder audience than her aural insurance adjuster. "I havenae idea how I'm supposed to spin this to C.R.O.W. Tell me Diego's a-a corporeal revenant. An illusion cast by the Morgen to keep you company, which, if so, is absolute shite parenting." When she didn't answer, Darkly growled unintelligibly at the sky and thrust his hands into his hair. "I'd even accept Ponce de Leon found the Fountain of Youth, Diego drank from it, and he's been living happily in St. Augustine for five-hundred-some-odd years. That he took you in after Ezra died—"

"He's not dead."

"Dinnae start that again." Darkly thrust a finger at her, falling two steps shy of being truly intimidating, considering he was only wearing pants and one sock and had an alarming array of welts rising on his neck and arms from the willow. "Tell me, Milla. Tell me he's a kindly immortal uncle who took you in." He grabbed her shoulders. "Please, I am begging you, tell me he is anything but what I think he is."

She looked into those clear green eyes and shook her head. "I don't want to lie to you."

Darkly exhaled, dropping his head. A beat passed, another, and then he drove a hand into her hair and pulled her into a harsh, demanding kiss. Her knees buckled in surprise, and he caught her with a hand between her shoulder blades, the kiss softening into something sweet but no less memorable.

He pulled away, gazing at her with smoke-stained eyes. "So ye ken, what we did wasnae due to candlesmoke."

"Noted," she gasped, lips still buzzing.

"Before this goes any further, Milla, I need tae—" A vantablack minivan with impenetrable windows squealed into the carriageway, screeching to a halt a hair's breadth from Darkly at the base of the steps. Milla frowned at their reflections in the glass: shocked, disheveled, and looking like a pair of shitty witches if she were being honest.

The window rolled down, taking their reflections with it, and the driver called out in a flat, neutral accent. "Get in, witches."

He took them to Taco Bell. She happily rattled off the entirety of the vegetarian menu before turning to Darkly, who had clambered onto the bench seat in the back, let fly a stream of Scottish cursing when he saw their bags in the trunk and had been scowling ever since. Milla took that in and told the driver to order the Classic Combo meal, an assorted box of popular items, and to upsize the melon soda.

The driver smiled, flashing a bit of fang, and ordered their food. The air in the minivan was tense, shadows pooling around Darkly until Milla couldn't see out the rear window. He sat in the middle of the seat, arms crossed and fuming in pitch-black sunglasses and one sock. From his bag, he had retrieved a black v-neck that clung to all the right parts of him, and Milla struggled against the very real urge to sneak a glance. Or five.

Obviously, she still did because, Horned God, look at the man. How did he even fit his arms in those tight sleeves?

The driver chatted with the server at the window, reaching out with gloved hands to grab their food. He passed bags and sodas to Milla, glancing between the two. "Gonna be about an hour."

"Where are we going?"

"Des Allemands." He nodded at Darkly. "The Madam has a job for you."

"Brilliant," the witch grumbled.

"Want me to roll up the partition?" Their driver gestured to the after-market installation separating the front seats from the rest of his minivan. That half-smile widened into a shit-eating grin; if vampires ate shit, that is, so maybe it was more of a blood-thirsty grin. "In case you two want to chat in private. Or not chat, this thing is soundproof."

"No, thank you," said Milla.

"Roll it up," barked Darkly.

She swiveled in her seat, narrowing her eyes at the cantankerous witch brooding like a hormonal teen. "I don't want—"

"To lie to me?" He finished for her. "Good, I was getting hoora tired of that."

"Says the Dark Witch." She threw a bag of burritos at him.

Darkly caught it and jerked his chin at the driver. "Roll it up."

The quiet motor of the partition whirred as a pane of fogged glass sealed Milla in with a Dark Witch.

A Dark Witch.

Her heart beat faster at the thought of what he was. Who he was. The minivan slid into motion, and Milla was pinned in her seat by the sunglasses glower of an honest-to-Goddess *Dark Witch*. Terror coiled, and a not-unpleasant shiver built in her spine. She tried to rally her anger at being deceived over the weeks she had spent in close conference with him. The runs, the sessions, and the flirting. But all she could manage was *hurt* at the unfairness of it all. He was a Dark Witch, a thing Forbidden and Foule, and he worked for C.R.O.W.

They allowed it; they allowed *him* while Milla had been hidden away like a dirty secret.

"I need to tell you something," he said.

"Unless you're about to tell me C.R.O.W. has re-evaluated their stance on Forbidden and Foule witches," she snapped, "I'm not so sure I want to hear it."

"Ken you need tae."

"You don't get to tell me what I think!" Milla slapped her seat, voice going shrill. "You *lied* to me, Darkly."

"Nae technically."

"*Yes*, technically!" She gripped the headrest to keep from throttling him. "You kept asking me my Way, baiting me into using magick when the whole time—the *whole* time—you were a Dark Witch."

"Still am."

"Stop that."

"Stop what?" He grinned at her, but the dimple failed to appear, and the edges were too sharp. Too sarcastic.

"Being cute," Milla grumbled, her shoulders dropping as anger fled her body. "I don't understand."

"Am nae so sure you want to." Darkly scratched his chest, right over his heart where Milla had spied the triple spirals of a triskelion shimmering a bioluminescent green. She had seen him scratch that exact spot time and time again, never giving much thought to the nervous trait until now. He took a deep breath and pulled the sunglasses away. They vanished as a swirl of smoke, and he leaned forward, bringing the doom cloud of shadow with him. "Before this goes any further, Milla, I need you to understand that I'm trying to help you—"

"By letting your ghosts crawl between my legs?"

"By keeping C.R.O.W. off your back!" He hollered, hitting his palm against her chair and slamming back against his seat. "And I cannae even manage that. Milla, I—" he scrubbed his hands over his face and mumbled into his palms.

"I'm sorry, what was that?"

"I said, I'm C.R.O.W., Milla."

"I knew that already," she scoffed. "You're my aural insurance adjuster."

"Nae, Milla. Listen to me," he entreated. "I'm C.R.O.W."

"You're …" *My aural insurance adjuster. My friend. You're Darkly and a Dark Witch. You're Forbidden and Foule like me.* All the words she wanted to say but couldn't because he was all of those things when he couldn't be, because to be all of those things didn't make sense unless he was—"No."

"I'm an Enforcer, Milla."

"No." She pressed against the partition, a hand reaching for the door, needing to put as much space between herself and the witch in the backseat as possible. "No, you can't be."

"I assure you, I am," he glowered. "Why d'ye ken I was so keen to get you out of St. Augustine?"

"No, you're a Dark Witch. You shouldn't exist. You're like me, and C.R.O.W. hates us. We can't, you can't—" Her chest was tight, ribs shrinking, compressing her lungs until only the thinnest stream of air could enter. A tingling began in her fingers, pulsing into her palms and crawling up her arms as a defensive, heated rise of magick because he wasn't an adjuster sent to survey and report on the state of her demesne. He was an Enforcer, a witch hunter, and he had been sent to hunt *her*.

"C.R.O.W. sent me to investigate; Lou wanted me to gain evidence of your Way—"

"Who the fuck is *Lou*?"

"Isnae important." He edged forward on the seat, reaching for her. Goddess, why was he always reaching for her? "Odd reports were coming from St. Augustine. Minor swells of magick pointing towards the Forbidden and Foule, followed by one massive burst of magick and then nothing. Nothing for a year beyond the odd ping of a Stitch Witch imbuing fabric or a Mix Witch working a wedding. The demesne had a new Witch with no discernible Way, and C.R.O.W. was happy to forget it, to forget *you*"—he looked pained by that, though for what reason Milla had no idea—"then in early January it happened again; a massive swell on the fringes of your demesne, and the Morgenhexe requested me."

Milla's heart plummeted into her belly, shock mixing with betrayal as a noxious cocktail. "My moth—Morgen requested you?"

Darkly either ignored her or didn't hear her, pressing on. "I need to know if what Marie—if what you said is true. I need to know so I can help you, Milla. All I've been doing since that bleeding *dip* is trying to help you, and I cannae … I cannae figure out what in the nine rings I'm supposed to tell C.R.O.W. without it being an outright lie." His eyes had gone wide and wild, staring through Milla as though the Dark Witch bore a scrap of her fractured Seeing and was reading the path ahead.

"After that colossal fuck-up with the raw-head … Lou saw you, and if they knew, *leannán*, if they ken for even a second that you were responsible for—that you … I need you to trust me. I need to know." His eyes fell on her, heavy and pleading. "What did you do?"

The air was too thin to breathe, the space between them too small to encompass the enormity of what he was asking. She pinned her eyes to the ceiling of the minivan, chewing her cheek and trying not to cry while anger bubbled in her chest. Rage and helplessness mired together, threatening to make her explode at the unfairness of it all.

All she had wanted was to return to the one place she had been moderately happy and disappear among the palm trees and the tourists. To live every day with her regrets and the not-ghost of Ezra. She made one stupid mistake in a moment of despair and weakness, using her Way and earning the title of Witch of the Demesne, and *this* was how it ended? In the back of a black minivan, in Horned God-damned New Orleans, with her not-adjuster, not-friend, not-her-Darkly revealing that he had been the true threat all along?

"I want to trust you," she began. The truth. He had worn her down over weeks, getting to know Milla as she was, not some idealized witch as Ezra would have her be. "I want to Darkly, but—you're an *Enforcer*."

"I'm a Dark Witch," he replied. "I was a Dark Witch first, and I'll be a Dark Witch last. Being an Enforcer is a stop in the middle and one I'm keen to leave behind." Again, he reached out, stopping just shy of her hand. Curling his fingers into a fist, he let his arm drop. "I've already told my handler you arenae a threat—"

"You don't know that."

He sent her a flat look before continuing. "I've done my best to explain how you tend the demesne and treat the desecrants, but after the raw-head I-I needed to get you out of the city, keep you out of C.R.O.W.'s reach until I could figure out what exactly you'd done to win the demesne and come up with a way to sell it, only now, I've nae—"

"I didn't mean to," she whispered. Darkly stilled, brow slowly knitting as his eyes widened. "It was an accident; I didn't mean to earn the demesne."

"What did you do?"

Milla drew her legs into the chair, hugging her knees and burying her face. Goddess, it was hot in here, and she was cold, and the walls were closing in. This was what she deserved. This was the punishment she'd been running from for two years, since she and Ezra and the lake. And then Diego.

Goddess, Diego.

What was going to happen to him? She would have to stand trial for Actes of Magick Forbidden and Foule, and the delicate lie crafted by two decades of training and Morgen's illusions would crumble to ash and *what would happen to Diego?*

"Leannán." Darkly must have leaned forward because his voice was soft and sweet, and his hand on her shoulder was a painful, gentle presence. "Tell me what you did, Milla. Please?"

Something in his tone about how he said *please* brought the words to her tongue.

"I had this dog," she began at the beginning, "Stinný. My dad gave him to me for Samhain when I was six. I couldn't handle the mortal schools, the lights, and the kids. My Seeing"—she waved a hand in front of her face, fingers splayed—"it was too much noise, I couldn't concentrate, couldn't make friends, so my dad gave me a dog. A fat little pillbug of a puppy with white fur everywhere, except for his face and a strip of fur at his shoulders that was the deepest midnight black. He was so beautiful."

Milla swallowed, eyes scanning the edge of Darkly's seat. He was utterly still, though a slip of shadow had pooled in his hand and begun winding up his forearm, like a snake or a … stoat.

"Every waking hour I wasn't at school, I was with Stinný. He had no idea I was different; he loved me for *me*, and there was only ever one him. Never three, never fractured, as if all the potential of Stinný was determined. A set fate." She lifted her gaze to meet that of Three Darklys in the back of a vampire's minivan, watching her with pain etched on every line of their faces. The shadows purled around him like a gentle fog, rapt and attentive to her every word. "I need you to understand, so C.R.O.W. can understand. I never meant for any of this to happen."

He gave a whisper of a nod, and the slip of shadow stretched across left-hand Darkly's shoulders.

"When I was eight, I left the gate open, and he—"

"Milla."

"You have to know I didn't mean to." She pleaded, eyes stinging with unshed tears. "He got out, and the bus—it dragged him down the road. I ran, but I didn't get there in time. My mom yelled for me to come home, get inside, and not look, but it was Stinný. *My* Stinný and the sound, Darkly. The cry he gave out when that fucking bus hit him, I still hear it, like someone ripped out my heart and bottled my screams." She looked down at her hand, the ruin of her head and heart.

The ruin of her life.

"A piece of me went with Stinný when he died. I-I could feel the impact, a shudder through my bones and down to my Soul—half a mile. I ran half a mile to get to my only friend—" her voice broke. The three Darklys collapsed into one, and his shadows spilled across the minivan floor, coiling around her ankles and legs.

A smoky, incorporeal hand reached from the mass of Shades. It brushed her knee, dispersing in a series of whorls, and Milla felt something like sympathy eking through the veil. Steadying and familiar and why wouldn't it be when the Dark Witch had been using his Shades to soothe her time and time again? At the lake when she saw the dead/not-dead seagull, in her room after drinking that Horned Godforsaken tea, and in his car when he drove her to the hospital.

"I felt him die," she continued, "and the Ways opened, allowing me to shave off part of myself and give it to Stinný."

The Shades slipped away from Milla, leaving a whisper in their absence and returning to their master. They coiled around his arms and legs, and his eyes found hers, so round and wide the whites were visible. His throat bobbed, and she rushed out:

"You have to understand, I was eight years old. I didn't know what I was doing or even know it was wrong. I was a strange and unusual little girl who watched too many Tim Burton movies." A harsh, dry laugh escaped, the sound of an autumn leaf crumpled beneath a boot. "I Frankenweenie'd my dog so I wouldn't be alone, and all it got me was a foster mother and an apprenticeship to an obnubilari."

"Is this how Diego…?"

"No. Yes?" She lay her hands on her knees, palms up, letting Darkly see the ruin of her life and the shimmer of the surgical scar running from wrist to elbow. "I'm not really sure how I did it, even now. Ezra gave me a fragment of bone on my twenty-third birthday. It could have been from anywhere; it was just a shard, but I thought it was his. I wore it around my neck like a lovesick dumbass." Milla curled her fingers, trailing the tips along her scars. "When the insurance came through, I bought myself a ticket to St. Augustine, set up my store, and waited until my Way burned from misuse.

"I thought I was bringing him back." The confession was bitter on her tongue, and a scornful laugh escaped. "Should have known better. You can't resurrect what isn't dead, and even if you *could*, we had Do Not Resurrects inscribed before the ritual at Lake Pontchartrain." Her fingers traced the surgical scar on her arm. "Neither of us wanted to be turned by Marie." Milla risked a glance at Darkly. He was staring at her knees, green eyes shuttered and lips pursed. "I got Diego instead. He was reborn from the tears of a broken heart, the sweat of desperation, and the anguish of solitude. Made flesh by my blood and my hand."

She hiccuped a laugh, remembering the utter shock on Diego's face. How he had whirled around, naked as the day he was born, which, she supposed, was that day. And then he'd hunched forward, blinking at her through near-sighted eyes.

"He took one look at me, crossed himself, and asked for a glass of wine. I panicked. I had been expecting Ezra, and what I got was my five-hundred-year-old ancestor telling me in barely comprehensible Spanish that he was thirsty. All the lies I'd told myself, the belief that Stinný was nothing more than a nightmare from my childhood, all of it fell apart. Unraveled by the tug of a life reborn and there"—Milla rubbed the tip of her nose with trembling fingers—"there Diego was; the proof of the Foule thing I am in the flesh." Darkly tracked the movement, narrowing his eyes on her nails, black and brittle from the raw-head. "It took fifteen minutes to explain the finer mechanics of dialing nine-one-one to a five-hundred-year-old conquistador."

"Milla," Darkly rasped, a look of exquisite pain on his face.

"I knew the swell of necro-energy would alert C.R.O.W. to what I was, what I had done. I knew I was fucked, and for the first time in a year, I wanted to live." She turned her right hand over, showing him the scars. "So I did what I had to do."

"You marred your aura," he breathed.

"*That* was the ritual which won me St. Augustine. The act of magick that secured my position as Witch of the Demesne and the last surge of energy C.R.O.W. should have tracked from the Ancient City. A desperate ritual performed by a desperate D—"

"Dinnae." He shot out a hand, clamping it down on her knee. "Dinnae say it. If you say it out loud, I'm nae so sure I can keep it from C.R.O.W. They'll ask me about this, about you, and no one lies to C.R.O.W—"

"—not even an Enforcer." Milla finished. It was a well-known phrase, one her father and Morgen had drilled into Milla time and time again. C.R.O.W. had the Ways and means to gain the truth and held no moral qualms with exercising those tactics to their fullest extent. "What will you tell them?"

"Dinnae ken." He gave her knee a gentle squeeze. His eyes fell to her leg, and he stilled, as though only then realizing where his hand lay. He slid it away, and Milla immediately missed the comforting weight. "As far as C.R.O.W. is concerned, Diego doesnae exist. There's no mention of him in your file, no record of a new Stitch Witch in the demesne—"

"Is that why you were so surprised to see him?"

"It was only supposed to be you," said Darkly. "How have you kept this from CR.O.W.?"

"Morgen. She called in a favor from an Ink Witch she knew to conjure documentation, and one of the obnubilari she was training on Big Torch bailed him from jail while I was in the hospital."

"Beginning to understand why she requested me." He settled in his seat, dropping his head back. "Have a bit of a history with the Forbidden and Foule."

"Considering that's what you are, I'm not surprised," Milla said. "Is that why you were benched?"

"Something like that." He sighed and raised his head. "You tend the demesne with your Way; there should be a surge, an energy swell the E.R.I.E. could track every time you—"

"What do you think my tea is for?" Milla shrugged. "Hawthorn, hellebore, hemlock, and clove."

"A nasty concoction," their driver chirped through the open partition. "Only an idiot would drown her Way like that. You two done back there?" He glanced over his shoulder, shallow eyes taking in Milla and Darkly. "No? Good. Because we're here."

Thirty One

HORSE Prior to their extermination by C.R.O.W., Dark Witches performed as the "horse", or vessel, in Voodoo ritual due to their unique ability to confer directly with the Dead and Otherwise, and compatibility with the Shades of those lost to us beyond the Gates.

- Letil, Manmou. Voodoo Nations, 1st ed., Český Sigil Press, 2006.

MUDDY WATER SPLASHED THE window as the minivan dipped and bobbed through a puddle and over a cattle grate. Milla pressed her nose to the glass, eyes drawn to the canal separating the mobile home park from the east-to-west run of the road.

"Heavily warded."

"What lives down here?" Darkly climbed into the seat beside Milla, hovering over her shoulder.

"Raw-head, Bloody Bones," the vampire supplied. She shuddered, pressing a finger to her lip. The throb of pain was nearly gone, any bit of soreness she felt there having been earned by an entirely different means. "Feu follets, grunch, lutin, letieche, witches, vampires"—he winked at them in the rearview mirror—"rougarou, take your pick."

"Rougarou?" Darkly croaked, his skin gone ashen. "How can you have werewolves?"

"Not werewolves," said Milla. "More like a Cajun loup garou."

"Chimera were ruled Forbidden and Foule over a century ago," he argued.

"Yet here I am with a Dark Witch," the vampire deadpanned. Darkly had no reply to that.

The mobile home park was a pleasant, bustling place despite the setting sun. Blue light bug lamps hung from posts framing a grass field where children played, kicking balls or running with their arms waving and tiny voices shrieking. Women sat under awnings in rocking chairs, chatting with half an eye on their children, and a few men tended a craw boil set up between a cluster of double-wides. Buoyant Creole filtered in through Darkly's open window, and none of the residents glanced at the black minivan rolling down their main road.

"Might be best if you let me make the introductions," the vampire instructed, throwing the minivan into park and unbuckling. "Tracy's notes listed an ICYMI rep she'd found living here, Lavelle DeMourtier. Fool witch snuck out of Ursulines to speak with Lavelle and promptly decided to shuffle off her mortal coil." He turned fully in the seat, pulling off his driver's cap and allowing Milla her first good look at him.

He was young-ish, like most vampires. The sort of young that skewed the line between twenty-four and thirty-four. Attractive, though pale with the subtle shallowness to his eyes that all vampires held. A short, sloping nose ended in a pert button over a pleasant mouth and almost elfin chin, which only lent itself towards his youthful appearance. He ruffled brown hair that Milla thought would lighten towards blonde if he were ever allowed back in the sun, loosening it from his scalp with his fingers and pulling on a black baseball hat with the letters N.O.P.D. emblazoned across the front. Leaning over, he rifled through the center console and pulled out a notebook and leather wallet.

"Marie said you recovered the body," said Milla. "Why are we here?"

"Because we only recovered the body."

"You must be fucking joking," Darkly whined.

"Wouldn't that be nice for you." He tugged the handle and kicked open the door, not waiting to see if the witches followed him up the steps of a tired double-wide. Police tape dangled from the door frame beneath a pair of half-burnt Dragon's Blood smudge sticks in a makeshift sconce. Milla stepped beside the vampire and dabbed a finger on the smudge sticks, pressing it to her tongue.

"Smudged this morning," she muttered.

"What is it?" Darkly sniffed the sticks, nose wrinkling.

"Dragon's Blood," Milla supplied, turning on the narrow porch to scan the yard. "For protection."

"Protection from what?"

"Certainly not an energy vampire," their driver snarked. "Of all the stupid …" He rapped his knuckles on the aluminum door, adjusting the umbrella and leaning close to listen. "C'est Detective Goodman, Orleans Parish."

Milla and Darkly traded a look, and she was satisfied to see that his eyebrows were as high on his face as she felt hers were.

"Vampire Voodoo Queen, Vampire Detective." He shook his head, bewildered. "Aye, that's brilliant. Bloody brilliant."

"At least we can assume he's the best at what he does," Milla chortled.

"Anybody home?" Detective Vampire knocked on the door a second time. "Êtes-vous là-dedans? Madame? Comment ça va?"

The deadbolt was thrown, and the door opened a crack, revealing half of a young woman's face. She scanned the vampire before opening the door wider. "Entrez." She waved him in, turning her back and disappearing to the rear of the mobile home. Milla caught sight of half-braided hair and rich, brown skin before she stepped into the bedroom and began conversing with someone unseen. A moment later, she stepped back into the hallway and gestured to the kitchen table. "C'est par là."

Detective Vampire looked from Milla to Darkly. "Do what you need to do."

She watched him saunter after the young woman, completely at a loss. A glance at Darkly was even less helpful. He stood in the doorway, hands in his pockets, staring at a square table shoved into a corner just off the kitchen.

"Thanks for the clarification," she muttered.

Though narrow and somewhat cramped, the trailer was comfortable in a shabby chic way. Well-loved sofas and pillows, blankets that looked hand-crocheted, and children's art taped to the wall. The bamboo blinds were lowered, and the air smelled of collards, yams, and muddled incense, likely from the Dragon Blood Sticks. Beads of blue light from the bug lamps outside speckled the walls in diagonal lines, a strand of which fell on a modest altar beside the worn, corduroy couch.

A yellow candle burnt to the nub was stuck to a small pewter plate by its own wax. Dried yellow and pink petals adorned the table, and the bouquet they had come from lay withered and curled at the altar's edge. An unlit cigarette sat beside a pink perfume bottle, and an artistic rendering of the household Loa was perched against the wall. As in the Sanderson household, the chosen portrait was a syncretized depiction of the Loa; Santa Ana, painted as an elderly woman in robes holding a young girl in her lap, framed on either side by champagne glasses with a dusty dredge of tan liquid in the bottom.

Serving the Loa was not uncommon in this part of Louisiana. The Delta was rich in the history of Voodoo as a faith and a Way. In both iterations, the practitioners served their Loa, and the Loa interfered on their behalf before Bondye—the Supreme

Creator in the Voodoo faith. Still, something about the fetish and adornments tickled the back of her brain.

She plucked a dried petal and rubbed it between two fingers, mulling the untended altar, which was odd in and of itself. The flowers should be fresh, and the champagne glasses should be filled regularly with rum or beer. While not symptomatic of all Loa, many desired regular, devout service. Even those who did not require daily affirmations deserved an altar that was kept and cared for. Respected, where this one had been ignored.

Milla picked up the perfume and sniffed the nozzle, promptly gagging at the over-powering stink of florals on the verge of rot. "Horned God."

She dropped the bottle, eyeing the altar with new, creeping suspicion. Dried flowers, champagne glasses with the dregs of beer at the bottom, that *stink*. She'd seen this before, recently, and the realization sent a dribble of dread down her spine. "Darkly, I think—" she twisted at the waist to address the witch and froze. He stood at the edge of the kitchen table, black eyes pinned on a chair cast in deep shadow and pulled out as if its occupant were still there. "Darkly?"

A deck of cards appeared in his hand, vanishing as he slid into the seat opposite the gloaming mass of shadows. His shoulders dropped, and he sighed. "I suppose it's showtime."

"What are you—"

In a fluid movement, Darkly pulled the shadow from under his jaw, covering his face in a smoky, black film. Milla flinched, and the shadows pulsed, seething broader and deeper black. Darkly swept his left arm over the table, revealing a spread of stygian black cards in the wake. He scooped them up and shuffled the deck with all the deftness of a cardician, dealing seven to the empty chair and seven to himself. The deep shadows in the empty chair darkened further at this, coalescing into a humanoid shape.

A Shade.

Darkly placed the remainder of the deck in the center of the table and drew four cards, placing one to the north, one to the east, one to the south, and one to the west. Milla edged closer, craning her neck to watch. She had never seen a Dark Witch work before; no one had if the stories were to be believed, which apparently they *weren't* because here he was, over-tall and in the flesh.

She remembered, then, the stories of Dark Witches she had heard. How they ushered Shades to the realms beyond, guiding the misguided home or, in the most malicious circumstances, bound them to bodies absent a Soul birthing a creature Forbidden and Foule.

Whispers of the Old World, eradicated and illegal.

Do you know what you both can do? Together?

The Voodoo Queen's words prickled the fine hairs at the base of her neck, and she crossed her arms, mulling the meaning behind the riddle as Darkly worked.

He waved a hand at the Shade, and a card was played from the deck in front of the empty chair—did she imagine that the mist moved? That a hand brushed the cards?—and laid on the southern stack directly before Darkly.

The image of a woman holding staves within a green wreath shimmered in the same luminescent mint and moss green as the sigil on his chest. Milla sucked a breath through her teeth, recognizing The World, a card representing completion or accomplishment, often regarding travel.

But the Shade had played it upside down, The World Reversed.

Incompletion.

Darkly pulled from his hand, laying Death reversed to the southeast. A fear of change cast aside, put away from the path. He was telling the Shade their journey was blessed, intended; urging them not to fear what the fates had allowed. He cocked his head, and though his face remained in shadow, Milla imagined she could see that gentle gaze falling on the lingering Shade.

The Shade pulled Justice, and Darkly nodded, only to go preternaturally still when the Shade reversed the card.

"Is it calling you dishonest?" Milla stepped closer, hovering behind Darkly.

"She," he corrected. "An injustice, if I understand her correctly." Something in his tone told Milla there was a slim-to-none chance he was misinterpreting. For whatever reason, her gaze tripped to the forgotten altar and its smattering of petals. "Something unaccounted for," he continued, his voice faint and fogged as though he called to her from a great distance. He played another card, laying it to the north.

Temperance.

Milla balked at the boldness. He was telling the Shade to walk the Middle Path. In a single card played by a clever-fingered hand, Darkly confirmed every rumor and whisper about the greatest magick a Dark Witch wielded. He was inviting the Shade to join him. To join his Shades until they were ready to move on to the eternal.

"You help them move on," she blurted. Darkly's featureless gaze turned as though he were looking at her out of the corner of his eye. "Is that what you do for C.R.O.W.? Help the Shades who aren't ready to pass through fully?"

"Something like that."

The Shade played The Emperor, dropping it without ceremony directly before him. An accusation, though Milla was fairly certain it came in jest. He jerked his attention back to the table and let out an indecorous snort. "Oh, I like you."

Pulling the Fool from his deck, indicative of new beginnings and a free spirit, he placed it on top of the Emperor. His fingers danced over the card as if he was undecided, and then it slowly reversed. He withdrew his hand and stared across the table at the Shade, who had just accused him of being reckless. "Cheeky."

The Shade responded with the Magician, laying it to the east—a test of will.

Darkly drew the Hermit—an appeal to inner guidance.

The partnership of the Lovers appeared on the edge of the table closest to Milla, and before either she or Darkly could react, it was ripped in two, and the pieces reversed. The shadows pulsed, and Darkly jumped from his seat, lurching in front of Milla as the Shade launched from the table. A deep, grey mist settled into the witch with a tremor that began at his shoulders, traveling to the top of his head and down through his legs. The shadows covering his face dissipated, revealing a black-eyed Darkly.

He looked between Milla and the now empty chair, brows lifting in surprise, and then he ran.

"Shit." Milla tore after him, stopping short to keep from colliding with the slamming front door. "Double shit. Hey, Vampire Driver Detective dude, a little help?" She wrenched the door open to the sound of terrified screams. The women relaxing under awnings were up and yelling, collecting their children as they scattered from the field like ants after their nest had been destroyed, revealing Darkly sprinting across the grass.

His gait was halting and ungainly, enough to have Milla hesitating. When they ran together in St. Augustine, he had been graceful, the miles passing under his feet easily. Now, he moved with all the finesse of a stork on stilts.

"Thank the Goddess for small favors." Milla kicked off her Birkenstocks and sprinted after the over-tall witch disappearing into a copse of trees at the far edge of the field. Gritting her teeth against what was sure to be painful on bare feet, it took her a few footfalls to realize the ground had been worn into a trail. Dappled moonlight bled through the grappling limbs of willow, beech, and live oak, enough for Milla to make out the darker shadow tearing down the path.

She was only half aware of the detritus in the trees: beads and mojo bags, poppets, coins, and combs. The fetish and gris-gris of Voodoo marking this space as holy ground. She burst into a clearing, skidding to a halt to keep from colliding with a black, wrought iron peristyle beside a cement cross. Thirteen headstones rimmed the glade in a teetering, misshapen circle, each adorned in more beads, ritual candles, liquor bottles, and flowers, all crumbling and riddled in green moss and lichen. A chipped and weather-stained Black Madonna stood beneath a massive live oak weeping curtains of Spanish moss, her hand raised in permanent blessing over her charges, and beside her was Darkly.

His chest rose and fell in heavy pants, and he stood with a stooped, weary posture, head cocked at an angle.

"Hey, you alright?" she called out.

His face twitched in her direction, and he raised his left hand, pointing to a broad headstone, the sort used to mark a spousal grave, half-shrouded in Spanish moss and lit by the warm glow of prayer candles. Unlike the forgotten altar in the mobile home, this one had been recently tended. The champagne glasses were filled with a sparkling, pale yellow liquid, and the bouquet was a fresh assortment of yellow daisies and pink carnations. An eyeshadow palette, an unopened package of cigarettes, and a plate of chocolate-dipped strawberries crowded around the prayer candle, and Milla knew the saint it would depict before she had stepped close enough to see.

"Santa Ana."

At her back, Darkly made a sound between a huff and a cough. A cool breeze pulled her hair as the witch marched through the veil of Spanish moss. He stumbled a step, two, limping for a third, and fell lifeless to the ground.

She rushed after Darkly, ducking under the Spanish moss and dropping to her knees. Looping her arms under his, Milla grunted and cursed until his head lay in her lap. The moss had formed a burial shroud over his features, and she cleared it away with gentle pinches, uncovering skin gone corpse pale. A touch of fingers to his throat revealed a pulse so slow and quiet she was tempted to call magick to hand and jolt the idiot witch back to consciousness so he could explain what in the nine rings all of *that* had just been.

She wouldn't need much, just a tiny pulse of her Way to gain a sense of his well-being. The same minor casting she had performed on Julie a day ago … two? Goddess, so much had happened so quickly that she was losing track.

Seconds passed to minutes—an hour. Milla's feet fell asleep, and his pulse remained molasses-slow, skin paling and growing cold. The air around them grew thick, unseasonably humid, and a swell of churning need rose from the ground, pulling sticky, feverish sweat to pebble her skin. An invisible weight draped itself over her shoulders, bowing Milla's head. She shuddered, pulling her hands away from Darkly as magick flared in her palms and arms. The pressure rose, clamping around Milla until black spots danced in her vision, a ghostly weight pressing down on the witch as if it could push all the magick out of her.

Her vision narrowed to a thin strip, her lungs unable to expand, and just when she thought she might pass out—the pressure slipped away, bleeding down her shoulders and over her arms as a slick, oily mass only felt and not seen.

The magick in her hands flared, burning beneath her scars, and she cried out at the deep, black substance coalescing in her palms.

"—the fuck?"

Milla shook her hands, trying to dislodge whatever-in-the-nine-rings *that* was, and Darkly shot up a hand, gripping Milla's wrist. She yelped, trying to jerk her arm away, and in a voice thick and smoky with intent, he said, *"Dinnae."*

Command laced through her, stilling the witch with a word. Moths fluttered in her belly, her heart racing at that *voice*. Slowly, so slowly, he captured her other wrist and brought both hands down on his chest, hissing and inhaling as the black trickled from her onto him—*into* him.

"Darkly, what're you—"

He locked eyes gone beyond midnight with Milla, the stygian depths swirling with a deep, heavy magick. His lips quirked into a knowing smirk and the flutter in her belly heated to a sinuous curl. *"Is mise an geata."*

The last of the pressure ebbed away, leaving Milla's arms tingling and her fingers trembling. She curled them against his chest, nails catching in the cotton of his shirt, only half registering the twitch and gasp it earned from the witch.

"Are you alright?" she asked when she was sure her voice would be steady. Darkly tightened his hold on her wrists, tugging gently. Milla bent forward, biting her lower lip as those black eyes trawled her face.

"I will be." He whispered, thumbs drawing circles over sensitive skin. "Gies a minute."

"Don't have a minute, Goody Witches." Vampire Detective strode into the glade, phone in hand. "Did you get her?"

"Aye." Darkly blinked, and the last of the smoke swirled and vanished like water down a drain. "And the other one." He squeezed Milla's wrists one last time before letting go and rolling onto his side.

"The other one?" She started to stand, only to crumple on dead legs from too long spent kneeling. Darkly caught her under her arms, hoisting Milla to her feet and tucking her close to his side.

"Lavelle," he murmured. "She was out here; Tracy wouldnae leave without her."

"I have no idea what any of that means."

"Why would you?" Vampire Detective scoffed. "He doesn't exist." He hooked a thumb at the headstone where Darkly had collapsed, frowning. "What was Lavelle doing at Belié Belcan's altar?"

"Belié Who?"

"Belcan." Milla stepped gingerly away from Darkly, her feet a tingling web of pins and needles. "He's a Loa invoked for protection."

"How on earth do you know that?"

She glanced at Darkly, enjoying the stupefied look on his face. "I told you, I did a section on Voodoo culture in college." She bent at the waist and squinted at the unlit prayer candle on the altar, unable to make out the icon. Vampire Detective stepped close, tapping the flashlight on his phone to illuminate the image on the glass: Saint Michael the Archangel wielding his sword against fallen angels. "He is tasked with casting judgment against malefactors and escorting Souls to Eternity; maybe that's why Lavelle was at his altar."

"She wasnae." Darkly half-heartedly pointed to the veil of moss. "She was on the other side and followed you through." Milla widened her eyes at all of *that*, choosing not to unpack any of it at this specific moment. Ducking under the Spanish moss, she studied the champagne glasses, flowers, and perfume. Again, there was a sickening sense of familiarity. The feeling that she ought to know what she was looking at, that she ought to understand.

"Ah, makes sense," the vampire stooped and poked a chocolate-covered strawberry, "the altar in her home is to Anaisa."

Milla reeled back on her heels, staggering into Darkly. "The flowers." Yellows and pinks, the sickly perfume, the oil diffusers and air fresheners. A lone champagne glass with a stale yellow liquid at the bottom. "Shit. Double shit, spite, and hell, *Anaisa*?"

Vampire Detective rolled his head on his neck, appealing to Darkly in a droll tone. "Does this mean anything to you?"

He shrugged, turning Milla to face him. "Care to explain?"

"The flowers, Darkly. In my store and Julie's apartment. And all those horrible oil diffusers. Marie said something got out when Ezra and I—at the lake—that Tracy was hunting it down, and then Tracy came down here to speak with Lavelle, who invoked Anaisa Pye, and no wonder all those ICYMI crazed, leggings-shilling Karens keep dropping like flies!"

"Still nae following."

"It's not Kayleigh at the top of this mess; it's Anaisa Pye! She got out, and she's—oh, Goddess." Milla wavered where she stood, true horror settling over her like a heavy cowl. "And she's in my demesne."

THIRTY TWO

ANAISA PYE, LOA OF the Seven Turns. Witch and nymph, protector of household happiness, love, and finances. Jealous and fickle, a demanding mistress requiring total devotion, and the only damn Loa able to manifest without a vessel.

"Milla?"

How, Horned God-dammit, *how* had she missed it?

I hope you are not allowing yourself to become distracted, Ludmilla.

It was so *obvious*, and it had been right in front of Milla for weeks. A rot in her demesne, a festering wound she had ignored because she'd been distracted by Julie and the store, by making things right with Diego and being a good *polednice* for Ana; distracted by Darkly and the threat of C.R.O.W.

I trained you better than this, Millapet.

"Milla, *leannán*, ken you've had a fright, but I need you to start talking sense."

"She's a Loa," Milla scrubbed her hands over her face.

"Gathered that."

"Goddess, how did I *miss* this?"

You never were very good with the Petro or the Rada.

"Better with the Gede," she mumbled. "Anaisa demands total devotion. Daily affirmations from those who serve, Goddess, I'm so stupid."

"Dinnae ken about stupid—"

"I don't know," Vampire Detective chirped. "She *did* posit the existence of an energy vampire."

"—but I'll need you to explain." The minivan took a sharp turn, wheels churning over gravel as their vampire chauffeur fled the mobile home park. Milla swayed in her seat, reaching for the Oh-shit Handle. Beside her, Darkly scrambled for his seat belt. Long shadows clung to the underside of his cheekbones and dragged at his eyes, sharpening the angles of his face. The dome light cast a yellow hue over the interior, turning the rich auburn of his hair a sickly brass.

"She's the Loa of Seven Turns. Sometimes, Anaisa is a maiden granting love and luck to the devout, or she's a crone called to bless a household or Anaisa Sangriñé, summoned for vengeance." The space behind her eyes prickled when she met his gaze, so Milla focused on his chest, right where the triskelion lay. "She is the consort of Belié Belcan and sibling to the Baron."

"So we're dealing with a-a Voodoo god?"

"Not a god," the vampire called back. "A Loa, and pray to whatever god *you* believe in that Bondye did not hear you utter such blasphemy."

"Noted." Darkly rolled his eyes and adjusted in the seat to face Milla. "How certain are you?"

"One hundred percent," she stated. Then frowned. "I think."

"Nae good enough."

"I know! I know, but … it fits, alright? Not in a woo-woo-vestic way, but okay, think about it. Ezra and I worked with Marie and her coven to perform that ritual—"

"Still dinnae ken what all that was about."

"Figure I've given you and C.R.O.W. enough ammunition to cleave me, don't you?"

Darkly's lips parted into a tiny *o*, but he kept quiet. She huffed and pressed on. He might be C.R.O.W., but he was a witch, a *Dark Witch*. If this was all going to end with her versus a Loa, Milla needed all the help she could get.

"Those who serve Anaisa Pye must do so *daily*. And what have we seen? Any time one of the women mentions quitting, she dies or ends up hospitalized. Any time she's distracted from her task of serving the Loa, Anaisa takes her vengeance. Jennifer Sanderson wanted to quit, and now she's dead. The McKenzie woman hosted a Galentine's dinner instead of an ICYMI event, and at least two of the women who attended, *including her*, are dead."

"I'll grant all points towards what you suggest, but the argument falls apart when we get to Julie."

Milla ignored the tiny flutter in her belly at how he said "we," forcing herself to maintain focus. "How so? Think about it: when did she start feeling sick?"

"I dinnae—"

"Whenever she wasn't entirely focused on ICYMI. She had to trade her shifts to get the time off for McKenzie's event, and then *boom*"—Milla clapped her hands—"she passes out in her car."

"And what then? You think Kayleigh Masterson is a Voodoo spirit in Karen form?"

Milla chewed her cheek, eyes darting over the leather stitching on the edge of Darkly's chair. "No," she shook her head. "No, I don't think it's her. When she was in my store, she felt human, wholly mortal, but I think she is the key to all this. Her, and her Upline. Annalisa."

"Annalisa," Vampire Detective echoed. "Now that almost feels *too* obvious."

"Thank you," Milla deadpanned, "for the opinion absolutely nobody asked for."

"Only here to help."

"Then get me home," she snapped. "There's a Loa loose in my demesne, and not just *any* Loa. Anaisa is a witch."

"Subtle," their driver muttered. Milla reached through the partition and knocked his baseball cap off.

"An actual witch, bloodbreath. In one of her turns she is Anaisa Fé GriGri, a medium, and vinefica, I think? Goddess, I should have listened to Ezra. He said not to focus so much on the Gede. Said we needed to bring the Rada, and the Petro would follow."

"Have nae idea what any of that means."

"It means there is a Loa, who is also a witch, in my demesne, and there's no one to defend St. Augustine." She finally looked at Darkly, and pain flared in her temples, driving deep into her skull. He slipped out of focus, and she grabbed his arm, seizing the present potential to keep the world from fracturing. "I stole the demesne from an augurist without even *trying*, Darkly. Anaisa is a step below a deity. If she steals the demesne while I'm gone, I don't think I could win it back."

His throat bobbed, acknowledgment tightening already weary features. "We'll think of something."

"It gets worse."

Darkly dropped his head and groaned. "'Course it does."

"I've been tending the demesne, Darkly. Not an augurist, not a meteomantic, *me*, do you understand? With the amount of magick I've fed into St. Augustine, the amount of power Anaisa would inherit … even if I stepped fully into my Way, she'd still outrank me."

"And in the attempt, the Enforcers sent by C.R.O.W. would know what you are." He clenched his fists tight enough to blanch the knuckles, then splayed his fingers. And back to fists, then splayed, like a fighter before a match. "We need to get back."

"We need to get back," she agreed.

"There's bound to be a late flight to Jacksonville." He touched her knee and leaned forward to address their driver. "Can you get us to an airport?"

"No can do," their driver answered. "I am under strict orders not to let you two out of my sight until this disaster is handled and you are delivered to St. Augustine. Guess which one takes precedence."

"So why can't we fly?" Milla asked.

"And leave my minivan in an airport parking lot?" The vampire's eyebrows climbed up to tickle the brim of his baseball hat. "Never."

"But it's an eight-and-a-half-hour drive!"

"I'm not the one who sat under a tree for hours waiting for her Dark Witch to come back to himself." He glanced over his shoulder, smirking at Milla. "Think how much further down the road we could be."

"You're an asshole."

"You wound me," he drawled, completely unoffended. "If only there were some way to speak with the dead so this didn't feel like a colossal waste of your precious time."

"What?"

"Ah," Darkly dropped back in his seat. "Yes. I suppose that would be good to do."

"Lord above, the lollpoop supposes." The vampire rolled his eyes. "You aren't very good at this, are you?"

"You havenae the slightest," Darkly muttered and unbuckled, clamoring into the back seat. He settled in the middle, long legs stretched between the pilot seats, and smoke began to swirl in his eyes. "Would rather you didnae watch if it's all the same."

"Watch what?"

"Shadestepping," the vampire answered. "Dark Witch specialty."

"How do you know about it?"

"As you may have gleaned from my situation, Goody Witch, I've lived long enough to remember a time when Dark Witches worked in every city."

"It's a means of conversing with Shades," Darkly explained resignedly. "I can gain more information from Tracy and Lavelle and use them to gather other women to question."

"But … they're dead," Milla stated the obvious.

"Aye, and I can get to them in the Neitherworld if they havenae moved on." He said this as though Milla really ought to have known the basics of how a Dark Witch functioned, which was absurd. How would she have known if he wasn't supposed to exist?

"The Neitherworld?" She raised her eyebrows. "Did you retain the rights to use that?"

"Land of the Dead wasnae quite right," Darkly replied, "and Shade Realm sounded too Dungeons and Dragons."

"It's called the Underdark," she corrected.

A smile flickered, sad and soft. "Havenae traversed the Neitherworld in a while, am nae sure how long this will take."

"How often do you Shadestep?"

"Not often," he admitted, a bit sheepish. "Even before I was benched, we kept it to a minimum, considering it treads too close to the Forbidden and Foule for C.R.O.W.'s liking." He paused. "Nae my favorite thing to do either, if I'm being honest."

"Why?" Milla pressed.

"It—" He paused again, considering. His eyes went unfocused and hazy, then he blinked and shook his head. "Takes a bit to come back to myself. Lou usually keeps close until I've recovered."

Again with that name. "Lou?"

"Another, ehm, Enforcer I work with." Darkly's cheeks went a touch pink.

"Well." Because what else did you say to that? She faced forward and patted Darkly's shin. "If you need anything, I'll be right here. I guess."

"Thank you," he murmured. A second later, his legs went slack. She gathered her backpack into her lap, counting to ten before turning in her seat. It wasn't every day a witch had the chance to observe a Way Forbidden and Foule, and she was the foster daughter of the Morgenhexe. It was practically in her upbringing to be nosy.

"You and Master Lightner certainly made a mess of things," their driver said.

Milla jumped, jerking around to glare at him. "Holy Horned God, do you have an opinion on everything?"

"When it involves the Madam? Yes."

"Then roll up the partition so I don't have to hear it." Milla dug in her bag, moving aside styrofoam cups and wads of napkins from their horrible tour of the French Quarter, searching for her phone. "Horned God, I can't remember the last time I got fucked this hard by someone whose name I don't even know."

"Dies-well."

"Doing the opposite of *well*, thank you very much." She peered in the front zipper pouch and checked the side pockets. "Where the hell is my phone?" An arm snaked through the partition at an awkward angle, and he waggled his fingers.

"Dies-well-with-remembrance Goodman."

"Goodman," she repeated. "As in the Hartford Goodmans who burned thirty women at the stake?"

"Thirty-seven," Dies-well corrected. "One and the same."

"You must've burned the wrong witch or six to earn a life sentence."

"Pity I'll never live up to my name," he hummed, seeming at ease with his circumstances. Milla supposed one would have to come to terms with immortality at some point, might as well do so after a few hundred years. "And I have your phones up here. Thought you might want them charged." He handed both hers and Darkly's phones through the partition. Milla sighed at her fractured screen as she powered the device on.

"Thank you."

"Don't mention it."

Missed calls and notifications filled her screen. Milla ignored them all, immediately dialing Diego's number. He answered on the second ring with, "Si esta llamada telefónica no es sobre ti acostándote con Darkly, juro por la Diosa que lo haré—"

"I didn't sleep with him."

"... why not!" The baffled exasperation in his voice had Milla laughing. "This is not funny, bruja. You left on a roadtrip with tall, Darkly, and handsome, you do not answer the phone, and now you are telling me last night did not end with you and him in bed?"

"I'm not sure last night ever ended."

Diego inhaled, and before he could unleash a stream of pent-up Iberian sexual frustration, Milla told him everything. When she was finished, feeling hollowed out and scraped raw, he inhaled again, letting the breath out in a slow, anxious stream.

"I told you not to go anywhere near the Delta," he hissed. "And you trust Darkly not to tell C.R.O.W.?"

"I know, you did, and I think … I think I do?" She hunched over, cupping her hand around the phone. "Even if I didn't, what choice do I have? Marie ratted me out—"

"She ratted him out," said Diego. "And from your story, she did not seem too surprised to know he existed, only that *you* brought him to New Orleans."

"I … had not considered that," Milla paced out. "All the more reason *to* trust him, I think. You know what Marie, Ezra, and I were trying to do. If she knew a Dark Witch existed and knew it was Darkly, then wouldn't that imply he might be … sympathetic?"

"Milla …"

"He's been nothing but helpful since I asked for a ride," she kept on, not entirely sure if she was trying to convince Diego or herself, "and he's doing this thing right now called shadestepping—"

"¿Qué es eso?"

"I have no idea."

"It is when a Dark Witch removes his Shade to traverse realms unknown," Dies-well supplied.

"Wait." Milla whirled around, eyes raking over the long body stretched out in the back seat. "He just *cleaved* himself?"

"Sort of."

"Who in the nine rings was that?" Diego hollered.

"Our vampire … chauffeur," Milla tried.

Dies-well snorted. "You could never afford me."

"Please, por Diosa, tell me he is driving you home," Diego whined. "I need you to tell this story in person so I can see if you have been obnubilated or hexed, and *then* I need your help in the store."

"Oh, shit, that reminds me—"

"That you purchased eight thousand dollars of ICYMI, and it is arriving tomorrow morning, and I have no idea where I am supposed to put it, much less when I will find the time to enter it into our system?"

Milla sucked in a breath. "... yes?"

"Diosa te bendiga," he sighed. "It has been a nightmare, and with Ana busy at the convention all day, there has not been anyone to—"

"Convention." Milla clapped a hand over her mouth and groaned. "Oh my Goddess, I forgot about the convention."

"Diego?" Ana's voice, chipper and bright, came over the line. "Diego, I need you up here!"

"Si, okay! In one minute!" He hollered back, exhaling hotly into the phone. "I am sorry, bruja, I need to go help her. The customers are relentless."

"Wait." She peered into the front seat, catching the time. "It's almost midnight, why are you still open?"

"The *convention*," he hissed as if that explained it. "Ana wanted to optimize our sales or something and is throwing an after-party. I had to assemble a hundred plastic champagne flutes this afternoon, and Julie has not been here to—"

"Where is Julie?"

"At the hospital," his voice held the tonal equivalent of a shrug.

"Diego!" Ana yelled again, her voice sharper. "Now, please, she's asking for you by name."

"Mierda, bruja, I need to go handle this customer. When are you back?"

"In the morning." She did the quick mental math. "Probably around nine."

"Si, okay." A door creaked and clicked closed, and the hum of voices filled the line. "You are taking me out for dinner when this convention is over. And I am ordering the *big* bottle of—oh."

"Diego? Is everything okay?"

"I do not … I am not sure," Diego whispered into the phone. "I have to go Milla, por favor llega rápido a casa." And then the line went dead.

THIRTY THREE

"HOLY HORNED GOD!" A corpse-cold death grip on her arm jolted Milla from an uneasy sleep. She thrashed upright, dropping her phone as she whirled around at a noise that was more death rattle than sepulchral groan.

"Milla?" Darkly rasped. If he'd looked harrowed before, he was downright haggard now. The circles under his eyes had deepened to purplish bruises, his pallor grey enough to have someone calling a coroner, and the hand at her arm was cold and clammy.

"Goddess, Darkly, are you alright?"

"Will be." He grabbed the empty pilot seat, pulled himself forward, and poured into the chair. "Tracy confirmed your suspicions." He slumped against the window, eyes fluttering closed. Early dawn light grayed his features further, and when he didn't elaborate, Milla set two fingers against his wrist. "Anaisa attacked her in Hattiesburg when she confronted the Loa in Jennifer Sanderson's boutique." Black eyes cracked open, falling to where she touched him.

"Just checking." She started to pull away, and Darkly spun his wrist, grabbing her hand and tangling their fingers together.

"And you were right about the Upline, Goddess, you were right about everything." He stared at the ceiling, eyes lightening to a gray-green. "Annalisa is Anaisa. Lavelle, the Shade from Des Allemands, was a Voodooist."

"Was?"

"Well, she's dead now, so I imagine that puts her on the outs with the Loa."

"Fair point." Milla squeezed his hand, earning a tiny smile from the witch. "Without the Baron and his *Maman* to deliver her to the Gates, she has nowhere to go."

"Makes one wonder how many other Voodooists are stuck in that Neitherworld of yours," Dies-well said. Milla shot him a narrow-eyed glare, silently willing him to kindly shut-the-fuck-up.

"She thinks," Darkly continued, missing the exchange between witch and vampire, "the, and I quote, 'pompous-ass white woman' misheard the Loa and never bothered to correct herself."

"Sounds like our Kayleigh."

He nodded, throat bobbing. "From what Tracy gathered, Kayleigh brought the Loa to Hattiesburg and worked with Jennifer Sanderson to shill ICYMI. The boutique opened, and the clothing sold, but Jennifer bought more than her books could recoup and wanted out."

"Tracy knew all of this?"

Darkly shook his head. "Lavelle was in Jennifer's downline; that's how Tracy found her. She pieced it together when Kayleigh took over Jennifer's group, but they both confirmed: Annalisa-Anaisa is at the top."

"So knowing that," Milla began, "I have good news and bad news."

"Brilliant." He held her hand tighter. The cool of his palm had warmed to something more akin to The Living, the stark contrast of her ever-present chill becoming more noticeable with every passing moment. "Bad news first, please."

"It, uh, it's kind of all the same."

"Fucking fantastic."

"The ICYMI Convention started," she said, retrieving her fallen smartphone without letting go of his hand. "Ana was throwing an after-party at the store when I called Diego. He said their sales had been insane."

"That's good for you and Julie then, innit?"

"Well, yes, but here's the thing." She took a deep breath. "I looked up the convention schedule. Last night was a kick-off, which sounded like an excuse for hundreds of huns to descend upon St. Augustine and wreak havoc, and tonight is the main event, keynote speech and all."

"Alright, and the bad-slash-good news?"

She opened the browser she'd been reading and showed it to Darkly. "Annalisa is the Keynote Speaker."

He scanned the lineup of the evening's festivities; his already wretched pallor turning as sickly as Milla felt. "A Loa, who thrives on the dedicated affirmations of those who serve her, is giving a keynote address to every ICYMI representative in the southeast, in the heart of your demesne. Tonight."

"Yes."

He screwed his face in frustration. "And how far away are we?"

Milla glanced out her window, catching a road sign just visible in the low morning light. "We should be coming up on Tallahassee, so … three and a half hours."

"Okay," he nodded. "Alright, we're there by half-nine, that gives us all day to track down Anaisa before her keynote and—"

the minivan changed lanes, and both witches watched in horror
as Dies-well navigated an off-ramp "—what in the nine rings do
you think you're doing?"

"Sun's coming up," he explained.

"Aye, we can see that; what does that have to do with"—he
glared at the windshield—"the Flamingo Roadside Inn?"

"Can't drive into direct sunlight." The vampire didn't bother
feigning eye contact through the rearview mirror. "I need to go
to coffin."

"But we're almost there!" Milla protested. "Let one of us drive."

"Let one of you drive *my* van?" Dies-well scoffed and threw the
minivan into park harder than was necessary. "I *never*. Of all the
ridiculous …" He grabbed an umbrella from the door well and
slid out of the car, muttering angrily as he ran for the shadows
hugging the peeling pink plaster wall of the Flamingo Roadside
Inn.

Darkly turned an incredulous stare at Milla. "He cannae be
fucking serious."

"I think he is." She grabbed her backpack and tugged on
the handle, scrutinizing Darkly as she waited for the door to
open. Though awake, his coloring had yet to return to anything
resembling healthy, and the bags under his eyes had grown darker
with each passing moment. "Maybe getting some sleep before we
swoop in hexes blazing is a good idea; you look half-dead, and
I'm … I'm going to need your help." She didn't wait to find out
what Darkly thought of that, slipping out of the minivan instead
and leaving him alone.

Dies-well returned not long after and dropped a key into her
hand. "I and my umbrella will fetch you sometime after solar
noon." His shallow eyes flicked over Milla with her backpack and
duffel bag, then traveled the length of Darkly, who had joined

her to stand in the weak morning light. "Please avail yourself of the facilities. Go," he shooed them with a hand. "Sleep, shower, have a drink. I know I will."

The vampire grinned broadly at them and sauntered under his umbrella, whistling off-key. Milla waited until she was certain he was out of earshot and then said somewhat admiringly, "I don't know if I want to stake him or invite him to my future son's bar mitzvah."

That earned a chuckle. He stole the key from her hands and swiped it at the door. "Dibs on the first shower."

"How come you get the first shower? I was accosted by Voodoo dolls."

"And *I* was possessed by the Shade of an ex-Enforcer and lain out on a forest floor for hours." He stepped inside the room and stopped abruptly. Milla ran face-first into his back, which, she must admit, had smelled better. Peering around him, she saw what had caused the sudden halt.

"What an asshole."

Darkly cleared his throat and tossed his bag onto the singular queen bed. "I'll sleep on the floor."

"No, take the bed, please." She sent him a little smile. In the growing light, he looked even closer to death than he had in the car. "You look like you're about to keel over."

"Good thing you're here then." He shot her the sarcastic grin that made Milla's stomach flutter, and it vanished just as quickly. "Milla, you should kn—"

"Please, Darkly, take it," she cut him off. "I've slept in worse places with much worse people."

✳

Three blankets and four pillows later, Milla was admiring her little nest on the floor when Darkly re-emerged from the bathroom in a cloud of steam. She tried not to look, really and truly, but the steam carried his spice and smoke scent to her nose, and, hand to Goddess, it turned her head.

No one could prove otherwise.

A glance at him in nothing but running shorts, skin still dewy from the steam, had her feeling like every idiot heroine in every young-adult fantasy novel she had ever read. In her youth. Certainly not as a grown-ass woman with a big-person job, a demesne, and a resurrected conquistador as a roommate.

The sheen of condensation did nothing to draw attention away from his sculpted form. Neither did the little beads of moisture navigating the swells of muscle and his taut stomach. It was *absurd*, and despite her best efforts, her mouth went dry, her stomach curled in over itself, and every sane thought eddied from her head. The only saving grace was that he was drying his hair with a hand towel, and she could ogle uninterrupted … until he pulled the towel away, locked those jade-green eyes with Milla, and winked. *Winked.*

"Asshole," she muttered, rifling through her duffel bag so he couldn't see the heat crawling up her neck.

Darkly chuckled, a deep, warm laugh that did nothing to help Milla's current state. Sunlight streaming through the blinds caught on the luminescent sigil, which disappeared and reappeared whenever light caught the loops and whorls. She was staring. He saw that she was staring, and then he glanced down at what she was staring at.

"Sorry, I just—" Milla stepped closer, hand outstretched. "I've never seen one like that."

"I'd be surprised if you had." He tensed in anticipation of her touch, and she jerked her hand back.

"I'm sorry."

"It's alright." The gentleness in his tone broke her a little. Shame flared, and she busied her hands, pulling her hair into a ponytail. Still, her eyes were drawn to the sigil. The way the light danced off each spiral and whorl, radiant emerald and luminous mint ebbed in shadow like the witch who wore it.

It didn't help that he took a step.

And another, closing the distance until they were less than an arm's length apart. His throat bobbed when she reached out again, drawn to the sigil like a moth to a flame.

"It's alright," Darkly repeated, urging her with a whispered consent. So she did.

He was cool to the touch. Considering the steam still billowing from the bathroom, it was surprisingly cool. Not clammy like she was. Chilled as though he had just stepped in from a winter storm. She traced the arc of a whorl, winding counterclockwise and spiraling in wider and wider turns, trying as hard as she could to ignore how his skin pebbled in the wake of her touch; how his breathing hitched when she neared the center of the sigil, heart thundering beneath her fingertip.

Darkly captured her hand, stilling it over his heart. Freckles danced along the tendons, a star scatter of a blemish from hours spent in the sun. Lean fingers at odds with misaligned boxer's knuckles curved under her palm, and a muscle tensed in his jaw when Milla looked up. He dragged his gaze over her face, trailing every line and leaving her laid open and bare before him.

"I should explain—" he began, and in those three words, all the little things she had fooled herself into forgetting came crashing down.

New Orleans, the vampires, Diego, Julie, the raw-head, Ana, Horned God—*New Orleans*, the silver Land Rover in his driveway, and the devastating blonde in his cottage.

Milla yanked her hand free and pressed it to her lips. "Oh my Goddess," she blurted, "I am so sorry. You have a girlfriend; this is so inappropriate."

"Come again?"

"I am so sorry, Darkly. I'm a selfish asshole, and I will apologize to Fiona and take whatever spite she sends my way, truly." Milla grabbed her duffel bag, preparing to dead march into the shower. Anything to get out of this room and away from him. Horned God, what was she even doing touching him like that?

"Fiona?" Darkly stood between her and the bathroom, scratching the center of his chest and generally being a lot of person in her way. She tried to step around him, but he huffed a tiny laugh and moved to block her path. So she went in the other direction. He did it again, and she feinted, darting around his left when he went right.

"Seriously, I'm trash." Milla rushed out, backing away. "I'm gonna go drown in the shower; call the hippocromantics when you think I'm close enough to dead."

"Not until you explain whatever"—he waggled his fingers over her—"this is."

"This is a supremely embarrassed witch who would like to shower off some of her awful," Milla replied.

"Milla." His voice was even and moderately amused, which just upset her further. "Who do you think Fiona is?"

"That leggy blonde wearing not-a-lot of your clothes."

Darkly's eyebrows flew up his face, and he had the gall to start chuckling. "Aye, well, your nae wrong."

"I am so sorry. She seems like a perfectly decent person, and Goddess knows she's gorgeous—"

"She's my handler."

"—in like a supermodel kind of way, wait." Milla blinked. "What?"

"She's my handler. We work together."

"You do see how that's worse, don't you?" Goddess, she was going to be ill. Or burst into flame. Darkly shrugged, his half-smile and shining eyes far too amused. "But … but she was at your cottage."

"Aye," he replied.

"On Valentine's Day."

"Well, your date was a raw-head, so I dinnae ken where the comparison lies."

"I don't … If she's not your girlfriend, what was she doing at your cottage?"

His eyes shuttered enough that Milla began to suspect a harsh truth was coming her way. "When I left you at Julie's," he began, "it was because Fiona had messaged about the signature swell we tracked to Refugio Cove where—"

"Where Anaisa had just attacked the Galentine's Dinner." She thought back, trying to recall any detail she could of that weird goodbye when he'd lingered, called her name, asked her to— "Wait. Is that why you told me to stay inside?" Darkly nodded, his mouth a thin, tight line. "There were Enforcers in the newsfeed; that's how I recognized Fiona the next morni-*HolyHornedGod* you were *there*." Her shoulders hit the wall, and Milla sank to the floor, mind reeling. Fiona had been yelling at a witch in that newscast. Livid and angry and jabbing an over-tall, broad-shouldered witch as she berated him. "What the *fuck*, Darkly."

"I told her it wasnae you, that I'd been with you all day," his words came out rushed, hurried, as though he were afraid if he didn't get them all out in one go, they would never have the chance to be heard. "And then you left on that run to tend the demesne and Milla—your *Way*. I'd been able to cover it when we ran, letting out my Shades to … but you ran, and the E.R.I.E.s picked it up." He dropped to the edge of the bed, elbows propped on his knees and head in his hands. Sitting right in front of Milla in running shorts that showed just a bit too much of his thigh.

Not that she was complaining, but this was hardly the time to be distracted by shorts that had no business being so short on a person so tall.

"I couldnae convince her otherwise, the signatures were too close. They're nearly identical, and I couldnae explain *why*. No one could, so we left Refugio Cove, following your signature across the city and then you—the raw-head … Goddess, *leannán*." He raised his head, eyes over-bright and red-rimmed. "I did what I could, but when the desecrant had you on the ground …"

"The bridge …" Milla pressed fingertips to her mouth, relishing the echo of pain from that night. "I—I felt something on the bridge like someone was trying to—" Darkly dropped his hands, guilt dragging at his features, and it hit. "That was *you* on the bridge. Grabbing my foot."

He rubbed a hand over the sigil and looked up at her. "Fiona doesnae know what you are. She suspects, but, Goddess be damned, Milla, you're a clever witch." A rueful smirk flashed, there and gone again. "She wanted to bait you into revealing your Way. I panicked and did what I could to warn you without Fiona realizing what I was doing."

"You tripped me." Goddess, he looked like he was going to be sick. Milla tried to rally her anger, but too many disparate pieces were coming together. Bits of red twine latching on to a snippet here and an exchange there. The shadows *had* tripped Milla, keeping her from running headlong into a raw-head. And the softness of the asphalt, its unnatural chill, and how it seemed to push her to her feet. The terror on Darkly's face when he saw her the next morning. How his hand darted to a wound hidden by her shirt, a wound he shouldn't have known was there.

"The lights?"

"Fiona." Darkly rasped. "She's a Light Witch." Fitting. Light and Dark Witches were two sides of the same coin … if one side had been scrubbed from the annals of Witchstory. "When you couldnae form a ward, Fiona started panicking, and then that raw-head had you on the ground. I couldnae get to you fast enough. She dropped a shield to keep the mortals safe, and I was running through the dark, drawing on my Shades, but I couldnae get to you through her shield and—"

"Darkly." He flinched at his name, fists clenching. Goddess, she wanted to be mad. She wanted to be *furious* with the witch for lying to her and deceiving her every step of the way. She wanted to hex him into a pile of festering rot for going along with his handler's—with *Fiona's*—plan to use her as bait for the raw-head, but if he hadn't been there, Milla would have run headlong into the desecrant's talon-tipped arms. "How long have you known?"

At that, all the color bled from his cheeks. "Since our fourth meeting," he swallowed thickly. "The Shades slipped free to get a look at you, and they recognized your Way."

"Our fourth session," Milla muttered, dumbfounded. She vaguely remembered that meeting. The room had gone dark, Darkly had been flirting, and then he'd received a phone call that left him spooked. "When you thought you'd kept me late?

Goddess, if you've known my Way this whole time, why didn't you—"

"The *leshy*," he stated. "And the *dip* and how you mediate for the *xana* and *rusalka* and a million different reasons. I thought I was about to watch you be flayed alive, Milla. I thought the wicked witch that had turned my head upside down was about to be ripped to shreds, and there was nothing I could do. And then that raw-head was dusted, and you were gone, vanishing into the Quarter. It was all Fiona could do to keep me from chasing after you.

"She stole my phone, forced me to go home and talk it out. She had a local Enforcer check on the store, and when they reported you were safe I think I cried, I'm nae sure. The night got hazy, and I woke on the couch at dawn. Fiona was already awake, putting coffee in my hands and talking sense. Box it out, she said. Spend the energy and clear your head."

"Oh."

"Oh?" He blinked at her. "*Oh?*"

"When you came out to talk to me, you were so sweaty I thought—" Darkly blushed from hairline to waistline; an adorable wave of red running the length of his body. They stared at one another, Darkly embarrassed and pleading and Milla too afraid to give voice to the one thought repeating itself in her head. "This whole time you've been—" He was Forbidden and Foule, like her, and Enforcer or not, he had tried to keep her away from his handler, had caught her when she fell, had sought to *understand* the witch rather than condemn or control her, and isn't that everything Milla had ever wanted? "—protecting me."

"Doing a shite job of i—"

She launched herself at him, and the witch met her halfway, strong arms clamping around Milla and drawing her tight enough to crack her spine. This was not the sweet, hesitant kiss they shared in that darkened bar. Oh no, this was weeks of pent-up frustration and want and desire. It was every small touch, wink, and laugh rolled into one exuberant crashing of tongues and teeth. His hand cupped the back of her head, twisting fingers in her hair and tugging just enough that she gasped and arched into him, the brief flash of pain vanishing beneath a sweep of his tongue in her mouth.

She ran her nails down his back, feeling his magick swell and chase her Way, her touch drawing a groan from Darkly. He pressed against her, letting Milla feel where this was going, before pulling his mouth from hers and dragging his teeth along her lip. A slow burn of sensation edged in pain that made Milla ache for the weight of him.

He tipped his forehead against hers, panting lightly, and murmured, "Cannae do this."

Bucket. Ice. Nice to meet you.

Milla wriggled out of his arms. "Excuse me?"

"Cannae." Darkly shook his head, looking bedraggled and bewildered. "Canne do this, Milla. I'm sorry, but—"

Another call she had overheard, another offhand comment, and another witch he kept mentioning bloomed in her memory. "Oh my Goddess, you thought I was a dude."

"What?"

"At the bar, at Drake's Fire. You said you thought a bloke had been sitting there." Milla started pacing. "Goddess, and you keep mentioning *Lou* when I've been so worried about *Fiona*—"

Darkly laughed. *Laughed.* "That's nae—"

"No, it's fine. Like, literally, not a problem. I just feel stupid that I've been lusting after the witch *investigating* me this whole time like a damn cliche, even while thinking you had a girlfriend when you're gay. I should have pieced it together. Really, this is fine, it's on me. I am so sorry."

"You really are a mess, you ken?"

Milla glared at him, thrusting a finger at the center of his chest, right in the middle of that gleaming sigil. "And you're shit at your job."

"I'm not gay, Milla. Unless you've already managed to forget the other night—"

"Hitchhiking ghost."

"And the steps outside the LaLaurie Mansion."

"Minor emotional trauma."

"And this." He palmed himself, which brought Milla's attention to a very obvious sign he was in fact not gay. She stared at him, head gone vacant for a moment. "I'm not gay, *leannán*," Darkly smiled, the one with the dimples. Then he shrugged. "Neither am I straight, but—"

"Oh." She frowned, equally relieved and confused. "So why"—she gestured to the disaster that was her—"me?"

Darkly stepped close and pinched her chin. His eyes went dark, and Milla swore she felt a strand of shadow trail across her lower back, under her shirt, and up the length of her spine. She shivered in the best way, and he favored her with the Dark Darkly grin that made her toes curl.

"It's not the Way or means I'm attracted to, Milla." He rumbled her name, sending that shiver in her spine right down into her belly. "It's the witch." He kissed her nose. "But this witch smells like death and tastes like Voodoo doll. And that is what I cannae do."

THIRTY FOUR

CLEAN, MOSTLY DRY, AND having brushed her teeth twice, Milla tugged on a tank top and navy blue underwear dotted with stars. She padded into the bedroom with her hair wrapped in a towel to find six-feet-and-change of Dark Witch passed out on the bed. Her heart thudded to a standstill, and she squirmed where she stood at the foot of the bed, running one bare foot over the back of the other.

The man was out cold, his chest barely rising and falling. Utter peace softened the harsh edges shadestepping had drawn and, taking in the length of him spread over the covers, Milla's blackened little heart beat a bit faster.

She grabbed one of the three blankets from her nest and draped it over him, lifting the dead weight of an arm that had fallen over the side of the bed and laying it across his stomach. Hovering in the room while Darkly slept felt creepy, but there was no way she was getting to sleep anytime soon.

Stomach growling, Milla tugged on a pair of shorts and slipped into her Birkenstocks, grabbing the key and her debit card and closing the door gently behind her. He was still asleep when she returned, arms laden with junk food from the vending machines near the motel office. Placing a packet of coconut-covered pink Sno-balls on the bedside table next to Darkly's phone, she tugged off her shorts and shoes, wrapped herself in a blanket, and plopped down in the armchair, tearing into a bag of cheese crackers and powering on the television.

Poltergeist played in the background; the best part where the little girl gets sucked into the television and the real fun begins, as she texted Diego, apologizing for the delay and promising she'd be home this evening. He didn't respond, which was abnormal for the witch, but he'd said they were busy. Being the second day of the convention and right at opening time, Milla had to assume he was busy picking up all the slack she had dropped. She went back to the movie, munching her cheese crackers and escaping into distraction to keep from nervously pacing the hotel or looking up how to hot-wire a late-market minivan, when Darkly lurched upright with a sepulchral groan.

Milla jumped, cheese crackers flying, and twisted in her seat. Impenetrable black pulsed from the bed, a seething mass of Shades stemming from the sleeping witch and devouring all light in the room. Crisp and wintry cold, the Shades manifested as a testing sort of wind, prodding this new plane and faltering when they approached the witch. At their heart was a darker shade of black against the gloom; the vague silhouette of a witch hunched over bent knees with his head in his hands.

"Darkly?" Milla unfolded herself from the chair, reaching into the dark until her hand hit the edge of the bed. Walking fingers along the mattress she found his hip, his thigh, his knee, and then lean, strong arms circled her waist. He pressed his face to her stomach, muttering in a voice gone hoarse and thick. Milla wrapped her arms around trembling shoulders, his skin chill to the touch. "Are you alright?"

"Nae," Darkly rasped. Tightening his arms, he pulled Milla into the bed, rolling to bring her down beside him, her chin on his head and his face against her chest. She went rigid, unsure what to do and what this was. Slowly, so slowly, the shadows withdrew into his person, and his trembling abated. Blue-green light from the television found them, and Milla tucked her chin, looking down at Darkly.

"Have you slept?" He stared up at her, eyes wholly black. She shook her head, rubbing her hands across the broadness of his back. "Will you?"

"I'll try." She kissed his forehead and wriggled down to cup his cheek and look him in the eye. "You?" He nodded, several days of stubble scratching pleasantly against her palm. "Let me turn off the TV."

"Let me," Darkly murmured. One hand drew lazy circles on her back, the chill roll of his magick tingling in the wake of his touch. With the other hand, he reached down and grabbed the blanket, dragging it over them and bringing with it a cloak of midnight.

"Are you ready?" Ezra tugged at her fingertips, smiling beneath his half-skull mask. His jacket was missing, and Milla drank in the sight of his sculpted frame beneath the fitted vest and those sinful pants. A chant rose behind them, and lotus-tinged smoke drifted lazily across the lake's surface. Milla's tongue tingled from the blend of valerian and graveyard dust she had licked from a bone.

"As I'll ever be." She smiled, letting herself be led deeper into the water, her skirt floating behind her. The stacked heel of her boots sank into the silt, but that wouldn't be an issue when their run to the Gates

began. Now, however, the water lapped at her thighs and hips as a cold prelude to the remainder of this late winter night.

Ezra guided her onto the square of cement submerged in the water, enveloping her in his heat.

"Stay with me, Milla." He tapped her temple with his forefinger, trailing it along her cheekbone and down to her jaw, while his other hand drew a line down her right arm, from shoulder to elbow. He pressed a talon-capped thumb against the apex of her scar. "No matter what you See, believe in me." Teal magick crackled in the void of his pupils, and he tipped his forehead to hers. She bit her lip as the talon bit into her flesh, drawing a line from elbow to wrist. He pulled away, running the same talon along his scar, and then gripped her at the crook of her elbow, mingling their blood, their flesh.

"I love you, Ludmilla Lightner," Ezra whispered, brushing his lips against hers. She staggered as the tether coiled around the bones in her arm, joining her to Ezra, body and Soul. He smiled against her mouth, and Milla whispered, "I love you, Ezra Lightner."

His lips found her ear, and he murmured his farewell. "You're my favorite thing in this old world."

Milla startled awake with Ezra's words spiraling in her head until they were everything and anything but the truth.

This old world.

For a moment, she allowed herself to imagine they hadn't failed. That they had returned a free and wild magick to the world, that she no longer needed to tread lightly on the fringes of two societies and instead could wield her magick freely and openly. Accepted.

Lauded, even.

Then she shivered and shoved the thought away. Packing it down down down until it slithered along the bones in her right arm and coiled back to sleep. Only then did she become aware of where she was and who she was with.

Darkly's arm was a comforting weight around her shoulders, and she lay with her cheek against his chest, an arm across his stomach, and a leg hitched over his. He moved in his sleep, rolling onto his side enough that Milla thought it best she slither out of his arms and let him sleep comfortably. She wriggled, his arm tightened around her shoulders, and he pulled her close, pressing Milla bodily against him.

Bodily.

She bit her tongue, eyes darting between their entwined legs and his chin in an attempt to assess if he was awake and, if so, how awake he actually was. She wriggled again, sliding a bit further down and trying to ignore the Very Awake part of Darkly that now pressed against the crook of her thigh and abdomen. Her fingers rested lightly at his waist, twitching against his skin. He squirmed at the touch, arching his back and pressing that Very Awake part of him harder against Milla. Her eyes went wide, she froze, and he murmured in a honey-sweet, sleep-thick voice, "Tha' tickles."

"Oh?" She wiggled her fingers, earning a squirm and a soft chuckle. He rolled onto his back, bringing Milla to lie on top of him, his eyes half-lidded and emerald-bright. So she tickled him again, turning the drowsy Dark Witch into a wriggling, giggling fiend. His knees bent, and she pushed upright, straddling his hips and dancing her fingers along his waist and ribs, fluttering over his belly button.

"Stop, ach, Goddess, stop!" He threw his head back, pawing at her hands, and lost to the fit of laughter. Emboldened, Milla tickled along the band of his running shorts, hooking her forefinger in the elastic. When he stilled, she dragged her eyes from the dusting of hair at his navel, up the lean, cut muscle of his stomach and chest, lingering on his mouth and the question there before finally meeting his eyes.

Darkly grazed her thigh with his fingers and rocked his hips, just enough to let her know where he stood.

Or lay.

Whatever.

"Is this what you want?" Milla trailed her finger along his waistband and down the length of his erection.

"Yesss." His hissed reply shivered between her ears. The muscles in his stomach flexed when he rocked his hips again. She smiled and leaned out of Darkly's reach, curling fingers around his girth. A whimper of want strangled from his throat as she pressed upward, teasing his head with her thumb. "Milla—"

She did it again, a languorous drag and tease, and Darkly's legs dropped behind her, muscles flexing beneath her backside. Hooking two fingers into his waistband, she tugged his shorts low, biting her lip when they revealed what she could now admit she'd been thinking about for weeks. Rock hard and beautiful and begging to be touched.

He wriggled, trying to pull his shorts off, and she shot him a glare.

"Be still." She didn't have the command in her voice that he did, but Milla could summon obedience when needed.

Darkly froze, his eyes molten and pinned on the witch straddling his legs. Wrapping her hand around him, she repeated the gesture, skin against skin. A tease of his silken head and a stroke. A test of his want and need as she heard his breathing turn ragged. Again, harder now, firmer. A draw on his person that had Darkly arching into her grip. He dug fingers into her thigh, capturing her wrist with his free hand to guide her movements. Forceful and authoritative, teaching her with a stroke and a pump how he liked to be touched, how he wanted *her* to touch *him*.

Milla bowed her lips into a smile and leaned over the witch, humming as she teased his head with her words. "Controlling little witch, aren't we?" She heard a sharp intake of breath and took him into her mouth, silencing whatever crafty reply had risen to that wicked tongue and showing him how cruel hers could be.

She ran her tongue around his head, sucking the tip as she stroked down his length, hard. Darkly bucked, groaning out a strained "Fuuuck." His hand trailed her side and cupped a breast. She straightened, sitting back on her knees and gripping him in full.

"Let me."

Darkly's lips parted, his eyes flicked green–black–green, but his hand fell away, fingers gripping the sheets as his chest rose and fell in deep bellows.

Satisfied, she leaned over him again, stroking as she worked his head and took him more fully into her mouth, smoothing each stroke with the wet swipe of her tongue, pulling him harder, taking him deeper.

That wandering hand found her head, cupping her skull. His hips rolled with each stroke and pull and whirl, fucking her mouth in a way that told Milla exactly how he would fuck her. She moaned, hollowing her cheeks and taking a long drag on his cock, loving the heat of the Dark Witch in her mouth and the singeing burn on her scalp as he guided her head. She reached up, splaying her hand over his chest, over the sigil, feeling the rapid beat of his heart as his body grew taut.

"Oh, Goddess, Milla," he panted.

She skimmed her teeth along the length of him and Darkly rammed his hips forward. And again. Again, until Milla's eyes watered at the sheer demand of this witch and his size in her mouth. She slapped her hand down on his hips, holding him still and slowing her strokes enough to look up and meet his eyes.

Watch me, she told him with a look. Sucking his cock from base to head, lathing the tip with her tongue and sliding him slowly, tortuously, achingly into her mouth until he was fully sheathed.

Something broke on Darkly's face, the last lock in a series of dams. Those wicked fingers knotted in her hair, gripping Milla just this side of pain, and he raised his hips, driving deeper into her mouth. His free hand slid beneath her tanktop, finding a breast and rolling the nipple between his fingers.

Milla moaned around his cock, sliding her hand between his legs and cupping his balls, squeezing gently. She trailed a nail along the flesh just behind, humming as she swallowed him whole. His legs twitched at the reverberation, and she did it again. Circling fingers in front of her mouth, stroking and sucking until his panting became uneven.

"Goddess." He worked her head, fucking her mouth, a controlling, devilish thing on the brink of madness. "Milla," he moaned, "Fuck, I'm gonnae—" his body tensed, hips thrusting, knocking the head of his cock against her throat as he came.

"Horned, fucking, God," Darkly panted, never letting up on that death grip in her hair. She swallowed his release and rolled her tongue along the underside of his shaft. He quivered, hand falling away when she withdrew to the tip. Meeting his heavy-lidded gaze, she swirled her tongue around his sensitive head. One last, lazy lathe that had him twitching in satisfaction.

Settling on her knees, Milla favored him with a self-satisfied smirk. She ran her thumb along her lower lip to catch the spillage and popped it into her mouth; closing her eyes as she sucked the last of him from her finger.

When she opened her eyes, Darkly was panting against the pillows, beholding her with something akin to awe and puzzlement. Milla cocked her head to say what; she had no idea, and he lurched upright, wrapping an arm around her shoulders and knocking her forward with his knees.

He caught her mouth, tongue sweeping and searing her inside out. A broad palm pressed between her shoulder blades, pinning Milla flush against him. Her nipples rubbed against his chest, a delicious ache nowhere near enough to lessen the harsh edge of arousal. Fingers dug into the back of her skull, angling Milla so he could take her mouth fully, his kiss turning into something possessive while his free hand trailed her waist, her hips, and dipped between her thighs.

She moaned in his mouth, wanting to feel all of him, knowing he was spent and not caring. She wanted him, wanted this. She wanted to feel him inside her, filling her.

Wanted to know what they could do, together.

Heat bubbled in her belly, shooting into Milla's limbs without warning. She pulled away from his kiss with a gasp, and then Darkly claimed her mouth again, his magick roiling chill and cold against hers. He drove his fingers between her underwear and skin, splitting moist lips and brushing against her clit in the sweetest, most agonizing tease. She whimpered and Darkly clenched the hand in her hair into a fist and circled her clit, again and again until she moaned into his mouth, her hips bucking. Satisfied, the witch released her from his all-consuming kiss, nipped her ear, and plunged two fingers deep.

A bestial groan strained from her throat, and she arched against him, riding his hand and wanting more. "Darkly, please …"

"Goddess, you're drippin'," he growled, probing deeper, harder. The strap of her tank top was pulled away, her breast freed, and then his tongue flicked her nipple, teeth grazing just to the point of pain. He drove his hand against her, and Milla plunged her fingers into his hair, holding Darkly to her chest. Grinding and writhing and moaning as he sucked and worked her from base to peak until she thought she might explode. That dangerous heat rose to boiling. She thought she heard Darkly curse, but the blood was rushing in her ears, her toes were tingling, and her Way—

Silk brushed her thighs and lower back, twining around Milla's waist and trailing over her ribs. Caressing her other breast until the nipple was teased and tickled to a point. Darkly moved his attention there, pulling the fabric away with his teeth and a snarl, capturing the ready nipple in his mouth. Milla's legs trembled as the cold air kissed her freed breast for a singular heartbeat before the silk of his shadows moved in, and she no longer knew where she ended and Darkly began.

Teeth buzzing, legs quaking, arching her body against him, every piece of her was drowned in Darkly and his shadows. His palm pressed against her clit, shadows lapped at her breast, and he crooked his fingers deep and slow. A wicked summons performed in the sweetest place, dragging his name from her throat as he beckoned her to fall over the edge.

"Please, Horned God, please—" she whimpered, body tensed on the precipice.

"*Do it, Milla,*" he urged her in that *voice*. Utter command ribboned through her veins and rattled along her bones. His teeth grazed her lip, her ear, her breasts. His shadows lapped and slithered over sensitive flesh, and Darkly drove his hand harder, pinning and possessing her body until she was unable to move, unable to think. "*Scream my name when you come.*"

Release had her howling his name. Darkly moaned his approval, unceasing in his relentless summons. He worked Milla until she lost her words and became a boneless, mewling thing thrown over the edge a second time.

THIRTY FIVE

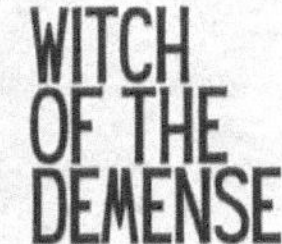

An earned title often secured among matrilineal lines with responsibility being passed from one witch to another via civil, organized ritual proceedings. In rare instances, the demesne may be stolen by a ritual act of high magnitude performed by a witch of equal, or greater power.

mortals would call this a "flex"

HOURS OR EONS LATER, a paced, repetitive knocking pulled Milla off of her witch. Darkly protested, clamping a hand on her ass to keep her where she'd collapsed, which was on him. The knocking increased in tempo, and he relented, but not without a muttered curse. Milla grabbed the blanket from the floor, smiling as she wrapped it around her shoulders and meandered to the door.

"Yes?"

"Invite me in." Dies-well shuffled underneath his umbrella, somehow managing to look both refreshed and still dead.

"Hello to you, too." Milla favored him with a true shit-eating grin, wondering if he understood what it meant. Deciding "no", she bent it towards bloodthirsty. Dies-well blinked at her.

"Invite me in," he repeated.

"No?"

"It is very bright out here." His shallow eyes widened, and Milla stifled a laugh at the poor vampire's panic. She glanced over her shoulder, snickering as Darkly pulled the comforter out from beneath him and up between his legs. He lay on his side and crooked a knee, sweeping a hand over his person and the barely concealed Honours of Scotland.

She pushed the door open wider, revealing the not-at-all decent Darkly. "Come on in."

"Oh for—" Dies-well darted inside, yanking his umbrella closed and kicking the door shut. "Can you witches not be decent for one God-damned minute?"

"You're the one who left us alone in here with one bed," Darkly crooned, flexing the muscles in his arms and stomach.

Dies-well's eyes shallowed a bit further, and he spun around, pinching the bridge of his nose. "Both of you are ordered to shower before we hit the road."

"We already showered."

"And you will shower again!" Dies-well glared at Darkly. "You reek of her, and she"—he turned his glare on Milla, who was biting the edge of her blanket to keep from laughing—"reeks of you. It's too much reeking!"

Darkly sat up under the guise of reaching for his running shorts, and the comforter slipped away. Dies-well turned a shade of purple Milla hadn't been aware was available to vampires and threw himself into the chair, cheese crackers crunching beneath his weight. He stood to check what he'd sat on and seethed at Milla, "How many crackers are there?"

She shrugged a shoulder. "Fifteen? Sixteen? Don't really know."

"Girly-gutted devil of a woman." Dies-well hissed and started counting the crackers, throwing a rude gesture in Milla's direction. She took that as a hint to grab her duffel bag and head to the shower.

Milla rejoined the witch and the vampire, clean and sore in all the right places. Darkly sat up in the bed, legs crossed at the ankles and munching on one of the Sno-Balls from the package she had bought. He scrolled his phone, eyes intent on the screen and a line drawn between his eyebrows. Organized piles of cheese cracker bits lined the table, and Dies-well appeared somewhat recovered, thanks to Darkly's wearing shorts and the now open window letting fresh air into the room.

"What's going on?" She tossed her duffel on the edge of the bed to pack.

"Have you checked your phone?" Dies-well asked. Milla shook her head. "Of course not, because this is some sort of weird witchy spring break to you two." He grabbed Milla's phone from the table and tossed it to her.

Multiple notifications filled the top of her screen—voicemails, missed calls, Yap! Reviews, news pings, and the icon for the chat group. She cocked her head, trying to remember the last time she'd seen a notice from the group chat. Was it in Des Allemands? No, her phone had been charging in the minivan. So, New Orleans? Milla tapped on the icon and immediately dropped her phone as a wicked stench filled the air. Burnt plastic, burning hair, chemical salt, and a curdling sweet that had witches and vampire gagging alike.

"Jesus Christ," Dies-well cried, "what is that?"

"Jesus has nothing to do with that," Darkly wheezed.

"It's the group chat." She pinched the corner of her phone between thumb and forefinger, arm outstretched. Dies-well grabbed the empty trashcan and ripped the bag free, holding it open. Milla dumped her phone in, and he spun the plastic, sealing away the worst of the stench. She pressed the bag tight across the screen, struggling to read through the film and shattered glass. The majority of the messages were sad emojis and weird images sparkling with fake glitter, depicting crying ponies and puppy dogs. Finally, she scrolled far enough back to find some text and wished she hadn't.

"What is it?" Darkly hovered over her shoulder, and Dies-well stared at them both.

"Hope you got some good rest, Dark Witch," he jeered. "You've got work to do." Darkly looked up at Dies-well, then down at Milla. She laced her fingers through his and gave a squeeze.

"Kayleigh died."

Darkly showered, and they were on the road within half an hour. Dies-well accommodated one stop at a chain coffee drive-thru, ordering Milla and Darkly half the breakfast menu, and tore out of the parking lot before she had placed their scalding drinks into the cupholders. Unwrapping her food, she cast a wary glance at Darkly in the seat beside her. Skin pale, pallor ashen, and body limp.

Without a complaint, without a flicker of emotion beyond determination he walked back into the darkness to retrieve Kayleigh Masterson. Milla was going to be damned before she let him walk out of that darkness alone. She hadn't needed to ask what had happened when she showered; he had offered it up for free when Milla had broken the news.

"I stretched out to wait for you and fell in."

Milla and Dies-well shared a look, the vampire appearing just as unsettled as she felt. "Does that happen often?"

"Never."

"Darkly, I can't ask you to go back in there."

"Dinnae fash, *leannán*, this is what I do." He cupped the back of her head, favoring Milla with a weak smile before stealing a quick kiss and pulling away with a wink and a resigned sigh. "It's showtime."

In the hour he'd been shadestepping, Milla had placed multiple unanswered calls and texts to Diego and Ana, eaten two egg-white and spinach wraps, and half the bear claw she'd asked Dies-well to order for Darkly. With every minute she was trapped in this minivan, unable to move them faster, unable to do *anything*, Milla's nerves frayed further. Her anxiety was nearing the stratosphere when, just outside of Greenville, her phone rang.

UNKNOWN CALLER

She sent it to voicemail, went back to her stolen bear claw, and the phone rang again.

UNKNOWN CALLER

"Ugh," she answered, ready to tear into whichever telemarketer was calling. "What?"

"Hi, is this, um, Ludmilla Probuditna?" The woman on the other end of the line said her name carefully, sounding out the consonants in a pleasant, if sad, voice.

"Whatever you're selling, I don't want it, and before you say anything, I don't even *have* a driver's license, so there's no extended warranty. Goodby—"

"This is about Kayleigh."

Milla went still. "What."

"My name is Madison, Madison Stewart. I'm Kayleigh Masterson's sister. Sarah recommended I call you about—"

"Sarah … Sanderson?" She swallowed an over-chewed lump of pastry and set the rest in the bag.

"She said she knew you," Madison explained. "I've been trying to get ahold of you for days, but your voicemail is full."

"Right, sorry." Milla took a bracing swallow of overly sweetened coffee. "And I'm, um, sorry for your loss."

"I … thank you." A sigh fluttered over the line. "Thank you, really. It's been a whirlwind; I just got into town last night. We're still processing everything, you know?"

"I can't begin to understand what you are going through, Madison. You or your family."

Another sigh, this one a bit more genuine than the last. "Thank you." She sighed again, paper shuffling over the line. "It's just that the coroner took the body, and I tried calling a few people, you know, in your circles."

"What sort of circles?"

"*Yours*," Madison stressed with the air of a hand being cupped around the receiver. "Sarah said you could help, you or your friend. I've done everything I can, but she *won't leave*."

"Who won't?"

"Kayleigh." Madison sounded more annoyed than Milla would have expected for a bereaved sibling calling the cantankerous shopowner her sister had doxxed online. "The kids arrive in a few days, and I can't have them living here with her haunting the place."

"Wait, I'm sorry. Are you telling me you called for an *exorcism?*"

"Isn't that what you *do?*"

"No!" She cried, then shrieked as Darkly lurched upright with a rasping, crackling death rattle. "Holy Horned God!"

"Ludmilla," Madison called over the line, "is everything alright?"

"Everything's perfectly alright, now," Milla rushed out. A shadowblind Darkly clamped a hand on her arm, his near-dead weight jerking her to the side. "We're all fine here, now. Thank you." He half-crawled, half-fell forward, grip tightening at her wrist as though confirming she was real and not a Shade. "How are you?"

"Um …"

Darkly plucked the phone from her hands, clearing his throat. "Hello, ma'am?"

Milla glared at him, then relented and rubbed her hand up and down his back while he finished the call. A few "mm-hmm's," a well-placed "my dearest condolences," in the richest Scottish that had ever rolled from his tongue, and then, "We can be there in a few hours if that's alright."

"What?" Milla sat up, alarmed. "No, we need to get to St. Augustine."

Darkly said his farewells to Madison, massaging his temples while muttering an address to Dies-well.

"Where are we going?" she asked again, peering through the partition at the new directions on Dies-well's GPS. "Why are we taking I-10? The beach traffic is going to be insane getting to St. Augustine. Cut south through Lake City and head east from Starke."

"His orders." Dies-well shrugged and kept driving.

"Beach traffic in February." Darkly shook his head, wearily mystified. "Goddess, I love Florida."

"What in the nine rings did you just agree to?" Milla grabbed his arm, jostling the witch from his rose-tinted daydream of the Sunshine State. He gazed back at her, eyes unfocused and shrouded in dark smoke. "Whoa, hey, everything okay?"

He wavered a smile and let it crumble like a sand sculpture. "She wouldnae come with me," he croaked. "Said she wasnae gonnae go with a strange man."

Milla snorted. "That sounds like the Kayleigh I met, but I wasn't asking about her."

"I ken." He closed his eyes, tilting his head back and rolling it against the headrest. His skin grayed, cheeks sinking and breaths slowing, so Milla reached out and pinched his thigh. Darkly jerked awake. "Ach, what was that for?"

"Just making sure you're still with me."

"Nae goin' anywhere." He laced their fingers together and raised the back of Milla's hand to his lips, brushing them against her knuckles and setting off a flurry of moths in her belly. He took a few more minutes to come back to himself, downing his tea, the remaining half a bear claw (which earned her an amused eye-roll), and an egg, sausage, and cheese sandwich. "I found her, but she wouldnae come with me, so we're going to her."

"And where *is* she?"

Darkly eyed her, his jaw moving side-to-side before he finally answered. "Vilano Beach."

The minivan trundled down a long, forgotten road tunneled by palms and black mangroves. Buttonwillow hugged the trunks of the taller trees, obscuring whatever suggestions of civilization existed beyond this long un-serviced road. White heat prickled behind Milla's eyes, matching the fluttering nerves in her belly. "Are you sure this is it?"

"Just following the GPS," Dies-well replied.

The witches shared a look, turning to their respective windows. Darkly rolled his down to shove his head out, gagging almost immediately at the stench. "Low-tide."

"In the middle of the afternoon?" Milla pinched her nose. "This time of year?

"Why do I have a bad feeling about this," Darkly murmured, craning his neck to scan the passing trees.

Milla traded her Birkenstocks for checkered slip-ons, shrugged into the sleeves of her moto jacket, and pulled out her phone to text Diego. Her last messages filled the screen, unread, just as the numerous calls had gone unanswered. She licked her lips, fingering her necklace as she texted Ana instead.

> In Vilano Beach, had to run an errand. Be there soon.

Her *čarodějnice* responded almost immediately, texting sales information, that she'd fixed one of the porcelain dolls to say "mama" when rocked back and forth, and to tell Milla she was making great connections at the convention. "I can't wait to tell you all about it!"

"Here we are." Dies-well slowed the minivan to a crawl. Milla looked up from her phone, and the uneasy tingling in her palms erupted into an outright blaze.

"What the fuck," she blurted.

An Everglades-style cottage loomed at the end of the lane; a teetering mass of stilts, wood, and shutters that was more homage to Baba Yaga than Floridian retirement property. More vines had crawled up the maze of stilts, breaching the balcony and tearing through the mosquito netting. They wound around the stair rail, weaving through the balusters. The wart-like pods had grown thick and veiny, the bloom within straining against the confines of the bright green sepals. Several had already burst open, revealing bright purple out-of-season flowers.

"Cannae be." Darkly slid out of the minivan, rushing around to Milla's side.

"I think we're both about to feel very stupid," she muttered.

Dies-well snickered. "Just now?"

Darkly opened her door, his mouth and nose buried in the crook of an elbow. Milla did the same as the sickly-sweet perfume of rot swarmed the car. "She's here."

"Well, shit."

"Any theories as to why Kayleigh's Shade and her very much-so-alive sister are at Ana's house?"

"I have a few uncomfortable theories ranging from 'potentially accurate' to 'raving mad'." Milla stepped onto the runner, one hand on the door. "Which would you like to hear f—" Her foot hit the gravel, and the demesne latched onto its absent witch, buckling her knee and dragging her down.

Darkly grabbed her by the elbow, and she jerked to a nauseating halt inches from the ground. "Milla?"

"I can—" Her tongue was slug thick and fat in her mouth, limbs disjointed as more and more of her was siphoned away by a hungry reservoir. "Ungh, Goddess."

The world tunneled down to only Darkly's face and smudges of black and gray. Her head lolled back, and he swept her into his arms, cradling Milla and holding her close. "Milla? What's happened?"

Color bled into her world the moment she was no longer in contact with the earth, with her demesne. Color and relief. She pressed a hand to the center of her chest, gasping like a fish on a dock and working a bit of her Way to slow her heart and quell the panic.

"Milla?" He jostled her lightly, his voice an echo shouted down a long hallway. "Milla, what was that?"

"My demesne," she croaked. Darkly faltered, his mouth dropping open to breathe a curse. "She's not tending it. I was gone too long, and she's—Anaisa's a *witch*."

"What do I—" he scanned her face for any hurt. He wouldn't find any. This was a Soul-deep hurt—the pain of betrayal. Milla was the Witch of the Demesne. She was St. Augustine, and St. Augustine was *her*, and Anaisa was stripping it away bit by bit without tending the demesne as it deserved.

Darkly looked to the minivan, up at the house, and back to Milla, so utterly befuddled and lost that she huffed a tiny laugh. His scowl was immediate, but if anything, he tightened his hold, charging for the steps. Long legs took them two at a time, and he paused at the landing. "Dinnae ken much about demesnes, so I'm working on a theory here."

He set her down gingerly, and Milla balanced on her tiptoes, gripping the railing with both hands.

"Milla?"

"I'm okay." A lie. Not even a pretty one, so naturally, he called her on it.

"Liar."

"Not technically." When she wasn't dragged to the ground, Milla lowered to her feet, testing and prodding the whisper-thin threads tying her to St. Augustine. She closed her eyes, seeking the cradling support of her demesne and finding only a whisper. An imprint. The bedded down leaves of a deer that had long ago risen and wandered away. A sob rose, and she swallowed it down, down, down, spinning away from Darkly, gripping the banister and gritting her teeth against the *nothing* in the aether. She dug her nails into the wood, taking a risk—just one little push of her Way. A test to see what yet remained, the Enforcer at her back be *damned*.

"*Trouchnivění*." The Forbidden and Foule hex left her lips as a plea. Her desire and intent twinned, her anonymity the sacrifice she was willing to pay. "*Trouchnivění*."

Rot.

Magick tingled over her palm, a heated web of her Way struggling to life only to fizzle and die.

"Did you just do something?" Darkly set his hand over hers. That was it. A simple, innocent touch and magick flared in Milla's veins. Her eyes flew wide, a tiny gasp escaping as the banister beneath her palm crumbled, moldering to nothing, and the strands of *her* wove themselves into the frayed threads of the demesne.

What the fuck was that.

Milla snuffed out her Way, eyes wide and mind reeling. She slipped her hand away from Darkly's, curling it into a fist and shoving it into her pocket. But not before he noticed the festering remains of the banister. The evidence of her Way, what she was, and what they could do.

Together.

Thirty Six

"She's in the kids' bedroom." Madison Stewart greeted them at the door with a frown. A little shorter and a little thinner than her sister, what she lacked in contour and highlights she made up for in sheer bluntness. "What the hell took you so long?"

"Excuse me?" Milla rocked back, bumping into Darkly. "What are you doing in my *car*—friend's house?"

"Shit, sorry." Madison blinked, and all bluster left the woman in an exhausted whoosh. "I didn't realize you two were close, I thought Sarah said she … doxxed your store?"

"Something like that."

"She's in the bedroom?" Darkly slipped past Milla, faltering at the end of a long hall leading to the rear of the house. Madison nodded.

"It's been days. The kids are getting in tomorrow, and I can't—" Her mouth twisted into a frown, making her look nearly identical to Kayleigh as Milla remembered her. "They shouldn't have to live here with their mother haunting the place."

"That's what I don't understand." Milla tried a softer approach, her head cocked and voice easy. Light. As much as she wanted to freak out and yell and demand answers, this was a woman who had just lost her sister. Common sense demanded she appeal to the woman's obvious grief. It felt … horrible. "Why would her kids be coming to live *here*?"

"Why shouldn't they? Their mom is dead, their dad is serving a three-year, and I travel for work. Mom and Dad are the only ones that can take them."

"Mom and …" Milla glanced around the living room, looking for clues. There were no pictures, no photo albums. No identifying stacks of mail to help her understand what in the nine rings was going on. "How do you know Sarah?"

"From Kayleigh's chat group," Madison sneered and pulled her phone from a pocket. "I just got access and found a slew of messages from Sarah sent from her mom's account."

"And … when did Kayleigh die?" Darkly asked.

"Two nights back, carbon monoxide poisoning." She *tsked* and shook her head. "I kept telling my mom to get detectors, but she said it wasn't worth the fuss at her age …" *Two nights back.* Madison's voice faded to white noise, the woman complaining about her mother and safety protocols while Milla's mind ran and ran. *Two nights back.* Where was she two nights back? The raw-head?

Too far.

So New Orleans, then.

Think, Millapet. You know when this happened.

"Shut up." She pressed the heels of her hands against her temples, needing Ezra to leave her alone for five fucking minutes so she could figure this out. White-hot pins prickled behind her eyes, the tell-tale crawl of a migraine blooming as Milla ran through the deaths, the Loa, and why the *fuck* this woman was in Ana's Gran's house, claiming it was Kayleigh's.

Two nights back, two nights back we were … we were in …

"... posted in the group chat. I don't know how her Upline knew it was Kayleigh before the officials released her name."

"When was that?" Darkly prodded.

"Just today."

Milla jerked her head up, the not-ghost of Ezra chuckling as he faded away. "Her Upline."

"God, I despise that woman," Madison sneered. "I told Kayleigh if her idiotic MLM didn't bankrupt her, Annalisa would. I can't believe she brought her here—"

The migraine roared across Milla's skull, and before she could close her eyes, the world split into three.

An elderly couple danced around each other in the kitchen. Milla followed Darkly down the hall. Two small children ran through the room in their bathing suits. Kayleigh set a bouquet of yellow flowers on the mantle and adjusted a statue. Teenaged Madison and Kayleigh lay on the floor, flipping through magazines, their heels kicking in the air. An older woman held Kayleigh amid suitcases and boxes cluttering the living room. Milla slammed into the wall, knocked aside by a fleeing shadow. Kayleigh waved from a bedroom, smiling at a young woman in black leggings and an oversized cardigan.

The triple images split and split and split again. The past, the present, and the future woven together into the tapestry of a family, a life, all the potential they held, and at the center was Milla waist-deep in frigid waters, reaching, seeking, summoning … and walking away.

"I did this," she breathed. The potentials folded in on one another, crumpling and clustering in collapsing fractals, the bloom of a flower in reverse until they become one, obvious truth.

A woman spun in place, around and around and around, her skirt flying out like a fan as her feet kicked up yellow and pink petals. She stopped, smiling at Milla across an impossible distance, her honey-amber eyes twinkling bright.

"Milla?" Darkly's fingers brushed her arm. She pulled away, charging for the mantel where a singular figurine stood among rotten, curling petals.

"I did this," she repeated. "This is all my fault."

"Is she okay?" Madison stage-whispered.

Milla missed Darkly's reply if he made one. She plucked the dancing, smiling figure from the mantel, the caramel-golden waves of her hair caught in the middle of a twirl. Milla knew the statue and her turns well. It had been part of her training with Ezra, and she'd focused an entire year of her degree on the branches of Voodoo, *Las 21 Divisions,* and the nation of the Rada, to which this figure belonged.

But Milla had always been better with the Gede, the Loa of Death. She had studied the Baron and his *Maman,* Papa Legba and Guede Nibo, neglecting the Petro and the Rada and failing to recognize the one Loa who could move among the nations unhindered and attend to her devotees without a vessel.

"Dammit, I thought I got the last of this crap." Madison stepped beside Milla, clearing debris from the mantel. None of it was unexpected. Petals, the burnt end of a cigarette, small sampler perfume vials, a photograph. "Can't believe she let that woman stay here."

"Gran Bwa," Milla whispered, clutching the statue. The fan of the figurine's skirt cut into her palm, and she let the pain ground her. "She called the *leshy* 'Gran Bwa.'"

"What woman?" Darkly's heat blanketed Milla's back, and she closed her eyes, counting backward from ten.

"Ana." Milla made it to five. "Annalisa, Anaisa, Ana Maria Metresa."

"Ana?" He startled, and Milla snatched the photograph from Madison, holding it up for Darkly to see what she already knew. "Get tae—"

"She wasn't in the picture because she took the *fucking* picture." Milla had seen this photograph before, or at least, the one taken just prior. The setting was the same, with the green and white awning and the clusters of chairs. Horned God, Milla had just been there, letting Darkly clean powdered sugar from her lips, in the same place where Kayleigh had posed with her beignets, only in this photograph, she wasn't alone.

The awning was the same, the angle of the sun, the artful dusting of powdered sugar. And Milla would know that city anywhere; how could she not when it was home to her worst memories? Goddess, she would know New Orleans anywhere, just as she knew the honey-amber eyes of Ana, beaming in a selfie next to Kayleigh Masterson. "How could I be so *stupid.*"

"You know Annalisa?" Madison took the photograph back, eyeing Milla with new suspicion.

"She's my apprentice," Milla spat, stomping in an angry circle. "She's my Horned God-damned *čarodějnice*, and this is *all my fault.*"

"No, Milla." Darkly used his calm and careful voice as if she were a doe easily startled. "How could this possibly be your fault? Dinnae—"

"Dinnae what, Darkly?" She shook the statue in his face. "I did this."

He didn't understand. She knew he didn't, and it was her fault. For being a fool and a liar in love. For following Ezra and thinking she wasn't blind. For believing the lies of a Mind Witch just because he made her feel—what—wanted? Needed? Special?

"*Leannán*, how could you have done this?"

"Because we let her *in!*" she cried. "I failed at the lake. I left him out there, and I let her in. *FUCK*. Don't you get it?"

"What does this have to do with the lake?"

"What lake?" Madison added.

"*Everything*." Milla stormed past Darkly, aiming for the hallway. "How has C.R.O.W. still not figured it out? We were attempting a mass summons, *Darkly*. We wanted to bring back magick as it was, and like an idiot, I let Ezra convince me to do it his way. He was so fucking certain." She slashed her hand through the air, heat building in her palms. "So Horned God damned sure of himself. 'We should start with the Loa,' he said. 'Summon the Baron and his *Maman*, open the Gates, and usher in a new era.'" Her tongue soured, acid spraying as she hissed the truth. Drops landed on the shag carpet, fizzing as they ate through the synthetic fibers. "Believe in me, he said, and I couldn't, and now he's Gone. He wanted to rewrite the rules we live by, wanted to prove that C.R.O.W. was wrong." She whirled around, coming face-to-chest with Darkly, which was just *perfect*. "I Saw it, Darkly. All of it. Everything that would come. The Loa, the chaos, a world without C.R.O.W., so I chose." Her next breath was ragged, scraping her throat raw. "I chose the least ruinous path. I chose to leave Ezra in the dark where no living soul can reach him, but I couldn't stop her from slithering in."

"You couldnae have known, Milla."

"*Yes, I could!*" The world went red, and Milla snapped, thrusting a finger at his chest and letting fly all of that rage in the face of her helplessness. "I could, and I *did*." Cotton brittled and browned beneath her fingertip, her Way escaping as she lost control. "You don't know what I am; you don't even know *who* I am. You think you know, but you *don't*, Darkly." Goddess, she'd already lost so much. Ezra, her aura, her *lifeline*, and now she was going to lose the demesne. "You see this broken little witch, and you want to-to what, cheer me up? Make me come with your clever fingers? Fix me? You can't fix this," she hissed, slapping her hand against her chest. The statue bit into her breastbone, and she sneered at the irony of deserved pain.

"I dinnae want to fix you, Milla, I want to *help* you, but I cannae if you dinnae—"

"Tell you the truth? Well," she scoffed. "You have it now. I'm responsible for Ezra being Gone. I'm responsible for the failed ritual at Lake Pontchartrain, *I'm* responsible for Anaisa Fucking Pye murdering a bunch of Karens, so take that back to C.R.O.W. and go home. I have a Loa to get rid of."

She stormed into the bedroom, immediately locating the Shade in the corner, huddled at the end of a bunk bed. He followed her. Why would he not? He needed her to rebuild his reputation with C.R.O.W. To return to whatever life he had outside St. Augustine, Milla, and her weeks of deceit.

A headache screamed across her brow, and her scars burned with magick. She needed an act large enough to call the attention of her demesne, an act Forbidden and Foule to keep her home *safe* from Anaisa. She needed *answers*, and there was one surefire way to get all that she needed.

"Am nae leaving you."

"Fine." Because of *course* he wouldn't leave. He was nice. Kind. Blind to Milla's special brand of wickedness because she'd been lying to him this entire time. She wheeled around, putting her back to the door and crowding Darkly into the room as she spoke with deadly calm. "If you won't leave then I'll treat you like the tool you are."

"Milla—" he started.

She slammed her palm against his chest, locking her eyes on the Shade hovering in the corner and hissing an intent she'd not spoken in years. Milla couldn't conjure salt and scissors, couldn't summon her phone, sunglasses, or water bottles, but she could summon *this*. "*Přijít.*" Come. "*Toto plavidlo je vaše.*" This vessel is yours. "*Přijít.*" Come.

It would have been better if he'd stepped away, grabbed her wrist, or fought back even a little. Darkly only looked down at the blackening tips of her fingers and the rot crawling across the front of his shirt, his eyes drifting closed as her intent took root. Shadows bloomed at his back, absorbing the lingering Shade, his body jolted, and with a high-pitched, tittering laugh, Kayleigh Masterson said, "Hooooooly *wow*, that was incredible."

"Hi, Kayleigh." Milla shook out her fingers and brushed ash away. "I think we need to have a chat."

"Yeah, yeah." Kayleigh twisted around to check herself—himself?—out in the mirror over a dresser. She pursed her lips, wiggled her eyebrows, and ran her hands down the body she was in. "He's a nice one, isn't he?"

"This is temporary, Masterson." Milla braced herself against the bookshelf, head spinning from the use of her Way. "Don't get too comfortable."

"Oh-ho-ho, does Miss Transylvania have a crush?"

Milla ground her teeth together, counting to three. "As a matter of fact, yes, I'm rather fond of him as he is, so let's get on with it." She placed the statue on the dresser. "Where did you get this?"

"Ew, I hate that thing." Kayleigh pinched the statue by the head, sneering in a way that distorted Darkly's features. His sneer was a subtle thing edged in sarcasm, whereas Kayleigh's was riddled with contempt. Milla hated what it did to his face.

"Why do you have it?"

"I bought it in New Orleans a few years ago." She strode across the room and stamped the trash can pedal, tossing the statue inside.

Milla rolled her eyes, shooed Kayleigh out of the way, and retrieved the statue. Placing it upright on the dresser, she turned it to face the Shade wearing Darkly's skin. "Talk, Masterson."

"Fiiine," she rolled her eyes and perched on the edge of the bunk bed. Legs and arms crossed, she tossed Darkly's head as if brushing waves of blonde hair over her shoulder and knocked it against the bedrail of the top bunk. Milla winced, and Kayleigh hissed, rubbing what was sure to be a bruise. "I was there for a convention."

"For ICYMI?"

Kayleigh/Darkly nodded, uncrossing their legs to try the other direction. "I had success with Dale cosmetics and did decently well with Nastat—"

"Nastat?"

"Facial care products. You know, with your complexion, a bronzer really would—"

"Sounds like off-brand UTI medicine."

"No need to be rude." Kayleigh pouted. Milla shrugged and tapped the top of the statue. "Anyways, I thought I would branch out into clothing, and one of the girls in the Nastat group had heard of ICYMI. Real good things, they were angel funded by some investment firm out of Silicon Valley, the designers had been poached from a few of the bigger fast fashion houses, and the test market in Australia went wild for the clothes."

"Get to the point."

"I aaammmm-uh." She smacked Darkly's lips, rolling his eyes. "Anyways, I turned it into a solo trip. Spent a whole day poking around the French Quarter." She gestured to the statue. "I found her in this tacky voodoo store, a real rundown place with shrunken heads and candles and odd artifacts. You know, your shop kinda reminds me of it?" Kayleigh cocked Darkly's head at Milla. "She was tucked behind a set of champagne glasses and pink silk flowers. I only went over there to find whatever perfume I smelled, and she just looked, I don't know, nice? The girl working the counter said she was a protector of family happiness and wealth, which sounded real good to me at the time."

"So you bought a Voodoo statue and brought it home?" Milla glanced between the statue and Kayleigh/Darkly, her mind churning. The timing fit, with Milla and Ezra attempting the ritual at the same time as the ICYMI convention; the beings at play fit, as Milla was pretty positive the store Kayleigh referenced was Marie Laveau's House of Voodoo, which, yes, alright, she could admit it, *had* been part of the decorative inspiration for Southern Gothic, but there was still something she was missing.

"That's where it gets weird." Kayleigh scratched at her chest, paused, and looked down, frantically patting the front of her body and then giggling. "Gosh, that was a fright."

"You alright?"

"Forgot I was a man for a minute." She let out another titter of nervous laughter, flexing and pointing Darkly's feet in a way that made Milla nervous. She could summon Shades no problem, but insofar as summoning them into a *person*, much less a Dark

Witch, she was working on a hunch and hadn't quite figured out the next bit.

"How did it get weird?"

"I couldn't get rid of the statue." Kayleigh/Darkly frowned. "Like, I'd leave her in my room to go to dinner, and she'd be in my purse when I went to grab my wallet. It freaked me out, so I left her in the bathroom at a bar, and when I got to the ICYMI After Party, she was back in my purse. So, I placed her in the center of our table, joking that she was the patron saint of our downlines before we went to dance."

"We?"

Kayleigh nodded vigorously, shaking loose a lock of Darkly's hair. "The girls I was seated with for dinner. Nice gals, most of them are in my downline, except for Jennifer."

"And this was two years ago?"

"Mm-hmm," Kayleigh nodded. "The night of that attack out on Lake Pontchartrain. We were all dancing around to that old Harry Belafonte song when the power went out. I tripped over a chair, and Annalisa helped me back up."

Click.

The final piece slid into place, and Milla stumbled, bracing herself against the dresser. "You danced to 'Banana Boat'?"

"Is that what that song is called?" Kayleigh looked thoughtful. "Always thought it was 'Day-oh.' Anyways, Annalisa and I drove home the next day and built out our downline in Hattiesburg. By the third month, we banked five thousand worth of residual income alone, and the rest is history. And you know what's weird?" Kayleigh/Darkly frowned at the statue. "She followed me everywhere, right? Like, she was in my bag when I went into your awful store—"

"Rude."

"—but when I was settling in on my cruise, she wasn't there."

Milla snapped straight. "What?"

"She didn't come with me." Kayleigh flexed her fingers and rolled Darkly's head on his/her neck. "She always popped up in my bag, but after I met you, she stayed put. I thought I'd finally gotten rid of her. God, the *relief*. I was able to relax and enjoy the cruise."

"Did you sell any ICYMI?"

"Hell no!" Kayleigh blurted, then paused, furrowing Darkly's brow. "I … you know, I didn't even *want* to."

"Thought as much," Milla sighed.

The Shade in Darkly's body watched her behind smoke-stained eyes, lips pursing as she assessed the slight witch. "I died."

"You did," Milla answered—no use lying about it when the woman wore an over-tall meatsuit.

"Did she kill me?"

"I think so." Milla fisted her hands, nerves fluttering wildly. This was going to get … awkward.

Kayleigh stared at Milla for a moment, mouth pinched to a tight button. She lowered her gaze and blinked, and when Kayleigh/Darkly looked up at Milla, their eyes were full black.

"She wants what you have," her voice went flat. Hollow, as though she were repeating something long forgotten. A hand rubbed over Darkly's chest, and Kayleigh bit his lip. "Not just this; she wants everything." A too-long exhale had the Shade angling her face at Milla. "Everything you promised. A place in the new world with her consort by her side and with a horse like this ..." Kayleigh leaned back, placing his body on display. That hand drifting lower.

Consort. A pounding like ritual drums flooded Milla's ears, tensing her shoulders and arms. *Horse.*

"When?"

"Tonight," Kayleigh/Darkly cocked their head, assessing Milla. "You'll never get in. She's made sure of that. The security is loyal to Anaisa, and you're not a Diamond Qualifying Executive. You don't have a badge."

"I'm not concerned." Milla offered a one-shoulder shrug, hoping it conveyed calm when she was anything but. "This is my demesne."

"Not for long." Kayleigh smiled, batting Darkly's eyelashes. And that was that.

She snarled and launched from the bed, grabbing Milla by the shoulders and hooking a foot behind her ankle. The damn woman must have done krav maga when she was alive, the move was so quick. She barely managed to wrap her arms around the Shade, bringing Kayleigh down with her.

They hit the ground, and Darkly's mass knocked the air from her lungs. Her arms loosened, and Kayleigh tore free, stumbling away while Milla scrambled to her feet and ran after him … her … whatever.

Her fingers caught his belt at the end of the hall, and she dug her heels into the carpet, slowing the Shade enough to grab hold of her shoulder and pull Darkly/Kayleigh back. She spun off balance, overcorrecting with arms thrown wide. Milla earned a backhand to the face, and Kayleigh slammed into the wall.

"Hey!" Madison rushed to her feet as Kayleigh/Darkly staggered into the living room, making it a half step before Milla threw herself at him, hugging the Shade around the waist and toppling Kayleigh to Darkly's knees. She scrabbled at his back like a rat, wrapping her arms and legs around him in a bear hug to get him into a half-nelson or something. She didn't really know; she was improvising. Give a witch a break.

Kayleigh/Darkly got their feet underneath them, rising into a sumo squat. They took a step and another, hands curling around Milla's arms to keep her on his back.

"No, nononono," Milla managed to get out before the Shade threw them both backward, slamming her to the ground for the second time. "Unnnggghhh." Her arms fell away, and the Shade rolled off her, staggering to the door.

Madison loomed into sight over Milla, furious. "What the hell?"

"Witch shit," Milla wheezed. She rolled onto her stomach, let out a *huurrrrk*, and pushed off the floor. Darkly's lank finally worked in her favor, keeping Kayleigh from achieving a full, dead-out sprint. She slipped on the welcome mat, pinwheeling his arms to keep her balance as Shade and body half fell/half ran off the covered porch, hitting the stairs and barely managing to keep upright as they skidded-slash-fled down the tightly twisted descent.

Milla lurched after him, gripping the railing and wincing with each footfall. She hit the landing as his right foot hit the gravel driveway, wobbling just enough to send Kayleigh skidding. Milla sent a prayer of thanks to the Goddess that the Shade had no idea what that body was capable of.

But Milla did.

Kayleigh might have spent the last fifteen minutes learning as much as she could about his strengths, which, if Milla was being honest with herself (and it was still a new thing she was trying), she had managed to an impressive degree, but Milla had spent weeks learning Darkly. Running beside him, behind him, watching him move and laugh and tease. Observing his strengths for herself.

And his weaknesses.

She jumped the last three steps, ankles barking as her feet hit the ground. The demesne reared up, latching onto Milla with the same abysmal drag as before but lessened. Manageable. She limped after Kayleigh, now running for the wooden dock, disappearing into the mangroves. Heat gathered in her palm, and she counted the Shade's footfalls before flinging out her right hand, aiming for the patch of gravel in front of Darkly's right foot.

"*Prach!*"

Dust!

She missed.

The ground churned behind the hijacked Dark Witch, bits of gravel bouncing and bursting into a fine powder.

"Motherfucker." Milla sprinted across the gravel driveway, slamming her palm against the driver's side door of the minivan as she passed by. A motor whirred, and Dies-well hollered, "Witch fight!" at her back.

Adrenaline fueled her stride, driving Milla by sheer panic alone. She kept intent burning in her casting hand, gritting her teeth against the constant drag of the demesne on her Way. She plunged into the trees, branches snagging her arms and legs, and a startled gasp left her lips when she set foot on the dock.

The *redwood* dock.

Not cypress. Not coastal oak or lodgepole pine. *Not* of her demesne. Milla could have cried for relief, would have cried if she had the time. But she didn't, so she wouldn't, and instead, she eyed the awkward stride of the Dark Witch. Her feet churned over wood that sought no claim, her hands sliced through the air like scythes, gaining on the witch she could catch on a good day, and *would* catch when he was being driven by an MLM Hun with *no idea* who she'd just pissed off.

"*Trouchnivění!*" Milla flung out her hand.

Rot!

Her hex flew as black lightning shot through with electric purple. Wood crackled and moldered, churning to advanced stages of rot as Kayleigh/Darkly's right leg came down on that old injury, the one he said had never quite healed all the way.

His knee buckled.

Milla launched at his back, pancaking Kayleigh face-first against the dock and holding on like a rodeo cowgirl as the woman rolled and clawed and hissed and spat. She wriggled onto her back, shrieking and swiping at Milla's face, grazing her cheek. For not the first time, Milla was thankful Darkly kept his nails trimmed. She ducked under a fist, straddling his hips and narrowly avoiding a hit to the temple.

"Horned God," she grunted, dodging a follow-up hook and jabbing Kayleigh/Darkly in the shoulder. "Did you used to box or something?"

"Kickboxing." Kayleigh darted out a hand, knotting it in Milla's hair. She wrenched, and Milla shrieked. A handful of black hair came away in Kayleigh's fist, and she lurched up to headbutt Milla. "And CrossFit."

Milla blocked the headbutt, catching the Shade in the nose with her elbow. Cartilage crunched at the impact, and Milla silently apologized to Darkly and his very cute nose for what she'd just done to it. Blood running down her upper lip, Kayleigh threw out her arms and gripped Milla's elbows with the Dark Witch's strength.

Arms pinned, Milla started wiggling her fingers along Kayleigh/Darkly's waist and the stretch of skin revealed by the pull of his shirt, bringing the woman to debilitating tears of laughter. She went wild, bucking her hips and arching back, howling at the relentless onslaught of Milla's fingers until her grip loosened.

Milla ripped her arms free and flung herself over Darkly's chest, using her weight to keep the flailing Kayleigh turtled on the ground. Digging her fingers and nails into his hair, she pinned those strong arms with her elbows. Kayleigh howled, beating at her back and kicking Darkly's legs, but Milla had spent a very fun few minutes figuring out where his center of gravity lay.

She tightened her thighs at his hips and leaned close to Kayleigh's face, hissing the reversal of summons with an intent that was not at all hard to come by.

"*Let', stín, a vrat' mi moji temnou čarodějnici,*" she hissed in Kayleigh/Darkly's face, magick bleeding from her fingertips into his person, burning away the taint of possession with a dark, Forbidden and Foule magick that was all her own. "*Let', stín!*"

Fly, shade.

Intent left her tongue as a fine cloud of graveyard dust.

"No!" Kayleigh shrieked, writhing wildly. Milla had to close her eyes against the sheer terror on Darkly's face. "You don't know what he's like!"

"*Let', stín, a vrat' mi moji temnou čarodějnici,*" she hissed again. "Give me back my Dark Witch." Milla brought her mouth to Darkly's and kissed him, harsh and cruel, a punishing embrace to draw the Shade from his person; ready and willing to take a further step into her magick than she'd ever gone.

The flailing slowed. Weak fists beat at Milla's back and then stopped altogether. An arm snaked around her shoulders, and

Darkly returned the kiss, following Milla's mouth with his until she pulled too far away. He dropped his head back, gulping at the air as Milla sat up, eyeing an errant fly buzzing near her head. A billow of smoke swirled from her mouth, and the cost of her Way hit Milla like six shots of vodka on the head of a hammer. She swayed, giggling when the horizon bobbed with her.

Darkly gripped her by the arms, his green eyes blazing with barely tempered rage. "Do *not* do that to me again."

THIRTY SEVEN

"HAVE TAE GET YOU out of here," Darkly grunted, easing Milla onto the dock. She hiccuped, arms and legs boneless and her head swimming from her Way. "Can you stand?"

"Prolly not," she drawled and hiccuped again. The redwood plank by her head heaved like it was caught on the swell of a wave, and the spit in her mouth turned sour. "Uh-oh."

"Uh-oh?" Darkly's shoes scuffed into view. He ducked low, brushing her bangs back.

"Might wanna—" Her stomach hitched and pinched; she burped and then scrabbled for the edge of the dock, emptying her stomach into the Tolomato River.

"Goddess," Darkly cursed and crouched beside her, buzzing phone in one hand. A text from the mysterious Lou lighted up the screen, the words large and angry, even to Milla's blurry vision.

WHERE ARE YOU

She pushed onto her knees, swaying as she knelt back. "Someone's textin' you."

Darkly glanced at his phone, snarled, and shoved it away. "We have about fifteen minutes before every Enforcer in the Panhandle Coven descends upon this house." He hoisted Milla into a fireman's carry, her head lolling against his arm with each angry step down the dock. "Dinnae ken you fancy explaining what you just did in there." *To me.* "But don't think for a *second* I willnae demand an explanation the minute you're through whatever"—he glanced at her, brow furrowed, mouth twisted into a frown, but his eyes were wide and worried, and something about that made her smile—"this is."

"You got it," she rasped and hiccuped again. "Boss."

"Dinnae *dare* heavin' on me."

"No promises."

"What the hell was *that?*" Madison met them at the end of the dock, hustling beside Darkly, who didn't bother to slow his stride. "You damn near put a hole through my wall!"

"Apologies," he grumbled. "Wasnae myself."

"I'll say," Milla chortled.

"Are you drunk?" Madison frowned at the upside-down witch, and Milla gave her a thumbs up. "I don't think I want to know." She jerked her head toward the house. "Did you get her?"

"I got her." Milla nodded, the motion making the upside-down world bob.

Madison pressed a hand against her chest, eyes fluttering closed. She mouthed "thank you" before moving to Dies-well's window and barking directions over the rising wail of sirens in the distance. "—an old service road. It should connect to Carcaba, and you can get lost in the neighborhood around Macie Lake."

Dies-well pushed the van to the limits of its suspension, tearing down the dirt road and nearly rolling up on two wheels when he turned them onto an overgrown service road. Milla clung to the armrests and Darkly white-knuckled the Oh-Shit handle with one hand, furiously swiping something into his phone. The van righted itself, Dies-well eased them into a suburban neighborhood of McMansions and SUVs, and Darkly's arm dropped to his leg.

Milla didn't mean to look, but her eyelids drooped, and he angled the screen just so, so she did.

"WHERE ARE YOU." The text screamed, timestamp less than five minutes old.

"Outside of Tallahassee," Darkly had replied. "Why?"

"Thank you," Milla whispered. He looked over at her, eyes flicking from her face to the blackened tips of her fingers. Without a word, he crawled into the rear seat and drew a curtain of midnight between them.

"West on Hypolita," Milla pointed through the partition and glanced at her phone, where yet another call to Diego had gone unanswered. *He's just busy*, she told herself. *The convention is in town, the store is overrun, and I'm late getting back. He has every right to ignore me.*

"It's really … bright," Dies-well muttered. He pressed back against the driver's seat, gloved hands gripping the steering wheel and arms locked straight, keeping as much of himself out of the setting sun as possible.

"There's an alley halfway down The Court; the balconies and trees keep it shaded."

"Thank you." He glanced over his shoulder at her, dour mouth twitching. "Are you alright, Little Lightner?"

"Marie concerned about her investment?"

Dies-well shook his head. "By all means, if that is what gets me a straight answer."

Milla shrugged one shoulder. "I've been better." Which seemed to satisfy the vampire.

"Did everyone know you and Ezra were married?" Darkly's voice, thicker and lazier than usual, dripped through his shadows. Milla twisted around as they fell away, purling like smoke and dissipating to nothing, revealing Darkly in repose and absolutely stoned out of his mind.

"Hooooooooly—"

"Fancy?" He held out a slick, black vape pen. Milla shook her head, utterly dumbfounded. His eyes were green and bloodshot, and the sweet incense of clove and clean smoke wafted from his person. He chuckled, which turned into a giggle, which melted into a groan. "I am in way over my head."

"Please don't have an existential crisis in the back of my car," Dies-well grumbled.

"Have you been stoned this whole time?" Milla balked. Darkly shrugged, the familiar lizard-lazy half smile curling his lips. "*That's* why your cottage always smells like incense!" she gasped, pointing at the witch. "Oh. My. Goddess and that stupid bean bag! Is this why you were benched?"

"Nae," he scowled and waggled a finger at her. "You've nae place to cast stones, Ludmilla. We all have our crutches."

"I don't have a—"

"Tea."

She slammed her mouth shut, cutting off her protest behind the clacking of her teeth.

"Hawthorne, hemlock and hellebore," he sang. "Ground in clove and juniper, steeped in ash and sprinkled with dandelion."

Hawthorn for the heart and to bind a witch in wood.

Hemlock to dampen, to poison, and purge.

Hellebore to banish the ache in the heart.

"How did you—"

"Dated a vinefica for a time," Darkly cut her off. "One tends to pick up a thing or two about herblore." To emphasize his point, he pressed the vape to his lips, inhaled, and blew a cloud of clove-scented smoke toward Milla. "That shite's poison, how are you still alive?"

"I use my Way and work a return that pings as a chrono-hex." Darkly's bloodshot eyes widened, and Milla felt a twinge of pride in her ability. A simple return disguised as a chrono-hex, useful for healing wounds, reversing the effects of cellular death, and turning desecrants to dust. "*Návrat.*"

"The raw-head," he rasped. Milla nodded. The vape pen danced over his knuckles and vanished. Darkly scrubbed a hand over his face before asking, "Why were you drowning your Way?"

"It was Ezra's idea," she blurted. "That trip to Hong Kong, we saw a vinefica in Kowloon; she designed it to keep my magick from flaring so if the worst happened if we failed and I …"

Tomb-like was not descriptive enough of a word to encompass the silence that fell. Darkly stared at her, his face utterly devoid of thought. Of feeling. And then he lurched forward, grabbing Milla by the arms and dragging her into the backseat onto his lap. Goddess, he was fast. She let out a singular squeak of surprise before his mouth crashed into hers.

Darkly's kiss was fierce, irate, and … hungry. Strong hands squeezed her arms and dropped to her waist, fingertips pressing hard against her ribs, her spine, and up into her hair only to drag back down, the pressure just this side of pain. Milla matched his fervor, shocked at the kiss and oh-so grateful. What she had done, the risk she had taken with his person in summoning that Shade, in *possessing* him on a theory and without consent ... Goddess, he had every right to be mad, to hate her, and this was his response? Her heart kicked up in hope. If this wasn't forgiveness, it was at least a statement of interest, suggesting where they could be without the Loa and CR.O.W. and Milla's status as a wicked witch, Forbidden and Foule.

But then again, so was he.

Her head dropped back as Darkly trailed his lips down her throat, across her collarbone. Her breath caught, a quiet hitch, and she forced out, "I thought you'd be mad at me."

"Furious." He nipped the crook of her neck. "Irate." His teeth snagged her earlobe. "Absolutely raging." His hands slid up her back, fingers stretching up her neck to brace the base of her skull. Keeping her right where he wanted her: on his lap and at his mercy. "Dinnae tell me you're nae acquainted with angry sex."

"Hardly," she huffed a tiny laugh and pressed against his hold, eyeing Darkly down the slope of her nose. "I was married to Ezra."

Mouth pressed against her skin, Darkly rumbled his mirth, sending shivers down her spine. He worked his lips across her jaw, and the cool breath of Shades bloomed from his palms. A path of goosebumps rose from his touch while the rest of his magick roiled beneath the surface, adding to the hypnotic swirls and relaxing, kneading pressure of his fingers.

"Thought you couldnae summon."

"I can't," she gasped as he nipped an earlobe.

"Liar."

"N-not technically." He did it again and blew gently at the patch of skin behind her ear, causing Milla to arch her back. "Can't s-summon things, just Shades."

"And New Orleans?"

"An accident." The truth. She'd lost control, they'd been affected by the candlesmoke, and Milla hadn't even known she'd done *anything* until Marie mentioned a summoning. Until the Voodoo Queen lobbed her question. Until that moment in the Voodoo glade.

Do you know what you both can do? Together?

"And just now?"

"A hunch."

"Hm." His Shades snaked into her hair, prickling her scalp. "Dinnae ken who I'm angrier with. You or Ezra."

"Ezra?" Milla leaned away to look him in the eye, but Darkly cupped her cheeks, pulling her lips to his.

"He wanted to hide you," Darkly whispered against her mouth. "Cannae believe they hid *you* from me." He slipped his tongue in when she started to reply, tasting of clove and smoke, a heady mixture that Milla greedily swallowed. Twining her tongue with his, she slipped her hands up his chest. Ash-tipped fingers stained his throat as they slipped behind his head, holding his mouth to hers, as captive as he held her.

Darkly groaned, adjusting his seat to drag her forward. Her thighs spread, knees hitting the seat, and he bucked his hips, drinking the moan she released at the swollen feel of him rubbing against the seam of her jeans.

She pulled away, just enough to form his name against his lips. "Darkly—"

"Dinnae talk," he rasped, hands gripping her ass as he jerked his hips again. "Dinnae think, *leannán*." She bit her lips to keep from moaning, fingernails pinching into his skin. Darkly growled and sought out her mouth. Cupping a breast, he swept his thumb over her nipple until Milla gasped outright. He plunged his tongue deep, lightly pinching her nipple through her bra and shirt, rocking against her again and again, drowning out whatever it was he thought Milla was going to say.

"Oh, Goddess," she gasped, eyes fluttering closed as he trailed lips down her throat, tonguing the hollow at the base. Milla held his head there, rolling her hips. Clever fingers tugged at the waist of her jeans, undoing the button and jarring Milla back into herself. She clenched her thighs around him, vanity lurching forward. "Darkly, you're stoned."

"Ahem."

"Aye, and livid," he replied. Calloused palms slipped under her shirt and up her sides, hands cupping her breasts as his Shades wound around her waist, drawing the witch closer.

"Sorry to interrupt, but—"

"Doesnae change what I want." A soft kiss followed. "Now help me by taking off these pants."

"We're here, damn your blood!" Dies-well barked. "And if you two are planning on having a hate-fuck in *my* minivan, I reserve the right to know and plan my absence accordingly."

The hall was dark, Milla's store as quiet as a mausoleum. She paused at the door, Dies-well and his umbrella bumping against her back. "He's not here," she murmured, flipping on the lights and walking forward in a daze. "Why isn't he here?"

"Who?" Dies-well collapsed his umbrella and squeezed around Milla, shoulders relaxing the moment he was out of the sun.

"Diego?" Darkly strode past Milla with both of their bags. "Mate, you good?"

"He's not here." She scrolled through the notifications on her phone. Every call she'd placed, every text she'd sent to the Stitch Witch, all unanswered and unread.

Goddess, when was the last time she'd spoken to Diego? So much had happened so *quickly*. The mobile home, Anaisa Pye, *Ana*—Ana had called for him; she'd held that after-party, keeping the store open late, and someone had asked for Diego by name. But who? Ana had been calling him, Ana had pulled him away from their conversation, and he'd asked Milla to come home quickly, so *who*?

Julie.

It had to be Julie; no one else in St. Augustine knew Diego, and as far as C.R.O.W. was concerned, he didn't exist. She fired off a text, ignoring Julie's previous messages.

Pocketing her phone, Milla joined Darkly in the sewing room and stumbled to a halt. Diego's workspace looked like the witch had just stepped out; bobbins, thimbles, and spools of thread were strewn over the table, a box of buttons sat unopened on the corner, and the drawer of zippers was ajar. A half-drunk glass of water was carefully perched on a Barefoot Bill's coaster next to the remains of a wilted salad, and an unfinished sleeve was half-fed through the sewing machine.

"This isn't right." Milla brushed past Darkly, grabbing the salad from the desk and tossing it into a trashcan. "Diego never leaves a mess."

"Milla—"

"He always cleans up. Every night. He hates a messy workspace; he likes his bobbins put away." Which she started doing one by one. And then the thimbles, sweeping them into her palm. "He's always yelling at me for leaving things out."

"*Leannán.*" Darkly placed his hand at her back, holding something out for Milla to take.

"I don't understand why he would just leave everything …"

"Maybe he was called away?" Dies-well spoke from the door.

"But he would clean this up first and finish that sleeve. You don't understand. He *always* cleans up. After himself, after me, he wouldn't—"

"Milla, you need to read this." Darkly shoved a piece of paper in her hands, crowding Milla's back. The paper was a soft, floral pink bordered by yellow flowers. Milla read it. Then read it again, willing the words to be different. "It was on his table."

I have him.

"It's Ana's paper." The sheet fell from trembling fingers, fluttering to the floor, and Milla went with it. Hunching over her knees and gripping her skull to stave off the rising panic.

I have him.

"It's Ana's paper, it's *fucking Anaisa.*"

"Milla, you dinnae ken that."

She began rocking back and forth, trying to stop the scream building in her throat, trying to keep from diving headfirst into her carefully controlled dread and unable to convince herself of anything but the worst.

"Is she all right?" Dies-well's voice was far away, an echo underneath the shrieking in her head.

This is all my fault.

"Dies-well, get out of here." Darkly's feet pounded against the floor.

"I'm not leaving, damn your blood," he argued. "Marie's orders."

*This is all **my fault.***

St. Augustine was full of women suckered into Ana's scheme. Women who would already be at the convention, ready to fall victim to whatever fresh hell the Loa had concocted. They'd been feeding her through the chat groups and their sales and events, affirming Anaisa Pye and Milla had been too stupid, too *blind* to recognize the threat. All the flowers, the perfumes, that Horned God Damned beer-in-a-champagne-glass schtick that she had thought so cute and *so Ana* at the time, and now Diego was gone.

I have him.

Milla had brought Diego back to this life, and he had become her purpose. Her being. Her *family*, and this was all her fault.

For believing Ezra's lies. For believing she could change the world for the better and not seeing the destruction and ruin it would bring until it was too late. Ezra was Gone, and she hadn't been able to stop the ritual, not entirely. A Loa had slipped through, and now it was trying to steal her demesne. Trying to steal from Milla everything she and Ezra had promised.

Her phone buzzed, a rancid, chemical burn filled the air, and Milla moaned. The women were at it again, celebrating Anaisa Pye, celebrating *Ana*; affirming and strengthening the Loa with

each

and

every

word.

And isn't this what Milla had wanted? Isn't this what she had trained for and fought for and betrayed her heart for?

A new world, a free flow of magick. Loa and Orisha. Domovoy, Huldufólk, and Húsvætti. A return to the old ways when witches like Darkly and Milla weren't forced to hide what they were. She had let Ezra twist her into a tool for his use, had let herself be blinded by the witch with his sparkling eyes and his pretty little lies—that he knew better, that he could change the world, and she had *believed* him.

"I hate him." Milla moaned to the floor, voicing a thought that had curdled in her heart and mind for years, far longer than the two he had been Gone. If she could pinpoint the when, the exact moment she had started to hate him, it would make it easier. But she couldn't, and Ezra was winning because he always won. It was the Way of the Witch; he saw what he wanted, and he took it and damn everyone else in the world. He always won, even when he gambled on the wrong little witch and lost. Because even now, exiled in the shadows and Gone, a Loa had slipped through and was finishing what he started.

"I hate him, I hate him, I hate him." Milla rocked, hugging her legs. Heat flooded her veins, itching beneath her scars and feeding the scream rising like noxious gas in a caldera.

"Goddess be damned, Dies-well, take the bags and go!"

A door slammed. A wave of churned wet earth, ash, and clove overpowered the rancid chemical stench from her phone. Cold air hit Milla like an arctic wind, pushing her to her knees and tearing around the witch, capturing her in a funnel of wild magick that swallowed her scream.

The howling release of fear and rage and injustice scraped her throat raw. It was a mournful bellow and a banshee's warning wail. Because it was her fault. The angry little witch who wanted to rewrite the world and fit it into her own chosen narrative. The liar she had become to fit the liar he was.

No one had done this to her. This was Milla paying the price for her arrogance and misdeeds, and she needed to set it right.

She needed to send Anaisa Pye back beyond the Gates and seal them properly. Needed to fix what was inherently broken so she could walk away from it all with a smudged conscience.

"I hate him!" She moaned aloud while in her head and her heart, she hated herself.

Milla threw her head back, cursing and spitting intent into the voided space and arctic winds surrounding her.

She crumpled to the ground as a miserable, weak thing.

Decrepit carpet hissed beneath her knees and her hands, crumbling to dust. Ash filled her mouth, and she held on hands and knees, panting and gasping as her mind worked through it all. Lake Pontchartrain and the ritual, the scar on her arm, her fractured Seeing, hawthorn, hellebore, hemlock, and clove. Kayleigh and ICYMI. Diego who hadn't been able to live free in his first life and was missing in his second. Julie and that empty bedroom for a child who would never come. Ezra, who had loved her, and Ezra, who had lied. Ezra, who was Gone, and the Dark Witch that was Here.

She thought of the women suckered into the scheme. Of Morgen and C.R.O.W. and a lifetime of hiding who she was. What she was.

She thought of that Dark Witch again, of the night she had spent in his arms, and she wondered what they could do.

Together.

She cried, she yelled, and she howled all of that to the festering rot blooming beneath her palms.

And then she took a Big Girl Breath and rose as a Death Witch.

Thirty Eight

Darkly was there when she stood, shrouding Milla's pain from the mortal and mundane in his blanket of midnight. She walked right through it, parting the Shades with a sweep of her hand and marching into the main room of Southern Gothic. Flowers rotted in her wake, fabric unraveled, and the reeds in the oil diffusers withered to blackened, twisted stems.

"While Ezra and I were on the lake, opening the gates and summoning Shades, Anaisa slipped through." She stated the facts as she knew them, wanting there to be abso-fucking-lutely zero question as to what would happen next. "Kayleigh bought a figurine of the Loa and took it to the ICYMI convention, where she and her Huns sang 'Banana Boat' and summoned her. From that point on, she began feeding off of her downline."

Dies-well whistled, pulling his phone from a pocket and typing a message. Darkly stood a few feet away, his shoulders tense and pupils dilated, ready and wary of Milla.

She supposed that was fair. He knew who she was. What she was. He had just watched her lose control of her Way and reduce Diego's sewing room to a mass of rot and ash. Her only question was: why did he shroud her in his Shades?

Why did he keep helping her?

He couldn't fix Milla, and the Enforcers were sure to come after that explosion of her Way. There was no more hiding to be done, not after *that*, which meant Milla was free to act until C.R.O.W. swarmed her demesne. She could take down Anaisa with the full force of her magick and ensure the Loa never hurt another woman.

Which was why she spoke carefully now.

"Kayleigh died two days ago because of me." Darkly opened his mouth to argue, and Milla silenced him with a finger raised. "I performed that ritual with Ezra. *I* summoned the Shades of your Neitherworld to myself to give Ezra a clear shot at the Gates, which begs the question … where were you?"

Darkly pursed his lips and dropped his eyes to the ground. A slip of smoke bloomed across his shoulders and coiled around his left arm. "In hospital."

"The hospital?"

"There was an incident in the Netherlands; I was put into a coma, and when I woke, the Shades told me there was someone at the Gates."

"We were told everything was ready," she replied. "I can only assume that meant you were out of the way."

He nodded, the color draining from his face. Freckles stood in stark relief on his nose and cheekbones, and, for a fleeting instant, Milla truly thought he was about to be ill. "When I woke, Ezra was Gone. No one knew what had happened, the Shades couldnae make sense of it all, and then …"

"You were benched." Milla nodded. "I was in hiding, and as far as C.R.O.W. was concerned, Ezra was no longer a problem. At least, not until Anaisa arrived in my demesne."

"Something like that."

She chewed her lip, thinking back through the weeks.

There was a surge of magick tracked by C.R.O.W. The sort this demesne hasn't seen in over a year, since you assumed the role of Witch of the Demesne.

"The night of the ritual was the first time I'd used my Way in public at such a scale. That ritual welcomed Anaisa into our realm, and I used the same ritual to summon Diego. Makes sense her manifestation in St. Augustine would have pinged as a similar surge on the E.R.I.E.s." Darkly's hand drifted to his phone, and Milla narrowed her eyes at him. "Really?"

"I powered it down."

"*Really?*"

"Honest." He pulled his phone from a pocket and tossed it onto the counter. The plastic case clacked against the glass surface and Darkly crowded into Milla's space. "Stopped running my E.R.I.E. after you drank your tea." He trailed his fingers over her hip. "Wasnae a lie, Milla. I want to help you."

"Alright," she exhaled, caught by his jade-green gaze.

A tiny smile flickered, the green darkened, and that infuriating smirk drove into Darkly's cheek. "What do you need?"

And if that weren't the sexiest Horned Goddamn thing Milla had ever heard.

Heat crawled up her breastbone, bleeding onto her neck. She grabbed her duffel from the floor and plopped on the counter, digging through the contents for something to do with her hands. "Kayleigh said Anaisa left her alone the day she came into my store, which means she's been planning this for longer than I initially thought. Whatever she's going to do, she's doing it tonight."

"At the ICYMI Convention?"

"Mm-hmm. The keynote begins in an hour. Kayleigh warned me that the security at the Fountain of Youth is loyal to Anaisa. She seemed convinced I wouldn't be able to get in. Lucky for us,"—Milla pulled out a handful of clothing and dumped it on the counter, finally spotting what she'd been digging for. She grabbed the graffitied hunk of concrete, placing it carefully on the counter—"I have a Jericho Stone."

"Get tae—!" Darkly hollered and leaped away.

"What has the Goody Death Witch done no—" Dies-well's eyes landed on the stone, then bugged wide. "Gory damn and hellfire, is that a *Jericho Stone?*"

I … yes?" Milla glanced at the concrete chunk.

Dies-well shoved himself behind Darkly, gripping the Dark Witch's sides and peering around his shoulder. "What in God's name are you doing with a Jericho Stone?"

"We're nae using a-a *that* to get into the Fountain of Youth," Darkly snapped.

"What else are we going to use?" Milla swept the concrete from the counter. Both witch and vampire flinched. "This thing can eat through walls, and it's already charged, and I—"

"Already *charged?*" Darkly near shrieked. "Are you mad?"

"You two can't seriously be afraid of this." She thrust the stone at the pair, who jumped a full foot back. "It's just a rock."

"It's a menace, that's what it is." Darkly whipped a scarf free from a rack and tossed it at Milla. "Wrap that thing up before it eats through—"

The bells over the front door jangled, their merry song drawing the attention of Dark Witch, Death Witch, and vampire to the mortal woman removing her keys from the lock, a pair of boots tucked in her arm.

"Jules?" Milla shoved her arm and the stone behind her back. "What are you doing here?"

"You texted." The nurse took in the odd scene: Dies-well clinging to Darkly, Milla obviously hiding something behind her back, and the pile of clothes on the counter. She set the boots down. "I came by to drop off your boots and see if you needed any help before heading to the convention."

"What? No." Milla darted out from behind the counter, rushing up to the nurse. "Nonono, Julie, you can't go."

"Why not?" She jerked her chin back, nostrils flaring. "I worked really hard to earn my badge."

"You have a badge?" Milla was aware her voice went a little too shrill, a little too excited. She just didn't care. "When did you get a badge?"

"Milla …" Darkly sidled close, his tone a warning.

"Yesterday," Julie smiled. "Wild, isn't it? I was ready to quit, didn't even think I was close to earning Diamond Qualifying Executive, but I guess the last-minute sales tipped me over. Ana brought it by this morning before heading to the Fountain of Youth."

"Yeah, that's"—Milla tracked Darkly, sliding behind Julie and frantically mouthing *No. Do not. Stop.*—"really cool. You must be so excited."

"I'm mostly going to support the girls," Julie sighed. "For closure, in a way. They planned a memorial for Kayleigh and McKenzie and the others during the keynote, and I really want to be there."

"Totally." Milla nodded, big dips of her chin paired with wide, overly genuine eyes. "Hey, did you see the new signs they put up in Toques Place?"

"The new …" Julie twisted, peering around Darkly, and Milla pressed a palm between her shoulder blades.

"*Běž spát.*" She muttered the go-to-sleep hex before she could think too hard about what she was doing. Julie wavered, hummed a little happy noise, and fell directly into Darkly's arms.

"What in the nine rings, Milla!" He lay the nurse down, pressing two fingers against her throat to check for a pulse.

"I didn't kill her, calm down." Milla crouched beside him, digging through Julie's bag and pulling out various brochures, tubes of chapstick and lipstick, an ICYMI branded folder, her wallet, and, finally, a colorful badge on a bright pink lanyard screaming ICYMI SPRING SALES KICK-OFF in bold, white letters.

"This wasnae part of the plan," he hiss-whispered. "Not that we *had* a plan, per se."

"Change your mind about the Jericho Stone?"

"Nae."

"Then stop complaining." Milla stood with the badges and a folio in her hand. "She's just asleep."

"Milla, *leannán*, this is wrong. You know that, right? It is very important to me that you know what you just did is wrong."

"We need to get into that event, Darkly." He straightened at her tone—cold, unfeeling. Analytical. "I have to stop Anaisa from doing whatever it is she's about to do and stealing my demesne. You and I both know there's enough residual magick in St. Augustine to allow her to blow the Gates wide open." Meeting his eyes, Milla straightened her shoulders, trying to add height and still about eight inches short of being threatening to the over-tall witch. "I didn't know what else to do. But what I *do* know is that—"she glanced at the badge in her hand—"Diamond Qualifying Executive Julie Alicia Kettler just saved our asses."

She withdrew a garish neon pink ticket edged in silver from the folder. It was greasy to the touch, and both witches wrinkled their noses at the sickly perfume wafting from the paper. Milla flashed it at Darkly and smiled knives. "Put her in my office and lock the door."

"Ooh, no. I draw the line at dragging bodies around your little shop of horrors."

Milla rolled her eyes and faced the vampire, who was not-so-subtly taking pictures of her store with his phone. "Dies-well? I need your help with a body."

He grinned, a slow roll of a thing that crawled his lips open like two caterpillars pulling apart. "Finally."

Most of the damage to Diego's sewing room was contained in a four-foot-wide circle of ash, withered synthetic carpet, and rot. Some of his fabric had been caught by her Way, as well as the corner of his table, but the sewing machine blessedly remained unscathed.

She rummaged through a few drawers and boxes, changing out of her filthy clothes and loading a messenger bag before kneeling in front of Diego's altar, appealing to the Triple Goddess for strength and courage. What she was about to do, what she had to do to protect those who had protected her, well … Milla was a witch, but she wasn't an asshole.

Snuffing out the candle, she slung her bag over a shoulder and paused as she glimpsed the corner of a cardboard box shoved under a ream of satin on his table. She pulled it free, vision blurring behind tears as she read the label.

Hostess City Tea & Spice

She set her hand on the label, closing her eyes and letting those quiet tears fall. "Where are you, Diego?"

There was no answer, not that she expected one, so Milla opened the box and shoved handfuls of tea into her messenger bag. She strode into the hall, head clear and resolve firm, stopping short to admire the six feet and change of Do Not Fuck With standing in her store.

The aural insurance adjuster in Chambray and shorts was wholly replaced by a C.R.O.W. Enforcer in worn, military-issue steel-toed boots and black BDU rip-stop pants. Tucked into his boots and fitted to a sinful degree, the pants were riddled with a vast array of pockets, loops, buckles, and sheaths, one of which hosted the obsidian handle of an athame. Hex-reinforced pads were sewn onto the knees, allure-stop cast into the seams, and they hung distractingly low on his trim hips. A Royal Marine-style black woolly-pully clung to every line and curve of his lean, muscular frame. Light hex-resistant padding in a brighter shade of black was sewn at the shoulders, elbows, and over his heart.

Milla had never seen him in all black, and the sight of it was enough to send a not-unpleasant shiver down her spine. It suited him, upsettingly so, turning the witch into a walking Shade.

Lethal and wicked and everything she wanted.

A whispered "Goddess" escaped, and Darkly turned his head, a knowing gleam flaring in green eyes. With shaking fingers, she began braiding her hair to have something to do with her hands.

Darkly smirked, rolling his shoulders back to better place himself on display, and then he saw what Milla was wearing and laughed.

"What." He stalked down the hallway to get a better look. "What?"

Milla looked down at her clothes, not seeing the issue. Boots, knee-high black-and-white striped socks, the least offensive pair of ICYMI leggings she could find—which amounted to a multi-colored lily print in muted gem tones—a hex-resistant compression top, and a cotton tank top. Darkly grinned at her, bemused, and leaned closer to get a better view of the graphic on her tank top.

"Is that a witch tied to a pyre?"

"Lighting her cigarette on the flames. Why?"

Darkly straightened and glanced over his shoulder at Dies-well, jamming a thumb in her direction.

"What?" Milla pushed.

"Just a little on the nose is all."

"Says the Enforcer wearing stygian black tactical gear designed to highlight his better assets," Milla grumbled.

"You fancy it, then?"

"Shut up." She slipped around him, neck flushing, and headed for a corner of her store where she kept an odd assortment of sporting equipment. Selecting wrist guards, elbow pads, and knee pads, she held out a set of hockey shoulder pads for Darkly.

"Nae wearing those."

"Your broken bones." Milla flicked the hex-resistant patch over his heart, adding a pinch of her Way for good measure.

Darkly smiled, close-lipped and cocky, as magick crackled and sparked over the hex-resistant fabric, which remained unscathed. "We've moved beyond plastic and styrofoam, Milla."

"What a pity we don't all have the deep coffers of C.A.R.B. to supply us with high-end gear." Milla tugged on the elbow pads and sashayed past him.

"I was thinking," he called after her, "when this is all ended, we should go to the beach."

"The beach?" Milla frowned. "You've been living at the beach for weeks."

"I'm talking a proper beach, or maybe an island, where it feels like the sun never sets, and you're surrounded by blue water on all sides." He closed the distance, green eyes bright and hopeful. "Somewhere quiet with no one else around so I can—"

"I am right here." Dies-well smacked the backrest of Diego's rococo chair.

Darkly flexed the fingers of his left hand, settling back on his hips and crossing his arms. "So, what is your plan?"

"Interrupt whatever ritual Anaisa is planning and keep her from stealing my demesne."

"You aim to detain?" Dies-well asked.

"Something like that."

"I can work with 'detained'." Darkly nodded, brows pulled together. He showed Milla the map pulled up on his phone. "I'll be waiting here." He tapped the corner of Myrtle and Magnolia Avenues. "Use the Jericho Stone to eat through the wall and get me in."

"Good thinking." Milla examined her nails, the chipped black polish, and the peachy-pale tips of her fingers, pleased that they weren't trembling. "Only, you forgot one thing."

"What's that?"

"Your alibi." Throwing her arms forward, Milla slammed her palms against each of their chests. Careful to avoid the hex-resistant patch on Darkly's woolly-pully, she spat ash with her hex. "*Zastavit.*"

Halt.

Neither witch nor vampire blinked, and while Dies-well only looked bored, Darkly's green eyes were frozen wide with surprise, his delicious lips parted in a tiny *o*.

"I'm sorry." She backed away, palms tingling and another hex at the ready. "You've done so much to help me, and I can't … I can't let anyone else get hurt because of my mistakes."

The index finger on his left hand twitched.

"*Zastavit!*" Milla hit him a second time.

And then she ran.

Thirty Nine

Milla channeled all of her rage, drawing on the helpless, panicked energy she had shoved down down down and throwing it into her legs. Darkly could dispel one of her halting hexes in under a minute. If, or when, this all blew up in her face, she needed it to look like a hex-and-run so that when Darkly followed her, it would look as though he were in active pursuit of his target.

And when the punishment Milla had been avoiding for years finally caught up with her, only she would pay the price. She owed him that much. He'd driven her to Hattiesburg without question and then to New Orleans. He'd protected her with his Shades, caught her, and *listened* to her when no one else would.

It was the least she could do for the witch who had seen the truth of her and asked, "What do you need?"

She flew through the Colonial Quarter, dust from decaying cobbles whorling behind each footfall as the witch fed the demesne with her run. Thighs screaming and lungs burning, her heart hammered at the thrill of communing with the demesne.

Her demesne.

Somewhere along the way, her accidental role had become a part of her. A defining piece of the witch and Horned God be damned if Milla wasn't going to throw every bit of herself into tending St. Augustine the way the ancient city deserved. All she had to do was perform an act of Forbidden and Foule magick large enough to fully re-stake her claim.

And banish a Loa.

And not get caught by C.R.O.W.

No big deal.

Milla veered onto Florida State Highway A1A, opening her stride for the last half mile. She ran her fingers along the warped, ridged trunk of the Old Senator Tree—a massive, ancient oak older than the city itself—and fell into a walk at Magnolia Avenue.

The street was packed with minivans and SUVs, most featuring stick-figure families and church stickers, all advertising ICYMI. As expected, the entrance to The Fountain of Youth was manned by security staff, their bright yellow windbreakers garish against the stucco and tile archway and artistically crumbling walls of the venue.

A row of barricades twisted back on itself, funneling women through the entrance. The last rays of Florida sunshine faded behind the palm trees, and the shadows lengthened, bleeding and deepening together in the wrong direction. Milla stared directly into the lens of the security camera she had positioned herself under, allowing one tiny smile as a faint chilled breeze tickled her neck, and those same shadows swallowed the camera whole.

The energy humming from the Fountain of Youth was unbelievable; a jittering wall of optimism and excitement that tickled Milla's nose. A part of her brain, the desperate lonely piece, clung to the idea of hope Anaisa spread among her devotees, and a disingenuous grin crawled across her face. She showed her stolen badge to the yellow-clad security detail, smiling and chit-chatting as he scanned the barcode on her ticket. The silver script flashed neon pink, and the guard waved Milla through. She sneezed, the smile fell away, and she scurried like a rat into the park.

One of the fliers in the ICYMI folder included a layout of the grounds, marking what events were occurring where. The central promenade, picnic area, and pier jutting out into the Matanzas River hosted DJs and a runway for the ICYMI Summer Style launch, and the keynote address (followed by dancing) was in the Magnolia Room, an all-weather pavilion-style structure near the middle of the grounds.

Food trucks, drinks kiosks, and merchandise tents were scattered through the grounds like breadcrumbs, tempting people to stop, laugh, drink, and dance. To spend money they didn't have, to exalt the glory that was ICYMI, and smile with drunken, reverent gazes at the numerous screens depicting pre-recorded insipid quotes from that evening's keynote speaker.

Milla stopped to study one of the screens, hung on a stand behind a table covered in half-filled champagne flutes.

"I see obstacles as an opportunity to *grow*," a digital Ana beamed. A pink flower was tucked behind one ear, her head invitingly tilted to the side. The Loa vamped for the camera, all sunshine and white teeth beneath a floppy yellow felt hat. "After all, the only approval *I* need is my own!"

Milla snatched a champagne flute from the table, throwing up her middle finger and a tiny little hex. She left the sparking, smoking screen behind and headed deeper into the Fountain of Youth, winding around tents and kiosks and narrowly avoiding a spray of perfume to the face. She paused at the edge of the central plaza and eyed the crowd, taking a sip from her champagne flute and immediately spitting it out. Holding the glass to the light, she turned it and squinted at the bubbles.

"Horned God-dammit, the beer thing again."

"Don't limit yourself," another on-screen Ana advised.

"Fucking spare me," Milla muttered and chugged her beer. The pulse of the music changed, and with it, the milling of the crowd. A tiny tremor ran through the park, the energy shifting. As one, the men and women twitched and turned to the east. "Weird."

She tucked close to a tree, hiding in the shadows as the crowd grew to a swarm, flooding the walkway with broad smiles and glassy eyes. Though zombies weren't a thing, especially not where Voodoo was concerned, she couldn't help but make the comparison between the movement of the crowd and the frankly offensive Hollywood creation. Their steps were stilted, absent any grace, and where before Milla had overheard conversation, now there was only muttered nonsense from the horde.

"Right," she exhaled, shaking out her hands. A weed tickled her legs, and she brushed it away. "Dull eyes, She-EO platitudes, stiff legs. I can do this." She dug in her messenger bag, brushing her fingers over the locket, a tiny wooden box, and smudge sticks. A scrap of ribbon or a sapling twig growing from the tree draped over her arm. She pulled away, tugging free from whatever it was. Taking one last Big Girl Breath, Milla stepped forward, ready to charge into the shambling horde.

Cold air burst at her back, and strong arms clamped around Milla's waist, pulling her back against a hard body and broad chest.

"What in the nine rings was that about?" Darkly snarled in her ear, sounding more frantic than angry.

"*Holy Horned God.*" Milla wriggled against his hold, heart firmly lodged in her throat. "It was an alibi to keep you safe. Where did you even *come from.*"

"Scotland."

His arms loosened, and she twisted around to face him. "Goddess, why are you so literal?"

"Dinnae fancy lies," he murmured. She expected him to argue. Expected to see a scowl or for him to huff angrily. Instead, he let his hands fall to her lower back, his expression softening. "Thank you."

"You're welcome." She lay her hands flat against his chest, his steady heartbeat calming against her palms. "You shouldn't be here, but since you are, one—how in the nine rings did you get in?"

"Shadestepping." He released her with a shrug but kept close.

"Okay, cool, that literally explains nothing, but I can live with that." Milla faced the grounds and the horde of Huns. "Two, where is Dies-well?"

"Left him in the store." Something feral flashed across his face, so Milla elbowed him in the side.

"The windows don't have any blinds! He'll burn to a crisp if we're not back before the sun comes up."

Darkly shrugged. "I threw a blanket on him."

"Horned God, Marie is gonna kill me." Milla massaged her temples. "Since you are here, we'd better get going." She pulled Darkly across the central plaza. "Dull eyes, awkward walk, don't draw attention to yourself."

Deeper in the grounds, the beat of house music pulsed in time to strobing lights silhouetting the trees. Bodies pressed together down the main artery of the Fountain of Youth, women and their plus ones streaming toward the pavilions and dance floors. Their eager faces were illuminated by the screens lining the broad dirt path, each displaying a looped tape of Ana spouting her flouncing affirmations in a cheery voice.

"Negative thoughts only have the power you allow them."

"The key to success is thinking in abundance, not scarcity."

"Load of rot, that." Darkly scowled at one of the screens while Milla squinted at the cracked screen on her phone. Annalisa Pighah was scheduled to give her keynote at seven, which gave them less than fifteen minutes to get to the Magnolia Room and seize the Loa before she could cause any more damage.

Ideally.

But Milla had never been one for ideals. The crowd was larger than she had assumed and moving at a glacial pace, and the press of energy was beginning to feel like walls closing in.

"There's an easier way to do this." Darkly pulled her off the path and behind a large tree. Bringing his left hand up in front of his chest, he curled his fingers towards his palm, tightening the shadows around them. In an instant, what had been a pleasant Florida evening harshened to a lightless arctic wasteland.

Wind howled in her ears and bit at the bare skin of her arms. Milla tucked closer to Darkly, using his body as a shield against the cold. "The sweater is making more sense," she yelled.

Darkly chuckled, and when he spoke, it was with a voice that Milla felt in her bones. "*Nae the time to ask for the shirt off my back, leannán.*"

"When I want that shirt off your back, I won't be asking."

Something silken and sensuous trailed across her cheek, followed by another deep, rolling chuckle from the Dark Witch. He adjusted his grip on her hand, lacing their fingers together and leading Milla through the shadows to the pavilion entrance twenty yards away in a single step. The wind died down, and she blinked, stunned.

"That's how you moved through the hallway!"

"Only works over short distances," Darkly said, sounding winded. "Honestly, didnae ken if I could bring you with me."

"What?" Milla gaped at him.

"Aye?" Darkly arched an eyebrow.

"Your energy is currency!" Ana quipped from a screen.

"You didn't even know if that was going to work? What if I'd gotten stuck in there?"

Darkly shrugged. "Likely would've made up for you summoning a Shade into my body."

Milla was allowed one second to be stunned, and then the crowd pressed in around them, forcing her to take a step or be crushed beneath the manic weight of Diamond Qualifying Executives.

The pavilion interior had been dressed in purples, pinks, teals, and gold, looking like an ICYMI shipment had vomited over the pillars and tables. Though the website and schedule of events had advertised a dinner followed by the keynote address, what Milla and Darkly walked into was anything but.

The music pulsed and pounded, urging men and women to drink, dance, and gyrate together on the dance floor. Altars strewn with flowers and lit candles lined the walls, each placed beneath a screen displaying Ana's constantly smiling face flirting with the crowd. The reek of clashing floral perfumes burrowed in Milla's nose, bringing a headache that threatened a migraine. Moving deeper into the Magnolia Room, what had looked on the surface to be a few hundred drunken middle-aged women and their husbands having a good time turned more sinister and lascivious.

A woman in red chugged a bottle of beer, throwing it to the ground, where it shattered into pieces. The men and women around her tore off their shoes to dance in the shards. Another woman sat on a chair with her legs crossed, sneering down at a man crawling towards her on his knees, pleading. Couples ground against each other on tables and chairs, and another woman was hoisted into the air by four men who pawed her clothes to shreds.

It was a scene of hedonistic delight turned up to eleven, and the wanton, carnal hit of intention had Milla staggering. Plunging her hand into the bag, she withdrew a smudge stick and shoved it to her nose, inhaling the citronella, clove, and horehound deeply to clear her head. She left Darkly wavering where he stood and stumbled to an altar shoved between two sets of doors choked with mortals. Ana grinned down at her from the screen hung on the wall with a soft, sympathetic smile meant to soothe.

"There is no perfection, only beautiful versions of brokenness."

Milla rolled her eyes and thrust the end of her smudge stick at a candle. Flame licked the bound herbs and thin tissue wrapping, teasing the bundle and refusing to catch. She snarled in frustration, glancing back to where she'd left Darkly.

He was gone.

"Shit."

She turned the candle and rotated the smudge stick, perhaps with less intent than she could have. The seductive call of the Loa's magick teased her nose, sweetening the rancid perfume in the room. She felt a tug at her side, and the Loa's promise filled her head with lies.

"You are worthy of what you desire," it whispered, sweet and soft and all things good. "Walk free and seen. No more hiding, no more wanting."

Milla wavered, shaking her head to dispel the thoughts and instead burrowing them deeper.

"You could have him on his knees and begging for you."

A match was struck, her smudge stick lit, and Darkly pulled Milla away from the altar, tucking the matchbox back into her bag. "Forget you had those?"

The siren song of promise slithered away, and she clenched her teeth, curling a hand into a fist so her nails bit against her skin. "Something like that."

She dragged Darkly beside the altar, using his over-tall body as a barrier between herself and the mortals. Grabbing his hips to keep him in place, she peered around the witch and scanned the crowd, chewing her lower lip as she considered the hundreds of people crammed into the hall, the layout, and the Loa. "I hate to suggest this, but—"

"We need to split up," Darkly finished, his voice ragged. Hungry. He tugged on the end of one of her braids, and she jerked her face up to him in surprise, watching black bleed out from the confines of his pupils. "The intent in here is running a number of my restraint."

"You good?"

A smirk drove the dimple deep into Darkly's cheek as his eyes darkened further. Placing his hands against the wall, he bent low and rumbled, "Ken I could be better."

"Right!" Milla ducked under his arms, sidestepping away and ignoring the swoop her stomach performed at the insinuation. "Right, piss-poor timing. Splitting up the party it is. Literally the worst idea, but here we go."

Darkly chuckled, starting after Milla and stopping short. He ran a hand down his face and shook his head to dispel what he could of the heady intent. "Nae the time for much else beyond a perimeter sweep. You take the western wall, I'll sweep to the east, and we'll meet there." He pointed at the stage.

"There's ready rooms back there for weddings. I'll go rot locks and see if I can spot Anaisa."

"How many?"

"Two."

"I can handle one of them. Any signal you can send if you're gonnae miss rendezvous?" To illustrate his point, a slip of shadow wound around Milla's arm, dragging her attention down to the manifestation of his Way. A tiny smile quirked her mouth as she watched the Shade.

"Death and destruction count as a signal?"

He pinched his lips but nodded, reaching out to squeeze the tips of her fingers. "Be careful, Milla."

More than the dark, seductive tone coloring his words, more than that tug on her braid and how he'd caged her against the wall with his body, that set her heart truly aflutter.

"You too," she whispered.

Darkly stalked along the wall, disappearing into the shadowy corners of the room as only a witch like him could. Milla slapped her cheek, bringing herself back to earth, and set off in the other direction.

FORTY

PICKING HER WAY OVER broken glass, Milla squeezed through writhing bodies and wormed behind the various altars, at one point climbing onto a table and hopping from one to another, all while seeking Ana's burnished gold waves among the crowd. The Loa remained unseen, but from her vantage on the table, Milla could see the stage at the far end of the room.

Sweeping gauze curtains decorated the stage in purples, pinks, and soft yellows. A podium stood beside a majestic throne at the center of the stage; the sort found in high school productions of *Camelot* or *Pippin*, all gold paint and maroon velveteen. The curtains running along the base of the stage were decorated in the cross-hatched heart vèvè of Anaisa Pye; a Voodoo symbol meant to represent the Loa and act as a waypoint during the summons—a light in the dark for the spirits to follow. In a typical Voodoo ritual, the vèvè was drawn on the ground or the altar in cornmeal, flour, or gunpowder, elements meant to concentrate the energies of the Loa and allow them to materialize in the body of the vessel.

Milla frowned at the design on the curtains, temples prickling and pinching. Her eyes fell to the dancefloor, packed full of mortals and covered in yellow rose petals.

"Today," the sound bite chirped over Milla's shoulder, "I choose to let go of that which no longer serves me."

"You and me both."

Skirting around the stage, she high-kneed over monitors, some pumping out dance music spun by a DJ in the rear of the hall, others hissing and humming quietly with power but not in active use. The LED lights painting the event hall in reds and purples didn't reach behind the stage, and dark shadows crowded along the wall, Milla's surroundings growing dimmer with each step. She tripped over a tangled mess of cables, eyeing where they plugged into the wall at her left and disappeared under the stage to her right. Ducking low, she spotted the silhouettes of three more monitors hidden out of sight, no doubt meant to project Anaisa's voice when she gave her "keynote" as Annalisa.

A keynote that was due to start any minute.

"Fuck." Milla kicked her booted foot free of the extension cords and edged along the rear wall, stopping beside a door. She wiggled the knob and lay her hand against the door, cursing a second time and then a third for good measure when it proved to be exactly what she'd predicted: locked and metal.

"Alright, little bug," she murmured, reaching within her bag and withdrawing the locket. She'd been caught off guard by Anaisa before, needing Darkly's help and his Way to get Julie to open a metal door. This time, there was no Darkly and no easily swayed mortal on the other side, so she came prepared. "Dinnertime."

The locket's clasp was a delicate piece of craftsmanship made from non-ferrous metal and easily bent out of shape. Sliding her nail between the nearly invisible lip of the aluminum, she crouched low and held it beside the keyhole, hoping beyond hope that the tumblers in the lock were iron.

Wood was easy, being organic, but metal was far trickier. Milla could cast rust on her own, but it was a deeper traveling of her Way than she was willing to risk. For one, it would absolutely alert Anaisa to her presence, and beyond that, her ability to function after stepping into her Way was directly related to the amount of magick she used. Rusting ferrous metal to dust to gain entry to the room would end with Milla drunk and near useless if and when they faced the Loa.

So, a creepy-crawlie Forbidden and Foule it was.

Gentle pressure had her fingernail slicing into the seam of the locket. She twisted and popped it open, expelling just a brush of Way—the tiniest little willful malediction sung as a Czech lullaby—on the bug within. A little rust-colored scarab, no bigger than the eye of a needle, skittered out of the locket. Antennae twerking left and right, it hesitated on the rim. Milla pressed it against the doorknob and murmured her malediction again.

"A já brouček, sekal souček, posekal si paleček, ŋel jsem k panu doktorovi, aby mi dal páseček."

And I, beetle, chopped a little stump, I cut my thumb, I went to the doctor to get a bandage.

The little bug rushed forward, spurred by her curse, and disappeared into the lock. Rustbugs worked quickly, hideous necrotic monsters that they were. Highly Forbidden and Foule, the parasitic little creatures ate through metal like termites ate wood.

Pressing her ear to the door, Milla pinched a little smile as she heard the grind of metal to rust to dust begin. Gripping the knob, she tested the lock, feeling more give than before. Just another moment, Triple Goddess bless the bug, and she'd be in.

Her smile fled as the door to the other ready room opened, the shadows surrounding it dissipating like smoke. Startled, she glanced for a place to hide, muscles tensing and about half a second away from launching herself beneath the risers when Darkly stepped out of the room.

"Were you just singing?"

"Were you just"—she fluttered a hand at the open door—"in there?"

"That I was."

"*How.*"

He looked back at the room, frowned, and stalked towards Milla. "It's empty. Nae sign of Ana."

"Where the fuck is she?" Milla rose, trying the knob again. It gave a quarter turn, and she stepped back. Raising her leg, she booted the door knob. Once, twice, Darkly yelped and hopped back, and thrice. The knob fell away in a cloud of dust, and Milla shouldered open the door.

"Did you just—"

"Kick a door knob off?" She bared her teeth at him. "That I did." Gathering Way in her right hand, she rushed into the room, ready to fling a hex at the first thing that moved. A mirror reflected her overly aggressive image, the looming shadow at her back, and nothing else.

"What the fuck." She snapped the locket closed, leaving the bug to eat the entire building if he so desired. Darkly eyed the locket, gaze drifting to the doorknob that was less knob and more a pile of rust on the ground.

"Was that a bleeding Rust Bug?"

"It was in my bag," she shrugged, "with the Jericho Stone."

His eyes bugged, and the witch gave a full-body shudder. "And you just had that with you?" He flapped a hand at her messenger bag. "In there?"

"It's not even the scariest thing in my bag."

"*A' bhan-dia thoir neart dhomh.*" Darkly made a protective sigil and pressed it over his heart. "I take it back; you are terrifying."

"I tried to tell you." Milla stalked out of the room, her fists clenched. Jaw clenched. Everything clenched. "What time is it?"

"Two 'til," the Dark Witch answered after a glance at his phone.

"Where in the nine rings is she?"

They worked their way over the confusion of cables and unused monitors, re-entering the dance floor of the pavilion. The crowd pressed around them, threatening to separate the witches. Milla grabbed his hand, attempting to shoulder through the crowd, unable to break through the writhing mass of bodies on the dance floor. Stepping onto a chair, she scanned the impassable sea of mortals between them and where Anaisa would speak.

Again, the vèvè on the riser curtain caught her attention, and again, warning prickled in her temples, crawling behind her eyes. A sense of wrongness to the scene that she couldn't place. The music cut, and she gripped Darkly's shoulder as the mortals froze in place. From the monitors, a tribal drumbeat began, low and quiet, and the unmistakable call of Harry Belafonte filled the room.

"Daaaaaaaaaay-oh!"

"Nae," Darkly breathed.

"Daaaaaaaaaaaaay-oh."

"Ach, nooo." He dropped a hand to the top of his head, stunned.

"Daylight come and—"

"Get tae fuck!" The Dark Witch gaped at the crowd, green eyes over-wide and shining with disbelief at the frozen crowd stretching out before them. "Cannae be." Milla hopped down from her chair, nudging him with an elbow. Darkly's startled expression darkened to a scowl when he realized what she intended to do. "This is nae the time."

"Yes, it is." Around them, the room had come to life. The men and women formed lines, twisting their wrists in the air and dropping their hands to twist them at their hips, each step of their Burton/Belafonte calypso bringing them closer to the stage. "It is most definitely the time."

She grabbed Darkly, pulling him into a passing conga line. The Anas on the screens over each altar smiled at the mortals caught in her intent and Darkly begrudgingly began doing the dance from *Beetlejuice*, truly getting into it after a few beats. Milla bit her lips to keep from guffawing. "You really do like that movie, don't you?"

He shot her a bewildered half-smile, eyes bright with pleasure, and she followed his lead. The Dark Witch knew each step, even turning at the right moment to playfully grab Milla's face just like the shrimp cocktails did to the dinner guests in the movie. She reared back and danced away, laughter bubbling, feeling … light. Happy.

And that wasn't right.

Alarmed, she spun toward Darkly, thoroughly caught by the sneaking influence of the Loa. The over-tall witch grinned wildly, laughter twisting toward manic as he threw his head back like the mortals in the crowd, seized by the music and feeding his intent into the ritual.

The ritual.

Fuck.

Realization clanged like a funeral bell, stopping Milla short. Darkly bumped into her, grabbing her waist to keep Milla from tumbling forward. He spun her around, swaying the witch in time to the music.

"Darkly, stop!" She reached up to grab his face, and he took both her hands in his, raising her arms higher and pulling Milla onto her tiptoes so she had no choice but to lean into him to maintain her balance.

Panic had her scanning the hall, noting the rabid, feral expressions the women wore. The way men swept their hands down their partners' bodies with reverent worship or dropped to their knees to crawl in plea. Jerking her attention back to Darkly, she noted the same feverish look in his eyes, Anaisa's power dragging him down with the mortals.

"Seriously, Simmons, snap out of it."

"Cannae," he mouthed, swinging their hips in time to the beat, twisting their hands in the air, each step moving them closer to the stage while all around them, the ICYMI representatives danced and sang, feeding the Loa with their devotion.

"Then we're fucked." Milla wriggled an arm free, looping it around Darkly's waist. Her fingers brushed something smooth and hard tucked into his pants, and she grinned, an idea forming.

"Isnae right," Darkly moaned through a pained grin, the fingers of his left hand working a sigil. His eyes smoked over, cleared, then smoked over again, the Dark Witch trying to do … something.

Golden-brown hair glinted in the strobing lights, and Milla whipped around, trying to lay eyes on the apparition already lost to a sea of strip mall pleather and chunky heels. "Did you see her?"

"Who?" Darkly threw his arms up, hopping forward and leading with his hips.

Another bright gleam, this time to her right. She twisted, seeking out Ana, and Darkly pulled her flush against him. Bell-like laughter tinkled over the music, the intent in the hall perfuming sweat-damp air with a sickly, floral scent like candied rose petals. Milla swayed as the surge of the Loa's magick dragged on the demesne and her own.

The urge to lean into Darkly's embrace, to let the music take her, rose until it was impossible to ignore. It would be so easy to dance with Darkly and forget, if only for a little while. So easy to give in, give up her demesne and let the Loa take what she was promised. Everything she was promised.

"Give a little," Anaisa whispered in her mind. "Relax, enjoy yourself, and let someone else bear the burden of the demesne. Of this *power*."

The pricking behind her eyes began to stab, steadying Milla in rejection of those intrusive thoughts. St. Augustine was *hers*. She was the Witch of the Demesne, not some upstart Loa who hadn't earned it. Not a charming young witch who stole from others, casting magick without cost or sacrifice.

What could Anaisa ever understand about what it meant to *give*?

All around them, men fell to their knees, caressing the thighs and hips of the women they worshiped, and the women held domineering command, empowered by the Loa who took and took and took.

Milla spun in Darkly's arms, her movement sure and seductive, a siren's call tempting him better than any allure or willful malediction could. She cupped the back of his neck, and he bent, willing and pliable to her touch.

"You have something I want." She flicked her tongue against his earlobe, relishing how he shivered before pulling away to let the Dark Witch read the desire plain on her face. The color on his cheeks rose, matching the flush crawling up Milla's neck and heating her ears.

Darkly's hands tightened at her hips, and she trailed her nails across the nape of his neck, causing him to bite that lower lip, his eyes flickering green-black-green. Trailing a finger along his jaw, Milla ran her hand down his chest, around his ribs, and lower to the hem of his sweater. He grazed her ear with his teeth, pressing his hand at the center of her back and pinning Milla to his chest, a favorite trick of his. She could feel his heartbeat booming rapidly. Could feel the thrum of blood in his veins, his heat warming away her chill.

Goddess, it would be so easy to give in to this, to have this, just like Anaisa promised.

And didn't she deserve it?

Hadn't Milla paid her dues and suffered enough?

Why shouldn't her bruised, blackened heart have Darkly after giving up Ezra?

"Overthinking kills your happiness," video Ana advised.

The music changed, a heavy drum line beating out in steady time, driving the room's pulse towards a climax. Milla dug her nails into Darkly's skin, ran her hand up his spine, and moaned when he kissed that spot beneath her ear, her neck, her collarbone. Moving lower and lower until he was on his knees where he belonged, kneeling before the goddess Death Witch.

He slid his hands over her hips and beneath her cotton tank. Skimming them up, up, up to cup her breasts. Milla dropped her head back as he swept thumbs across her nipples, relishing the wicked curl of pleasure that settled between her hips. He did it again, pressing a kiss just below her navel, and her eyes flew wide, nails digging into his shoulders and pushing against Darkly. Willing him lower, needing his mouth low enough to—

A flash of burnished gold glinted in the dark, lascivious tapestry of the hall, and the earth tilted beneath her feet, more of the demesne slipping away and draining the witch. She teetered forward, landing against Darkly, and snarled. Digging her fingers into his arms, she dragged him to his feet and forced him back against a table.

His ass hit the edge, and Darkly gripped the rim with both hands.

"Please, Milla," he begged, wanting her to command him. Control him. "Whatever you want, whatever you need."

And that was Anaisa's mistake.

Never once had Darkly begged. He had *asked.*

Milla settled between his legs, snaking one arm around his back while her right hand trailed the waist of his pants. He bucked his hips at her touch, grinding against her. She pressed her lips to his, fingers curling around that rock-hard object tucked into the hidden sheath on his pants.

"Anything?" She nipped his lower lip and swallowed his ensuing groan with a kiss.

"Anything," he rolled his hips again. "Anything you need, *leannán.*"

"I need you to get your shit together." Milla snapped, ripping an obsidian-handled athame free and slicing the blade along her thigh.

Forty One

She staggered away from Darkly, sweeping the blade out of his reach and shoving free her hand into the messenger bag at her side. The slice on her thigh burned, warmth rushing from the wound.

"Goddess, Milla …" Darkly gaped at the welling blood. He extended a hand as if to staunch the wound with his palm. "You're bleeding."

"Don't make this weird." Milla barked the order, bending the cruel magick Anaisa had spun into something of her own. If Darkly wanted orders, then orders she would give. "'Cos shit's about to get a whole lot weirder."

He straightened, waiting for Milla to continue. Withdrawing a fistful of tea from her bag, she gestured for him to move away from the table. Darkly melted to his knees, which was sort of what she wanted him to do, crawling for Milla as she backed away. "Please, Milla," he wheedled at her in a needy, nasally voice. "Let me help you."

"Horned God, this is not a good look for you." Spinning to face the crowd, she swept the bloody athame across the tea bags and muttered a rushed intent. "*Odsvětit.*"

Desecrate.

She lobbed the handful of blood-stained herbs, and the desecration hex set in at the crest of their flight. Filter paper dried and crumbled, releasing a cloud of hawthorn, hellebore, hemlock, and clove over the mortals. Darkly made a choked sound at her back, coughing as he inhaled the activated dispersant and, thank the Triple Goddess, recovered himself quickly.

"You good?" Milla shouted over her shoulder, tucking the athame in her boot.

"Bloody embarrassed," he muttered. A burst of cold brushed against her legs and back, and the Dark Witch rushed past, flinging shadows at the herbal cloud and applying intent to make them corporeal. Milla's jaw dropped at the display, and a cloud of tea dust settled over the crowd, inhaled by the panting mortals and disrupting the Loa's sway.

"Again?" Darkly hollered, snapping Milla out of her shock. He had moved so *quickly*. Darting forward and flinging Shades without a second thought, every inch the Enforcer.

"Right," she swallowed a lump in her throat. "Right, yeah." Repeating the move, Milla tossed bags in a circle, creating a sphere of safety in front of the stage. Some erupted in the air, others hit the ground and spewed gray smoke like a witchy gas bomb, and soon, the pavilion was under a semblance of control.

If mortal bodies dropping to the ground was "control." A cluster of women at the edge of the dance floor staggered together like hens at feeding time, colliding and hitting the ground in a mass of lycra, spandex, and push-up bras. Yellow rose petals danced up from the floor and settled on the bodies.

"Oh, shit."

Darkly spun in a slow circle, horrified by the bodies hitting the floor. He turned a wan eye at Milla. "What all is in that tea?"

Three couples to her left tipped over like they'd been flicked in the forehead, teetering back and falling stiff as boards.

"Double shit." Milla scratched her cheek. "That must be the dandelion … or maybe a reaction between the binding agents? I don't really know."

"Right, I'm nae gonnae let you drink that anymore." Darkly twisted his wrists, drawing shadows from under the tables and creating a midnight wall between the mortals and the witches.

"I don't tell you what to do." Milla pressed another bag to the wound on her leg, whispering "*Odsvětit*" under her breath and tossing it in an under-arm softball pitch at the stage.

"Beg to differ."

"Still—" the tea bag squelched at the foot of the risers, her pitch falling short, but the wet earth, mineral, and murk scent of catacombs filled the pavilion, masking the acrid perfume and lessening her growing headache. "You don't get to tell me what to do."

"Ach, aye, because asking nicely has worked so well." Darkly dropped into a wide-legged stance, knees bent and arms thrown out straight. His fingers curled in the air, and he pulled at the shadows, scooping one arm to wind the dark around his sleeve until he'd amassed a ball of onyx around his forearm. He gathered it in his palms, twisting and stretching until he had something resembling saltwater taffy on a pull.

Stretching arms wide, he pulled a veil of midnight thin enough that Milla could make out the tables and chairs on the other side. Like a fire eater in a carnival, he lowered into a lunge, inhaled deeply, and blew on the shadow. The crisp scent of clean smoke and clove followed the shadow as it belled and filled like a sail, forming a wall of twilight between the witches and the mortals.

He uttered something in Irish, and the shadow-wall detached from his hands in geometric whorls.

"I deserve to be happy." Ana's voice kept up its obnoxious affirmations, her bubbly timbre muffled by Darkly's Shades.

"That should hold for a few." He brushed off his hands and stalked to Milla, kicking up rose petals and leaving footprints in the desecrated herbal dust. "You alright?

"I've had worse." Milla pressed her hand against her thigh, thinking rather than saying *návrat, návrat, návrat*. A low-level allure, a regression, a return, not enough to get her drunk, and useful for healing wounds. Like cuts from an athame or slices on her lip. When the wound had stitched closed, she looked up. "And you?"

"Doing what needs to be done." He scanned their area. "What was that?"

"Invocation," Milla answered. "I think. It felt like what Ezra and I did at the lake, the start of the summons."

"Then where is she?" He arched a brow at Milla over his shoulder. There was a regality to his posture and the cool, almost bored expression he wore.

From somewhere to their left, one of the screens answered. "I am creating my life exactly as I want it."

"She's here, somewhere. She must be, or I don't know how she managed all this." She swept the athame over the bodies on the floor. "But why a summons? She's already *here*."

"You can manifest anything your heart desires," another screen announced. Milla scowled in its direction, her gaze shifting to the dissipating smoke from her tea bag bombs wafting to the rafters and thinning as it was drawn from the room. Darkly toed the rose petals on the ground, kicking them up in a flurry of trampled yellow to reveal the geometric design on the dance floor. A light on a motor swung overhead, painting the Dark Witch in a deep red.

"Doesnae make any sense." He frowned at her, black eyes reflecting the light. "All of that effort, and for what?"

"Believe that great things are coming your way."

"Goddess, those are annoying." Milla flicked her fingers in the direction of the latest affirmation. The fuzz and crackle of corroded wire and fried circuitry sizzled, yet through it all, the DJ kept spinning his tunes—head down, noise-canceling headphones on, dancing away to Nelly Furtado's "Maneater."

"So, what's her play?" She joined Darkly in the center of the dance floor, pooling intent in her hands. "If that was the invocation, we're at step two—"

"Two?"

"A Voodoo ritual has four parts," Milla explained. "Preparation, Invocation, Possession, but there's no horse, and the Farewell."

"Take calculated risks, not random risks," televised Ana offered.

"But the energy she's gathered only lasts so long, so where is she? Why is she delaying?"

"There is time enough for everything," the Loa chirped from another screen. Milla narrowed her eyes in the direction of Ana's voice, prickles of heat popping behind her eyes.

"Could be she wasnae expecting you to bring an Enforcer," Darkly offered. "Maybe she's changed her mind?"

"Maybe." Milla pressed the pad of her thumb to the center of her forehead as the little pops of heat heightened to painful jabs. She toed the flower petals, eyes following the lines of the design painted on the dancefloor and thought … thought … thought … grasping at an idea just out of reach.

"How is your connection to the de—"

"Ssh!" Milla slapped her hand against Darkly's arm, whipping her head around when another screen flared bright and sunny through the smoke.

"I embrace change and welcome challenges."

And then it hit.

"Oh, fuck." Milla breathed, gripping Darkly's bicep. To steady herself, or him, who knew.

"What?"

"She's here."

"Where?" He spun around, scanning the room as if he could manifest the Loa himself.

"Today," Ana stated from every screen at once. Her usually chipper voice was deeper. Firmer. "My thoughts are gathered, and I am focused like never before."

The screens around the room flared bright, Ana's hair burning a caustic yellow, her teeth a painful white. The pinks harshened from the soft floral color to an abrasive, over-saturated neon burning through Milla's smoke.

"Tracy was a technomantic," she groaned. "Oh, Goddess, I really should have seen this coming."

"*Seen what?*" Darkly's voice turned the question into a demand, and the answer spilled from Milla's tongue before she could swallow it down.

"Broad Cast."

"I am committed to my success"—the gobos in the rafters swung at once, their motors whirring as each light focused on the stage. Reds, purples, pinks, and yellows joined as a sickly, bilious hue—"I will not back down."

"Cannae be," Darkly breathed beside her. Milla felt a rush of chilled air as he released some of his Way, ready to charge into action.

"Horned God dammit, she told us what she was doing!" She thumped fists against her temples. "Casting intent through the chat group, all those Horned God-damned screens over the altars. As the witch behind the Broad Cast, she's been gathering intent this whole time, and I—we —"

The smoke in front of the risers began to twirl, spin and separate like a hand running through fine hair. Milla stared at the stage in horror, wanting to rub her eyes to dispell what she was seeing.

"We walked right into it," Darkly finished. Cursing under his breath as he caught up to Milla's logical leap. "We fed the ritual." He stared down at her, skin blood-red beneath the gobo, black eyes round as marbles. "Which means that wasnae the invocation—"

"It was the summons to possession," Milla rasped, looking at the geometric design in horror. She was going to be sick. Just violently ill all over herself, those fucking rose petals, and the dreadful design on the dance floor.

"I will take action when I have a goal"—the bitter kaleidoscope coalesced on the throne, solidifying into a recognizable shape as the voices in stereo shifted channels and thinned to one set of vocal cords—"so that I can acquire the lifestyle I dream of."

Ana leaned forward on the throne, all sunshine and smiles, laughter in her eyes and lush hair falling like a molten wave down her shoulders and back. Clad in a shimmering shift dress of the softest pink, she was the picture of femininity, generosity, and lies.

"Blessed be, *polednice*."

"Blessed be," Milla called back. "Let these people go, Ana."

"Blunt," Darkly muttered.

Ana cocked her head, biting her lower lip and smiling at them both. "No."

Milla stared down the Loa. "Let them go, or we'll have to make you let them go."

"Really?" Darkly snorted in disbelief. "Is that the best you could come up with?"

"Figured it was worth a shot." She shrugged and scuffed her boot at the ground. Darkly followed the motion, his attention falling to the patch of dance floor her kick uncovered.

"Hunh." He crouched low, clearing away more of the petal and herb dust, capturing Ana's attention. She shifted her eyes from Milla, glaring at Darkly with an intensity that clenched something in Milla's chest. With a tiny twist of her lips, her gaze lifted past him, landing on a pile of women just beyond where his shadow veil had fallen.

"Did you enjoy my ritual, *polednice?*" Ana rose from her throne with effortless grace. "I've had a long time to decide just how I would do this. I suppose I should thank you for the idea."

"Monologuing already, Anaisa?"

The Loa pursed her lips, shaking her head lightly. A silken curl fell out of place, making the ageless spirit look even younger. "Only trying to explain," she blinked innocently at the witch, "so you aren't upset by what happens next."

"And that is?"

The softness drained from Ana's face like water from a tub. Her cheekbones sharpened into blades, honey-amber eyes glinting with an internal flame.

"I want what I was promised," she hissed, repeating what Kayleigh had shared. "A new demesne in the mortal realm. My consort by my side." Extending an arm, she reached for Milla, offering her hand. "*Ven, mi amor.*"

Her eyes flashed with hunger, and Milla realized too late that the Loa wasn't reaching for her. She spun in time to see Darkly jerk his face up, panic distorting his features.

"No!" He lurched to his feet, throwing his arms forward as Ana curled her fingers into a fist. The wall of shadow he had cast crashed down, billowing in whorls of smoke that curled in on themselves and vanished. "Done!" He staggered as though the Loa's intent had been a direct blow, clutching at his chest. "Done, for fuck's sake, done!"

"*Rozpárat!*" Milla threw out her left hand and flung an unraveling hex, acting without any thought beyond protecting Darkly from whatever Ana was doing … had done. The hex went wild, tangling in the gauze curtains and shredding them to spiderwebs.

The Loa tossed her head back, laughing with glee. "I will have my Belié with me," she taunted, crooking a finger at the Dark Witch. Darkly moaned, pawing at his chest, the collar of his woolly-pully. Frantically trying to back away and only managing a stumbling step.

Milla spat acid and flung another hex, this time with her right hand. "*Rozložit!*"

Decompose.

It landed at Ana's feet, and the stench of sweet rot joined with the Loa's noxious perfume. She squealed and yanked her foot away from the moldering puddle eating the stage. "You dare!"

"Fuck yeah, I do!" Milla yelled back, throwing another hex with her right hand and running her left arm around Darkly's back. He leaned heavily on her, nearly toppling them both.

"Done," he croaked for whatever reason, "donedonedone." His eyes were a wide, terrified green as he repeated the word over and over and over again. Shadows bloomed and vanished in his palms, and veins throbbed in his neck and at his temples.

"Goddess, what did she do?"

"I cannae," he wheezed, black smoke curling from his mouth. "Gonnae no dae—"

"Can you dispell it?"

"I will have my consort!" Ana shrieked, stomping her foot on the rapidly decomposing stage.

"Don't see how!" Milla shot back, pooling more intent. Her fingertips burned, and ash clawed up her throat, but seriously—*what the fuck, Ana.* "Where's your horse?"

Beside her, Darkly stiffened, choking mid-fish-gape. On the stage, Anaisa tittered, covering her mouth with a hand.

"Oh, *polednice.*" Derision dripped from her honeyed tongue. "Haven't you figured it out yet?"

Tightening her arm around Darkly, Milla used all her strength to haul the Dark Witch back from the stage, away from Ana's sphere of influence and whatever hex she'd hit him with. "Figured out what?"

"You brought the horse to me." The Loa spread her arms wide. A gust of trash perfume air swept out from the stage, blowing away the rose petals and herbal dust to reveal the entirety of the geometric design painted on the dance floor.

No, not a design.

A vèvè.

Milla skated her gaze over the floor, dread dragging her gut six feet under as she recognized the design. Two swords splayed at their joined points with crosses as their pommels, the blades wrapped in a sinuous line, with Anaisa's cross-hatched heart in the center.

The vèvè of Belié Belcan.

Intent crackled in the air, raising the fine hairs on Milla's arms. The painted lines began to glow a deep, bloody crimson, and Ana's words bounced around in her skull.

You brought the horse to me.

She whipped her face up, watching the Dark Witch struggle to compose himself. Unable to dispell, unable to cast, or fling a hex; held by Ana's wicked magick and all of the heady intent she'd raised with the mortals, the dancing, and the—"Oh, Goddess."

"The original oungan and manbo," Milla had once explained to the Dark Witch. *"The Voodoo witches who performed the ritual were Dark and Death Witches."*

"No, nononono." She dropped her arm, backing away from Darkly and reaching back back back into her past, searching for anything that might help her help him. But she'd never been strong with the Petro and the Rada. She'd been better with the Gede, and her oversight would get Darkly possessed.

"A Dark Witch." Marie had practically frothed at the prospect. *"The perfect vessel. I had heard rumors one still walked among us, but to see him in person?"*

"Oooohhhh, I fucked up." Milla darted forward, intending to grab Darkly and—what, drag his over-tall self out of the pavilion? "I fucked up so bad."

He swept his arm at her, forcing Milla back and away. His shoulders twitching, his movements jerky, but still, he managed to throw out his casting hand, hastily flinging a hex at Ana, the move absent any of the grace Milla had come to associate with the witch. What looked like a blade made of shadow struck the top of the throne, crashing and curling into smoke. Anaisa crooked her finger again, summoning the Dark Witch nearer and her consort into the chosen vessel. She inhaled as her fingers curled, and Milla heard the death rattle it pulled from Darkly. The black was sucked from his eyes, and for a heartbeat, he looked so frightened, so mortal …

…so Milla hexed the witch.

FORTY TWO

"*NEHÝBEJTE SE.*"

The halting hex hit Anaisa square in the chest. She froze with a hideous scowl, twisting her lovely features into something truly heinous. Milla darted for Darkly, hands fluttering up and down his arms, cradling his face, and dancing down his front as he twitched and jerked, mouth still forming the word "done" for some inane reason as he repeatedly tapped the center of his chest.

"What do I do, what do I do, what do I do?" she chanted, racking her brain for any hex, any curse, any allure that would stop a Loa mid-possession. Shades, she knew. Twisting her deadly hexes into something new, she *knew*, but a Loa? "This wasn't what I learned, Darkly, I—oh, Goddess, I never learned this."

"Sssssstiiiiii," he rasped, hissing in pain as a shoulder jerked up. Teeth gnashing, tongue pressed against their backs, struggling to get a word out before Belié Belcan took him altogether. "T'sssstttt."

Another burst of static crackled in the pavilion, followed by a bloom of sickly, floral perfume as Anaisa dispelled Milla's hex.

"You're only making it worse for him, *polednice!*" The Loa taunted from the stage, switching into the language of her intent to continue the possession. "*Acepta este caballo, mi amor.*"

Darkly surged forward, the force of it enough to send Milla stumbling backward, closer to the stage. His head fell back, mouth open in a silent scream, and somewhere, in places beyond the mortal realm, a balance tipped.

Anaisa's hiss fizzed at Milla's back, and she whirled in time to witness the Loa flick her fingers at a swathe of gauze curtain, sending it flying. The rough rayon snaked around Milla's face, enshrouding her in scratchy tulle again and again and again, forcing itself down her throat and tightening at her neck.

Milla staggered back, clawing at the gauze and trying to call intent to hand to rot the fabric. Darkly groaned, she felt a hand brush her arm, and a woman cried out from somewhere in the room. And then another and another, shouts of shock, pain, and fright, and Anaisa laughed.

Goddess, but this was all Milla's fault. The Loa, the freaking pyramid scheme that had gotten its poisonous fingers into her demesne, all of it was her fault. Her mistake, one that would see this Loa stealing St. Augustine away. The rayon tightened. Milla's eyes bugged, spots danced, and then she heard it—six feet and change of Dark Witch hitting the floor to her right.

The shock of that sound, of bone and muscle and flesh collapsing lifeless, the echoing horror of what was occurring, jolted Milla into action. The decade of hand-to-hex training from the Morgenhexe, the years she spent under Ezra's not-so-gentle tutelage, all surged to the forefront.

Rozpárat! Milla shouted in her mind, calling on every lesson, every torment Ezra had put her through to make sure his little Death Witch was as strong in body as she was in mind. *Rozpárat!*

Anaisa shrieked as the rayon unraveled strand by strand. Milla clawed at her face, brittle nails scratching her skin, but she didn't care. There was a Dark Witch to de-possess, and she was a Death Witch with a serious grudge.

She dove for Darkly's lifeless form, rolling onto her knees and catching the energy Anaisa sent flying after her. The weight of it, the sheer force of the malintent in that hex, knocked Milla off balance. She threw out a leg to remain upright, muscles protesting as she compressed the ball in her hands, reshaping and reforming the intent. A sweat broke out over her brow, and Milla shouted as she sent the energy hurtling back at Anaisa as a spear. It caught the Loa on the hip, and she staggered.

"How are you doing that!" Anaisa hissed.

"Trade secrets," Milla panted, winded from the exertion. Horned God, she used to do this *daily* with Morgen, for hours on end, and one little siphon-to-redirection of a hex had her seeing spots. Ana reached for the collapsed mortals on the dancefloor through the haze, crooking her fingers and muttering intent. Her eyes glowed, hair lifting as she drained the women, using their energy, life force, *whatever,* to strengthen her power.

In the momentary reprieve, Milla's attention drifted to the Dark Witch. He'd been trying to tell her something, trying to get her to do something, but what?

She pressed her hands to Darkly's shoulders, sending a pulse through his body to check for any wounds, any physical injury in need of healing, but there was nothing, and these women and men were dying, and it was Milla's fault.

If she hadn't been so rude to Kayleigh, if she had paid more attention to Julie, if Ana's sunny optimism hadn't blinded her, if she had trusted Darkly earlier, getting to know the witch and his Shades, she could—*Shades.*

Frantic, Milla switched intents. She couldn't heal whatever had gone wrong, didn't know the first thing about banishing a Loa, but Shades … Shades she knew.

She and Ezra had worked with them and practiced possessing bugs, rats, and toads with them all in preparation for the big moment when she would summon the Baron into Ezra, joining them Shade and Soul so the powerful Loa could walk the earth again.

"T'sttttiiiiiii…"

The hissing word Darkly had tried to force made sense then. The Dark Witch, perfect vessel that he was, understood the Shades better than anyone, and he'd been trying to tell her what to do, tell her how to keep him safe. Keep him active as she stood against the Loa.

Even staring down his possession, the clever witch wanted to help.

"I'm really sorry about this," Milla rushed out, switching intents for a third time. A fly buzzed around her head, and the world spun as the cost of her Way surged, her vision blurring. "Jus' 'member it was yer idea." Taking a shaking breath, Milla dug her nails into his woolly-pully. Intent leaked out of her palms as she took hold of the one damn thing she could. *"Let', stín!"*

Fly, Shade!

The slightest twitch of his left index finger was Milla's only warning before a wall of cold rushed from the Dark Witch, knocking her back. A Shade clamored free, hovering over both witches—one on her knees, the other supine and vulnerable.

"Go!" she rasped, hoping his Shade was as willing to follow orders as the witch was. The Darkly-sized shadow didn't acknowledge her; he simply disappeared into the shadows pooled under the stage. Instinct had Milla darting forward, stopping herself just shy of diving after him.

Ana saw all of this and tittered, "Clever. Almost too clever. But you forgot one thing."

"Oh, Goddess, what now?"

"A Dark Witch may be the perfect vessel," she dropped the arm that had been siphoning from the mortals, cocking her head and smiling at Milla, "but for my consort to take root, the vessel must be empty."

"Well, shit." The body on the ground twitched, and the hex escaped before Milla could reconsider. "*Nehýbejte se.*"

She swayed, vision doubling, but kept her feet, mentally sending a silent apology to the Dark Witch she kept hexing.

Anaisa growled, aether in the sickly-perfumed air rising. Another crackling pink ball sped at Milla. She ducked, electric heat singeing across her back, and straightened to find the Loa again working a summoning sigil at Darkly. Drawing on the fine threads binding her to the demesne, Milla thrust both hands forward in a vicious desecration hex—"*Odsvětit!*"—and hit Anaisa in the center of her chest, sending the Loa rocking back into the throne.

Out of the corner of her eye, she spotted a lean shadow darting along the walls, dancing around the light from flickering candles on the altars and the DJ setup. Her pulse quickened as a thin string of shadows rose in his wake; a mass of Shades called to heel by the Dark Witch. She allowed herself one relieved sigh at the confirmation that on some plane, Darkly was hale, somewhat whole, and gathering the other Shades, keeping them safe and out of Ana's reach. Cutting off the Loa as best he could, or at least, keeping her from using the mortals to make her stronger. She needed to buy him time, keep the Loa's attention off of him.

Ana wheezed from the throne, fingers plucking at the destroyed fabric on her chest. Confusion flashed over her face, wrinkling the youthful brow, her lips silently forming the word, "What?"

Placing herself between the stage and Darkly's body, Milla hollered, "Why?"

"Why?" Anaisa jerked her face up, dumbfounded, though whether that was from the manifestation of Milla's magick or her question, she had no idea. The stench of grilled meat joined the stank of cheap perfume, and Milla gagged. "You who opened the gate wish to know why?" Intoxicating laughter bubbled, rich, and sweet. Milla caught herself smiling along and twisted the expression into a sneer. "Because these women begged me to, little witch. Because it is in my nature to be kind and generous. To reward the faithful."

"I always thought the beneficent Anaisa Pye to be better than a pyramid scheme. Why prey on the weak when you could celebrate your return to the world as the loving and kind Anaisa Pye Mandro? The Metresa?"

"You think these women are weak?" Anaisa splayed her hand at the bodies on the floor.

"At the moment, or in general?"

"You think them weak and depressed and hurting. You ascribe to them the very things that keep you hiding in your store, *polednice*, when these women are strong! They yearn, they desire, they want, and they devote themselves to me." She stepped to the edge of the stage, her hands curled into fists and held over her heart. "So quick to judge, *polednice*. To disregard the quiet nurse and the smiling apprentice. So ready to cast us into our roles when we could be so much more."

"So you spin this turn as Anaisa Pye Dantó, cast a glamour on hideous leggings, and murder innocent women you claim are strong?"

Anaisa smiled at Milla, sharp and cruel—the Dantó Turn incarnate: fierce, aggressive, arrogant, and spiteful.

"What glamour?" She threw her head back, laughing at Milla's momentary shock. "The Rada Nation would have followed the Gede; you must know that. Such gifts you both offered. Such treasures, such promises." She descended a step at the front of the stage, eyes pinned on Milla, which was frankly terrifying. But fine. Better than the alternative, which was her attention falling on the lifeless Dark Witch on the ground. "The *Baron del Cementerio* and his *Maman*, calling us back from the Gates. And then you turned your back. You walked away and left him in the dark just as they turned their backs on me. On *usss*." She hissed that last word, a sibilant fizzing of teeth and tongue.

And that was when Milla realized her mistake: she had allowed herself to become distracted.

A plate hit her in the middle of her back. She yelled and stumbled forward, bringing her elbow up to deflect a fork only to be hit in the side by an ice bucket. Anaisa twitched her fingers, bloated with stolen power, and flung inanimate objects at Milla from every angle.

She staggered to the left at the punch of a chair to her leg and was knocked back by a large ICYMI tote packed with what felt like cannonballs. Flinging hexes, only a quarter of which landed to deflect or disintegrate Anaisa's projectiles, Milla was slowly, steadily separated from Darkly's body and pommeled to the front of the stage.

"They turned us into saints of the colonizers' faith," Anaisa spat, monologuing as she barraged Milla with banquet utensils and women's effects. "Enslaved the Loa as they enslaved my people, and then you witches locked us away. The world does not deserve the kind turns of Anaisa Pye. No, they deserve the Dantó, the Mandé, all the wicked turns of Anaisa to bring about their ruin."

She flicked her fingers as if Milla were no more than a buzzing fly, and a speaker hidden by the skirt on the stage flew forward and slammed into her stomach. She hit the ground with a pained grunt, rolling onto her side and jerking her face up at a flicker of movement.

Darkly's shadow skipped along the eastern wall, collecting the Shades of the fallen women and stealing them away from Anaisa, picking his way closer to his body.

Anaisa followed where Milla's attention fell, and she giggled with mad glee.

At that, Milla realized her second mistake: she had vastly underestimated Ana Maria Metresa.

The Loa swung an arm up, Milla scrabbled for Darkly, the DJ spun into Cher's "Dark Lady," and every candle in the pavilion flared to life, burning away the shadows along the walls and cutting the living Shade off from his body.

Forty Three

"Oh, fuck," Milla wheezed, reaching for Darkly as Anaisa rushed out a litany of Dominican Spanish. Intent charged the air, crackling along the underside of the lingering smoke like pink lightning. A bolt struck the dancefloor, and Milla jerked her hand back, curling in on herself to avoid the strike. She peered through her fingers as another bolt struck down, closer this time, and she blindly thrust her hand at the stage, sending an old-fashioned necrotic blast at the Loa.

Anaisa's furious shriek was the only prompt Milla needed to get up, get moving. She struggled to her feet, wincing as she stood. The entirety of her front felt like one giant bruise, and it was an effort to swallow a lungful of air. Fluttering fingers at her chest, Milla worked a nasty bit of magick, killing off the tissue in her lungs to ease the strain of breathing.

A glance at the stage showed her the Loa had taken Milla's last hex in the chest, the force of it sending her crashing into the curtains. Metal beams creaked and bent, the gauzy fabric fluttering from the rafters to puddle on the stage.

She wove towards Darkly's body on drunken legs, and a woman flew out of the bodies on the outskirts of the dance floor.

She tackled Milla at the ankles, and the witch hit the ground, elbows first and then her jaw, biting her tongue. Hot salt and metal filled her mouth as the woman scrambled up Milla's legs, pinning her down. They rolled together, and Milla wriggled free before another Diamond Qualifying Executive pile-drove her into the ground.

Digging an elbow between the witch's shoulder blades, the weight of the middle-aged woman crushed Milla's leg as acrylic nails clawed at her tank top. Milla wriggled onto her side and swept her free leg in a wide arc, silently thanking Diego for every forty-five-minute workout video he'd ever made her do. She caught the woman with a steel-toed boot at the back of her head. She grunted and rolled off of Milla, allowing her to crawl free.

At her back, the curtains and beams of the stage pulled away from where Anaisa had fallen, drawn up by invisible strings to construct a battered peristyle over the Loa. Anaisa clawed free of the detritus, hair mussed, makeup smeared, and lips curled into a feral snarl. She conjured a ball of hot pink light into her hands, flinging it at Milla with a flick of her wrist. The Death Witch turned, deflecting the orb with her elbow pad. It exploded in a shower of sparks and heat, blistering her skin.

"We only have you to thank, *polednice*," Ana repeated her early taunt, throwing two more searing orbs at Milla. "My consort and I, we owe this all to you!"

A caustic hex splashed against Milla's shoulder, fizzing like hydrogen peroxide in a wound, the heat of it burrowing bone deep and earning a cry from the witch. She caught the second orb in her right hand, cringing against the pain and twisting the intent, ruining it into something of her own and lobbing it back with a shot-put throw. Anaisa held out her hand to stop the venomous green necro-hex mid-air. It splattered against her palm instead, and she shrieked in pain, clutching her wrist as a blight-hex ate at her flesh.

A fire ignited in her eyes, and Anaisa seethed. Shoulders heaving, she took deep, steadying breaths. Light gleamed beneath her skin, the faintest blush giving the Loa a dusky, rosy glow. Milla tensed at the rise of magick, startling when Anaisa spoke again, intent crackling in every word.

"I want what I was *promised*."

"Yeah, well." Milla withdrew the athame from her boot, hissing as she sliced it across her left palm, just the worst place to draw blood for more reasons than Milla could list, save for the one damn hex she could think of at this particular moment.

Before she could think too hard about what she was doing, Milla brought her bleeding palm to her chest, limping towards Anaisa, every muscle tensed and ready to fling a hex Forbidden and Foule.

"Too stupid to give up," the Loa jeered at her. A noxious pink cloud hovered over her head and shoulders, magick lighting up the veins in her limbs. Raising her arms, she shrieked in rapid Spanish, splayed fingers curling to fists as she threw her arms down.

A wall of power flew from the Loa, buffeting Milla back a step. At her feet, the vèvè throbbed an angry red, the visceral heat of it flaring brightest behind the witch and crawling across the floor, turning the pavilion into a blood-lensed hellscape. She felt the shift as Anaisa drew on all of her amassed power, the further tipping of scales, and ignored it. Determined to get off one last hex, she flooded intent in her palm, the force of her Way burning her veins to char.

"*Moje*— ack!" Piston-like arms wrapped around Milla's legs, pulling them out from under her. She hit the ground, *hard*, the meager breath she had regained emptying in a whoosh.

Stars danced, her head swam, and she kept falling. Dragged down, down, down into an empty well. Thread after thread snapped and frayed, withering to nothing; leaving the witch and whatever magick still pulsed in her veins so very, very alone.

"No," Milla wheezed, blinking rapidly to clear her vision. Denying with every fiber of her being what had just happened. "No, it's mine, you can't—"

"I did," Ana gloated. She inhaled, humming and stretching her arms wide, shivering in delight. "Such a reservoir you've built for me, *polednice*. Such a glorious act of devotion."

Gleaming, honey-yellow eyes settled on Milla as an over-tall figure limped into view. Far, so far away from the witch lying at the bottom of her well. It loomed over her, face twisted into a righteous sneer, eyes a deep, terrifying black.

"All right, mi amor?" A faintly accented voice left Darkly's mouth. Rich like a humid summer evening thickened by the music of the islands and restless seas.

"No," Milla wept and Darkly frowned.

"Not you." A swift kick caught her in the side, and he limped away, satisfied that the witch on the ground had nothing left. Was nothing. Just another failure. Another fool who had attempted to fly for the sun and still had so far to fall.

The room blurred behind her tears, sour bile puddled on her tongue, and Milla spat, curling in on herself, burrowing deep into the defeat. She cradled her left hand to her chest, only half aware of the curl of smoke rising from where her blood and saliva pooled on the floor.

The two Loa conferred near the stage, their voices deepening and ripening with a power that was both their own as Voodoo spirits and that stolen from the demesne Milla had charged with every bit of her heart, Soul, and Shade, glutting themselves on the reservoir of magick that she had built.

It wasn't fair that it all came to this. Wasn't fair that all Milla had wanted to do was hide. To spend the rest of her days spiraling into her misery. It wasn't fair that she'd won the demesne through an accident. That she'd found herself caring again. For St. Augustine. For the witches and mortals in it. For the desecrants and the wayward Dark Witch. It wasn't fair that she had just started to live again after wanting to disappear and die, and this is how it ended?

Lying in a puddle of her own blood and spit, choking on the acrid smoke rising as her caustic self ate through the floor?

Milla blinked, eyes crossing and uncrossing as her vision cleared and zeroed in on that bubbling, festering puddle eating through the floor. A fly buzzed around the curl of smoke, bobbing on a phantom breeze.

"She is a dishonorable witch," Anaisa purred from the stage. Milla craned her neck, spotting the Loa in their conference. Ana was pressed against Darkly, arms wrapped around his waist and chin propped on the center of his chest, pouting up at the Dark Witch her consort rode. "It was her lies that left you stranded at the Gates." She clawed her hands into his back. "Her deceit which kept you from me."

"She is the witch who left us separated?" He gazed down at Anaisa, a hand sweeping up her back. Strands of thick, glossy hair fell through clever fingers as black eyes, cold with righteous fury, drifted over the witch on the floor. When he beheld the Loa in his arms again, a love-drunk smile softened his expression.

Milla was going to be sick.

"Bind her with your chains, my love," Anaisa purred. "Punish her as she deserves. It is only just."

Another cloud of her sickly perfume bloomed. Darkly's head tipped back, eyes drifting closed as he inhaled deeply of his consort. "Anything for my Anaisa."

"Ewww," Milla groaned, rolling onto her back only to be stopped by the messenger bag shoved under her spine. She groped blindly, slowing her movements to avoid notice from the lovesick Loa while racking her memory for anything she could of Belié Belcan.

He was justice personified, swift in his judgment. He acted with extreme prejudice, as ready to defend one from their enemies as he was to defeat them on their behalf.

And according to the witch who had summoned him, Milla was enemy number one.

He limped from an injury won in battle; he was a Loa who preferred rum and cigars. Consort of Anaisa (unhelpful) and the Loa one called upon for revocations.

Revocations!

Helpful bit of magick, revocations. Augurists loved them, constantly charging crystals with revocations disguised as protection charms to send ill intent back on the casting witch.

She could use that to her advantage if she could get Belié away from Anaisa. If she could get him to see that his consort was the wicked witch and not the drained, bleeding, bruised witch one second away from crying herself to pieces on the floor.

Worming onto her side, Milla dug in her bag, fingers curling around a fistful of teabags. She scanned the hall for any diversion, any idea, any advantage she could use to draw them apart. To get Belié to see—

The fly buzzed in front of her eyes, drawing Milla's gaze to where a shadow flickered beside an altar. The slightest swelling of a Shade beckoning from behind one of the now blank screens. Milla saw that, tracked it, and in the deepest, darkest parts of her, a match was struck. A candle lit.

And she moved.

Milla had made many mistakes. She had underestimated her opponent; she had gotten distracted. She had started to care about someone other than herself.

But Anaisa had made a bigger mistake: she had never learned what Milla truly was.

Swallowing a pained groan, she rolled onto her knees and called on whatever intent remained. Weakened, lessened, humbled, and pissed.

"Anaisa," Milla rasped, drawing the attention of both Loa.

"Oh, sweetheart," the object of her ire pouted, unwrapping herself from Darkly's body. "Don't you ever give up?"

Belié Belcan bristled, shadows pooling in his hands. He blinked and glanced down, mildly surprised. Shaking the shadows away, he let them pool again and threw his head back in a laugh. "It has been centuries since I last rode a Dark Witch."

"Well, double dang," Milla came to a standstill, left hand shoved deep in her bag, "I was hoping you wouldn't know how to use him."

"All the more reason you should have devoted yourself to me." Anaisa curved her hands over empty air, summoning another noxious pink ball. "I would have helped you turn your dreams into reality. I would have taught you how to manifest—"

"Manifest this." She ripped her hand free from the bag, sending a fistful of bloodied tea flying at the Loa and throwing all of herself into one last hex. "*Odsvětit!*"

Weaker hand aside, her throw was good. The hex—fueled by wicked intent, driven by cruel desire, and blooded with her sacrifice—was as cursed as they come. It hit the teabags as they neared the Loa, exploding into a cloud of fester and rot. Anaisa shrieked and ducked low, rolling on the ground with far more evasive prowess than Milla expected. Belié, on the other hand, looked up too late from his shadow play. Black eyes rounded to orbs at the moment before the cloud hit him dead on.

He coughed, sneezed, summoned a broadsword of fucking midnight to his hands, and, for the second time that night, Milla heard the wet-meat sound of Darkly's over-tall body crashing to the floor.

She winced—this was really going to do a number on the witch—the dregs of her Way forced a hiccup, and she set off after Anaisa.

The Loa had regained her feet, attempting to sprint across the dance floor in four-inch platform espadrilles. Ankles wobbling, she tripped over a pile of Diamond Qualifying Executives and went down in a heap of ragged neon pink and matted golden curls.

Swallowing a rise of nausea from what felt like drinking an entire shotski by herself, Milla stumbled after Anaisa. Hand in her bag, searching … searching … searching … there!

Her fingers brushed the edges of a wooden box, and she ripped it free, prying open the lid. Cupping her palm, she scooped the origami tiger from her bookshelf out of his box, bringing it up to eye level as she swayed. "Hello, you."

The tiger bristled in her palm, shaking his triangular paper face at the witch whose grin was a slow crawling thing. He'd been a last-minute purchase, a souvenir obtained on a whim by a husband trying to make his gloomy wife smile.

A little origami tiger, innocuous enough to sit overlooked on a shelf by both Dark Witch and Morgenhexe. A useful little tool for a cautious witch who packed too much and thought she might burn out her magick before the night was through.

Where Soul was the truth of memory as a witness, the facts of the life that was lived, and Shade was the emotive memory, the color of life; paper was written memory, able to be imbued with all sorts of things. Like, for instance, a little bit of the Forbidden and Foule when a witch was hard up and needed some help.

"*Jit.*" she whispered.

Go.

The tiger leaped from her hand, skittering across the dance floor and bounding up the pile of multi-level-marketing moms in less time than it took Milla to blink. Anaisa's shrill cry when he made his first cut was music to her ears, the glorious sound enough to fuel her legs as she trudged forward.

Anaisa popped her head up from the pile of soccer moms, eyes round and mouth open in a surprised little *o*. The tiger had opened a gash on her cheekbone, angry red lines striped her throat, and the sleeve of her dress was in shreds. She glanced past Milla, no doubt spotting the crumpled six feet and change of Dark Witch on the ground, and a furious howl escaped.

"You wicked witch!"

"Yeah," Milla smiled, shaking blood from her palm and vaguely recognizing the sizzle as it struck the floor. "Yeah, I am." Her head spun wildly, legs weak, and veins near empty of magick. She wiped the back of her hand under her nose, tipped headfirst into her Way, and got to work. "*Třást se.*"

Fear me.

She flicked her hand at Anaisa, the hex landing between her eyes. The Loa reeled from the fradey-hex, tumbling from the hun huddle and crab-walking away from certain death stalking across the dancefloor.

The witch marched forward, hands moving on their own. Her fingertips grayed and began shedding ash. She flung hexes that clouded her vision and started a low ringing in her ears. Her mouth went dry, and smoke curled from her lips with each word. Anaisa took some, deflected others, gaining her espadrilled feet to fling hot pink poison at Milla.

The Loa performed a perfect summons-to-hex, hitting Milla with a ball of heat. She twisted and caught it with the messenger bag, shrugging it off and throwing another hex as she spun. Dropping to a knee, Milla directed the force of her rage at the stage and spat, "*Rozložit!*"

Her fingers blackened to the first knuckle, the room tilted at a forty-five-degree angle, and the rapidly corroding surge protector beneath the stage started hissing and fizzing. Sparks caught the cheap, highly flammable curtains, and a ring of flame surrounded the stage, burning away the repeating cross-hatched heart of Anaisa's vèvè.

Funny thing about vèvè. They were a beacon in the dark for the Loa, a means of summoning them to this world, but in any standard Voodoo ritual, the vèvè was kept pristine until the possession was complete and the farewell performed.

To smudge or alter the vèvè in any way barred the path for the Loa to return to Guinee, their residence, thus trapping the Loa in the mortal realm in a body that could bleed.

Even better, and just as she assumed when she'd peered under the stage earlier, Milla's hex hit the main power source for the lights in the room. Cher's wailing died away, and the DJ jerked his head up, scanning the room and letting out a pitiful whimper. Milla held on one knee, glaring at Anaisa and pointing a decaying finger at the door as bulbs crackled and popped, sparks raining down. Filaments burnt out at the surge of energy through their electrical wiring, killing the light keeping the shadows away. The DJ's footfalls grew faint, and Milla spun, flinging another blighting hex at an altar.

"*Rozložit.*"

Anaisa howled, hitting Milla square in the back with another blast. It sent her sprawling forward, but her decomposition hex landed true.

The candles crumbled and fell to the altar's surface, flame licking across the cheap silk flowers and setting them ablaze. Light flickered, orange, red, and angry against the tables, pillars, and bodies in the room, casting long shadows and opening a path for her Dark Witch.

His Shade wasted no time, clever thing that it was. Surging from behind the dead screen and cutting across the walls, strobing shadow to shadow and closing the distance between it and his body with a legion of Shades following in his wake. Milla rolled onto her back and stared into the manic, preemptively victorious face of Anaisa Danto Pye, Loa of Spite.

She opened her mouth to say … well, whatever it was, Milla really didn't care.

"*Poškození,*" Milla breathed, thrusting an open, bloodied palm at the Loa. *Damage.* Smoke clouded her vision, so she heard rather than saw the Loa thrown back from the very basic, very easy damage-hex … on the surface.

But Milla was a Death Witch, and she applied her own little spin to the intent behind the word.

Rolling onto her stomach, she drew up one knee and then the other, forcing herself to rise, to face the thing that had snuck through the Gates and killed innocent women. The wretch that had stolen her demesne and used her Dark Witch as a vessel.

"I let you in my home," Milla wheezed at the heinous witch who had lied and made her care. "I let you into my life." The bitch that had wheedled her way into Milla's carefully balanced, isolated existence and earned the admiration of her friends and her singular family. "I let you run my *store*."

The Loa that had tried to kill her.

Anaisa lay crumpled against the risers, flesh mottled in various states of decay from Milla's hex. She pushed against the stairs, trying to rise and falling back.

Milla limped up to the wreckage, panting heavily as she stared down the Loa. "I'm sending you back," she stated, voice thick and the words escaping through a cloud of funerary smoke.

"No," Anaisa wheezed. She dropped her head back, shoulders twitching. "No, you won't."

"Won't I?" Milla's shoulders sagged. The skin on her temples pinched something fierce, and her eyes watered from a low, ghastly burn. Goddess, she wanted to sit down, drop her head between her knees, and catch her breath. It would be so easy to crumple to the ground and give up, but the job wasn't done. She'd walked away before, turned her back, and shirked her responsibility, and look what had happened. This all might end with Milla arrested by C.R.O.W., with her Soul and Shade cleaved from the witch, but, Horned God dammit, Milla was going to finish this before Anaisa did any more damage.

The Loa shook her head, her matted, bloodied hair painting the ruined stage with gore. Her shoulders twitched as she laughed, and Milla lifted her chin, squaring her shoulders. "You think this is a joke?"

"I think you're a joke, *polednice*." Anaisa raised her head. Blood from the wound on her cheek rained down the length of her throat, and a score of gashes from the paper tiger were visible through the many tears in her once fashionable pink dress. "You've lost. The demesne is mine, and you're running on ash."

"So you say." She made a brief effort of eyeing her skeletal fingers, flicking ash from the tips and abandoning cockiness in favor of remaining upright. That damned fly wove in and out of her bones, bobbing on a phantom breeze. "You may have stolen my demesne, but there's still one thing I can do."

Frothing at the mouth, Anaisa pushed herself from the stage, gaining her feet with teeth bared and neon sparks bursting from her fingertips.

Milla should have known the Loa wouldn't give up easily. Mainly because of pretty much everything that preceded this moment, but really because she knew in her blackest heart of hearts that she would never truly be free of her past mistakes.

She had wanted a de-regulation of magick. A new, free world where a Death Witch needn't hide what she was. A return to the Old Ways.

Her intent had been true, borne from a yearning to breathe and be.

Her desire had been undeniable. For Ezra, for freedom. For a new world.

But she had failed to consider the cost—the sacrifice.

All rituals demanded sacrifice, and in her foolish, misguided hope for a new world and her haste to stop the Armageddon she would have wrought, Milla had left the Gates open long enough for this thing to be summoned. She had sacrificed her safety and allowed this Loa to taint her demesne with its poisonous presence and *that* was the Loa's mistake.

"And what is that, *polednice*?" Anaisa twisted her wrist. Noxious hot pink bled along her palms as she gathered her stolen power, burning through the head and heart lines and bursting the seam of her life. The blood in her hair dried and flaked away, silken curls unraveling the matted knots. With a press of her palm, the gash on her cheekbone vanished, and the bright, sunny *čarodějnice* smiled beatifically at her *polednice*.

"What could you possibly do to me? You have nothing left. No demesne to draw from, no Stitch Witch to offer a pithy remark, no Way left in your veins to siphon what I throw at you. No Dark Witch—and yes, I knew what he was. From the moment I laid eyes on the oungan, I knew what he was. The Perfect Vessel. A horse for my consort, and what a horse." She dragged her lower lip through perfect, white teeth, honey-amber eyes gleaming. "I can't wait to take him for a ride."

"That's …" Milla panted, hitching her leg in a weary step and shaking blood from her left hand to spatter against the vèvè painted floor. "That's not an image I needed today."

"Give up, Milla." Anaisa brought her hands together, cupping them around the caustic ball she conjured. Sickly perfume wafted over Milla, a thousand promises of a thousand wonderful things trickling into her ears. "Take the punishment you are owed, like a good little witch. Kneel. Devote yourself to me and mine. If you're lucky, Belié will convince me to go easy on you."

"Not interested in the easy way out." She shook her hand again, sliding her left foot back into a defensive hand-to-hex stance. Her bootsole slipped in the spatter of her blood, and the stench of chemical rot and burnt plastic wrinkled her nose.

The Loa narrowed her eyes at Milla. "Who are you that you're so stubborn."

"Ludmilla Saxana Probuditna," she replied with a shrug. Anaisa scoffed. "Lightner."

The Loa's face fell. Just for an instant. Just long enough to show Milla that she understood. "He's Gone."

"I expect you'll see him soon," Milla replied. Taking as deep a breath as she could manage, she pooled the dregs of her Way to hand, kindling it to a semblance of life. A tingle, a sunburn slap, a suggestion of warmth from a single match. What she had planned … it would take everything she was. Everything she had. Every bit of latent Way that still sparked in her veins.

But she could do it, oh, of that, she was abso-fucking-lutely positive.

"You're a-a vestic. You can't even summon; you couldn't possibly have joined his line. She never would have let you—"

Milla spread her hands at her hips. "And yet."

"No." Anaisa yielded a step, finally putting the pieces together. All the hints, the false leads, the layers of lies that Milla shrouded herself in to hide the truth of the witch. "No, it's impossible."

"Improbable."

The Loa recovered quickly from her shock, tossing her golden hair back. She sneered at Milla's blackened fingers and the wound weeping on her thigh, honey-amber eyes reading the blackened, charred veins crawling along Milla's temples and cheeks. "What are you?"

"A witch," Milla's voice resonated with the echo of the catacombs, "with a Way Forbidden and Foule." She cocked her head, listening to the shambling footfalls at her back. Anaisa saw it an instant later, the hunched Dark Witch limping his way across the floor.

"Belié!" she called to her consort, throwing out her arm. Palm out, wrist up, hex flying. A frantic, last-ditch effort to avoid the death that barred her way. Milla caught it with her bleeding palm, redirecting the caustic, spitting ball and slamming it to the ground, twisting the intent into something of her own.

Something wretched and wicked. Ruinous.

Keep it simple, Millapet, Ezra directed, watching her from a safe distance, in another time, as he always did. *A low-level manipulation, something you can do again and again and again.*

"*Rozložit,*" she spat. The acid pink ball flared and guttered out, the Way dying under Milla's practiced onslaught. Darkly's footsteps drew closer, gaining surety as Belié recovered from her poisonous tea. Cold bloomed at her back, the shadow-sword drawn again. Intent crackled in the air, strobing as a blue light as the Loa fed his power into the Dark Way.

"*Rozložit.*" Ash crawled from her hairline, joining the blackened veins worming from her temples and knitting together over the bridge of her nose in a funeral mask. Rot rose on her tongue, and Milla stepped further into her Way, shredding the uneasy tether that had kept her hidden all these years. Beneath her palm, the blood spatter bubbled and smoked, festering on the tile and eating through the geometric design that made up Belié Belcan's vèvè.

The rot caught, crawling over the floor like cancer. She whipped her head around at Belié's startled gasp only a few feet away. Close, far closer than she'd assumed. He lowered his arm, and the tip of his midnight sword, now dancing in blue lightning, dropped to the floor as he witnessed the destruction of the vèvè. A trap laid by a witch who had nothing left but her acid spit, caustic blood, and the one damn thing she'd always been able to do.

The low-level manipulation, the cantrip that had lost her a husband, gifted her a Stitch Witch and won her a demesne.

A summoning.

"Who are *you* to challenge the Rada?" Anaisa shrieked.

With the last of her ability, Milla jumped to her feet and flung her arms out wide, fingers clawed at the two Loa she'd trapped in their mostly mortal bodies. That obnoxious fly landed on her arm, and she did Anaisa the honor of looking her in the eye as she smiled.

"I'm a Horned God-damned Death Witch."

"Oh—" Belié breathed.

"—snap." Anaisa winced.

"*Pojd'te a zničte.*" The Death Witch muttered a textbook-perfect hex, adding her own special brand of hate into the mix.

Come and destroy.

Darkly screamed, his knees hit the ground, and Milla held on, summoning his Shade and bringing it crashing back into his body. His shoulders twitched, tendons spasming in his neck as the spirit of the Loa and the Shade of the Dark Witch battled for supremacy. It wouldn't be enough. He wouldn't be enough. Not against Belié Belcan. Not unless Milla could force the revocation and turn the Loa of Justice against his consort. So she held on, fingers rotting to the bone, teeth grinding to dust until the scream lodged in her throat was too much to restrain.

The cry that left Milla was a sepulchral howl meant for a charnel house. She held onto her Way, clinging to those fine, gossamer-thin threads of her as she teetered head-first into the dark, recalling one very poignant phrase spoken in a very foreign tongue as she summoned each and every Shade that Darkly had collected.

Is mise an geata.

I am the gate.

"*Pojd'te*," she bid them, *come*, and they obeyed, pounding into his back one by one by one. A sea of Shade drowned the Dark Witch and overwhelmed the Loa. Their woes were too many, their accusations against Anaisa too loud to ignore. Milla saw the moment Belié believed. Saw the instant those black marble eyes fixed his consort and, oh, was her cry of horror a delight.

"No, mi amor, please, I only wanted to bring you through the Gates! I only wanted you with me, and these women, they gave of themselves freely. For you!"

"You have been wicked, Anaisa Danto Pye." Belié advanced, his hand grasping for a sword it no longer held.

Milla narrowed her eyes, straining against the urge to close them entirely and fall. Twisting her wrist, she curled her clawed hand into a fist, switching intent. "*Zničit*," she commanded.

Destroy.

The Dark Witch surged forward as if yanked by a string tied to his ribcage, head dropping back and arms thrown wide. Held upright by the Shades torn from him one by one, crowding Milla and the promise she offered, and all too happy to comply. They clawed eagerly at Anaisa, shadow hands tearing at her dress, her hair, and her arms.

So many dead.

So many women caught up in this scheme.

Milla couldn't save them; Darkly could only help them find an uneasy peace. There would be no moving on for these women, no eternity until the wretched thing that had damned them was destroyed.

"No!"

Milla whipped her head around to see Anaisa throw her hands up. Pink glowed at her palms, and Death stalked forward, closing a skeletal hand around the Loa's throat and hissing, "*Zničit*."

The Shades descended, taking from Anaisa what she had stolen from them. The Loa screamed, the world tilted on its axis, and the scales tipped with it. Threads erupted from the demesne, winding around Milla and connecting her once again to St. Augustine. Power rushed up her legs, a surging welcome that heated in her belly and breathed strength into her arms. Her Way throbbed and pulsed, a riot of energy and exaltation as she became the creature nature intended her to be. The creature she had always been.

A Death Witch.

She bared her teeth and tightened her grip, feeling the feeble hit of the Loa's final hex and letting the threat of death fuel her. Anaisa moaned, and the Shades devoured, crashing over the Loa like a wave. Over and over and over, they came, a funnel of shadow and midnight smoke.

They consumed the life that was stolen. Anaisa's glorious hair brittled and frayed, her apple cheeks sunk, and those honey-amber eyes dimmed and dulled.

"Pojd'te a zničte. Pojd'te a zničte. Pojd'te a zničte." Milla held on, the bones of her skeletal hand digging into Anaisa's throat as she chanted her intent again and again and again. Never letting go as that vitriolic hex spewed from her mouth as ash and corpse-dust and all things Forbidden and Foule.

The last of the Shades purled against the husk of the Loa, and Milla let go, watching her waver for a heartbeat. Just long enough to ensure Milla would never forget this moment. She raised her blackened and shriveled hand, the middle finger and thumb hooked together.

"Blessed be." She flicked Anaisa at the center of her chest, and the Loa collapsed as nothing more than a pile of cigar-scented ash.

Forty Four

Milla spat acid and venom at the ash, a perk of being a witch, and then she collapsed.

The pavilion spun overhead, and her stomach roiled, but there was nothing to throw up, no poison to rid from her body. She had spent it all, and now she was done. Now, she could close her eyes and sleep.

She was done.

"Oh, no you dinnae." Darkly looped his arms under hers, hoisting Milla up to her feet and hooking an arm under her legs. He cradled her close to his chest, and the scent of burnt wool and sweet rot made Milla sneeze. They stumbled from the pavilion, Darkly's legs giving out on the Fountain of Youth's picnic lawn. She spilled from his arms and lay in the grass, breathing in her demesne and feeling its power kindle in her veins. Darkly knelt beside her, the ruined messenger bag sloughing off his shoulder. "What do you need?"

To die.

It was over. That much she knew. The amount of necromantic energy she'd manipulated in there would have set off every E.R.I.E. in a one-hundred-mile radius, and she wore the evidence of it on her skin. Her thigh burned, and her palm screamed from the athame; the fingers of her left hand were blackened to the third knuckle, her right was ashen and skeletal, and the painful pulsing at her temples told Milla she wore the funeral mask of a Death Witch.

She rolled onto her back, gazing at the stars twinkling to life overhead. Darkly's face blurred into her field of vision; his cheekbones smudged with herbal tea dust, his neck and shoulder mottled and starting to fester. Still, he pressed his hand against her cheek and rubbed a thumb under her eye, tracing the blackened veins and cursing in that unintelligible Scottish. He jerked his hand away, squinting at his palm with a frown.

"Are you you?" she wheezed.

"Milla, *leannán*." He wrapped his arms around her, hissing as he pulled Milla to his chest. "Sweetheart, what did you do?"

"She took you," she rasped, letting the thunderous beat of his heart drown out the screaming in her head. "She took you, and she took the demesne; I couldn't—"

"But what did you do?" She looked up at him then, reading the terror and the confusion. He'd had no idea, not an inkling of what they could do together. A piece of Milla's heart shriveled, killed by the knowledge that her Dark Witch had no true idea what he was.

"I got the idea from watching Poltergeist," Milla whispered, fingers toying with a burn on his sweater. Fabric crumbled at her touch, and she withdrew.

"Ach, hen." He pressed his lips to her head, hands traveling up to her cheeks, and then his mouth was on hers, the desperate kiss of a man who knew she was damned. Milla let herself enjoy it, knowing it would be a long time, if ever, before she was embraced like this again. She used what strength she had to hold

Darkly close, dear. He pulled away with a gasp and uttered, "Cannae do this."

Milla dragged her eyes up to his face, blinking at the disgusted twist of his mouth. His lips were puffy and red, but he managed a tiny smile.

"Your breath tastes like death." He winked. *Winked.* Milla chuckled, and his phone started screeching.

The E.R.I.E. app was going insane, messages flying in, notifications from the A.I.I. team positioned nearby, C.A.R.B. issuing alerts, and the shrill electronic ring of a call. He ripped the phone from a pocket on his leg, swiping to answer the call and wincing when a familiar, lilting female voice began tearing into him.

"Keir Darkly Simmons, what the hell have you been up to? I have been trying to get ahold of you for hours. All our equipment's acting the maggot, and I know you're at the source of that necro-surge we just tracked—"

"Lou," he croaked, holding his phone flat in front of his mouth. Milla felt her eyebrows crawl up her forehead in shock.

"Lou?" she mouthed.

"I am having a bloody time keeping the boys from legging it over. Horned God help me, Keir, if you are still there with her when they arrive—"

"Lou, Big Yin, if you would haud yer wheesht for a second—"

"You did not just tell me to blag off!"

Darkly winced, caught Milla's eye and shook his head. "We need five minutes tae clear the scene."

"Oooh no, Keir. You stay right where you are and wait for the dispatched team. This is going to fall back on me, and I vouched for you—"

Darkly hung up and dropped his phone to the ground. "Cannae thole her pish the day." He ran a hand over his face and let out a long-suffering sigh. The phone immediately began ringing, and this time Milla's eyes damn near bugged out of her skull at the image of long-legged, dewy blonde Fiona flashing on the screen.

"Lou is your ... Fiona?"

"My sister, Lou." He nodded, tension tightening the corners of weary eyes. "Luminescence Fiona Simmons."

Milla pursed her lips, worming them together until the pressure grew too great to restrain. She burst out laughing. "Your sister is your handler? Your sister is Fiona!" Darkly narrowed his eyes at her, and Milla cackled, "Your *sister* was your Valentine's Day date!"

"Goan' yerself," he grumbled, sweeping his phone from the ground and shoving it in a pocket. "Wee Miss My Date Was a Raw-head."

She shook her head, wiping a glob of ash from under an eye. "And Keir, was it?"

"Old Irish name," he supplied, scanning her face and hands, her legs, and looking a little ill. "I've nae idea how I'm going to get you out of here."

"Just go, Darkly," Milla sighed, dropping back into the grass. "They already know I'm here and what I am; I can't ask you to put yourself at risk for me."

"Dinnae fash," he groaned and stood, moving to hook his arms under hers and haul Milla to her feet. He got about as far as the "arms under hers part" when the screech of tires and metal clanging against metal resounded from the entrance to the grounds. A singular headlight burned through the dark, falling on a half-standing Milla and Darkly stooping over her. They jerked their faces in unison, jaws dropping as a minivan barreled down. One light was busted, the side mirrors dangled from wires, the fender was dented beyond belief, and a worrying amount of steam came through the grille.

Dies-well slammed on the brakes, his face hovering behind the wheel as a pale orb cast in maniacal glee. The minivan skid to a halt beside them, tail-end swinging wide, and the vampire rolled down the window, propping an arm on the sill with a flash of fang. "Get in, witches."

✳

"How." Darkly demanded, blotting a cotton ball that had been drowned in rubbing alcohol against Milla's palm. She hissed and scrunched her eyes at the sting and stench of rotting cotton.

"A leggy blonde," Dies-well responded, "and a solid hunch."

The GPS added, "Your destination is on your right."

Milla and Darkly glanced out his window, noting the darkened street and a pier stretching over the Matanzas River. Then Darkly looked down at himself, at the phone in his pocket, and choked. "Did you place a locator on my phone?"

"Hardly," Dies-well chuffed, tapping the GPS to silence the kind British woman. "I used the Find My Fam app."

"Agh," The Dark Witch dropped his chin, silently counting to three. When he raised his head, it was to look Milla in the eye. "And you said the Morgenhexe arranged the apprenticeship?"

"She did," Milla gritted through her teeth as Darkly dribbled more rubbing alcohol on her palm. "It's her right as my *jezibaba*; why do you ask?"

"Seems a wee bit suspect." He cupped the back of her hand, fingers gently circling her wrist as he angled her palm to the light.

"She sets you up with Lightner and then the Loa. Being who she is, I would have thought the Morgenhexe to be more discerning."

"A coincidence," Milla whispered, too afraid to give voice to the same suspicion she harbored.

"Are you implying Morgen Tage, of all witches, believes in coincidence?"

"She was Ezra's *jezibaba* for a while, and she trained Tracy, who C.R.O.W. thought was Ana's first *polednice*, on Big Torch Key. I'm a witch of convenience."

Darkly snorted and gave her a soft look. "Hardly convenient."

Milla twisted her mouth in a mock scowl, readying a retort when her phone started ringing. She glanced at the screen, and a not-at-all-brave sound came out of her mouth, one Milla had never thought herself capable of making.

Diego.

In a flash, the phone was at her ear, and she was sobbing at the sound of his voice.

"Where have you been, bruja? I have been trying to get ahold of you all day."

"Diego, oh my Goddess, Diego, are you alright?" Darkly released her hand, letting Milla turn away from him, and started cleaning the cut on her leg instead. "Ssss, ow—please tell me you're alright."

"Well, I am a little sunburned from the eight-hour drive in a convertible, but nothing some aloe will not fix."

"Oh, my Goddess." Milla slumped in the seat, the stress of the last few days rushing from her body and puddling at her feet. In the wake of all that frustration and fear, she was exhausted to the bone, more than she had been on the lawn of the Fountain of Youth. Diego was alright. He was alive. Anaisa had not taken him, but then—"Where are you?"

"Key West."

She sat up, screeching into the phone. "What?!"

"Remember that customer asking for me by name?"

"Yes, and if you tell me you jetted down to the Keys for a fuckation you can start apologizing right now. You nearly gave me several heart attacks."

"Morgen grabbed me and made a compelling case for why I needed to take a last-minute trip down to the tower and lie low. She left a note. Did you not see it?"

"Did she not think to *sign it?*" Milla bellowed.

Diego was silent for a beat before replying in a measured tone, "I can see how her not signing the note may have caused some confusion."

"You think?"

"Si, you are right. I am sorry, we should have been more clear, but Milla, listen—"

"Why?"

"Que?"

"Why did you need to go to Key West?" Milla moved the phone to her other ear, sharing a look with Darkly. Witch of convenience she may be, but even a wicked witch didn't believe in coincidence, and Morgen showing up to remove Diego from harm's way reeked of it. "She's never taken you down there before."

"She received, as she put it, 'completely unfounded conjecture warranting an abundance of caution.' Namely, about a certain pequeña bruja conducting an illegal Seeing in New Orleans, of all places," Diego chided. "I told you not to go down there."

"And that's why she grabbed you?"

"Si." He smacked his lips. "Also, she wants me to alter a few pieces of her wardrobe."

"You—" Milla's jaw dropped. She stared out the minivan window, watching but not seeing the lights of her city pass by. "You went to Key West because my foster mother wanted you to alter her wardrobe?"

Darkly snorted, coughing into a fist to stifle further laughter.

"I am a bespoke tailor, bruja," Diego sniffed. "If a terrifying witch wants to whisk me away to the Keys to alter her Katherine Hepburn cosplay and agrees to pay my rush fees, who am I to argue?"

Milla dropped her head into the crook of her palm, bemused and bewildered. "Oh my Horned God, I am far too drunk for this."

"Ooh, do tell. The tower is beyond boring; you never warned me how austere her aesthetic is, although now that I am seeing it, a whole lot of you makes sense," Diego chattered. "So, drinks. Not alone, I presume?"

"No." Milla glanced at the Dark Witch, who was now typing on his phone. "No, I'm with Darkly."

The Stitch Witch whooped, a trilling, piercing exclamation that had Milla pulling the phone away from her ear with a whimper. Darkly jerked his face up, checking to see if she was alright. Milla rolled her eyes at him, pointing at the phone and twisting in the seat for privacy.

"Tell me everything," Diego demanded. "The where, the when, the how. I know the why and who."

"There's nothing to tell."

"Disagree," Darkly stated, loud enough that Diego heard it and started cackling in the phone.

"Okay, okay, we can save the story for our next movie night if you can drag yourself away from tall, Darkly, and handsome long enough to remember your friends exist."

"It's not like that."

"Liar." Diego's smile was audible. "It was New Orleans that did it, si? Please tell me it was New Orleans. Ana is going to be furious; we had a bet going."

"Ana," Milla's voice flatlined. "About that, Diego, Ana was the energy vampire."

"Que?"

"Seriously," Dies-well hollered back through the partition, "stop calling it that. It's offensive."

"What do you mean she was an energy vampire? And what is an energy vampire?"

"I can hear you!" The vampire pounded his fist against the steering wheel.

"I, wow, it's a whole story, tío." She took a breath, intending to steady herself enough to tell Diego everything, but her throat felt too tight, the minivan too small, and suddenly all Milla wanted to do was push the door open and run off into the night, disappearing into the woods and swamps of her demesne to hide from the reality of what she'd done. "She, um, she was a Loa that escaped when Ezra and I-when we, um"—the minivan trundled over a pothole, and the phone cracked against her cheekbone, tumbling from her hand—"It was all my fault."

Milla stared down at the ongoing call, hands tremoring wildly. Darkly plucked the phone from the ground, squeezing her knee gently to get her to look at him and holding her over-wide stare as he assured Diego in the calm, steadying voice he was so fond of.

She couldn't hear Diego's questions, only the frantic tone. "Aye," Darkly nodded. "C.R.O.W. is handled for now. The grounds are old enough they'd emit a necro-signature even without Milla having been there—course I ken what her Way is, do you think me a fool?" He paused and then chuffed at something Diego said. "Was a rhetorical question." His mouth formed a tight line, and he dropped his eyes to the floor. "Until you get back, of course. That is," head still ducked low, the Dark Witch looked up at Milla, silver flecks in his eyes gleaming brightly in the dome light, "if she'll have me."

"Yes," Milla breathed, amazed that she had ever thought of this kind, considerate witch was a cocky, self-assured, Highland coo-loving, asshole. Darkly hit her with a wide, dimpled grin. And then he winked.

"Gies a call on the morn," he told Diego. "I'll answer if she doesnae." A pause, a tiny chuckle, and then, "You too, mate."

The phone was tucked in a cupholder, and Milla stared at Darkly, the Forbidden and Foule Dark Witch that C.R.O.W. had sent. The last few weeks replayed themselves in her mind, every little touch and gesture, every joke, every scowl. Their catastrophic first meeting and their arguments about C.R.O.W. and the laws ruling their witchy world. Every lunch and every mile they had run through her demesne, all leading up to this moment where Darkly chose her. Again.

"You lied to C.R.O.W.?"

"No one lies to C.R.O.W.," he replied, fingers twitching. "They're gonnae have questions, but it should buy us a day or two to recover from the worst of it."

"That easy?" Her voice felt far too small for the weight of her question.

Darkly closed the space between them, dusting a soft, fleeting kiss to her lips and dropping his forehead against hers. "That easy."

He pulled away, rubbing the heel of his palm against his forehead, and crawled into the back seat. "Come here." He dragged her back with him. Legs stretched out, he summoned a blanket from nowhere, tucking it around her shoulders and drawing her to his side.

"I can't help but feel we're forgetting something," she murmured. "Diego's in Key West, Anaisa and Belié are banished, the demesne is secured …"

"Not that you've asked," Dies-well added, "but Marie is satisfied."

"There's the glamour on the ICYMI merchandise," she began.

"Problem for another day," Darkly ended.

"So what else is there?" Milla mused aloud. Darkly tipped his head forward to look down at her, his hand gliding up her thigh, her hip and skimming her ribcage.

"I can think of a thing or two."

"Oh, my Horned God," she pushed away from him. "You are disgusting. I'm disgusting!" She raised her casting hand as evidence, pointing a skeletal index finger at him. "That's disgusting."

"So you say," he smarmed, fingers drifting higher up her side.

"I hate to interrupt, which is a blatant lie, obviously," Dies-well chirped from the driver's seat, "but as delightfully quaint as your demesne is, I would like to know where you'd like me to drive you."

Milla side-eyed Dies-well, unable to stifle her smile at the vampire's now familiar glower.

"We should avoid the cottage." Darkly straightened in his seat. "It's a C.R.O.W. safehouse, wouldnae be wise for anyone in this auto right now." He glanced at Milla. "To yours, then?"

She opened her mouth, ready to say yes. Wanting her shower, her bed. Wanting more than anything to go home and knowing it wouldn't be home at all. Not without Diego. Not without the witch who had stitched her back together and kept the not-ghost away. As much as she loved her butter yellow Victorian with peeling paint on the lattice and ached to see the electric candles flickering in the windows as a beacon for the wicked, the weird, the Forbidden, and the Foule, the prickling behind her eyes told her it wouldn't be right.

Not just yet.

"No." She eyed the sign for Florida State Highway A1A South and the arrow pointing across the Bridge of Lions. An idea sparked in the depths of her exhausted mind. "Dies-well, turn left."

"Left?"

"Left."

"I'm all the way in the right lane!" he whined, jerking on the wheel and cutting off the four-door sedan next to them.

"*HolyHornedGod*." Darkly gripped the Oh-Shit handle, heels planted firmly on the floor. "Where are we going?"

"Where are we—" she laughed at the over-tall witch in his fright. "The beach, obviously."

He gaped owlishly at her, jaw working as he struggled to comprehend. "The beach?"

"Or maybe an island," she dropped her head against his shoulder, inhaling the soothing clove and smoke scent unique to the Dark Witch, "where it feels like the sun never sets and you're surrounded by blue water on all sides." Milla tugged on his belt buckle. "Somewhere quiet with no one else around so I can—"

Dies-well smacked the steering wheel, glaring at them in the rearview mirror, his shallow eyes lit with amusement disguised as outrage. "I am right here."

Epilogue

Sunset painted the mountains in varying swathes of blue backlit by a sherbet sky. Hidden in the undergrowth, a quartet of crickets strung their symphony as an Appalachian breeze whistled through the reeds on a nearby crick. She let her head drop back against the rim of the hot tub, eyes lazily following one of the boys as they paraded through the glade in low-cut swim trunks. All thighs and rippling muscles beaded with sweat in the humid evening air. She bit her lower lip as a tray appeared in the corner of her eye, laden with a fish bowl margarita, a platter of freshly fried tortilla chips, and steaming queso.

"I could get used to this," she muttered, accepting the margarita with both hands.

"Don't get too comfortable," Chad grinned, feeding her a chip dripping with spicy, melted cheese.

Her eyes flew open, and she glared at the lumpy, muscled hunk. "What was that?"

"Doesn't that hurt your neck?" He grinned and handed her the margarita. Julie sat up, eyeing the drink in her—

"Here." Again, Chad offered her the over-large margarita. "Just the way you like it."

"Thanks…" Julie eyed him, accepting the glass and holding it under her nose. She inhaled deeply and lurched upright at the stench of burnt plastic and chemical sear.

Her neck pinched, the talons of a headache digging in at her temples. She skittered across the floor, back hitting a stack of cardboard.

"Oh, gosh."

It was pitch black wherever she was, minus the tiny red light glowing a few feet away. She felt along the floor, fingers brushing something slick and greasy. Imagining the worst, like a jacket made from human skin, or, actually, no, that was the worst thing she could imagine, Julie rushed to her feet, spinning to brace the boxes as the wretched stench grew stronger.

"Cheese and crackers." She pressed a hand to her mouth, frantically feeling up the cardboard. Her fingers found the corner and slid along the side until they hit a wall, a door jamb, and finally the knob. "Please don't be locked, please don't be locked."

She turned the knob, sobbing with relief when the door swung open. Muted light spilled down a narrow hall in dim, flickering oranges and a dull, steady yellow, giving shape to her surroundings. She took a shaky step forward, recognizing the silhouettes of half-empty clothing racks and a mannequin in a shop window.

"What in the world." Julie frowned, her head fuzzy and skull aching as she tried to piece together her day. She'd woken from a nap to that text from Milla, gotten dressed, and grabbed her badges and ticket for the ICYMI Convention. She had driven into the Colonial Quarter to check on the store and see if Diego needed help, and then—nothing. She'd gone to the store, talked to Milla, and woken up in the office. But how could she have fallen asleep? She'd *just* taken a nap to be well-rested for the convention.

The convention.

Julie rushed down the hall, bursting onto the cramped sales floor and navigating the labyrinth of clothes racks. The gas lamps of the Colonial Quarter cast odd shadows in the room, and out of the corner of her eye, she could have sworn she saw the mannequin in the window move. "Milla?" Scanning the shop, she spotted her bag on the display case beside the register, but no Milla, no Darkly, no Diego. "This doesn't make any sense."

"You're telling me," a voice replied, broad and nasal, like an old radio announcer.

Julie froze, eyes about to pop out of her skull. "Is someone there?"

"Always, toots," the voice answered from somewhere over her head. It was either someone very, very tall or someone hiding near the ceiling, and neither option gave much in the way of comfort. "You just ain't heard us before."

"Stop calling dames 'toots,'" another voice snapped. This one was deeper like the words were being formed in the back of a throat. "Dem broads don't like it none."

"Oh, God." Her stomach dropped.

"Nah, the name's Valentine, see?"

Julie whirled around, phone held out like a crucifix. The beam of her LED flashlight landed on two ventriloquist dummies perched on a shelf. They stared down at her with vacant eyes, their painted smiles wide and too red, their suits crisp and pressed.

Silent.

Unmoving.

"Carbon monoxide poisoning," she muttered. "It's only been a couple days. I'm still recovering. I passed out, and they put me in the stockroom to sleep it off."

It sounded plausible enough, and the dummy on the left nodded in agreement.

Julie shrieked and dropped her phone. Her hip slammed into the corner of the display, rattling the case and knocking rings and headdresses off of their stands. A clock in the hutch beside the register started clanging wildly, and the mannequin in the window turned to face her, a handless arm raised in front of the space where a head should be—shushing her.

"Oh my *GOD!*" She grabbed her bag, snatched her phone from the floor, and darted for the front door.

"I already told ya!" the dummy shouted after her. "The name's Valentine!"

"I don't think she's interested, buddy."

"Stop calling me buddy, Winthorpe."

Julie screamed and wailed, pounding her fist on the glass and working the lock on the door. Something skittered over her feet, and she saw a series of interlocked paper clips with chalk for hands drawing awful designs on her shoes.

"Please, please, please let me oooouut." The nurse sobbed, slapping her palm against the door and staring in horror at her smiling, waving reflection in a gilded mirror. She sank to the floor, hugging her knees and rocking back and forth, utterly deaf to the clank and roll of tumblers and the pleasant jangling of the bells.

A firm hand grabbed her by the shoulder and pulled her to her feet, followed by a friendly arm draping across her shoulders and guiding Julie into the Colonial Quarter, the entire district abandoned at whatever ungodly hour it was.

"It's a good thing we found you when we did," a woman spoke, her lilting accent like a lullaby. "Carbon monoxide poisoning is hardly a joke; the hallucinations alone are enough to drive one mad."

Julie raised her head, blinking at a pair of the largest, brightest blue-green eyes she'd ever seen. "How did you—"

"Know you were in there?" The woman frowned. "We didn't. There was an explosion at the Fountain of Youth; the gas lines run straight through the Quarter, and we're clearing the whole area. It's lucky we heard you when we did, isn't it, Cyrus?"

The woman moved her gaze past Julie, who startled when she noticed the man standing beside her.

"Lucky thing, indeed." His accent was thicker, warmer. Greek, she thought, or something Mediterranean. "How long were you in there, miss?"

"I, oh …" Julie blinked, shaking her head and trying to remember. "A little before sunset, six o'clock or so?"

"Six hours." The woman sighed in a way Julie interpreted as an old weariness. "Of course, my brother and that witch couldn't find it within themselves to come back and check on you." The arm around her shoulders slipped away, and the blonde woman stepped aside. Her gentle expression hardened to headmistress levels of sternness as she eyed Julie head-to-toe. "Cyrus. Can you work with that?"

The man, Cyrus, raised both hands. One held a phone making tiny chirping sounds, and the other featured stubby fingers crooked like he was spinning a dial. "Come now, Lou, it is like you do not know me at all."

"What are you—"

"Trust us," the woman, Lou, stood beside him, and Julie noticed they were dressed alike. Black sweaters with tactical patches at their shoulders and over their hearts. Fitted pants with an insane amount of buckles and pockets.

"Are you the F.B.I.?" She wrung her hands, needing to latch onto something that made any sort of sense.

"No." Lou's bright eyes gleamed from within, an ethereal light calling Julie's attention like a moth to a flame. "No, you poor little Staid, we are something much, much more."

DEATH

Milla and Darkly will return in

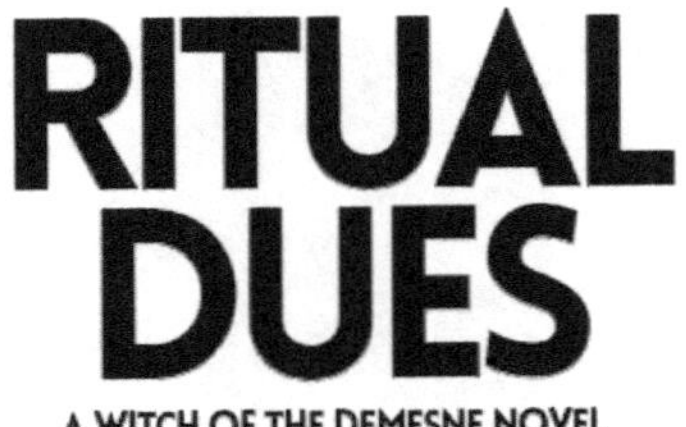

ELSEWHERE, IN THE WORLD OF C.R.O.W.

STITCHING PALMS

A WITCHES OF C.R.O.W. NOVELLA

Diego Gregorio de Bimini needs a vacation.

After his roommate stirs up trouble with the Enforcers of witch law, he decides to do just that.

Heeding the summons to the Conch Republic, the Stitch Witch spends his days lounging in the sun and trawling Key West for curious items occult and otherwise. When the discovery of a cursed item from his past places the Stitch Witch at risk of being discovered by the very Enforcers he hopes to avoid, Diego makes a deal with a local pawnbroker to spare the mortal world from an ancient threat.

Available Now

SHADY DEPTHS

A WITCHES OF C.R.O.W. NOVELLA

*A witch running from heartbreak, a merman who hunts the stars,
and the Shade which binds them both.*

Keir Simmons, a bounty hunter for the Coven for the Regulation and Oversight of Witches, has made a career out of running away from his problems. Blindsided by a break-up, he leaps at the first assignment he's offered, one that will take him far away from his ex: chasing a rogue lorelei to the edge of the European continent.

When a chance encounter with a midnight diver leaves the pair inextricably linked, Keir is caught between his responsibilities as a C.R.O.W. Enforcer, his past as a questionably wicked witch, and his broken, but beating heart. With C.R.O.W. breathing down his neck and the lorelei continuing to evade capture, it becomes harder and harder to turn away from his unlikely ally — a man with a secret lurking just beneath the surface.

Find out why Darkly was benched in *Shady Depths*

Available Now

ALSO BY B.L. BROWN

Witch of the Demesne
Ritual Income
Ritual Dues

Witches of C.R.O.W.
Shady Depths
Stitching Palms

Camp Cryptid
Faun Over Me
Shifting Hearts

Beerhall Brides
Ravished by the Rasselbock

THANKS, Y'ALL!

There are so many people to thank for their patience, their insight, their repeated readings of passages, and, in the case of the World's Best Hype Woman™, multiple readings of an entire manuscript.

Oliver – You told me to "shut up and write" without understanding what you were truly unleashing. I love you for that and so many other things. Thank you for brainstorming ideas, fixing plots, arguing about the pros and cons of mind control (none, unless you are a dick; and surprisingly a lot), digging through your vast knowledge of corporate lingo and financial terms for the sake of a good (bad?) pun, and for not saying "no" when I told you I wanted to vanish to New Orleans for "research". The Sazeracs were delicious.

Ana – The World's Best Hype Woman™. I am immeasurably grateful for your multiple readings of Ritual Income, from that first eight-hundred-page behemoth to the final five-hundred-ish-page version. Milla, Darkly, and the team have been brought to life thanks to you. I'm sorry my characters trash on Jamon so much. Thank you for listening to me ramble over uncountable glasses of wine and shark cootchie boards. I am the luckiest person to have you in my corner.

Molly – Here it is, the book I pitched to you a million years ago after a pregnancy-induced fever dream. Ludmilla has come a long way from that first glimpse of "a middle-aged witch in some sort of antique store and a secret kind of magic versus a life-force-sucking monster." Your insight, critical eye, and sick ability to spot a plothole a million miles away were invaluable. Thank you for believing in my cantankerous little witch from the beginning and for putting up with me for 30+ years.

Theresa – you took my words and slashed them into a sort of sense. And then you did it again and again. I am in awe.

The Ladies of Fort Smut – I could not ask for better company on this writing, retreating, and charcuterie-eating life. From the time the story first planted its seeds in my head, we have added three tiny humans, survived a pandemic, group-read numerous terrible and not-so-terrible books, and crafted the most rewarding and routinely hilarious group chat. Sorry for all the TikToks, I love you all, where are we going next?

Jen – Some people are forever people; you're one of them. The bottle of Writer's Tears you sent after I finished the first draft saw me through to the finish line. On-on, you beautiful human.

Bald Chris – Another forever person. Thank you for meeting me in New Orleans and silently suffering through a walking tour of the city to visit the locations in my book. When are we going back? Snake and Jake's is calling.

KoaW – You believed in me. Can I keep you?

My Beta Team – Ana, Trier, Callie, Molly, Whitney, Megan. For whatever amount you made it through, whether it be multiple long hauls or a few chapters, I am forever grateful for your time, patience, and feedback. Y'all are the best around, and I'm a better writer because of you.

The Monster Fudgers Book Club – Y'all saw my call for ARC Readers and embraced *Shady Depths* with your whole hearts. I hope you enjoyed seeing Keir on the other side. He'll be okay, I promise (and you'll get more Toby soon).

The Authors over at Blood&Pulp – I've joined more than a few author servers, and none of them have felt like home in the way Blood&Pulp does. Martin, you've created something truly special, my friend, and I am grateful to be a part of it. Krista, you are a living legend. I aspire to be 1/10th of the author you are. Bob, man, how do you do it time and time again? Forever impressed. Michael, I feel like I should be paying for the knowledge you give away for free. 10/10 dentists agree: no notes. Sarah, it has been a true honor to debut a novel beside you. I can't wait to see what's next for Calynn.

You – you lovely, lovely human being who read this book. I feel like we frequent the same corners of Goodreads, KU, and TikTok. I feel like we could almost be friends. I hope you stick around for more.

About the Author

Britta is the worst. She doesn't even publish under her real name and responds to things like, "Mom", "B", and "Brown".

As B. L. Brown, she publishes urban fantasy and paranormal romance. Her debut novella, *Shady Depths*, was released in April 2023 and her short fiction can be found in *Tails, Trysts, and Tentacles: One Monstrous Summer*, *Fireside: Modern Legends and Lore*, and *The Future of Us, A Moms Who Write Anthology*.

As Britta, she is a human-wrangling, word-wielding, musical theatre and beer-loving runner with a passion for fairy tales and folklore. She can be found under a pile of digital literature or begging her friends in academia for their JSTOR logins.

Otherwise, she is in no particular order: lost in the woods, scanning the shelves at the bottle shop, flicking through a classic cookbook, or chasing a kiddo around the neighbor's yard.

You can follow her on Amazon, Goodreads, Twitter, Instagram, and TikTok. For less obnoxious updates, join her infrequent newsletter at www.brittawritesthings.com